Can You Forgive Her? Vol. II

by

Anthony Trollope

Double 9
BOOKS

Can You Forgive Her?
Vol. II
by Anthony Trollope

ISBN: 978-93-61154-11-9

Published by

DOUBLE 9 BOOKS
2/13-B, Ansari Road
Daryaganj, New Delhi – 110002
info@double9books.com
www.double9books.com
Tel. 011-40042856

This book is under public domain

ABOUT THE AUTHOR

Anthony Trollope was an English novelist and government official during the Victorian era. His best-known works include the Chronicles of Barsetshire, a series of novels set in the fictional county of Barsetshire. He also authored novels about politics, social issues, and gender, among other topics. Trollope's literary fame plummeted in his final years, but he regained some popularity by the mid-twentieth century. Anthony Trollope was the son of barrister Thomas Anthony Trollope and Frances Milton Trollope, a novelist and travel writer. Despite being a brilliant and well-educated man and a Fellow of New College, Oxford, Thomas Trollope failed at the Bar because of his nasty temper. Farming ventures proved unproductive, and he missed out on an expected bequest when an elderly childless uncle remarried and had children. Thomas Trollope was the son of Rev. (Thomas) Anthony Trollope, rector of Cottered in Hertfordshire, and the sixth son of Sir Thomas Trollope, 4th Baronet. The baronetcy was later passed down to the descendants of Anthony Trollope's second son, Frederick.

CONTENTS

CHAPTER XLI
A NOBLE LORD DIES..9

CHAPTER XLII
PARLIAMENT MEETS...17

CHAPTER XLIII
MRS. MARSHAM..27

CHAPTER XLIV
THE ELECTION FOR THE CHELSEA DISTRICTS..........................40

CHAPTER XLV
GEORGE VAVASOR TAKES HIS SEAT...47

CHAPTER XLVI
A LOVE GIFT..54

CHAPTER XLVII
MR. CHEESACRE'S DISAPPOINTMENT...65

CHAPTER XLVIII
PREPARATIONS FOR LADY MONK'S PARTY...............................78

CHAPTER XLIX
HOW LADY GLENCORA WENT TO
LADY MONK'S PARTY...85

CHAPTER L
HOW LADY GLENCORA CAME BACK
FROM LADY MONK'S PARTY...95

CHAPTER LI
BOLD SPECULATIONS ON MURDER..107

CHAPTER LII
WHAT OCCURRED IN SUFFOLK
STREET, PALL MALL...113

CHAPTER LIII
THE LAST WILL OF THE OLD SQUIRE 123

CHAPTER LIV
SHOWING HOW ALICE WAS PUNISHED 132

CHAPTER LV
THE WILL 141

CHAPTER LVI
ANOTHER WALK ON THE FELLS 150

CHAPTER LVII
SHOWING HOW THE WILD BEAST
GOT HIMSELF BACK
FROM THE MOUNTAINS 160

CHAPTER LVIII
THE PALLISERS AT BREAKFAST 168

CHAPTER LIX
THE DUKE OF ST. BUNGAY IN
SEARCH OF A MINISTER 179

CHAPTER LX
ALICE VAVASOR'S NAME GETS INTO
THE MONEY MARKET 188

CHAPTER LXI
THE BILLS ARE MADE ALL RIGHT 197

CHAPTER LXII
GOING ABROAD 204

CHAPTER LXIII
MR. JOHN GREY IN QUEEN ANNE STREET 213

CHAPTER LXIV
THE ROCKS AND VALLEYS 222

CHAPTER LXV
THE FIRST KISS 235

CHAPTER LXVI
LADY MONK'S PLAN 244

CHAPTER LXVII
THE LAST KISS 252

CHAPTER LXVIII
FROM LONDON TO BADEN 263

CHAPTER LXIX
FROM BADEN TO LUCERNE 273

CHAPTER LXX
AT LUCERNE 282

CHAPTER LXXI
SHOWING HOW GEORGE VAVASOR
RECEIVED A VISIT 292

CHAPTER LXXII
SHOWING HOW GEORGE VAVASOR
PAID A VISIT 302

CHAPTER LXXIII
IN WHICH COME TIDINGS OF GREAT
MOMENT TO ALL PALLISERS 310

CHAPTER LXXIV
SHOWING WHAT HAPPENED IN
THE CHURCHYARD 319

CHAPTER LXXV
ROUGE ET NOIR 328

CHAPTER LXXVI
THE LANDLORD'S BILL 339

CHAPTER LXXVII
THE TRAVELLERS RETURN HOME 348

CHAPTER LXXVIII
MR. CHEESACRE'S FATE 356

CHAPTER LXXIX
DIAMONDS ARE DIAMONDS 368

CHAPTER LXXX
THE STORY IS FINISHED WITHIN
THE HALLS OF THE DUKE OF OMNIUM 37

CHAPTER XLI
A NOBLE LORD DIES

George Vavasor remained about four days beneath his grandfather's roof; but he was not happy there himself, nor did he contribute to the happiness of any one else. He remained there in great discomfort so long, being unwilling to leave till an answer had been received to the request made to Aunt Greenow, in order that he might insist on Kate's performance of her promise with reference to Alice, if that answer should be unfavourable. During these five days Kate did all in her power to induce her brother to be, at any rate, kind in his manner towards his grandfather, but it was in vain. The Squire would not be the first to be gracious; and George, quite as obstinate as the old man, would take no steps in that direction till encouraged to do so by graciousness from the other side. Poor Kate entreated each of them to begin, but her entreaties were of no avail. "He is an ill-mannered cub," the old man said, "and I was a fool to let him into the house. Don't mention his name to me again." George argued the matter more at length. Kate spoke to him of his own interest in the matter, urging upon him that he might, by such conduct, drive the Squire to exclude him altogether from the property.

"He must do as he likes," George said, sulkily.

"But for Alice's sake!" Kate answered.

"Alice would be the last to expect me to submit to unreasonable ill-usage for the sake of money. As regards myself, I confess that I'm very fond of money and am not particularly squeamish. I would do anything that a man can do to secure it. But this I can't do. I never injured him, and I never asked him to injure himself. I never attempted to borrow money from him. I have never cost him a shilling. When I was in the wine business he might have enabled me to make a large fortune simply by settling on me then the reversion of property which, when he dies, ought to be my own. He was so perversely ignorant that he would make no inquiry, but chose to think that I was ruining myself, at the only time of my life when I was really doing well."

"But he had a right to act as he pleased," urged Kate.

"Certainly he had. But he had no right to resent my asking such a favour at his hands. He was an ignorant old fool not to do it; but I should never have quarrelled with him on that account. Nature made him a fool, and it wasn't his fault. But I can't bring myself to kneel in the dirt before him simply because I asked for what was reasonable."

The two men said very little to each other. They were never alone together except during that half-hour after dinner in which they were supposed to drink their wine. The old Squire always took three glasses of port during this period, and expected that his grandson would take three with him. But George would drink none at all. "I have given up drinking wine after dinner," said he, when his grandfather pushed the bottle over to him. "I suppose you mean that you drink nothing but claret," said the Squire, in a tone of voice that was certainly not conciliatory. "I mean simply what I say," said George—"that I have given up drinking wine after dinner." The old man could not openly quarrel with his heir on such a point as that. Even Mr. Vavasor could not tell his grandson that he was going to the dogs because he had become temperate. But, nevertheless, there was offence in it; and when George sat perfectly silent, looking at the fire, evidently determined to make no attempt at conversation, the offence grew, and became strong. "What the devil's the use of your sitting there if you neither drink nor talk?" said the old man. "No use in the world, that I can see," said George; "if, however, I were to leave you, you would abuse me for it." "I don't care how soon you leave me," said the Squire. From all which it may be seen that George Vavasor's visit to the hall of his ancestors was not satisfactory.

On the fourth day, about noon, came Aunt Greenow's reply. "Dearest Kate," she said, "I am not going to do what you ask me,"—thus rushing instantly into the middle of her subject.

> You see, I don't know my nephew, and have no reason for
> being specially anxious that he should be in Parliament.
> I don't care two straws about the glory of the Vavasor
> family. If I had never done anything for myself, the
> Vavasors would have done very little for me. I don't care
> much about what you call 'blood.' I like those who like me,
> and whom I know. I am very fond of you, and because you
> have been good to me I would give you a thousand pounds
> if you wanted it for yourself; but I don't see why I am to
> give my money to those I don't know. If it is necessary to
> tell my nephew of this, pray tell him that I mean no offence.
> Your friend C. is still waiting—waiting—waiting, patiently;
> but his patience may be exhausted.
>
> Your affectionate aunt,

"Of course she won't," said George, as he threw back the letter to his sister. "Why should she?"

"I had hoped she would," said Kate.

"Why should she? What did I ever do for her? She is a sensible woman. Who is your friend C., and why is he waiting patiently?"

"He is a man who would be glad to marry her for her money, if she would take him."

"Then what does she mean by his patience being exhausted?"

"It is her folly. She chooses to pretend to think that the man is a lover of mine."

"Has he got any money?"

"Yes; lots of money—or money's worth."

"And what is his name?"

"His name is Cheesacre. But pray don't trouble yourself to talk about him."

"If he wants to marry you, and has plenty of money, why shouldn't you take him?"

"Good heavens, George! In the first place he does not want to marry me. In the next place all his heart is in his farmyard."

"And a very good place to have it," said George.

"Undoubtedly. But, really, you must not trouble yourself to talk about him."

"Only this,—that I should be very glad to see you well married."

"Should you?" said she, thinking of her close attachment to himself.

"And now, about the money," said George. "You must write to Alice at once."—"Oh, George!"

"Of course you must; you have promised. Indeed, it would have been much wiser if you had taken me at my word, and done it at once."—"I cannot do it."

Then the scar on his face opened itself, and his sister stood before him in fear and trembling. "Do you mean to tell me," said he, "that you will go back from your word, and deceive me;—that after having kept me here by this promise, you will not do what you have said you would do?"

"Take my money now, and pay me out of hers as soon as you are married. I will be the first to claim it from her,—and from you."

"That is nonsense."

"Why should it be nonsense? Surely you need have no scruple with me. I should have none with you if I wanted assistance."

"Look here, Kate; I won't have it, and there's an end of it. All that you have in the world would not pull me through this election, and therefore such a loan would be worse than useless."

"And am I to ask her for more than two thousand pounds?"

"You are to ask her simply for one thousand. That is what I want, and must have, at present. And she knows that I want it, and that she is to supply it; only she does not know that my need is so immediate. That you must explain to her."

"I would sooner burn my hand, George!"

"But burning your hand, unfortunately, won't do any good. Look here, Kate; I insist upon your doing this for me. If you do not, I shall do it, of course, myself; but I shall regard your refusal as an unjustifiable falsehood on your part, and shall certainly not see you afterwards. I do not wish, for reasons which you may well understand, to write to Alice myself on any subject at present. I now claim your promise to do so; and if you refuse, I shall know very well what to do."

Of course she did not persist in her refusal. With a sorrowful heart, and with fingers that could hardly form the needful letters, she did write a letter to her cousin, which explained the fact—that George Vavasor immediately wanted a thousand pounds for his electioneering purposes. It was a stiff, uncomfortable letter, unnatural in its phraseology, telling its own tale of grief and shame. Alice understood very plainly all the circumstances under which it was written, but she sent back word to Kate at once, undertaking that the money should be forthcoming; and she wrote again before the end of January, saying that the sum named had been paid to George's credit at his own bankers.

Kate had taken immense pride in the renewal of the match between her brother and her cousin, and had rejoiced in it greatly as being her own work. But all that pride and joy were now over. She could no longer write triumphant notes to Alice, speaking always of George as one who was to be their joint hero, foretelling great things of his career in Parliament, and saying little soft things of his enduring love. It was no longer possible to her now to write of George at all, and it was equally impossible to Alice. Indeed, no letters passed between them, when that monetary correspondence was over, up to the end of the winter. Kate remained down in Westmoreland, wretched and ill at ease, listening to hard words spoken by her grandfather against her brother, and feeling herself unable to take her brother's part as she had been wont to do in other times.

George returned to town at the end of those four days, and found that the thousand pounds was duly placed to his credit before the end of the month. It is hardly necessary to tell the reader that this money had come from the stores of Mr. Tombe, and that Mr. Tombe duly debited Mr. Grey with the amount. Alice, in accordance with her promise, had told her father that the money was needed, and her father, in accordance with his promise, had procured it without a word of remonstrance. "Surely I must sign some paper," Alice had said. But she had been contented when her father told her that the lawyers would manage all that.

It was nearly the end of February when George Vavasor made his first payment to Mr. Scruby on behalf of the coming election; and when he called at Mr. Scruby's office with this object, he received some intelligence which surprised him not a little. "You haven't heard the news," said Scruby. "What news?" said George.

"The Marquis is as nearly off the hooks as a man can be." Mr. Scruby, as he communicated the tidings, showed clearly by his face and voice that they were supposed to be of very great importance; but Vavasor did not at first seem to be as much interested in the fate of "the Marquis" as Scruby had intended.

"I'm very sorry for him," said George. "Who is the Marquis? There'll be sure to come another, so it don't much signify."

"There will come another, and that's just it. It's the Marquis of Bunratty; and if he drops, our young Member will go into the Upper House."

"What, immediately; before the end of the Session?" George, of course, knew well enough that such would be the case, but the effect which this event would have upon himself now struck him suddenly.

"To be sure," said Scruby. "The writ would be out immediately. I should be glad enough of it, only that I know that Travers's people have heard of it before us, and that they are ready to be up with their posters directly the breath is out of the Marquis's body. We must go to work immediately; that's all."

"It will only be for part of a Session," said George.

"Just so," said Mr. Scruby.

"And then there'll be the cost of another election."

"That's true," said Mr. Scruby; "but in such cases we do manage to make it come a little cheaper. If you lick Travers now, it may be that you'll have a walk-over for the next."

"Have you seen Grimes?" asked George.

"Yes, I have; the blackguard! He is going to open his house on Travers's side. He came to me as bold as brass, and told me so, saying that he never liked gentlemen who kept him waiting for his odd money. What angers me is that he ever got it."

"We have not managed it very well, certainly," said Vavasor, looking nastily at the attorney.

"We can't help those little accidents, Mr. Vavasor. There are worse accidents than that turn up almost daily in my business. You may think yourself almost lucky that I haven't gone over to Travers myself. He is a Liberal, you know; and it hasn't been for want of an offer, I can tell you."

Vavasor was inclined to doubt the extent of his luck in this respect, and was almost disposed to repent of his Parliamentary ambition. He would now be called upon to spend certainly not less than three thousand pounds of his cousin's money on the chance of being able to sit in Parliament for a few months. And then, after what a fashion would he be compelled to negotiate that loan! He might, to be sure, allow the remainder of this Session to run, and stand, as he had intended, at the general election; but he knew that if he now allowed a Liberal to win the seat, the holder of the seat would be almost sure of subsequent success. He must either fight now, or give up the fight altogether; and he was a man who did not love to abandon any contest in which he had been engaged.

"Well, Squire," said Scruby, "how is it to be?" And Vavasor felt that he detected in the man's voice some diminution of that respect with which he had hitherto been treated as a paying candidate for a metropolitan borough.

"This lord is not dead yet," said Vavasor.

"No; he's not dead yet, that we have heard; but it won't do for us to wait. We want every minute of time that we can get. There isn't any hope for him, I'm told. It's gout in the stomach, or dropsy at the heart, or some of those things that make a fellow safe to go."

"It won't do to wait for the next election?"

"If you ask me, I should say certainly not. Indeed, I shouldn't wish to have to conduct it under such circumstances. I hate a fight when there's no chance of success. I grudge spending a man's money in such a case; I do indeed, Mr. Vavasor."

"I suppose Grimes's going over won't make much difference?"

"The blackguard! He'll take a hundred and fifty votes, I suppose; perhaps more. But that is not much in such a constituency as the Chelsea districts. You see, Travers played mean at the last election, and that will be against him."

"But the Conservatives will have a candidate."

"There's no knowing; but I don't think they will. They'll try one at the general, no doubt; but if the two sitting Members can pull together, they won't have much of a chance."

Vavasor found himself compelled to say that he would stand; and Scruby undertook to give the initiatory orders at once, not waiting even till the Marquis should be dead. "We should have our houses open as soon as theirs," said he. "There's a deal in that." So George Vavasor gave his orders. "If the worst comes to the worst," he said to himself, "I can always cut my throat."

As he walked from the attorney's office to his club he bethought himself that that might not unprobably be the necessary termination of his career. Everything was going wrong with him. His grandfather, who was eighty years of age, would not die,—appeared to have no symptoms of dying;—whereas this Marquis, who was not yet much over fifty, was rushing headlong out of the world, simply because he was the one man whose continued life at the present moment would be serviceable to George Vavasor. As he thought of his grandfather he almost broke his umbrella by the vehemence with which he struck it against the pavement. What right could an ignorant old fool like that have to live for ever, keeping the possession of a property which he could not use, and ruining those who were to come after him? If now, at this moment, that wretched place down in Westmoreland could become his, he might yet ride triumphantly over his difficulties, and refrain from sullying his hands with more of his cousin's money till she should become his wife.

Even that thousand pounds had not passed through his hands without giving him much bitter suffering. As is always the case in such matters, the thing done was worse than the doing of it. He had taught himself to look at it lightly whilst it was yet unaccomplished; but he could not think of it lightly now. Kate had been right. It would have been better for him to take her money. Any money would have been better than that upon which he had laid his sacrilegious hands. If he could have cut a purse, after the old fashion, the stain of the deed would hardly have been so deep. In these days,—for more than a month, indeed, after his return from Westmoreland,—he did not go near Queen Anne Street, trying to persuade himself that he stayed away because of her coldness to him. But, in truth, he was afraid of seeing her without speaking of her money, and afraid to see her if he were to speak of it.

"You have seen the *Globe*?" someone said to him as he entered the club.

"No, indeed; I have seen nothing."

"Bunratty died in Ireland this morning. I suppose you'll be up for the Chelsea districts?"

CHAPTER XLII
PARLIAMENT MEETS

Parliament opened that year on the twelfth of February, and Mr. Palliser was one of the first Members of the Lower House to take his seat. It had been generally asserted through the country, during the last week, that the existing Chancellor of the Exchequer had, so to say, ceased to exist as such; that though he still existed to the outer world, drawing his salary, and doing routine work,—if a man so big can have any routine work to do,—he existed no longer in the inner world of the cabinet. He had differed, men said, with his friend and chief, the Prime Minister, as to the expediency of repealing what were left of the direct taxes of the country, and was prepared to launch himself into opposition with his small bodyguard of followers, with all his energy and with all his venom.

There is something very pleasant in the close, bosom friendship, and bitter, uncompromising animosity, of these human gods,—of these human beings who would be gods were they not shorn so short of their divinity in that matter of immortality. If it were so arranged that the same persons were always friends, and the same persons were always enemies, as used to be the case among the dear old heathen gods and goddesses;—if Parliament were an Olympus in which Juno and Venus never kissed, the thing would not be nearly so interesting. But in this Olympus partners are changed, the divine bosom, now rabid with hatred against some opposing deity, suddenly becomes replete with love towards its late enemy, and exciting changes occur which give to the whole thing all the keen interest of a sensational novel. No doubt this is greatly lessened for those who come too near the scene of action. Members of Parliament, and the friends of Members of Parliament, are apt to teach themselves that it means nothing; that Lord This does not hate Mr. That, or think him a traitor to his country, or wish to crucify him; and that Sir John of the Treasury is not much in earnest when he speaks of his noble friend at the "Foreign Office" as a god to whom no other god was ever comparable in honesty, discretion, patriotism, and genius. But the outside Briton who takes a delight in politics,—and this description should include ninety-nine educated Englishmen out of every hundred,—should not be desirous of peeping behind the scenes. No beholder at any theatre should do so. It is good to believe in these friendships and these enmities, and very pleasant to watch their changes. It is delightful when Oxford embraces Manchester, finding that it cannot live without support in that quarter; and very delightful when the uncompromising assailant of all men in power receives the legitimate reward of his energy by being taken in among the bosoms of the blessed.

But although the outer world was so sure that the existing Chancellor of the Exchequer had ceased to exist, when the House of Commons met that gentleman took his seat on the Treasury Bench. Mr. Palliser, who had by no means given a general support to the Ministry in the last Session, took his seat on the same side of the House indeed, but low down, and near to the cross benches. Mr. Bott sat close behind him, and men knew that Mr. Bott was a distinguished member of Mr. Palliser's party, whatever that party might be. Lord Cinquebars moved the Address, and I must confess that he did it very lamely. He was once accused by Mr. Maxwell, the brewer, of making a great noise in the hunting-field. The accusation could not be repeated as to his performance on this occasion, as no one could hear a word that he said. The Address was seconded by Mr. Loftus Fitzhoward, a nephew of the Duke of St. Bungay, who spoke as though he were resolved to trump poor Lord Cinquebars in every sentence which he pronounced,—as we so often hear the second clergyman from the Communion Table trumping his weary predecessor, who has just finished the Litany not in the clearest or most audible voice. Every word fell from Mr. Fitzhoward with the elaborate accuracy of a separate pistol-shot; and as he became pleased with himself in his progress, and warm with his work, he accented his words sharply, made rhetorical pauses, even moved his hands about in action, and quite disgusted his own party, who had been very well satisfied with Lord Cinquebars. There are many rocks which a young speaker in Parliament should avoid, but no rock which requires such careful avoiding as the rock of eloquence. Whatever may be his faults, let him at least avoid eloquence. He should not be inaccurate, which, however, is not much; he should not be long-winded, which is a good deal; he should not be ill-tempered, which is more; but none of these faults are so damnable as eloquence. All Mr. Fitzhoward's friends and all his enemies knew that he had had his chance, and that he had thrown it away.

In the Queen's Speech there had been some very lukewarm allusion to remission of direct taxation. This remission, which had already been carried so far, should be carried further if such further carrying were found practicable. So had said the Queen. Those words, it was known, could not have been approved of by the energetic and still existing Chancellor of the Exchequer. On this subject the mover of the Address said never a word, and the seconder only a word or two. What they had said had, of course, been laid down for them; though, unfortunately, the manner of saying could not be so easily prescribed. Then there arose a great enemy, a man fluent of diction, apparently with deep malice at his heart, though at home,—as we used to say at school,—one of the most good-natured fellows in the world; one ambitious of that godship which a seat on the other side of the House bestowed, and greedy to grasp at the chances which this disagreement in the councils of the gods might give him. He was quite content, he said, to vote for the Address, as, he believed, would be all the gentlemen on his side of the House. No one could suspect them or him of giving a factious opposition to Government. Had they not borne and forborne beyond all precedent known in that House? Then he touched lightly, and almost with grace to his opponents, on many subjects, promising support, and barely hinting that they were totally and manifestly wrong in all things. But—. Then the tone of his voice changed, and the well-known look of fury was assumed upon his countenance. Then great Jove on the other side pulled his hat over his eyes, and smiled blandly. Then members put away the papers they had been reading for a moment, and men in the gallery began to listen. But—. The long and the short of it was this; that the existing Government had come into power on the cry of a reduction of taxation, and now they were going to shirk the responsibility of their own measures. They were going to shirk the responsibility of their own election cry, although it was known that their own Chancellor of the Exchequer was prepared to carry it out to the full. He was willing to carry it out to the full were he not restrained by the timidity, falsehood, and treachery of his colleagues, of whom, of course, the most timid, the most false, and the most treacherous was—the great god Jove, who sat blandly smiling on the other side.

Great Jove.

No one should ever go near the House of Commons who wishes to enjoy all this. It was so manifestly evident that neither Jove nor any of his satellites cared twopence for what the irate gentleman was saying; nay, it became so evident that, in spite of his assumed fury, the gentleman was not irate. He intended to communicate his look of anger to the newspaper reports of his speech; and he knew from experience that he could succeed in that. And men walked about the House in the most telling moments,—enemies shaking hands with enemies,—in a way that showed an entire absence of all good, honest hatred among them. But the gentleman went on and finished his speech, demanding at last, in direct terms, that the Treasury Jove should state plainly to the House who was to be, and who was not to be, the bearer of the purse among the gods.

Then Treasury Jove got up smiling, and thanked his enemy for the cordiality of his support. "He had always," he said, "done the gentleman's party justice for their clemency, and had feared no opposition from them;

and he was glad to find that he was correct in his anticipations as to the course they would pursue on the present occasion." He went on saying a good deal about home matters, and foreign matters, proving that everything was right, just as easily as his enemy had proved that everything was wrong. On all these points he was very full, and very courteous; but when he came to the subject of taxation, he simply repeated the passage from the Queen's Speech, expressing a hope that his right honourable friend, the Chancellor of the Exchequer, would be able to satisfy the judgement of the House, and the wishes of the people. That specially personal question which had been asked he did not answer at all.

But the House was still all agog, as was the crowded gallery. The energetic and still existing Chancellor of the Exchequer was then present, divided only by one little thin Secretary of State from Jove himself. Would he get up and declare his purposes? He was a man who almost always did get up when an opportunity offered itself, — or when it did not. Some second little gun was fired off from the Opposition benches, and then there was a pause. Would the purse-bearer of Olympus rise upon his wings and speak his mind, or would he sit in silence upon his cloud? There was a general call for the purse-bearer, but he floated in silence, and was inexplicable. The purse-bearer was not to be bullied into any sudden reading of the riddle. Then there came on a general debate about money matters, in which the purse-bearer did say a few words, but he said nothing as to the great question at issue. At last up got Mr. Palliser, towards the close of the evening, and occupied a full hour in explaining what taxes the Government might remit with safety, and what they might not, — Mr. Bott, meanwhile, prompting him with figures from behind with an assiduity that was almost too persistent. According to Mr. Palliser, the words used in the Queen's Speech were not at all too cautious. The Members went out gradually, and the House became very thin during this oration; but the newspapers declared, next morning, that his speech had been the speech of the night, and that the perspicuity of Mr. Palliser pointed him out as the coming man.

He returned home to his house in Park Lane quite triumphant after his success, and found Lady Glencora, at about twelve o'clock, sitting alone. She had arrived in town on that day, having come up at her own request, instead of remaining at Matching Priory till after Easter, as he had proposed. He had wished her to stay, in order, as he had said, that there might be a home for his cousins. But she had expressed herself unwilling to remain without him, explaining that the cousins might have the home in her absence, as well as they could in her presence; and he had given way. But, in truth, she had learned to hate her cousin Iphy Palliser with a hatred that was unreasonable,—seeing that she did not also hate Alice Vavasor, who had done as much to merit her hatred as had her cousin. Lady Glencora knew by what means her absence from Monkshade had been brought about. Miss Palliser had told her all that had passed in Alice's bedroom on the last night of Alice's stay at Matching, and had, by so doing, contrived to prevent the visit. Lady Glencora understood well all that Alice had said: and yet, though she hated Miss Palliser for what had been done, she entertained no anger against Alice. Of course Alice would have prevented that visit to Monkshade if it were in her power to do so. Of course she would save her friend. It is hardly too much to say that Lady Glencora looked to Alice to save her. Nevertheless she hated Iphy Palliser for engaging herself in the same business. Lady Glencora looked to Alice to save her, and yet it may be doubted whether she did, in truth, wish to be saved.

While she was at Matching, and before Mr. Palliser had returned from Monkshade, a letter reached her, by what means she had never learned. "A letter has been placed within my writing-case," she said to her maid, quite openly. "Who put it there?" The maid had declared her ignorance in a manner that had satisfied Lady Glencora of her truth. "If such a thing happens again," said Lady Glencora, "I shall be obliged to have the matter investigated. I cannot allow that anything should be put into my room surreptitiously." There, then, had been an end of that, as regarded any steps taken by Lady Glencora. The letter had been from Burgo Fitzgerald, and had contained a direct proposal that she should go off with him. "I am at Matching," the letter said, "at the Inn; but I do not dare to show myself, lest I should do you an injury. I walked round the house yesterday, at night, and I know that I saw your room. If I am wrong in thinking that you love me, I would not for worlds insult you by my presence; but if you love me still, I ask you to throw aside from you that fictitious marriage, and give yourself to the man whom, if you love him, you should regard as your husband." There had been more of it, but it had been to the same effect. To Lady Glencora it had seemed to convey an assurance of devoted love,—of that love which, in former days, her friends had told her was not within the compass of Burgo's nature. He had not asked her to meet him then, but saying that he would return to Matching after Parliament was met, begged her to let him have some means of knowing whether her heart was true to him.

She told no one of the letter, but she kept it, and read it over and over again in the silence and solitude of her room. She felt that she was guilty in thus reading it,—even in keeping it from her husband's knowledge; but though conscious of this guilt, though resolute almost in its commission, still she determined not to remain at Matching after her husband's departure,— not to undergo the danger of remaining there while Burgo Fitzgerald should be in the vicinity. She could not analyse her own wishes. She often told herself, as she had told Alice, that it would be better for them all that she should go away; that in throwing herself even to the dogs, if such must be the result, she would do more of good than of harm. She declared to herself, in the most passionate words she could use, that she loved this man with all her heart. She protested that the fault would not be hers, but theirs, who had forced her to marry the man she did not love. She assured herself that her husband had no affection for her, and that their marriage was in every respect prejudicial to him. She recurred over and over again, in her thoughts, to her own childlessness, and to his extreme desire for an heir. "Though I do sacrifice myself," she would say, "I shall do more of good than harm, and I cannot be more wretched than I am now." But yet she fled to London because she feared to leave herself at Matching when Burgo Fitzgerald should be there. She sent no answer to his letter. She made no preparation for going with him. She longed to see Alice, to whom alone, since her marriage, had she ever spoken of her love, and intended to tell her the whole tale of that letter. She was as one who, in madness, was resolute to throw herself from a precipice, but to whom some remnant of sanity remained which forced her to seek those who would save her from herself.

Mr. Palliser had not seen her since her arrival in London, and, of course, he took her by the hand and kissed her. But it was the embrace of a brother rather than of a lover or a husband. Lady Glencora, with her full woman's nature, understood this thoroughly, and appreciated by instinct the true bearing of every touch from his hand. "I hope you are well?" she said.

"Oh, yes; quite well. And you? A little fatigued with your journey, I suppose?"

"No; not much."

"Well, we have had a debate on the Address. Don't you want to know how it has gone?"

"If it has concerned you particularly, I do, of course."

"Concerned me! It has concerned me certainly."

"They haven't appointed you yet; have they?"

"No; they don't appoint people during debates, in the House of Commons. But I fear I shall never make you a politician."

"I'm almost afraid you never will. But I'm not the less anxious for your success, since you wish it yourself. I don't understand why you should work so very hard; but, as you like it, I'm as anxious as anybody can be that you should triumph."

"Yes; I do like it," he said. "A man must like something, and I don't know what there is to like better. Some people can eat and drink all day; and some people can care about a horse. I can do neither."

And there were others, Lady Glencora thought, who could love to lie in the sun, and could look up into the eyes of women, and seek their happiness there. She was sure, at any rate, that she knew one such. But she said nothing of this.

"I spoke for a moment to Lord Brock," said Mr. Palliser. Lord Brock was the name by which the present Jove of the Treasury was known among men.

"And what did Lord Brock say?"

"He didn't say much, but he was very cordial."

"But I thought, Plantagenet, that he could appoint you if he pleased? Doesn't he do it all?"

"Well, in one sense, he does. But I don't suppose I shall ever make you understand." He endeavoured, however, to do so on the present occasion, and gave her a somewhat longer lecture on the working of the British Constitution, and the manner in which British politics evolved themselves, than would have been expected from most young husbands to their young wives under similar circumstances. Lady Glencora yawned, and strove lustily, but ineffectually, to hide her yawn in her handkerchief.

"But I see you don't care a bit about it," said he, peevishly.

"Don't be angry, Plantagenet. Indeed I do care about it, but I am so ignorant that I can't understand it all at once. I am rather tired, and I think I'll go to bed now. Shall you be late?"

"No, not very; that is, I shall be rather late. I've a lot of letters I want to write to-night, as I must be at work all to-morrow. By-the-by, Mr. Bott is coming to dine here. There will be no one else." The next day was a Wednesday, and the House would not sit in the evening.

"Mr. Bott!" said Lady Glencora, showing by her voice that she anticipated no pleasure from that gentleman's company.

"Yes, Mr. Bott. Have you any objection?"

"Oh, no. Would you like to dine alone with him?"

"Why should I dine alone with him? Why shouldn't you eat your dinner with us? I hope you are not going to become fastidious, and to turn up your nose at people. Mrs. Marsham is in town, and I dare say she'll come to you if you ask her."

But this was too much for Lady Glencora. She was disposed to be mild, but she could not endure to have her two duennas thus brought upon her together on the first day of her arrival in London. And Mrs. Marsham would be worse than Mr. Bott. Mr. Bott would be engaged with Mr. Palliser during the greater part of the evening. "I thought," said she, "of asking my cousin, Alice Vavasor, to spend the evening with me."

"Miss Vavasor!" said the husband. "I must say that I thought Miss Vavasor—" He was going to make some allusion to that unfortunate hour spent among the ruins, but he stopped himself.

"I hope you have nothing to say against my cousin?" said his wife. "She is my only near relative that I really care for;—the only woman, I mean."

"No; I don't mean to say anything against her. She's very well as a young lady, I dare say. I would sooner that you would ask Mrs. Marsham to-morrow."

Lady Glencora was standing, waiting to go away to her own room, but it was absolutely necessary that this matter should be decided before she went. She felt that he was hard to her, and unreasonable, and that he was treating her like a child who should not be allowed her own way in anything. She had endeavoured to please him, and, having failed, was not now disposed to give way.

"As there will be no other ladies here to-morrow evening, Plantagenet, and as I have not yet seen Alice since I have been in town, I wish you would let me have my way in this. Of course I cannot have very much to say to Mrs. Marsham, who is an old woman."

"I especially want Mrs. Marsham to be your friend," said he.

"Friendships will not come by ordering, Plantagenet," said she.

"Friendships will not come by ordering," said Lady Glencora.

"Very well," said he. "Of course, you will do as you please. I am sorry that you have refused the first favour I have asked you this year." Then he left the room, and she went away to bed.

CHAPTER XLIII
MRS. MARSHAM

But Lady Glencora was not brought to repentance by her husband's last words. It seemed to her to be so intolerably cruel, this demand of his, that she should be made to pass the whole of her first evening in town with an old woman for whom it was impossible that she should entertain the slightest regard, that she resolved upon rebellion. Had he positively ordered Mrs. Marsham, she would have sent for that lady, and have contented herself with enduring her presence in disdainful silence; but Mr. Palliser had not given any order. He had made a request, and a request, from its very nature, admits of no obedience. The compliance with a request must be voluntary, and she would not send for Mrs. Marsham, except upon compulsion. Had not she also made a request to him, and had not he refused it? It was his prerogative, undoubtedly, to command; but in that matter of requests she had a right to expect that her voice should be as potent as his own. She wrote a line, therefore, to Alice before she went to bed, begging her cousin to come to her early on the following day, so that they might go out together, and then afterwards dine in company with Mr. Bott.

"I know that will be an inducement to you," Lady Glencora said, "because your generous heart will feel of what service you may be to me. Nobody else will be here,—unless, indeed, Mrs. Marsham should be asked, unknown to myself."

Then she sat herself down to think,—to think especially about the cruelty of husbands. She had been told over and over again, in the days before her marriage, that Burgo would ill-use her if he became her husband. The Marquis of Auld Reekie had gone so far as to suggest that Burgo might probably beat her. But what hard treatment, even what beating, could be so unendurable as this total want of sympathy, as this deadness in life, which her present lot entailed upon her? As for that matter of beating, she ridiculed the idea in her very soul. She sat smiling at the absurdity of the thing as she thought of the beauty of Burgo's eyes, of the softness of his touch, of the loving, almost worshipping, tones of his voice. Would it not even be better to be beaten by him than to have politics explained to her at one o'clock at night by such a husband as Plantagenet Palliser? The British Constitution, indeed! Had she married Burgo they would have been in sunny Italy, and he would have told her some other tale than that as they sat together under the pale moonlight. She had a little water-coloured drawing called Raphael and Fornarina, and she was infantine enough to tell herself that the so-called Raphael was like her Burgo—no, not her Burgo, but the Burgo that was not hers. At any rate, all the romance of the picture she might have enjoyed had they allowed her to dispose as she had wished of her own hand. She might have sat in marble balconies, while the vines clustered over her head, and he would have been at her knee, hardly speaking to her, but making his presence felt by the halo of its divinity. He would have called upon her for no hard replies. With him near her she would have enjoyed the soft air, and would have sat happy, without trouble, lapped in the delight of loving. It was thus that Fornarina sat. And why should not such a lot have been hers? Her Raphael would have loved her, let them say what they would about his cruelty.

Poor, wretched, overburthened child, to whom the commonest lessons of life had not yet been taught, and who had now fallen into the hands of one who was so ill-fitted to teach them! Who would not pity her? Who could say that the fault was hers? The world had laden her with wealth till she had had no limb free for its ordinary uses, and then had turned her loose to run her race!

"Have you written to your cousin?" her husband asked her the next morning. His voice, as he spoke, clearly showed that his anger was either over or suppressed.

"Yes; I have asked her to come and drive, and then to stay for dinner. I shall send the carriage for her if she can come. The man is to wait for an answer."

"Very well," said Mr. Palliser, mildly. And then, after a short pause, he added, "As that is settled, perhaps you would have no objection to ask Mrs. Marsham also?"

"Won't she probably be engaged?"

"No; I think not," said Mr. Palliser. And then he added, being ashamed of the tinge of falsehood of which he would otherwise have been guilty, "I know she is not engaged."

"She expects to come, then?" said Lady Glencora.

"I have not asked her, if you mean that, Glencora. Had I done so, I should have said so. I told her that I did not know what your engagements were."

"I will write to her, if you please," said the wife, who felt that she could hardly refuse any longer.

"Do, my dear!" said the husband. So Lady Glencora did write to Mrs. Marsham, who promised to come,—as did also Alice Vavasor.

Lady Glencora would, at any rate, have Alice to herself for some hours before dinner. At first she took comfort in that reflection; but after a while she bethought herself that she would not know what to tell Alice, or what not to tell. Did she mean to show that letter to her cousin? If she did show it, then,—so she argued with herself,—she must bring herself to endure the wretchedness of her present lot, and must give up for ever all her dreams about Raphael and Fornarina. If she did not show it,—or, at any rate, tell of it,—then it would come to pass that she would leave her husband under the protection of another man, and she would become—what she did not dare to name even to herself. She declared that so it must be. She knew that she would go with Burgo, should he ever come to her with the means of going at his and her instant command. But should she bring herself to let Alice know that such a letter had been conveyed to her, Burgo would never have such power.

I remember the story of a case of abduction in which a man was tried for his life, and was acquitted, because the lady had acquiesced in the carrying away while it was in progress. She had, as she herself declared, armed herself with a sure and certain charm or talisman against such dangers, which she kept suspended round her neck; but whilst she was in the post-chaise she opened the window and threw the charm from her, no longer desiring, as the learned counsel for the defence efficiently alleged, to be kept under the bonds of such protection. Lady Glencora's state of mind was, in its nature, nearly the same as that of the lady in the post-chaise. Whether or no she would use her charm, she had not yet decided, but the power of doing so was still hers.

Alice came, and the greeting between the cousins was very affectionate. Lady Glencora received her as though they had been playmates from early childhood; and Alice, though such impulsive love was not natural to her as to the other, could not bring herself to be cold to one who was so warm to her. Indeed, had she not promised her love in that meeting at Matching Priory in which her cousin had told her of all her wretchedness? "I will love you!" Alice had said; and though there was much in Lady Glencora that she could not approve,—much even that she could not bring herself to like,— still she would not allow her heart to contradict her words.

They sat so long over the fire in the drawing-room that at last they agreed that the driving should be abandoned.

"What's the use of it?" said Lady Glencora. "There's nothing to see, and the wind is as cold as charity. We are much more comfortable here; are we not?" Alice quite acquiesced in this, having no great desire to be driven through the parks in the gloom of a February afternoon.

"If I had Dandy and Flirt up here, there would be some fun in it; but Mr. Palliser doesn't wish me to drive in London."

"I suppose it would be dangerous?"

"Not in the least. I don't think it's that he minds; but he has an idea that it looks fast."

"So it does. If I were a man, I'm sure I shouldn't like my wife to drive horses about London."

"And why not? Just because you'd be a tyrant,—like other husbands? What's the harm of looking fast, if one doesn't do anything improper? Poor Dandy, and dear Flirt! I'm sure they'd like it."

"Perhaps Mr. Palliser doesn't care for that?"

"I can tell you something else he doesn't care for. He doesn't care whether Dandy's mistress likes it."

"Don't say that, Glencora."

"Why not say it,—to you?"

"Don't teach yourself to think it. That's what I mean. I believe he would consent to anything that he didn't think wrong."

"Such as lectures about the British Constitution! But never mind about that, Alice. Of course the British Constitution is everything to him, and I wish I knew more about it;—that's all. But I haven't told you whom you are to meet at dinner."

"Yes, you have—Mr. Bott."

"But there's another guest, a Mrs. Marsham. I thought I'd got rid of her for to-day, when I wrote to you; but I hadn't. She's coming."

"She won't hurt me at all," said Alice.

"She will hurt me very much. She'll destroy the pleasure of our whole evening. I do believe that she hates you, and that she thinks you instigate me to all manner of iniquity. What fools they all are!"

"Who are they all, Glencora?"

"She and that man, and—. Never mind. It makes me sick when I think that they should be so blind. Alice, I hardly know how much I owe to you;

I don't, indeed. Everything, I believe." Lady Glencora, as she spoke, put her hand into her pocket, and grasped the letter which lay there.

"That's nonsense," said Alice.

"No; it's not nonsense. Who do you think came to Matching when I was there?"

"What;—to the house?" said Alice, feeling almost certain that Mr. Fitzgerald was the person to whom Lady Glencora was alluding.

"No; not to the house."

"If it is the person of whom I am thinking," said Alice, solemnly, "let me implore you not to speak of him."

"And why should I not speak of him? Did I not speak of him before to you, and was it not for good? How are you to be my friend, if I may not speak to you of everything?"

"But you should not think of him."

"What nonsense you talk, Alice! Not think of him! How is one to help one's thoughts? Look here."

Her hand was on the letter, and it would have been out in a moment, and thrown upon Alice's lap, had not the servant opened the door and announced Mrs. Marsham.

"Oh, how I do wish we had gone to drive!" said Lady Glencora, in a voice which the servant certainly heard, and which Mrs. Marsham would have heard had she not been a little hard of hearing,—in her bonnet.

"How do, my dear?" said Mrs. Marsham. "I thought I'd just come across from Norfolk Street and see you, though I am coming to dinner in the evening. It's only just a step, you know. How d'ye do, Miss Vavasor?" and she made a salutation to Alice which was nearly as cold as it could be.

Mrs. Marsham was a woman who had many good points. She was poor, and bore her poverty without complaint. She was connected by blood and friendship with people rich and titled; but she paid to none of them egregious respect on account of their wealth or titles. She was staunch in her friendships, and staunch in her enmities. She was no fool, and knew well what was going on in the world. She could talk about the last novel, or—if need be—about the Constitution. She had been a true wife, though sometimes too strong-minded, and a painstaking mother, whose children, however, had never loved her as most mothers like to be loved.

The catalogue of her faults must be quite as long as that of her virtues. She was one of those women who are ambitious of power, and not very scrupulous as to the manner in which they obtain it. She was hardhearted, and capable of pursuing an object without much regard to the injury she might do. She would not flatter wealth or fawn before a title, but she was not above any artifice by which she might ingratiate herself with those whom it suited her purpose to conciliate. She thought evil rather than good. She was herself untrue in action, if not absolutely in word. I do not say that she would coin lies, but she would willingly leave false impressions. She had been the bosom friend, and in many things the guide in life, of Mr. Palliser's mother; and she took a special interest in Mr. Palliser's welfare. When he married, she heard the story of the loves of Burgo and Lady Glencora; and though she thought well of the money, she was not disposed to think very well of the bride. She made up her mind that the young lady would want watching, and she was of opinion that no one would be so well able to watch Lady Glencora as herself. She had not plainly opened her mind on this matter to Mr. Palliser; she had not made any distinct suggestion to him that she would act as Argus to his wife. Mr. Palliser would have rejected any such suggestion, and Mrs. Marsham knew that he would do so; but she had let a word or two drop, hinting that Lady Glencora was very young,—hinting that Lady Glencora's manners were charming in their childlike simplicity; but hinting also that precaution was, for that reason, the more necessary. Mr. Palliser, who suspected nothing as to Burgo or as to any other special peril, whose whole disposition was void of suspicion, whose dry nature realized neither the delights nor the dangers of love, acknowledged that Glencora was young. He especially wished that she should be discreet and matronly; he feared no lovers, but he feared that she might do silly things,— that she would catch cold,—and not know how to live a life becoming the wife of a Chancellor of the Exchequer. Therefore he submitted Glencora,— and, to a certain extent, himself,—into the hands of Mrs. Marsham.

Lady Glencora had not been twenty-four hours in the house with this lady before she recognized in her a duenna. In all such matters no one could be quicker than Lady Glencora. She might be very ignorant about the British Constitution, and, alas! very ignorant also as to the real elements of right and wrong in a woman's conduct, but she was no fool. She had an eye that could see, and an ear that could understand, and an abundance of that feminine instinct which teaches a woman to know her friend or her enemy at a glance, at a touch, at a word. In many things Lady Glencora was much quicker, much more clever, than her husband, though he was to be Chancellor of the Exchequer, and though she did know nothing of the Constitution. She knew, too, that he was easily to be deceived,—that though his intelligence was keen, his instincts were dull,—that he was gifted with no fineness of touch, with no subtle appreciation of the characters of men and women;

and, to a certain extent, she looked down upon him for his obtusity. He should have been aware that Burgo was a danger to be avoided; and he should have been aware also that Mrs. Marsham was a duenna not to be employed. When a woman knows that she is guarded by a watch-dog, she is bound to deceive her Cerberus, if it be possible, and is usually not ill-disposed to deceive also the owner of Cerberus. Lady Glencora felt that Mrs. Marsham was her Cerberus, and she was heartily resolved that if she was to be kept in the proper line at all, she would not be so kept by Mrs. Marsham.

Alice rose and accepted Mrs. Marsham's salutation quite as coldly as it had been given, and from that time forward those two ladies were enemies. Mrs. Marsham, groping quite in the dark, partly guessed that Alice had in some way interfered to prevent Lady Glencora's visit to Monkshade, and, though such prevention was, no doubt, good in that lady's eyes, she resented the interference. She had made up her mind that Alice was not the sort of friend that Lady Glencora should have about her. Alice recognized and accepted the feud.

"I thought I might find you at home," said Mrs. Marsham, "as I know you are lazy about going out in the cold, —unless it be for a foolish midnight ramble," and Mrs. Marsham shook her head. She was a little woman, with sharp small eyes, with a permanent colour in her face, and two short, crisp, grey curls at each side of her face; always well dressed, always in good health, and, as Lady Glencora believed, altogether incapable of fatigue.

"The ramble you speak of was very wise, I think," said Lady Glencora; "but I never could see the use of driving about in London in the middle of winter."

"One ought to go out of the house every day," said Mrs. Marsham.

"I hate all those rules. Don't you, Alice?" Alice did not hate them, therefore she said nothing.

"My dear Glencora, one must live by rules in this life. You might as well say that you hated sitting down to dinner."

"So I do, very often; almost always when there's company."

"You'll get over that feeling after another season in town," said Mrs. Marsham, pretending to suppose that Lady Glencora alluded to some remaining timidity in receiving her own guests.

"Upon my word I don't think I shall. It's a thing that seems always to be getting more grievous, instead of less so. Mr. Bott is coming to dine here to-night."

There was no mistaking the meaning of this. There was no pretending even to mistake it. Now, Mrs. Marsham had accepted the right hand of fellowship from Mr. Bott,—not because she especially liked him, but in compliance with the apparent necessities of Mr. Palliser's position. Mr. Bott had made good his ground about Mr. Palliser; and Mrs. Marsham, as she was not strong enough to turn him off from it, had given him the right hand of fellowship.

"Mr. Bott is a Member of Parliament, and a very serviceable friend of Mr. Palliser's," said Mrs. Marsham.

"All the same; we do not like Mr. Bott—do we, Alice? He is Doctor Fell to us; only I think we could tell why."

"I certainly do not like him," said Alice.

"It can be but of small matter to you, Miss Vavasor," said Mrs. Marsham, "as you will not probably have to see much of him."

"Of the very smallest moment," said Alice. "He did annoy me once, but will never, I dare say, have an opportunity of doing so again."

"I don't know what the annoyance may have been."

"Of course you don't, Mrs. Marsham."

"But I shouldn't have thought it likely that a person so fully employed as Mr. Bott, and employed, too, on matters of such vast importance, would have gone out of his way to annoy a young lady whom he chanced to meet for a day or two in a country-house."

"I don't think that Alice means that he attempted to flirt with her," said Lady Glencora, laughing. "Fancy Mr. Bott's flirtation!"

"Perhaps he did not attempt," said Mrs. Marsham; and the words, the tone, and the innuendo together were more than Alice was able to bear with equanimity.

"Glencora," said she, rising from her chair, "I think I'll leave you alone with Mrs. Marsham. I'm not disposed to discuss Mr. Bott's character, and certainly not to hear his name mentioned in disagreeable connection with my own."

But Lady Glencora would not let her go. "Nonsense, Alice," she said. "If you and I can't fight our little battles against Mr. Bott and Mrs. Marsham without running away, it is odd. There is a warfare in which they who run away never live to fight another day."

"I hope, Glencora, you do not count me as your enemy?" said Mrs. Marsham, drawing herself up.

"But I shall,—certainly, if you attack Alice. Love me, love my dog. I beg your pardon, Alice; but what I meant was this, Mrs. Marsham; Love me, love the best friend I have in the world."

"I did not mean to offend Miss Vavasor," said Mrs. Marsham, looking at her very grimly. Alice merely bowed her head. She had been offended, and she would not deny it. After that, Mrs. Marsham took herself off, saying that she would be back to dinner. She was angry, but not unhappy. She thought that she could put down Miss Vavasor, and she was prepared to bear a good deal from Lady Glencora—for Mr. Palliser's sake, as she said to herself, with some attempt at a sentimental remembrance of her old friend.

"She's a nasty old cat," said Lady Glencora, as soon as the door was closed; and she said these words with so droll a voice, with such a childlike shaking of her head, with so much comedy in her grimace, that Alice could not but laugh. "She is," said Lady Glencora. "I know her, and you'll have to know her, too, before you've done with her. It won't at all do for you to run away when she spits at you. You must hold your ground, and show your claws,—and make her know that if she spits, you can scratch."

"But I don't want to be a cat myself."

"She'll find I'm of the genus, but of the tiger kind, if she persecutes me. Alice, there's one thing I have made up my mind about. I will not be persecuted. If my husband tells me to do anything, as long as he is my husband I'll do it; but I won't be persecuted."

"You should remember that she was a very old friend of Mr. Palliser's mother."

"I do remember; and that may be a very good reason why she should come here occasionally, or go to Matching, or to any place in which we may be living. It's a bore, of course; but it's a natural bore, and one that ought to be borne."

"And that will be the beginning and the end of it."

"I'm afraid not, my dear. It may perhaps be the end of it, but I fear it won't be the beginning. I won't be persecuted. If she gives me advice, I shall tell her to her face that it's not wanted; and if she insults any friend of mine, as she did you, I shall tell her that she had better stay away. She'll go and tell him, of course; but I can't help that. I've made up my mind that I won't be persecuted."

After that, Lady Glencora felt no further inclination to show Burgo's letter to Alice on that occasion. They sat over the drawing-room fire, talking chiefly of Alice's affairs, till it was time for them to dress. But Alice, though she spoke much of Mr. Grey, said no word as to her engagement with George Vavasor. How could she speak of it, inasmuch as she had already resolved,—already almost resolved,—that that engagement also should be broken?

Alice, when she came down to the drawing-room, before dinner, found Mr. Bott there alone. She had dressed more quickly than her friend, and Mr. Palliser had not yet made his appearance.

"I did not expect the pleasure of meeting Miss Vavasor to-day," he said, as he came up, offering his hand. She gave him her hand, and then sat down, merely muttering some word of reply.

"We spent a very pleasant month down at Matching together;—didn't you think so?"

"I spent a pleasant month there certainly."

"You left, if I remember, the morning after that late walk out among the ruins? That was unfortunate, was it not? Poor Lady Glencora! it made her very ill; so much so, that she could not go to Monkshade, as she particularly wished. It was very sad. Lady Glencora is very delicate,—very delicate, indeed. We, who have the privilege of being near her, ought always to remember that."

"I don't think she is at all delicate."

"Oh! don't you? I'm afraid that's your mistake, Miss Vavasor."

"I believe she has very good health, which is the greatest blessing in the world. By delicate I suppose you mean weak and infirm."

"Oh, dear, no,—not in the least,—not infirm certainly! I should be very sorry to be supposed to have said that Lady Glencora is infirm. What I mean is, not robust, Miss Vavasor. Her general organization, if you understand me, is exquisitely delicate. One can see that, I think, in every glance of her eye."

Alice was going to protest that she had never seen it at all, when Mr. Palliser entered the room along with Mrs. Marsham.

The two gentlemen shook hands, and then Mr. Palliser turned to Alice. She perceived at once by his face that she was unwelcome, and wished herself away from his house. It might be all very well for Lady Glencora to fight with Mrs. Marsham,—and with her husband, too, in regard to the Marsham persecution,—but there could be no reason why she should do so. He just touched her hand, barely closing his thumb upon her fingers, and asked her how she was. Then he turned away from her side of the fire, and began talking to Mrs. Marsham on the other. There was that in his face and in his manner which was positively offensive to her. He made no allusion to his former acquaintance with her,—spoke no word about Matching, no word about his wife, as he would naturally have done to his wife's friend. Alice felt the blood mount into her face, and regretted greatly that she had ever come among these people. Had she not long since made up her mind that she would avoid her great relations, and did not all this prove that it would have been well for her to have clung to that resolution? What was Lady Glencora to her that she should submit herself to be treated as though she were a poor companion,—a dependent, who received a salary for her attendance,—an indigent cousin, hanging on to the bounty of her rich connection? Alice was proud to a fault. She had nursed her pride till it was very faulty. All her troubles and sorrows in life had come from an overfed craving for independence. Why, then, should she submit to be treated with open want of courtesy by any man; but, of all men, why should she submit to it from such a one as Mr. Palliser,—the heir of a ducal house, rolling in wealth, and magnificent with all the magnificence of British pomp and pride? No; she would make Lady Glencora understand that the close intimacies of daily life were not possible to them!

"I declare I'm very much ashamed," said Lady Glencora, as she entered the room. "I shan't apologize to you, Alice, for it was you who kept me talking; but I do beg Mrs. Marsham's pardon."

Mrs. Marsham was all smiles and forgiveness, and hoped that Lady Glencora would not make a stranger of her. Then dinner was announced, and Alice had to walk down stairs by herself. She did not care a doit for that, but there had been a disagreeable little contest when the moment came. Lady Glencora had wished to give up Mr. Bott to her cousin, but Mr. Bott had stuck manfully to Lady Glencora's side. He hoped to take Lady Glencora down to dinner very often, and was not at all disposed to abate his privilege.

During dinner-time Alice said very little, nor was there given to her opportunity of saying much. She could not but think of the day of her first arrival at Matching Priory, when she had sat between the Duke of St. Bungay and Jeffrey Palliser, and when everybody had been so civil to her! She now occupied one side of the table by herself, away from the fire, where she felt cold and desolate in the gloom of the large half-lighted room. Mr. Palliser occupied himself with Mrs. Marsham, who talked politics to him; and Mr. Bott never lost a moment in his endeavours to say some civil word to Lady Glencora. Lady Glencora gave him no encouragement; but she hardly dared to snub him openly in her husband's immediate presence. Twenty times during dinner she said some little word to Alice, attempting at first to make the time pleasant, and then, when the matter was too far gone for that, attempting to give some relief. But it was of no avail. There are moments in which conversation seems to be impossible,—in which the very gods interfere to put a seal upon the lips of the unfortunate one. It was such a moment now with Alice. She had never as yet been used to snubbing. Whatever position she had hitherto held, in that she had always stood foremost,—much more so than had been good for her. When she had gone to Matching, she had trembled for her position; but there all had gone well with her; there Lady Glencora's kindness had at first been able to secure for her a reception that had been flattering, and almost better than flattering. Jeffrey Palliser had been her friend, and would, had she so willed it, have been more than her friend. But now she felt that the halls of the Pallisers were too cold for her, and that the sooner she escaped from their gloom and hard discourtesy the better for her.

Mrs. Marsham, when the three ladies had returned to the drawing-room together, was a little triumphant. She felt that she had put Alice down; and with the energetic prudence of a good general who knows that he should follow up a victory, let the cost of doing so be what it may, she determined to keep her down. Alice had resolved that she would come as seldom as might be to Mr. Palliser's house in Park Lane. That resolution on her part was in close accordance with Mrs. Marsham's own views.

"Is Miss Vavasor going to walk home?" she asked.

"Walk home;—all along Oxford Street! Good gracious! no. Why should she walk? The carriage will take her."

"Or a cab," said Alice. "I am quite used to go about London in a cab by myself."

"I don't think they are nice for young ladies after dark," said Mrs. Marsham. "I was going to offer my servant to walk with her. She is an elderly woman, and would not mind it."

"I'm sure Alice is very much obliged," said Lady Glencora; "but she will have the carriage."

"You are very good-natured," said Mrs. Marsham; "but gentlemen do so dislike having their horses out at night."

"No gentleman's horses will be out," said Lady Glencora, savagely; "and as for mine, it's what they are there for." It was not often that Lady Glencora made any allusion to her own property, or allowed any one near her to suppose that she remembered the fact that her husband's great wealth was, in truth, her wealth. As to many matters her mind was wrong. In some things her taste was not delicate as should be that of a woman. But, as regarded her money, no woman could have behaved with greater reticence, or a purer delicacy. But now, when she was twitted by her husband's special friend with ill-usage to her husband's horses, because she chose to send her own friend home in her own carriage, she did find it hard to bear.

"I dare say it's all right," said Mrs. Marsham.

"It is all right," said Lady Glencora. "Mr. Palliser has given me my horses for my own use, to do as I like with them; and if he thinks I take them out when they ought to be left at home, he can tell me so. Nobody else has a right to do it." Lady Glencora, by this time, was almost in a passion, and showed that she was so.

"My dear Lady Glencora, you have mistaken me," said Mrs. Marsham; "I did not mean anything of that kind."

"I am so sorry," said Alice. "And it is such a pity, as I am quite used to going about in cabs."

"Of course you are," said Lady Glencora. "Why shouldn't you? I'd go home in a wheelbarrow if I couldn't walk, and had no other conveyance. That's not the question. Mrs. Marsham understands that."

"Upon my word, I don't understand anything," said that lady.

"I understand this," said Lady Glencora; "that in all such matters as that, I intend to follow my own pleasure. Come, Alice, let us have some coffee,"—and she rang the bell. "What a fuss we have made about a stupid old carriage!"

The gentlemen did not return to the drawing-room that evening, having, no doubt, joint work to do in arranging the great financial calculations of the nation; and, at an early hour, Alice was taken home in Lady Glencora's brougham, leaving her cousin still in the hands of Mrs. Marsham.

CHAPTER XLIV
THE ELECTION FOR THE CHELSEA DISTRICTS

March came, and still the Chancellor of the Exchequer held his position. In the early days of March there was given in the House a certain parliamentary explanation on the subject, which, however, did not explain very much to any person. A statement was made which was declared by the persons making it to be altogether satisfactory, but nobody else seemed to find any satisfaction in it. The big wigs of the Cabinet had made an arrangement which, from the language used by them on this occasion, they must be supposed to have regarded as hardly less permanent than the stars; but everybody else protested that the Government was going to pieces; and Mr. Bott was heard to declare in clubs and lobbies, and wherever he could get a semi-public, political hearing, that this kind of thing wouldn't do. Lord Brock must either blow hot or cold. If he chose to lean upon Mr. Palliser, he might lean upon him, and Mr. Palliser would not be found wanting. In such case no opposition could touch Lord Brock or the Government. That was Mr. Bott's opinion. But if Lord Brock did not so choose, why, in that case, he must expect that Mr. Palliser, and Mr. Palliser's friends, would—. Mr. Bott did not say what they would do; but he was supposed by those who understood the matter to hint at an Opposition lobby, and adverse divisions, and to threaten Lord Brock with the open enmity of Mr. Palliser,—and of Mr. Palliser's great follower.

"This kind of thing won't do long, you know," repeated Mr. Bott for the second or third time, as he stood upon the rug before the fire at his club, with one or two of his young friends around him.

"I suppose not," said Calder Jones, the hunting Member of Parliament whom we once met at Roebury. "Planty Pall won't stand it, I should say."

"What can he do?" asked another, an unfledged Member who was not as yet quite settled as to the leadership under which he intended to work.

"What can he do?" said Mr. Bott, who on such an occasion as this could be very great,—who, for a moment, could almost feel that he might become a leader of a party for himself, and some day institute a Bott Ministry. "What can he do? You will very shortly see what he can do. He can make himself the master of the occasion. If Lord Brock doesn't look about him, he'll find that Mr. Palliser will be in the Cabinet without his help."

"You don't mean to say that the Queen will send for Planty Pall!" said the young Member.

"I mean to say that the Queen will send for any one that the House of Commons may direct her to call upon," said Mr. Bott, who conceived himself to have gauged the very depths of our glorious Constitution. "How hard it is to make any one understand that the Queen has really nothing to do with it!"

"Come, Bott, draw it mild," said Calder Jones, whose loyalty was shocked by the utter Manchesterialism of his political friend.

"Not if I know it," said Mr. Bott, with something of grandeur in his tone and countenance. "I never drew it mild yet, and I shan't begin now. All our political offences against civilization have come from men drawing it mild, as you call it. Why is it that Englishmen can't read and write as Americans do? Why can't they vote as they do even in Imperial France? Why are they serfs, less free than those whose chains were broken the other day in Russia? Why is the Spaniard more happy, and the Italian more contented? Because men in power have been drawing it mild!" And Mr. Bott made an action with his hand as though he were drawing up beer from a patent tap.

"But you can't set aside Her Majesty like that, you know," said the young Member, who had been presented, and whose mother's old-world notions about the throne still clung to him.

"I should be very sorry," said Mr. Bott; "I'm no republican." With all his constitutional love, Mr. Bott did not know what the word republican meant. "I mean no disrespect to the throne. The throne in its place is very well. But the power of governing this great nation does not rest with the throne. It is contained within the four walls of the House of Commons. That is the great truth which all young Members should learn, and take to their hearts."

"And you think Planty Pall will become Prime Minister?" said Calder Jones.

"I haven't said that; but there are more unlikely things. Among young men I know no man more likely. But I certainly think this,—that if Lord Brock doesn't take him into the Cabinet, Lord Brock won't long remain there himself."

In the meantime the election came on in the Chelsea districts, and the whole of the south-western part of the metropolis was covered with posters bearing George Vavasor's name. "Vote for Vavasor and the River Bank."

That was the cry with which he went to the electors; and though it must be presumed that it was understood by some portion of the Chelsea electors, it was perfectly unintelligible to the majority of those who read it. His special acquaintances and his general enemies called him Viscount Riverbank, and he was pestered on all sides by questions as to Father Thames. It was Mr. Scruby who invented the legend, and who gave George Vavasor an infinity of trouble by the invention. There was a question in those days as to embanking the river from the Houses of Parliament up to the remote desolations of further Pimlico, and Mr. Scruby recommended the coming Member to pledge himself that he would have the work carried on even to Battersea Bridge. "You must have a subject," pleaded Mr. Scruby. "No young Member can do anything without a subject. And it should be local;— that is to say, if you have anything of a constituency. Such a subject as that, if it's well worked, may save you thousands of pounds—thousands of pounds at future elections."

"It won't save me anything at this one, I take it."

"But it may secure the seat, Mr. Vavasor, and afterwards make you the most popular metropolitan Member in the House; that is, with your own constituency. Only look at the money that would be spent in the districts if that were done! It would come to millions, sir!"

"But it never will be done."

"What matters that?" and Mr. Scruby almost became eloquent as he explained the nature of a good parliamentary subject. "You should work it up, so as to be able to discuss it at all points. Get the figures by heart, and then, as nobody else will do so, nobody can put you down. Of course it won't be done. If it were done, that would be an end of it, and your bread would be taken out of your mouth. But you can always promise it at the hustings, and can always demand it in the House. I've known men who've walked into as much as two thousand a year, permanent place, on the strength of a worse subject than that!"

Vavasor allowed Mr. Scruby to manage the matter for him, and took up the subject of the River Bank. "Vavasor and the River Bank" was carried about by an army of men with iron shoulder-straps, and huge pasteboard placards six feet high on the top of them. You would think, as you saw the long rows, that the men were being marshalled to their several routes; but they always kept together—four-and-twenty at the heels of each other. "One placard at a time would strike the eye," said Mr. Vavasor, counting the expense up to himself. "There's no doubt of it," said Mr. Scruby in reply. "One placard will do that, if it's big enough; but it takes four-and-twenty to touch the imagination." And then sides of houses were covered with that shibboleth—"Vavasor and the River Bank"—the same words repeated in columns down the whole sides of houses. Vavasor himself declared that he was ashamed to walk among his future constituents, so conspicuous had his name become. Grimes saw it, and was dismayed. At first, Grimes ridiculed the cry with all his publican's wit. "Unless he mean to drown hisself in the Reach, it's hard to say what he do mean by all that gammon about the River Bank," said Grimes, as he canvassed for the other Liberal candidate. But, after a while, Grimes was driven to confess that Mr. Scruby knew what he was about. "He is a sharp 'un, that he is," said Grimes in the inside bar of the "Handsome Man;" and he almost regretted that he had left the leadership of Mr. Scruby, although he knew that on this occasion he would not have gotten his odd money.

George Vavasor, with much labour, actually did get up the subject of the River Bank. He got himself introduced to men belonging to the Metropolitan Board, and went manfully into the matter of pounds, shillings, and pence. He was able even to work himself into an apparent heat when he was told that the thing was out of the question; and soon found that he had disciples who really believed in him. If he could have brought himself to believe in the thing,—if he could have been induced himself to care whether Chelsea was to be embanked or no, the work would not have been so difficult to him. In that case it would have done good to him, if to no one else. But such belief was beyond him. He had gone too far in life to be capable of believing in, or of caring for, such things. He was ambitious of having a hand in the government of his country, but he was not capable of caring even for that.

But he worked. He worked hard, and spoke vehemently, and promised the men of Chelsea, Pimlico, and Brompton that the path of London westwards had hardly commenced as yet. Sloane Street should be the new Cheapside. Squares should arise around the Chelsea barracks, with sides open to the water, for which Belgravia would be deserted. There should be palaces there for the rich, because the rich spend their riches; but no rich man's palace should interfere with the poor man's right to the River Bank. Three millions and a half should be spent on the noble street to be constructed, the grandest pathway that the world should ever yet have seen; three millions and a half to be drawn from,—to be drawn from anywhere except from Chelsea;—from the bloated money-bags of the City Corporation, Vavasor once ventured to declare, amidst the encouraging shouts of the men of Chelsea. Mr. Scruby was forced to own that his pupil worked the subject well. "Upon my word, that was uncommon good," he said, almost patting Vavasor on the back, after a speech in which he had vehemently asserted that his ambition to represent the Chelsea districts had all come of his long-fixed idea that the glory of future London would be brought about by the embankment of the river at Chelsea.

But armies of men carrying big boards, and public-houses open at every corner, and placards in which the letters are three feet long, cost money. Those few modest hundreds which Mr. Scruby had already received before the work began, had been paid on the supposition that the election would not take place till September. Mr. Scruby made an early request, a very early request, that a further sum of fifteen hundred pounds should be placed in his hands; and he did this in a tone which clearly signified that not a man would be sent about through the streets, or a poster put upon a wall, till this request had been conceded. Mr. Scruby was in possession of two very distinct manners of address. In his jovial moods, when he was instigating his clients to fight their battles well, it might almost be thought that he was doing it really for the love of the thing; and some clients, so thinking, had believed for a few hours that Scruby, in his jolly, passionate eagerness, would pour out his own money like dust, trusting implicitly to future days for its return. But such clients had soon encountered Mr. Scruby's other manner, and had perceived that they were mistaken.

The thing had come so suddenly upon George Vavasor that there was not time for him to carry on his further operations through his sister. Had he written to Kate,—let him have written in what language he would,— she would have first rejoined by a negative, and there would have been a correspondence before he had induced her to comply. He thought of sending for her by telegram, but even in that there would have been too much delay. He resolved, therefore, to make his application to Alice himself, and he wrote to her, explaining his condition. The election had come upon him quite suddenly, as she knew, he said. He wanted two thousand pounds instantly, and felt little scruple in asking her for it, as he was aware that the old Squire would be only too glad to saddle the property with a legacy to Alice for the repayment of this money, though he would not have advanced a shilling himself for the purpose of the election. Then he said a word or two as to his prolonged absence from Queen Anne Street. He had not been there because he had felt, from her manner when they last met, that she would for a while prefer to be left free from the unavoidable excitement of such interviews. But should he be triumphant in his present contest, he should go to her to share his triumph with her; or, should he fail, he should go to her to console him in his failure.

Within three days he heard from her, saying that the money would be at once placed to his credit. She sent him also her candid good wishes for success in his enterprise, but beyond this her letter said nothing. There was no word of love,—no word of welcome,—no expression of a desire to see him. Vavasor, as he perceived all this in the reading of her note, felt a triumph in the possession of her money. She was ill-using him by her coldness, and there was comfort in revenge. "It serves her right," he said to himself. "She should have married me at once when she said she would do so, and then it would have been my own."

When Mr. Tombe had communicated with John Grey on the matter of this increased demand,—this demand which Mr. Tombe began to regard as carrying a love-affair rather too far,—Grey had telegraphed back that Vavasor's demand for money, if made through Mr. John Vavasor, was to be honoured to the extent of five thousand pounds. Mr. Tombe raised his eyebrows, and reflected that some men were very foolish. But John Grey's money matters were of such a nature as to make Mr. Tombe know that he must do as he was bidden; and the money was paid to George Vavasor's account.

He told Kate nothing of this. Why should he trouble himself to do so? Indeed, at this time he wrote no letters to his sister, though she twice sent to him, knowing what his exigencies would be, and made further tenders of her own money. He could not reply to these offers without telling her that money had been forthcoming from that other quarter, and so he left them unanswered.

In the meantime the battle went on gloriously. Mr. Travers, the other Liberal candidate, spent his money freely,—or else some other person did so on his behalf. When Mr. Scruby mentioned this last alternative to George Vavasor, George cursed his own luck in that he had never found such backers. "I don't call a man half a Member when he's brought in like that," said Mr. Scruby, comforting him. "He can't do what he likes with his vote. He ain't independent. You never hear of those fellows getting anything good. Pay for the article yourself, Mr. Vavasor, and then it's your own. That's what I always say."

Mr. Grimes went to work strenuously, almost fiercely, in the opposite interest, telling all that he knew, and perhaps more than he knew, of Vavasor's circumstances. He was at work morning, noon, and night, not only in his own neighbourhood, but among those men on the river bank of whom he had spoken so much in his interview with Vavasor in Cecil Street. The entire Vavasorian army with its placards was entirely upset on more than one occasion, and was once absolutely driven ignominiously into the river mud. And all this was done under the direction of Mr. Grimes. Vavasor himself was pelted with offal from the sinking tide, so that the very name of the River Bank became odious to him. He was a man who did not like to have his person touched, and when they hustled him he became angry. "Lord love you, Mr. Vavasor," said Scruby, "that's nothing! I've had a candidate so mauled,—it was in the Hamlets, I think,—that there wasn't a spot on him that wasn't painted with rotten eggs. The smell was something quite awful. But I brought him in, through it all."

And Mr. Scruby at last did as much for George Vavasor as he had done for the hero of the Hamlets. At the close of the poll Vavasor's name stood at the head by a considerable majority, and Scruby comforted him by saying that Travers certainly wouldn't stand the expense of a petition, as the seat was to be held only for a few months.

"And you've done it very cheap, Mr. Vavasor," said Scruby, "considering that the seat is metropolitan. I do say that you have done it cheap. Another thousand, or twelve hundred, will cover everything—say thirteen, perhaps, at the outside. And when you shall have fought the battle once again, you'll have paid your footing, and the fellows will let you in almost for nothing after that."

A further sum of thirteen hundred pounds was wanted at once, and then the whole thing was to be repeated over again in six months' time! This was not consolatory. But, nevertheless, there was a triumph in the thing itself which George Vavasor was man enough to enjoy. It would be something to have sat in the House of Commons, though it should only have been for half a session.

CHAPTER XLV
GEORGE VAVASOR TAKES HIS SEAT

George Vavasor's feeling of triumph was not unjustifiable. It is something to have sat in the House of Commons, though it has been but for one session! There is on the left-hand side of our great national hall, — on the left-hand side as one enters it, and opposite to the doors leading to the Law Courts, — a pair of gilded lamps, with a door between them, near to which a privileged old dame sells her apples and her oranges solely, as I presume, for the accommodation of the Members of the House and of the great policeman who guards the pass. Between those lamps is the entrance to the House of Commons, and none but Members may go that way! It is the only gate before which I have ever stood filled with envy, — sorrowing to think that my steps might never pass under it. There are many portals forbidden to me, as there are many forbidden to all men; and forbidden fruit, they say, is sweet; but my lips have watered after no other fruit but that which grows so high, within the sweep of that great policeman's truncheon.

Ah, my male friend and reader, who earnest thy bread, perhaps, as a country vicar; or sittest, may-be, at some weary desk in Somerset House; or who, perhaps, rulest the yard behind the Cheapside counter, hast thou never stood there and longed, — hast thou never confessed, when standing there, that Fate has been unkind to thee in denying thee the one thing that thou hast wanted? I have done so; and as my slow steps have led me up that more than royal staircase, to those passages and halls which require the hallowing breath of centuries to give them the glory in British eyes which they shall one day possess, I have told myself, in anger and in grief, that to die and not to have won that right of way, though but for a session, — not to have passed by the narrow entrance through those lamps, — is to die and not to have done that which it most becomes an Englishman to have achieved.

There are, doubtless, some who come out by that road, the loss of whose society is not to be regretted. England does not choose her six hundred and fifty-four best men. One comforts one's self, sometimes, with remembering that. The George Vavasors, the Calder Joneses, and the Botts are admitted. Dishonesty, ignorance, and vulgarity do not close the gate of that heaven against aspirants; and it is a consolation to the ambition of the poor to know that the ambition of the rich can attain that glory by the strength of its riches alone. But though England does not send thither none but her best men, the best of her Commoners do find their way there. It is the highest and most legitimate pride of an Englishman to have the letters M.P. written after his name. No selection from the alphabet, no doctorship, no fellowship, be it of ever so learned or royal a society, no knightship,—not though it be of the Garter,—confers so fair an honour. Mr. Bott was right when he declared that this country is governed from between the walls of that House, though the truth was almost defiled by the lips which uttered it. He might have added that from thence flow the waters of the world's progress,—the fullest fountain of advancing civilization.

George Vavasor, as he went in by the lamps and the apple-stall, under the guardianship of Mr. Bott, felt all the pride of which I have been speaking. He was a man quite capable of feeling such pride as it should be felt,— capable, in certain dreamy moments, of looking at the thing with pure and almost noble eyes; of understanding the ambition of serving with truth so great a nation as that which fate had made his own. Nature, I think, had so fashioned George Vavasor, that he might have been a good, and perhaps a great man; whereas Mr. Bott had been born small. Vavasor had educated himself to badness with his eyes open. He had known what was wrong, and had done it, having taught himself to think that bad things were best. But poor Mr. Bott had meant to do well, and thought that he had done very well indeed. He was a tuft-hunter and a toady, but he did not know that he was doing amiss in seeking to rise by tuft-hunting and toadying. He was both mean and vain, both a bully and a coward, and in politics, I fear, quite unscrupulous in spite of his grand dogmas; but he believed that he was progressing in public life by the proper and usual means, and was troubled by no idea that he did wrong.

Vavasor, in those dreamy moments of which I have spoken, would sometimes feel tempted to cut his throat and put an end to himself, because he knew that he had taught himself amiss. Again he would sadly ask himself whether it was yet too late; always, however, answering himself that it was too late. Even now, at this moment, as he went in between the lamps, and felt much of the honest pride of which I have spoken, he told himself that it was too late. What could he do now, hampered by such a debt as that which he owed to his cousin, and with the knowledge that it must be almost indefinitely increased, unless he meant to give up this seat in Parliament, which had cost him so dearly, almost before he had begun to enjoy it? But his courage was good, and he was able to resolve that he would go on with the business that he had in hand, and play out his game to the end. He had achieved his seat in the House of Commons, and was so far successful. Men who had ever been gracious to him were now more gracious than ever, and they who had not hitherto treated him with courtesy, now began to smile and to be very civil. It was, no doubt, a great thing to have the privilege of that entrance between the lamps.

Mr. Bott had the new Member now in hand, not because there had been any old friendship between them, but Mr. Bott was on the look-out for followers, and Vavasor was on the look-out for a party. A man gets no great thanks for attaching himself to existing power. Our friend might have enrolled himself among the general supporters of the Government without attracting much attention. He would in such case have been at the bottom of a long list. But Mr. Palliser was a rising man, round whom, almost without wish of his own, a party was forming itself. If he came into power, — as come he must, according to Mr. Bott and many others, — then they who had acknowledged the new light before its brightness had been declared, might expect their reward.

Vavasor, as he passed through the lobby to the door of the House, leaning on Mr. Bott's arm, was very silent. He had spoken but little since they had left their cab in Palace Yard, and was not very well pleased by the garrulity of his companion. He was going to sit among the first men of his nation, and to take his chance of making himself one of them. He believed in his own ability; he believed thoroughly in his own courage; but he did not believe in his own conduct. He feared that he had done, — feared still more strongly that he would be driven to do, — that which would shut men's ears against his words, and would banish him from high places. No man believes in himself who knows himself to be a rascal, however great may be his talent, or however high his pluck.

"Of course you have heard a debate?" said Mr. Bott.

"Yes," answered Vavasor, who wished to remain silent.

"Many, probably?"

"No."

"But you have heard debates from the gallery. Now you'll hear them from the body of the House, and you'll find how very different it is. There's no man can know what Parliament is who has never had a seat. Indeed no one can thoroughly understand the British Constitution without it. I felt, very early in life, that that should be my line; and though it's hard work and no pay, I mean to stick to it. How do, Thompson? You know Vavasor? He's just returned for the Chelsea Districts, and I'm taking him up. We shan't divide to-night; shall we? Look! there's Farringcourt just coming out; he's listened to better than any man in the House now, but he'll borrow half-a-crown from you if you'll lend him one. How d'ye do, my lord? I hope I have the pleasure of seeing you well?" and Bott bowed low to a lord who was hurrying through the lobby as fast as his shuffling feet would carry him. "Of course you know him?"

Vavasor, however, did not know the lord in question, and was obliged to say so.

"I thought you were up to all these things?" said Bott.

"Taking the peerage generally, I am not up to it," said Vavasor, with a curl on his lip.

"But you ought to have known him. That was Viscount Middlesex; he has got something on to-night about the Irish Church. His father is past ninety, and he's over sixty. We'll go in now; but let me give you one bit of advice, my dear fellow—don't think of speaking this session. A Member can do no good at that work till he has learned something of the forms of the House. The forms of the House are everything; upon my word they are. This is Mr. Vavasor, the new Member for the Chelsea Districts."

Our friend was thus introduced to the doorkeeper, who smiled familiarly, and seemed to wink his eye. Then George Vavasor passed through into the House itself, under the wing of Mr. Bott.

Vavasor, as he walked up the House to the Clerk's table and took the oath and then walked down again, felt himself to be almost taken aback by the little notice which was accorded to him. It was not that he had expected to create a sensation, or that he had for a moment thought on the subject, but the thing which he was doing was so great to him, that the total indifference of those around him was a surprise to him. After he had taken his seat, a few men came up by degrees and shook hands with him; but it seemed, as they did so, merely because they were passing that way. He was anxious not to sit next to Mr. Bott, but he found himself unable to avoid this contiguity. That gentleman stuck to him pertinaciously, giving him directions which, at the spur of the moment, he hardly knew how not to obey. So he found himself sitting behind Mr. Palliser, a little to the right, while Mr. Bott occupied the ear of the rising man.

There was a debate in progress, but it seemed to Vavasor, as soon as he was able to become critical, to be but a dull affair, and yet the Chancellor of the Exchequer was on his legs, and Mr. Palliser was watching him as a cat watches a mouse. The speaker was full of figures, as becomes a Chancellor of the Exchequer; and as every new budget of them fell from him, Mr. Bott, with audible whispers, poured into the ear of his chief certain calculations of his own, most of which went to prove that the financier in office was altogether wrong. Vavasor thought that he could see that Mr. Palliser was receiving more of his assistance than was palatable to him. He would listen, if he did listen, without making any sign that he heard, and would occasionally shake his head with symptoms of impatience. But Mr. Bott was a man not to be repressed by a trifle. When Mr. Palliser shook his head he became more assiduous than ever, and when Mr. Palliser slightly moved himself to the left, he boldly followed him.

No general debate arose on the subject which the Minister had in hand, and when he sat down, Mr. Palliser would not get up, though Mr. Bott counselled him to do so. The matter was over for the night, and the time had arrived for Lord Middlesex. That nobleman got upon his feet, with a roll of papers in his hand, and was proceeding to address the House on certain matters of church reform, with great energy; but, alas, for him and for his feelings! before his energy had got itself into full swing, the Members were swarming away through the doors like a flock of sheep. Mr. Palliser got up and went, and was followed at once by Mr. Bott, who succeeded in getting hold of his arm in the lobby. Had not Mr. Palliser been an even-tempered, calculating man, with a mind and spirit well under his command, he must have learned to hate Mr. Bott before this time. Away streamed the Members, but still the noble lord went on speaking, struggling hard to keep up his fire as though no such exodus were in process. There was but little to console him. He knew that the papers would not report one sentence in twenty of those he uttered. He knew that no one would listen to him willingly. He knew that he had worked for weeks and months to get up his facts, and he was beginning to know that he had worked in vain. As he summoned courage to look round, he began to fear that some enemy would count the House, and that all would be over. He had given heart and soul to this affair. His cry was not as Vavasor's cry about the River Bank. He believed in his own subject with a great faith, thinking that he could make men happier and better, and bring them nearer to their God. I said that he had worked for weeks and months. I might have said that he had been all his life at this work. Though he shuffled with his feet when he walked, and knocked his words together when he talked, he was an earnest man, meaning to do well, seeking no other reward for his work than the appreciation of those whom he desired to serve. But this was never to be his. For him there was in store nothing but disappointment. And yet he will work on to the end, either in this House or in the other, labouring wearily, without visible wages of any kind, and, one may say, very sadly. But when he has been taken to his long rest, men will acknowledge that he has done something, and there will be left on the minds of those who shall remember him a conviction that he served a good cause diligently, and not altogether inefficiently. Invisible are his wages, yet in some coin are they paid. Invisible is the thing he does, and yet it is done. Let us hope that some sense of this tardy appreciation may soothe his spirit beyond the grave. On the present occasion there was nothing to soothe his spirit. The Speaker sat, urbane and courteous, with his eyes turned towards the unfortunate orator; but no other ears in the House seemed to listen to him. The corps of reporters had dwindled down to two, and they used their pens very listlessly, taking down here a sentence and there a sentence, knowing that their work was naught. Vavasor sat it out to the last, as it taught him a lesson in those forms of the House which Mr. Bott had truly told him it would be well that he should learn. And at last he did learn the form of a "count-out." Some one from a back seat muttered something, which the Speaker understood; and that high officer, having had his attention called to a fact of which he would never have taken cognizance without such calling, did count the House, and finding that it contained but twenty-three Members, he put an end to his own labours and to those of poor Lord Middlesex. With what feelings that noble lord must have taken himself home, and sat himself down in his study, vainly opening a book before his eyes, can we not all imagine? A man he was with ample means, with children who would do honour to his name; one whose wife believed in him, if no one else would do so; a man, let us say, with a clear conscience, to whom all good things had been given. But of whom now was he thinking with envy? Early on that same day Farringcourt had spoken in the House,—a man to whom no one would lend a shilling, whom the privilege of that House kept out of gaol, whose word no man believed; who was wifeless, childless, and unloved. But three hundred men had hung listening upon his words. When he laughed in his speech, they laughed; when he was indignant against the Minister, they sat breathless, as the Spaniard sits in the critical moment of the bull-killing. Whichever way he turned himself, he carried them with him. Crowds of Members flocked into the House from libraries and smoking-rooms when it was known that this ne'er-do-well was on his legs. The Strangers' Gallery was filled to overflowing. The reporters turned their rapid pages, working their fingers wearily till the sweat drops stood upon their brows. And as the Premier was attacked with some special impetus of redoubled irony, men declared that he would be driven to enrol the speaker among his colleagues, in spite of dishonoured bills and evil reports. A man who could shake the thunderbolts like that must be paid to shake them on the right side. It was of this man, and of his success, that Lord Middlesex was envious, as he sat, wretched and respectable, in his solitary study!

Mr. Bott had left the House with Mr. Palliser; and Vavasor, after the count-out, was able to walk home by himself, and think of the position which he had achieved. He told himself over and over again that he had done a great thing in obtaining that which he now possessed, and he endeavoured to teach himself that the price he was paying for it was not too dear. But already there had come upon him something of that feeling, — that terribly human feeling, — which deprives every prize that is gained of half its value. The mere having it robs the diamond of its purity, and mixes vile alloy with the gold. Lord Middlesex, as he had floundered on into terrible disaster, had not been a subject to envy. There had been nothing of brilliance in the debate, and the Members had loomed no larger than ordinary men at ordinary clubs. The very doorkeepers had hardly treated them with respect. The great men with whose names the papers are filled had sat silent, gloomy, and apparently idle. As soon as a fair opportunity was given them they escaped out of the House, as boys might escape from school. Everybody had rejoiced in the break-up of the evening, except that one poor old lord who had worked so hard. Vavasor had spent everything that he had to become a Member of that House, and now, as he went alone to his lodgings, he could not but ask himself whether the thing purchased was worth the purchase-money.

But his courage was still high. Though he was gloomy, and almost sad, he knew that he could trust himself to fight out the battle to the last. On the morrow he would go to Queen Anne Street, and would demand sympathy there from her who had professed to sympathize with him so strongly in his political desires. With her, at any rate, the glory of his Membership would not be dimmed by any untoward knowledge of the realities. She had only seen the play acted from the boxes; and to her eyes the dresses would still be of silk velvet, and the swords of bright steel.

CHAPTER XLVI
A LOVE GIFT

When Alice heard of her cousin's success, and understood that he was actually Member of Parliament for the Chelsea Districts, she resolved that she would be triumphant. She had sacrificed nearly everything to her desire for his success in public life, and now that he had achieved the first great step towards that success, it would have been madness on her part to decline her share in the ovation. If she could not rejoice in that, what source of joy would then be left for her? She had promised to be his wife, and at present she was under the bonds of that promise. She had so promised because she had desired to identify her interests with his,—because she wished to share his risks, to assist his struggles, and to aid him in his public career. She had done all this, and he had been successful. She strove, therefore, to be triumphant on his behalf, but she knew that she was striving ineffectually. She had made a mistake, and the days were coming in which she would have to own to herself that she had done so in sackcloth, and to repent with ashes.

But yet she struggled to be triumphant. The tidings were first brought to her by her servant, and then she at once sat down to write him a word or two of congratulation. But she found the task more difficult than she had expected, and she gave it up. She had written no word to him since the day on which he had left her almost in anger, and now she did not know how she was to address him. "I will wait till he comes," she said, putting away from her the paper and pens. "It will be easier to speak than to write." But she wrote to Kate, and contrived to put some note of triumph into her letter. Kate had written to her at length, filling her sheet with a loud pæan of sincere rejoicing. To Kate, down in Westmoreland, it had seemed that her brother had already done everything. He had already tied Fortune to his chariot wheels. He had made the great leap, and had overcome the only obstacle that Fate had placed in his way. In her great joy she almost forgot whence had come the money with which the contest had been won. She was not enthusiastic in many things;—about herself she was never so; but now she was elated with an enthusiasm which seemed to know no bounds. "I am proud," she said, in her letter to Alice. "No other thing that he could have done would have made me so proud of him. Had the Queen sent for him and made him an earl, it would have been as nothing to this. When I think that he has forced his way into Parliament without any great friend, with nothing to back him but his own wit"—she had, in truth, forgotten Alice's money as she wrote;—"that he has achieved his triumph in the metropolis, among the most wealthy and most fastidious of the richest city in the world, I do feel proud of my brother. And, Alice, I hope that you are proud of your lover." Poor girl! One cannot but like her pride, nay, almost love her for it, though it was so sorely misplaced. It must be remembered that she had known nothing of Messrs. Grimes and Scruby, and the River Bank, and that the means had been wanting to her of learning the principles upon which some metropolitan elections are conducted.

"And, Alice, I hope that you are proud of your lover!" "He is not my lover," Alice said to herself. "He knows that he is not. He understands it, though she may not." And if not your lover, Alice Vavasor, what is he then to you? And what are you to him, if not his love? She was beginning to understand that she had put herself in the way of utter destruction;—that she had walked to the brink of a precipice, and that she must now topple over it. "He is not my lover," she said; and then she sat silent and moody, and it took her hours to get her answer written to Kate.

On the same afternoon she saw her father for a moment or two. "So George has got himself returned," he said, raising his eyebrows.

"Yes, he has been successful. I'm sure you must be glad, papa."

"Upon my word, I'm not. He has bought a seat for three months; and with whose money has he purchased it?"

"Don't let us always speak of money, papa."

"When you discuss the value of a thing just purchased, you must mention the price before you know whether the purchaser has done well or badly. They have let him in for his money because there are only a few months left before the general election. Two thousand pounds he has had, I believe?"

"And if as much more is wanted for the next election he shall have it."

"Very well, my dear;—very well, If you choose to make a beggar of yourself, I cannot help it. Indeed, I shall not complain though he should spend all your money, if you do not marry him at last." In answer to this, Alice said nothing. On that point her father's wishes were fast growing to be identical with her own.

"I tell you fairly what are my feelings and my wishes," he continued. "Nothing, in my opinion, would be so deplorable and ruinous as such a marriage. You tell me that you have made up your mind to take him, and I know well that nothing that I can say will turn you. But I believe that when he has spent all your money he will not take you, and that thus you will be saved. Thinking as I do about him, you can hardly expect that I should triumph because he has got himself into Parliament with your money!"

Then he left her, and it seemed to Alice that he had been very cruel. There had been little, she thought, nay, nothing of a father's loving tenderness in his words to her. If he had spoken to her differently, might she not even now have confessed everything to him? But herein Alice accused him wrongfully. Tenderness from him on this subject had, we may say, become impossible. She had made it impossible. Nor could he tell her the extent of his wishes without damaging his own cause. He could not let her know that all that was done was so done with the view of driving her into John Grey's arms.

But what words were those for a father to speak to a daughter! Had she brought herself to such a state that her own father desired to see her deserted and thrown aside? And was it probable that this wish of his should come to pass? As to that, Alice had already made up her mind. She thought that she had made up her mind that she would never become her cousin's wife. It needed not her father's wish to accomplish her salvation, if her salvation lay in being separated from him.

On the next morning George went to her. The reader will, perhaps, remember their last interview. He had come to her after her letter to him from Westmoreland, and had asked her to seal their reconciliation with a kiss; but she had refused him. He had offered to embrace her, and she had shuddered before him, fearing his touch, telling him by signs much more clear than any words, that she felt for him none of the love of a woman. Then he had turned from her in anger, declaring to her honestly that he was angry. Since that he had borrowed her money,—had made two separate assaults upon her purse,—and was now come to tell her of the results. How was he to address her? I beg that it may be also remembered that he was not a man to forget the treatment he had received. When he entered the room, Alice looked at him, at first, almost furtively. She was afraid of him. It must be confessed that she already feared him. Had there been in the man anything of lofty principle he might still have made her his slave, though I doubt whether he could ever again have forced her to love him. She looked at him furtively, and perceived that the gash on his face was nearly closed. The mark of existing anger was not there. He had come to her intending to be gentle, if it might be possible. He had been careful in his dress, as though he wished to try once again if the rôle of lover might be within his reach.

Alice was the first to speak. "George, I am so glad that you have succeeded! I wish you joy with my whole heart."

"Thanks, dearest. But before I say another word, let me acknowledge my debt. Unless you had aided me with your money, I could not have succeeded."

"Oh, George! pray don't speak of that!"

"Let me rather speak of it at once, and have done. If you will think of it, you will know that I must speak of it sooner or later." He smiled and looked pleasant, as he used to do in those Swiss days.

"Well, then, speak and have done."

"I hope you have trusted me in thus giving me the command of your fortune?"

"Oh, yes."

"I do believe that you have. I need hardly say that I could not have stood for this last election without it; and I must try to make you understand that if I had not come forward at this vacancy, I should have stood no chance for the next; otherwise, I should not have been justified in paying so dearly for a seat for one session. You can understand that; eh, Alice?"

"Yes; I think so?

"Anybody, even your father, would tell you that; though, probably, he regards my ambition to be a Member of Parliament as a sign of downright madness. But I was obliged to stand now, if I intended to go on with it, as that old lord died so inopportunely. Well, about the money! It is quite upon the cards that I may be forced to ask for another loan when the autumn comes."

"You shall have it, George."

"Thanks, Alice. And now I will tell you what I propose. You know that I have been reconciled,—with a sort of reconciliation,—to my grandfather? Well, when the next affair is over, I propose to tell him exactly how you and I then stand."

"Do not go into that now, George. It is enough for you at present to be assured that such assistance as I can give you is at your command. I want you to feel the full joy of your success, and you will do so more thoroughly if you will banish all these money troubles from your mind for a while."

"They shall, at any rate, be banished while I am with you," said he. "There; let them go!" And he lifted up his right hand, and blew at the tips of his fingers. "Let them vanish," said he. "It is always well to be rid of such troubles for a time."

It is well to be rid of them at any time, or at all times, if only they can be banished without danger. But when a man has overused his liver till it will not act for him any longer, it is not well for him to resolve that he will forget the weakness of his organ just as he sits down to dinner.

It was a pretty bit of acting, that of Vavasor's, when he blew away his cares; and, upon the whole, I do not know that he could have done better. But Alice saw through it, and he knew that she did so. The whole thing was uncomfortable to him, except the fact that he had the promise of her further moneys. But he did not intend to rest satisfied with this. He must extract from her some meed of approbation, some show of sympathy, some spark of affection, true or pretended, in order that he might at least affect to be satisfied, and be enabled to speak of the future without open embarrassment. How could even he take her money from her, unless he might presume that he stood with her upon some ground that belonged mutually to them both?

"I have already taken my seat," said he.

"Yes; I saw that in the newspapers. My acquaintance among Members of Parliament is very small, but I see that you were introduced, as they call it, by one of the few men that I do know. Is Mr. Bott a friend of yours?"

"No,—certainly not a friend. I may probably have to act with him in public."

"Ah, that's just what they said of Mr. Palliser when they felt ashamed of his having such a man as his guest. I think if I were in public life I should try to act with people that I could like."

"Then you dislike Mr. Bott?"

"I do not like him, but my feelings about him are not violent."

"He is a vulgar ass," said George, "with no more pretensions to rank himself a gentleman than your footman."

"If I had one."

"But he will get on in Parliament, to a certain extent."

"I'm afraid I don't quite understand what are the requisites for Parliamentary success, or indeed of what it consists. Is his ambition, do you suppose, the same as yours?"

"His ambition, I take it, does not go beyond a desire to be Parliamentary flunkey to a big man,—with wages, if possible, but without, if the wages are impossible."

"And yours?"

"Oh, as to mine;—there are some things, Alice, that a man does not tell to any one."

"Are there? They must be very terrible things."

"The schoolboy, when he sits down to make his rhymes, dares not say, even to his sister, that he hopes to rival Milton; but he nurses such a hope. The preacher, when he preaches his sermon, does not whisper, even to his wife, his belief that thousands may perhaps be turned to repentance by the strength of his words; but he thinks that the thousand converts are possible."

"And you, though you will not say so, intend to rival Chatham, and to make your thousand converts in politics."

"I like to hear you laugh at me,—I do, indeed. It does me good to hear your voice again with some touch of satire in it. It brings back the old days,—the days to which I hope we may soon revert without pain. Shall it not be so, dearest?"

Her playful manner at once deserted her. Why had he made this foolish attempt to be tender? "I do not know," she said, gloomily.

For a few minutes he sat silent, fingering some article belonging to her which was lying on the table. It was a small steel paper-knife, of which the handle was cast and gilt; a thing of no great value, of which the price may have been five shillings. He sat with it, passing it through his fingers, while she went on with her work.

"Who gave you this paper-cutter?" he said, suddenly.

"Goodness me, why do you ask? and especially, why do you ask in that way?"

"I asked simply because if it is a present to you from any one, I will take up something else."

"It was given me by Mr. Grey."

He let it drop from his fingers on to the table with a noise, and then pushed it from him, so that it fell on the other side, near to where she sat.

"George," she said, as she stooped and picked it up, "your violence is unreasonable; pray do not repeat it."

"I did not mean it," he said, "and I beg your pardon. I was simply unfortunate in the article I selected. And who gave you this?" In saying which he took up a little ivory foot-rule that was folded up so as to bring it within the compass of three inches.

"It so happens that no one gave me that; I bought it at a stupid bazaar."

"Then this will do. You shall give it me as a present, on the renewal of our love."

"It is too poor a thing to give," said she, speaking still more gloomily than she had done before.

"By no means; nothing is too poor, if given in that way. Anything will do; a ribbon, a glove, a broken sixpence. Will you give me something that I may take, and, taking it, may know that your heart is given with it?"

"Take the rule, if you please," she said.

"And about the heart?" he asked.

He should have been more of a rascal or less. Seeing how very much of a rascal he was already, I think it would have been better that he should have been more,—that he should have been able to content his spirit with the simple acquisition of her money, and that he should have been free from all those remains of a finer feeling which made him desire her love also. But it was not so. It was necessary for his comfort that she should, at any rate, say she loved him. "Well, Alice, and what about the heart?" he asked again.

"I would so much rather talk about politics, George," said she.

The cicatrice began to make itself very visible in his face, and the debonair manner was fast vanishing. He had fixed his eyes upon her, and had inserted his thumbs in the armholes of his waistcoat.

"Alice, that is not quite fair," he said.

"I do not mean to be unfair."

"I am not so sure of that. I almost think that you do mean it. You have told me that you intend to become my wife. If, after that, you wilfully make me miserable, will not that be unfair?"

"I am not making you miserable,—certainly not wilfully."

"Did that letter which you wrote to me from Westmoreland mean anything?"

"George, do not strive to make me think that it meant too much."

"If it did, you had better say so at once."

But Alice, though she would have said so had she dared, made no answer to this. She sat silent, turning her face away from his gaze, longing that the meeting might be over, and feeling that she had lost her own self-respect.

"Look here, Alice," he said, "I find it very hard to understand you. When I look back over all that has passed between us, and to that other episode in your life, summing it all up with your conduct to me at present, I find myself at a loss to read your character."

"I fear I cannot help you in the reading of it."

"When you first loved me;—for you did love me. I understood that well enough. There is no young man who in early life does not read with sufficient clearness that sweetest morsel of poetry.—And when you quarrelled with me, judging somewhat harshly of my offences, I understood that also; for it is the custom of women to be hard in their judgement on such sins. When I heard that you had accepted the offer made to you by that gentleman in Cambridgeshire, I thought that I understood you still,—knowing how natural it was that you should seek some cure for your wound. I understood it, and accused myself, not you, in that I had driven you to so fatal a remedy." Here Alice turned round towards him sharply, as though she were going to interrupt him, but she said nothing, though he paused for her to speak; and then he went on. "And I understood it well when I heard that this cure had been too much for you. By heavens, yes! there was no misunderstanding that. I meant no insult to the man when I upset his little toy just now. I have not a word to say against him. For many women he would make a model husband, but you are not one of them. And when you discovered this yourself, as you did, I understood that without difficulty. Yes, by heavens! if ever woman had been driven to a mistake, you had been driven to one there." Here she looked at him again, and met his eyes. She looked at him with something of his own fierceness in her face, as though she were preparing herself to fight with him; but she said nothing at the moment, and then he again went on. "And, Alice, I understood it also when you again consented to be my wife. I thought that I still understood you then. I may have been vain to think so, but surely it was natural. I believed that the old love had come back upon you, and again warmed your heart. I thought that it had been cold during our separation, and I was pleased to think so. Was that unnatural? Put yourself in my place, and say if you would not have thought so. I told myself that I understood you then, and I told myself that in all that you had done you had acted as a true, and good, and loving woman. I thought of you much, and I saw that your conduct, as a whole, was intelligible and becoming." The last word grated on Alice's ears, and she showed her anger by the motion of her foot upon the floor. Her cousin noted it all, but went on as though he had not noted it. "But now your present behaviour makes all the rest a riddle. You have said that you would be my wife, declaring thereby that you had forgiven my offences, and, as I suppose, reassuring me of your love; and yet you receive me with all imaginable coldness. What am I to think of it, and in what way would you have me behave to you? When last I was here I asked you for a kiss." As he said this he looked at her with all his eyes, with his mouth just open, so as to show the edges of his white teeth, with the wound down his face all wide and purple. The last word came with a stigmatizing hiss from his lips. Though she did not essay to speak, he paused again, as if he were desirous that she might realize the full purport of such a request. I think that, in the energy of his speaking, a touch of true passion had come upon him; that he had forgotten his rascaldom, and his need of her money, and that he was punishing her with his whole power of his vengeance for the treatment which he had received from her. "I asked you for a kiss. If you are to be my wife you can have no shame in granting me such a request. Within the last two months you have told me that you would marry me. What am I to think of such a promise if you deny me all customary signs of your affection?" Then he paused again, and she found that the time had come in which she must say something to him.

"I asked you for a kiss."

"I wonder you cannot understand," she said, "that I have suffered much."

"And is that to be my answer?"

"I don't know what answer you want."

"Come, Alice, do not be untrue; you do know what answer I want, and you know also whether my wanting it is unreasonable."

"No one ever told me that I was untrue before," she said.

"You do know what it is that I desire. I desire to learn that the woman who is to be my wife, in truth, loves me."

She was standing up, and so was he also, but still she said nothing. He had in his hand the little rule which she had told him that he might take, but he held it as though in doubt what he would do with it. "Well, Alice, am I to hear anything from you?"

"Not now, George; you are angry, and I will not speak to you in your anger."

"Have I not cause to be angry? Do you not know that you are treating me badly?"

"I know that my head aches, and that I am very wretched. I wish you would leave me."

"There, then, is your gift," said he, and he threw the rule over on to the sofa behind her. "And there is the trumpery trinket which I had hoped you would have worn for my sake." Whereupon something which he had taken from his waistcoat-pocket was thrown violently into the fender, beneath the fire-grate. He then walked with quick steps to the door; but when his hand was on the handle, he turned. "Alice," he said, "when I am gone, try to think honestly of your conduct to me." Then he went, and she remained still, till she heard the front door close behind him.

When she was sure that he was gone, her first movement was made in search of the trinket. I fear that this was not dignified on her part; but I think that it was natural. It was not that she had any desire for the jewel, or any curiosity even to see it. She would very much have preferred that he should have brought nothing of the kind to her. But she had a feminine reluctance that anything of value should be destroyed without a purpose. So she took the shovel, and poked among the ashes, and found the ring which her cousin had thrown there. It was a valuable ring, bearing a ruby on it between two small diamonds. Such at least, she became aware, had been its bearing; but one of the side stones had been knocked out by the violence with which the ring had been flung. She searched even for this, scorching her face and eyes, but in vain. Then she made up her mind that the diamond should be lost for ever, and that it should go out among the cinders into the huge dust-heaps of the metropolis. Better that, though it was distasteful to her feminine economy, than the other alternative of setting the servants to search, and thereby telling them something of what had been done.

When her search was over, she placed the ring on the mantelpiece; but she knew that it would not do to leave it there, — so she folded it up carefully in a new sheet of note-paper, and put it in the drawer of her desk. After that she sat herself down at the table to think what she would do; but her head was, in truth, racked with pain, and on that occasion she could bring her thoughts to no conclusion.

CHAPTER XLVII
MR. CHEESACRE'S DISAPPOINTMENT

When Mrs. Greenow was left alone in her lodgings, after the little entertainment which she had given to her two lovers, she sat herself down to think seriously over her affairs. There were three paths open before her. She might take Mr. Cheesacre, or she might take Captain Bellfield—or she might decide that she would have nothing more to say to either of them in the way of courting. They were very persistent, no doubt; but she thought that she would know how to make them understand her, if she should really make up her mind that she would have neither one nor the other. She was going to leave Norwich after Easter, and they knew that such was her purpose. Something had been said of her returning to Yarmouth in the summer. She was a just woman at heart, and justice required that each of them should know what was to be his prospect if she did so return.

There was a good deal to be said on Mr. Cheesacre's behalf. Mahogany-furnitured bedrooms assist one's comfort in this life; and heaps of manure, though they are not brilliant in romance, are very efficacious in farming. Mrs. Greenow by no means despised these things; and as for the owner of them, though she saw that there was much amiss in his character, she thought that his little foibles were of such a nature that she, as his wife, or any other woman of spirit, might be able to repress them, if not to cure them. But she had already married for money once, as she told herself very plainly on this occasion, and she thought that she might now venture on a little love. Her marriage for money had been altogether successful. The nursing of old Greenow had not been very disagreeable to her, nor had it taken longer than she had anticipated. She had now got all the reward that she had ever promised herself, and she really did feel grateful to his memory. I almost think that among those plentiful tears some few drops belonged to sincerity. She was essentially a happy-tempered woman, blessed with a good digestion, who looked back upon her past life with contentment, and forward to her future life with confidence. She would not be greedy, she said to herself. She did not want more money, and therefore she would have none of Mr. Cheesacre. So far she resolved,—resolving also that, if possible, the mahogany-furnitured bedrooms should be kept in the family, and made over to her niece, Kate Vavasor.

But should she marry for love; and if so, should Captain Bellfield be the man? Strange to say, his poverty and his scampishness and his lies almost recommended him to her. At any rate, it was not of those things that she was afraid. She had a woman's true belief in her own power, and thought that she could cure them,—as far as they needed cure. As for his stories about Inkerman, and his little debts, she cared nothing about that. She also had her Inkermans, and was quite aware that she made as good use of them as the Captain did of his. And as for the debts,—what was a man to do who hadn't got any money? She also had owed for her gloves and corsets in the ante-Greenow days of her adventures. But there was this danger,—that there might be more behind of which she had never heard. Another Mrs. Bellfield was not impossible; and what, if instead of being a real captain at all, he should be a returned ticket-of-leave man! Such things had happened. Her chief security was in this,—that Cheesacre had known the man for many years, and would certainly have told anything against him that he did know. Under all these circumstances, she could not quite make up her mind either for or against Captain Bellfield.

Between nine and ten in the evening, an hour or so after Mr. Cheesacre had left her, Jeannette brought to her some arrowroot with a little sherry in it. She usually dined early, and it was her habit to take a light repast before she retired for the night.

"Jeannette," she said, as she stirred the lumps of white sugar in the bowl, "I'm afraid those two gentlemen have quarrelled."

"Oh, laws, ma'am, in course they have! How was they to help it?"

Jeannette, on these occasions, was in the habit of standing beside the chair of her mistress, and chatting with her; and then, if the chatting was much prolonged, she would gradually sink down upon the corner of a chair herself,—and then the two women would be very comfortable together over the fire, Jeannette never forgetting that she was the servant, and Mrs. Greenow never forgetting that she was the mistress.

"And why should they quarrel, Jeannette? It's very foolish."

"I don't know about being foolish, ma'am; but it's the most natural thing in life. If I had two beaux as was a-courting me together, in course I should expect as they would punch each other's heads. There's some girls do it a purpose, because they like to see it. One at a time's what I say."

"You're a young thing, Jeannette."

"Well, ma'am—yes; I am young, no doubt. But I won't say but what I've had a beau, young as I look."

"But you don't suppose that I want beaux, as you call them?"

"I don't know, ma'am, as you wants 'em exactly. That's as may be. There they are; and if they was to blow each other's brains out in the gig to-night, I shouldn't be a bit surprised for one. There's nothing won't quiet them at Oileymead to-night, if brandy-and-water don't do it." As she said this, Jeannette slipt into her chair, and held up her hands in token of the intensity of her fears.

"Why, you silly child, they're not going home together at all. Did not the Captain go away first?"

"The Captain did go away first, certainly; but I thought perhaps it was to get his pistols and fighting things ready."

"They won't fight, Jeannette. Gentlemen have given over fighting."

"Have they, ma'am? That makes it much easier for ladies, no doubt. Perhaps them peaceable ways will come down to such as us in time. It'd be a comfort, I know, to them as are quiet given, like me. I hate to see men knocking each other's heads about,—I do. So Mr. Cheesacre and the Captain won't fight, ma'am?"

"Of course they won't, you little fool, you."

"Dear, dear; I was so sure we should have had the papers all full of it,— and perhaps one of them stretched upon his bloody bier! I wonder which it would have been? I always made up my mind that the Captain wouldn't be wounded in any of his wital parts—unless it was his heart, you know, ma'am."

"But why should they quarrel at all, Jeannette? It is the most foolish thing."

"Well, ma'am, I don't know about that. What else is they to do? There's some things as you can cry halves about, but there's no crying halves about this."

"About what, Jeannette?"—"Why, about you, ma'am."

"Jeannette, I wonder how you can say such things; as if I, in my position, had ever said a word to encourage either of them. You know it's not true, Jeannette, and you shouldn't say so." Whereupon Mrs. Greenow put her handkerchief to her eyes, and Jeannette, probably in token of contrition, put her apron to hers.

"To be sure, ma'am, no lady could have behaved better through it than you have done, and goodness knows you have been tried hard."

"Indeed I have, Jeannette."

"And if gentlemen will make fools of themselves, it isn't your fault; is it, ma'am?"

"But I'm so sorry that they should have quarrelled. They were such dear friends, you know;—quite all in all to each other."

"When you've settled which it's to be, ma'am, that'll all come right again,—seeing that gentlefolks like them have given up fighting, as you say." Then there was a little pause. "I suppose, ma'am, it won't be Mr. Cheesacre? To be sure, he's a man as is uncommonly well to do in the world."

"What's all that to me, Jeannette? I shall ever regard Mr. Cheesacre as a dear friend who has been very good to me at a time of trouble; but he'll never be more than that."

"Then it'll be the Captain, ma'am? I'm sure, for my part, I've always thought the Captain was the nicer gentleman of the two,—and have always said so."

"He's nothing to me, girl."

"And as for money,—what's the good of having more than enough? If he can bring love, you can bring money; can't you, ma'am?"

"He's nothing to me, girl," repeated Mrs. Greenow.

"But he will be?" said Jeannette, plainly asking a question.

"Well, I'm sure! What's the world come to, I wonder, when you sit yourself down there, and cross-examine your mistress in that way! Get to bed, will you? It's near ten o'clock."

"I hope I haven't said anything amiss, ma'am;" and Jeannette rose from her seat.

"It's my fault for encouraging you," said Mrs. Greenow. "Go downstairs and finish your work, do; and then take yourself off to bed. Next week we shall have to be packing up, and there'll be all my things to see to before that." So Jeannette got up and departed, and after some few further thoughts about Captain Bellfield, Mrs. Greenow herself went to her bedroom.

Mr. Cheesacre, when he drove back to Oileymead alone from Norwich, after dining with Mrs. Greenow, had kept himself hot, and almost comfortable, with passion against Bellfield; and his heat, if not his comfort, had been sustained by his seeing the Captain, with his portmanteau, escaping just as he reached his own homestead. But early on the following morning his mind reverted to Mrs. Greenow, and he remembered, with anything but satisfaction, some of the hard things which she had said to him. He had made mistakes in his manner of wooing. He was quite aware of that now, and was determined that they should be rectified for the future. She had rebuked him for having said nothing about his love. He would instantly mend that fault. And she had bidden him not to be so communicative about his wealth. Henceforth he would be dumb on that subject. Nevertheless, he could not but think that the knowledge of his circumstances which the lady already possessed, must be of service to him. "She can't really like a poor beggarly wretch who hasn't got a shilling," he said to himself. He was very far from feeling that the battle was already lost. Her last word to him had been an assurance of her friendship; and then why should she have been at so much trouble to tell him the way in which he ought to address her if she were herself indifferent as to his addresses? He was, no doubt, becoming tired of his courtship, and heartily wished that the work were over; but he was not minded to give it up. He therefore prepared himself for another attack, and took himself into Norwich without seeking counsel from any one. He could not trust himself to think that she could really wish to refuse him after all the encouragement she had given him. On this occasion he put on no pink shirt or shiny boots, being deterred from doing so by a remembrance of Captain Bellfield's ridicule; but, nevertheless, he dressed himself with considerable care. He clothed his nether person in knickerbockers, with tight, leathern, bright-coloured gaiters round his legs, being conscious of certain manly graces and symmetrical proportions which might, as he thought, stand him in good stead. And he put on a new shooting-coat, the buttons on which were elaborate, and a wonderful waistcoat worked over with foxes' heads. He completed his toilet with a round, low-crowned hat, with dog's-skin gloves, and a cutting whip. Thus armed he went forth resolved to conquer or to die,—as far as death might result from any wound which Mrs. Greenow might be able to give him. He waited, on this occasion, for the coming of no market-day; indeed, the journey into the city was altogether special, and he was desirous that she should know that such was the case. He drove at a great pace into the inn-yard, threw his reins to the ostler, took just one glass of cherry-brandy at the bar, and then marched off across the market-place to the Close, with quiet and decisive steps.

"Is that you, Cheesacre?" said a friendly voice, in one of the narrow streets. "Who expected to see you in Norwich on a Thursday!" It was Grimsby, the son of old Grimsby of Hatherwich, a country gentleman, and one, therefore, to whom Cheesacre would generally pay much respect; but on this occasion he did not even pull up for an instant, or moderate his pace. "A little bit of private business," he said, and marched onwards with his head towards the Close. "I'm not going to be afraid of a woman—not if I know it," he said to himself; but, nevertheless, at a certain pastrycook's, of whose shop he had knowledge, he pulled up and had another glass of cherry-brandy.

"Mrs. Greenow is at home," he said to Jeannette, not deigning to ask any question.

"Oh, yes, sir; she is at home," said Jeannette, conscious that some occasion had arrived; and in another second he was in the presence of his angel.

"Mr. Cheesacre, whoever expected to see you in Norwich on a Thursday?" said the lady, as she welcomed him, using almost the same words as his friend had done in the street. Why should not he come into Norwich on a Thursday, as well as any one else? Did they suppose that he was tied for ever to his ploughs and carts? He was minded to conduct himself with a little spirit on this occasion, and to improve the opinion which Mrs. Greenow had formed about him. On this account he answered her somewhat boldly.

"There's no knowing when I may be in Norwich, Mrs. Greenow, or when I mayn't. I'm one of those men of whom nobody knows anything certain, except that I pay as I go." Then he remembered that he was not to make any more boasts about his money, and he endeavoured to cover the error. "There's one other thing they may all know if they please, but we won't say what that is just at present."

"Won't you sit down, Mr. Cheesacre?"

"Well,—thank you,—I will sit down for a few minutes if you'll let me, Mrs. Greenow. Mrs. Greenow, I'm in such a state of mind that I must put an end to it, or else I shall be going mad, and doing somebody a damage."

"Dear me! what has happened to you? You're going out shooting, presently; are you not?" and Mrs. Greenow looked down at his garments.

"No, Mrs. Greenow, I'm not going out shooting. I put on these things because I thought I might take a shot as I came along. But I couldn't bring myself to do it, and then I wouldn't take them off again. What does it matter what a man wears?"

"Not in the least, so long as he is decent."

"I'm sure I'm always that, Mrs. Greenow."

"Oh, dear, yes. More than that, I should say. I consider you to be rather gay in your attire."

"I don't pretend to anything of that kind, Mrs. Greenow. I like to be nice, and all that kind of thing. There are people who think that because a man farms his own land, he must be always in the muck. It is the case, of course, with those who have to make their rent and living out of it." Then he remembered that he was again treading on forbidden ground, and stopped himself. "But it don't matter what a man wears if his heart isn't easy within him."

"I don't know why you should speak in that way, Mr. Cheesacre; but it's what I have felt every hour since—since Greenow left me."

Mr. Cheesacre was rather at a loss to know how he should begin. This allusion to the departed one did not at all assist him. He had so often told the widow that care killed a cat, and that a live dog was better than a dead lion; and had found so little efficacy in the proverbs, that he did not care to revert to them. He was aware that some more decided method of proceeding was now required. Little hints at love-making had been all very well in the earlier days of their acquaintance; but there must be something more than little hints before he could hope to bring the matter to a favourable conclusion. The widow herself had told him that he ought to talk about love; and he had taken two glasses of cherry-brandy, hoping that they might enable him to do so. He had put on a coat with brilliant buttons, and new knickerbockers, in order that he might be master of the occasion. He was resolved to call a spade a spade, and to speak boldly of his passion; but how was he to begin? There was the difficulty. He was now seated in a chair, and there he remained silent for a minute or two, while she smoothed her eyebrows with her handkerchief after her last slight ebullition of grief.

"Mrs. Greenow," he exclaimed at last, jumping up before her; "dearest Mrs. Greenow; darling Mrs. Greenow, will you be my wife? There! I have said it at last, and I mean it. Everything that I've got shall be yours. Of course I speak specially of my hand and heart. As for love;—oh, Arabella, if you only knew me! I don't think there's a man in Norfolk better able to love a woman than I am. Ever since I first saw you at Yarmouth, I've been in love to that extent that I've not known what I've been about. If you'll ask them at home, they'll tell you that I've not been able to look after anything about the place,—not as it should be done. I haven't really. I don't suppose I've opened the wages book half a dozen times since last July."

"And has that been my fault, Mr. Cheesacre?"

"Upon my word it has. I can't move about anywhere without thinking about you. My mind's made up; I won't stay at Oileymead unless you will come and be its mistress."

"Not stay at Oileymead?"

"No, indeed. I'll let the place, and go and travel somewheres. What's the use of my hanging on there without the woman of my heart? I couldn't do it, Mrs. Greenow; I couldn't, indeed. Of course I've got everything there that money can buy,—but it's all of no use to a man that's in love. Do you know, I've come quite to despise money and stock, and all that sort of thing. I haven't had my banker's book home these last three months. Only think of that now."

"But how can I help you, Mr. Cheesacre?"

"Just say one word, and the thing'll be done. Say you'll be my wife? I'll be so good to you. I will, indeed. As for your fortune, I don't care that for it! I'm not like somebody else; it's yourself I want. You shall be my pet, and my poppet, and my dearest little duck all the days of your life."

"No, Mr. Cheesacre; it cannot be."

"And why not? Look here, Arabella!" At these words he rose from his chair, and coming immediately before her, went down on both knees so close to her as to prevent the possibility of her escaping from him. There could be no doubt as to the efficacy of the cherry-brandy. There he was, well down on his knees; but he had not got down so low without some little cracking and straining on the part of the gaiters with which his legs were encompassed. He, in his passion, had probably omitted to notice this; but Mrs. Greenow, who was more cool in her present temperament, was painfully aware that he might not be able to rise with ease.

"Mr. Cheesacre, don't make a fool of yourself. Get up," said she.

"Never, till you have told me that you will be mine!"

"Then you'll remain there for ever, which will be inconvenient. I won't have you take hold of my hand, Mr. Cheesacre. I tell you to have done." Whereupon his grasp upon her hand was released; but he made no attempt to rise.

"I never saw a man look so much like a fool in my life," said she. "If you don't get up, I'll push you over. There; don't you hear? There's somebody coming."

But Cheesacre, whose senses were less acute than the lady's, did not hear. "I'll never get up," said he, "till you have bid me hope."

"Bid you play the fiddle. Get away from my knees, at any rate. There;— he'll be in the room now before—"

Mr. Cheesacre disturbed.

Cheesacre now did hear a sound of steps, and the door was opened while he made his first futile attempt to get back to a standing position. The door was opened, and Captain Bellfield entered. "I beg ten thousand pardons," said he, "but as I did not see Jeannette, I ventured to come in. May I venture to congratulate my friend Cheesacre on his success?"

In the meantime Cheesacre had risen; but he had done so slowly, and with evident difficulty. "I'll trouble you to leave the room, Captain Bellfield," said he. "I'm particularly engaged with Mrs. Greenow, as any gentleman might have seen."

"There wasn't the slightest difficulty in seeing it, old fellow," said the Captain. "Shall I wish you joy?"

"I'll trouble you to leave the room, sir," said Cheesacre, walking up to him.

"Certainly, if Mrs. Greenow will desire me to do so," said the Captain.

Then Mrs. Greenow felt herself called upon to speak.

"Gentlemen, I must beg that you will not make my drawing-room a place for quarrelling. Captain Bellfield, lest there should be any misconception, I must beg you to understand that the position in which you found Mr. Cheesacre was one altogether of his own seeking. It was not with my consent that he was there."

"I can easily believe that, Mrs. Greenow," said the Captain.

"Who cares what you believe, sir?" said Mr. Cheesacre.

"Gentlemen! gentlemen! this is really unkind. Captain Bellfield, I think I had better ask you to withdraw."

"By all means," said Mr. Cheesacre.

"As it is absolutely necessary that I should give Mr. Cheesacre a definite answer after what has occurred —"

"Of course," said Captain Bellfield, preparing to go. "I'll take another opportunity of paying my respects to you. Perhaps I might be allowed to come this evening?"

To this Mrs. Greenow half assented with an uncertain nod, and then the Captain went. As soon as the door was closed behind his back, Mr. Cheesacre again prepared to throw himself into his former position, but to this Mrs. Greenow decidedly objected. If he were allowed to go down again, there was no knowing what force might be necessary to raise him. "Mr. Cheesacre," she said, "let there be an end to this little farce between us."

"Farce!" said he, standing with his hand on his heart, and his legs and knickerbockers well displayed.

"It is certainly either a farce or a mistake. If the latter, — and I have been at all to blame, — I ask your pardon most sincerely."

"But you'll be Mrs. Cheesacre; won't you?"

"No, Mr. Cheesacre; no. One husband is enough for any woman, and mine lies buried at Birmingham."

"Oh, damn it!" said he, in utter disgust at this further reference to Mr. Greenow. The expression, at such a moment, militated against courtesy; but even Mrs. Greenow herself felt that the poor man had been subjected to provocation.

"Let us part friends," said she, offering him her hand.

But he turned his back upon her, for there was something in his eye that he wanted to hide. I believe that he really did love her, and that at this moment he would have taken her, even though he had learned that her fortune was gone.

"Will you not give me your hand," said she, "in token that there is no anger between us?"

"Do think about it again—do!" said he. "If there's anything you like to have changed, I'll change it at once. I'll give up Oileymead altogether, if you don't like being so near the farm-yard. I'll give up anything; so I will. Mrs. Greenow, if you only knew how I've set my heart upon it!" And now, though his back was turned, the whimpering of his voice told plainly that tears were in his eyes.

She was a little touched. No woman would feel disposed to marry a man simply because he cried, and perhaps few women would be less likely to give way to such tenderness than Mrs. Greenow. She understood men and women too well, and had seen too much both of the world's rough side and of its smooth side to fall into such a blunder as that; but she was touched. "My friend," she said, putting her hand upon his arm, "think no more of it."

"But I can't help thinking of it," said he, almost blubbering in his earnestness.

"No, no, no," said she, still touching him with her hand. "Why, Mr. Cheesacre, how can you bring yourself to care for an old woman like me, when so many pretty young ladies would give their eyes to get a kind word from you?"

"I don't want any young lady," said he.

"There's Charlie Fairstairs, who would make as good a wife as any girl I know."

"Psha! Charlie Fairstairs, indeed!" The very idea of having such a bride palmed off upon him did something to restore him to his manly courage.

"Or my niece, Kate Vavasor, who has a nice little fortune of her own, and who is as accomplished as she is good-looking."

"She's nothing to me, Mrs. Greenow."

"That's because you never asked her to be anything. If I get her to come back to Yarmouth next summer, will you think about it? You want a wife, and you couldn't do better if you searched all England over. It would be so pleasant for us to be such near friends; wouldn't it?" And again she put her hand upon his arm.

"Mrs. Greenow, just at present there's only one woman in the world that I can think of."

"And that's my niece."

"And that's yourself. I'm a broken-hearted man,—I am, indeed. I didn't ever think I should feel so much about a thing of the kind—I didn't, really. I hardly know what to do with myself; but I suppose I'd better go back to Oileymead." He had become so painfully unconscious of his new coat and his knickerbockers that it was impossible not to pity him. "I shall always hate the place now," he said,—"always."

"That will pass away. You'd be as happy as a king there, if you'd take Kate for your queen."

"And what'll you do, Mrs. Greenow?"

"What shall I do?"—"Yes; what will you do?"

"That is, if you marry Kate? Why, I'll come and stay with you half my time, and nurse the children, as an old grand-aunt should."

"But about—." Then he hesitated, and she asked him of what he was thinking.

"You don't mean to take that man Bellfield, do you?"

"Come, Mr. Cheesacre, that's rank jealousy. What right can you have to ask me whether I shall take any man or no man? The chances are that I shall remain as I am till I'm carried to my grave; but I'm not going to give any pledge about it to you or to any one."

"You don't know that man, Mrs. Greenow; you don't, indeed. I tell it you as your friend. Does not it stand to reason, when he has got nothing in the world, that he must be a beggar? It's all very well saying that when a man is courting a lady, he shouldn't say much about his money; but you won't make me believe that any man will make a good husband who hasn't got a shilling. And for lies, there's no beating him!"

"Why, then, has he been such a friend of yours?"

"Well, because I've been foolish. I took up with him just because he looked pleasant, I suppose."

"And you want to prevent me from doing the same thing."

"If you were to marry him, Mrs. Greenow, it's my belief I should do him a mischief; it is, really. I don't think I could stand it;—a mean, skulking beggar! I suppose I'd better go now?"

"Certainly, if that's the way you choose to talk about my friends."

"Friends, indeed! Well, I won't say any more at present. I suppose if I was to talk for ever it wouldn't be any good?"

"Come and talk to Kate Vavasor for ever, Mr. Cheesacre."

To this he made no reply, but went forth from the house, and got his gig, and drove himself home to Oileymead, thinking of his disappointment with all the bitterness of a young lover. "I didn't ever think I should ever care so much about anything," he said, as he took himself up to bed that night.

That evening Captain Bellfield did call in the Close, as he had said he would do, but he was not admitted. "Her mistress was very bad with a headache," Jeannette said.

CHAPTER XLVIII
PREPARATIONS FOR LADY MONK'S PARTY

Early in April, the Easter recess being all over, Lady Monk gave a grand party in London. Lady Monk's town house was in Gloucester Square. It was a large mansion, and Lady Monk's parties in London were known to be very great affairs. She usually gave two or three in the season, and spent a large portion of her time and energy in so arranging matters that her parties should be successful. As this was her special line in life, a failure would have been very distressing to her;—and we may also say very disgraceful, taking into consideration, as we should do in forming our judgement on the subject, the very large sums of Sir Cosmo's money which she spent in this way. But she seldom did fail. She knew how to select her days, so as not to fall foul of other events. It seldom happened that people could not come to her because of a division which occupied all the Members of Parliament, or that they were drawn away by the superior magnitude of some other attraction in the world of fashion. This giving of parties was her business, and she had learned it thoroughly. She worked at it harder than most men work at their trades, and let us hope that the profits were consolatory.

It was generally acknowledged to be the proper thing to go to Lady Monk's parties. There were certain people who were asked, and who went as a matter of course,—people who were by no means on intimate terms with Lady Monk, or with Sir Cosmo; but they were people to have whom was the proper thing, and they were people who understood that to go to Lady Monk's was the proper thing for them. The Duchess of St. Bungay was always there, though she hated Lady Monk, and Lady Monk always abused her; but a card was sent to the Duchess in the same way as the Lord Mayor invites a Cabinet Minister to dinner, even though the one man might believe the other to be a thief. And Mrs. Conway Sparkes was generally there; she went everywhere. Lady Monk did not at all know why Mrs. Conway Sparkes was so favoured by the world; but there was the fact, and she bowed to it. Then there were another set, the members of which were or were not invited, according to circumstances, at the time; and these were the people who were probably the most legitimate recipients of Lady Monk's hospitality. Old family friends of her husband were among the number. Let the Tuftons come in April, and perhaps again in May; then they will not feel their exclusion from that seventh heaven of glory,—the great culminating crush in July. Scores of young ladies who really loved parties belonged to this set. The mothers and aunts knew Lady Monk's sisters and cousins. They accepted so much of Lady Monk's good things as she vouchsafed them, and were thankful. Then there was another lot, which generally became, especially on that great July occasion, the most numerous of the three. It comprised all those who made strong interest to obtain admittance within her ladyship's house,—who struggled and fought almost with tooth and nail to get invitations. Against these people Lady Monk carried on an internecine war. Had she not done so she would have been swamped by them, and her success would have been at an end; but yet she never dreamed of shutting her doors against them altogether, or of saying boldly that none such should hamper her staircases. She knew that she must yield, but her effort was made to yield to as few as might be possible. When she was first told by her factotum in these operations that Mr. Bott wanted to come, she positively declined to have him. When it was afterwards intimated to her that the Duchess of St. Bungay had made a point of it, she sneered at the Duchess, and did not even then yield. But when at last it was brought home to her understanding that Mr. Palliser wished it, and that Mr. Palliser probably would not come himself unless his wishes were gratified, she gave way. She was especially anxious that Lady Glencora should come to her gathering, and she knew that Lady Glencora could not be had without Mr. Palliser.

It was very much desired by her that Lady Glencora should be there. "Burgo," said she to her nephew, one morning, "look here." Burgo was at the time staying with his aunt, in Gloucester Square, much to the annoyance of Sir Cosmo, who had become heartily tired of his nephew. The aunt and the nephew had been closeted together more than once lately, and perhaps they understood each other better now than they had done down at Monkshade. The aunt had handed a little note to Burgo, which he read and then threw back to her. "You see that she is not afraid of coming," said Lady Monk.

"I suppose she doesn't think much about it," said Burgo.

"If that's what you really believe, you'd better give it up. Nothing on earth would justify such a step on your part except a thorough conviction that she is attached to you."

Burgo looked at the fireplace, almost savagely, and his aunt looked at him very keenly. "Well," she said, "if there's to be an end of it, let there be an end of it."

"I think I'd better hang myself," he said.

"Burgo, I will not have you here if you talk to me in that way. I am trying to help you once again; but if you look like that, and talk like that, I will give it up."

"I think you'd better give it up."

"Are you becoming cowardly at last? With all your faults I never expected that of you."

"No; I am not a coward. I'd go out and fight him at two paces' distance with the greatest pleasure in the world."

"You know that's nonsense, Burgo. It's downright braggadocio. Men do not fight now; nor any time would a man be called upon to fight, because you simply wanted to take his wife from him. If you had done it, indeed!"

"How am I to do it? I'd do it to-morrow if it depended on me. No one can say that I'm afraid of anybody or of anything."

"I suppose something in the matter depends on her?"

"I believe she loves me,—if you mean that?"

"Look here, Burgo," and the considerate aunt gave to the impoverished and ruined nephew such counsel as she, in accordance with her lights, was enabled to bestow. "I think you were much wronged in that matter. After what had passed I thought that you had a right to claim Lady Glencora as your wife. Mr. Palliser, in my mind, behaved very wrongly in stepping in between you and—you and such a fortune as hers, in that way. He cannot expect that his wife should have any affection for him. There is nobody alive who has a greater horror of anything improper in married women than I have. I have always shown it. When Lady Madeline Madtop left her husband, I would never allow her to come inside my doors again,—though I have no doubt he ill-used her dreadfully, and there was nothing ever proved between her and Colonel Graham. One can't be too particular in such matters. But here, if you,—if you can succeed, you know, I shall always regard the Palliser episode in Lady Glencora's life as a tragical accident. I shall indeed. Poor dear! It was done exactly as they make nuns of girls in Roman Catholic countries; and as I should think no harm of helping a nun out of her convent, so I should think no harm of helping her now. If you are to say anything to her, I think you might have an opportunity at the party."

Burgo was still looking at the fireplace; and he sat on, looking and still looking, but he said nothing.

"You can think of what I have said, Burgo," continued his aunt, meaning that he should get up and go. But he did not go. "Have you anything more that you wish to say to me?" she asked.

"I've got no money," said Burgo, still looking at the fireplace.

Lady Glencora's property was worth not less than fifty thousand a year. He was a young man ambitious of obtaining that almost incredible amount of wealth, and who once had nearly reached it, by means of her love. His present obstacle consisted in his want of a twenty-pound note! "I've got no money." The words were growled out rather than spoken, and his eyes were never turned even for a moment towards his aunt's face.

"You've never got any money," said she, speaking almost with passion.

"How can I help it? I can't make money. If I had a couple of hundred pounds, so that I could take her, I believe that she would go with me. It should not be my fault if she did not. It would have been all right if she had come to Monkshade."

"I've got no money for you, Burgo. I have not five pounds belonging to me."

"But you've got—?"

"What?" said Lady Monk, interrupting him sharply.

"Would Cosmo lend it me?" said he, hesitating to go on with that suggestion which he had been about to make. The Cosmo of whom he spoke was not his uncle, but his cousin. No eloquence could have induced his uncle, Sir Cosmo, to lend him another shilling. But the son of the house was a man rich with his own wealth, and Burgo had not taxed him for some years.

"I do not know," said Lady Monk. "I never see him. Probably not."

"It is hard," said Burgo. "Fancy that a man should be ruined for two hundred pounds, just at such a moment of his life as this!" He was a man bold by nature, and he did make his proposition. "You have jewels, aunt;— could you not raise it for me? I would redeem them with the very first money that I got."

Lady Monk rose in a passion when the suggestion was first made, but before the interview was over she had promised that she would endeavour to do something in the way of raising money for him yet, once again. He was her favourite nephew, and the same almost to her as a child of her own. With one of her own children indeed she had quarrelled, and of the other, a married daughter, she rarely saw much. Such love as she had to give she gave to Burgo, and she promised him the money though she knew that she must raise it by some villanous falsehood to her husband.

On the same morning Lady Glencora went to Queen Anne Street with the purpose of inducing Alice to go to Lady Monk's party; but Alice would not accede to the proposition, though Lady Glencora pressed it with all her eloquence. "I don't know her," said Alice.

"My dear," said Lady Glencora, "that's absurd. Half the people there won't know her."

"But they know her set, or know her friends,—or, at any rate, will meet their own friends at her house. I should only bother you, and should not in the least gratify myself."

"The fact is, everybody will go who can, and I should have no sort of trouble in getting a card for you. Indeed I should simply write a note and say I meant to bring you."

"Pray don't do any such thing, for I certainly shall not go. I can't conceive why you should wish it."

"Mr. Fitzgerald will be there," said Lady Glencora, altering her voice altogether, and speaking in that low tone with which she used to win Alice's heart down at Matching. She was sitting close over the fire, leaning low, holding up her little hands as a screen to her face, and looking at her companion earnestly. "I'm sure that he will be there, though nobody has told me."

"That may be a reason for your staying away," said Alice, slowly, "but hardly a reason for my going with you."

Lady Glencora would not condescend to tell her friend in so many words that she wanted her protection. She could not bring herself to say that, though she wished it to be understood. "Ah! I thought you would have gone," said she.

"It would be contrary to all my habits," said Alice: "I never go to people's houses when I don't know them. It's a kind of society which I don't like. Pray do not ask me."

"Oh! very well. If it must be so, I won't press it." Lady Glencora had moved the position of one of her hands so as to get it to her pocket, and there had grasped a letter, which she still carried; but when Alice said those last cold words, "Pray do not ask me," she released the grasp, and left the letter where it was. "I suppose he won't bite me, at any rate," she said, and she assumed that look of childish drollery which she would sometimes put on, almost with a grimace, but still with so much prettiness that no one who saw her would regret it.

"He certainly can't bite you, if you will not let him."

"Do you know, Alice, though they all say that Plantagenet is one of the wisest men in London, I sometimes think that he is one of the greatest fools. Soon after we came to town I told him that we had better not go to that woman's house. Of course he understood me. He simply said that he wished that I should do so. 'I hate anything out of the way,' he said. 'There can be no reason why my wife should not go to Lady Monk's house as well as to any other.' There was an end of it, you know, as far as anything I could do was concerned. But there wasn't an end of it with him. He insists that I shall go, but he sends my duenna with me. Dear Mrs. Marsham is to be there!"

"She'll do you no harm, I suppose?"

"I'm not so sure of that, Alice. In the first place, one doesn't like to be followed everywhere by a policeman, even though one isn't going to pick a pocket. And then, the devil is so strong within me, that I should like to dodge the policeman. I can fancy a woman being driven to do wrong simply by a desire to show her policeman that she can be too many for him."

"Glencora, you make me so wretched when you talk like that."

"Will you go with me, then, so that I may have a policeman of my own choosing? He asked me if I would mind taking Mrs. Marsham with me in my carriage. So I up and spoke, very boldly, like the proud young porter, and told him I would not; and when he asked why not, I said that I preferred taking a friend of my own,—a young friend, I said, and I then named you or my cousin, Lady Jane. I told him I should bring one or the other."

"And was he angry?"

"No; he took it very quietly,—saying something, in his calm way, about hoping that I should get over a prejudice against one of his earliest and dearest friends. He twits at me because I don't understand Parliament and the British Constitution, but I know more of them than he does about a woman. You are quite sure you won't go, then?" Alice hesitated a moment. "Do," said Lady Glencora; and there was an amount of persuasion in her accent which should, I think, have overcome her cousin's scruples.

"It is against the whole tenor of my life's way," she said, "And, Glencora, I am not happy myself. I am not fit for parties. I sometimes think that I shall never go into society again."

"That's nonsense, you know."

"I suppose it is, but I cannot go now. I would if I really thought—"

"Oh, very well," said Lady Glencora, interrupting her. "I suppose I shall get through it. If he asks me to dance, I shall stand up with him, just as though I had never seen him before." Then she remembered the letter in her pocket,—remembered that at this moment she bore about with her a written proposition from this man to go off with him and leave her husband's house. She had intended to show it to Alice on this occasion; but as Alice had refused her request, she was glad that she had not done so. "You'll come to me the morning after," said Lady Glencora, as she went. This Alice promised to do; and then she was left alone.

Alice regretted,—regretted deeply that she had not consented to go with her cousin. After all, of what importance had been her objection when compared with the cause for which her presence had been desired? Doubtless she would have been uncomfortable at Lady Monk's house; but could she not have borne some hour or two of discomfort on her friend's behalf? But, in truth, it was only after Lady Glencora had left her that she began to understand the subject fully, and to feel that she might possibly have been of service in a great danger. But it was too late now. Then she strove to comfort herself with the reflection that a casual meeting at an evening party in London could not be perilous in the same degree as a prolonged sojourn together in a country house.

CHAPTER XLIX
HOW LADY GLENCORA WENT TO LADY MONK'S PARTY

Lady Monk's house in Gloucester Square was admirably well adapted for the giving of parties. It was a large house, and seemed to the eyes of guests to be much larger than it was. The hall was spacious, and the stairs went up in the centre, facing you as you entered the inner hall. Round the top of the stairs there was a broad gallery, with an ornamented railing, and from this opened the doors into the three reception-rooms. There were two on the right, the larger of which looked out backwards, and these two were connected by an archway, as though made for folding-doors; but the doors, I believe, never were there. Fronting the top of the staircase there was a smaller room, looking out backwards, very prettily furnished, and much used by Lady Monk when alone. It was here that Burgo had held that conference with his aunt of which mention has been made. Below stairs there was the great dining-room, on which, on these occasions, a huge buffet was erected for refreshments,—what I may call a masculine buffet, as it was attended by butlers and men in livery,—and there was a smaller room looking out into the square, in which there was a feminine battery for the dispensing of tea and such like smaller good things, and from which female aid could be attained for the arrangement or mending of dresses in a further sanctum within it. For such purposes as that now on foot the house was most commodious. Lady Monk, on these occasions, was moved by a noble ambition to do something different from that done by her neighbours in similar circumstances, and therefore she never came forward to receive her guests. She ensconced herself, early in the evening, in that room at the head of the stairs, and there they who chose to see her made their way up to her, and spoke their little speeches. They who thought her to be a great woman,—and many people did think her to be great,—were wont to declare that she never forgot those who did come, or those who did not. And even they who desired to describe her as little,—for even Lady Monk had enemies,—would hint that though she never came out of the room, she would rise from her chair and make a step towards the door whenever any name very high in fashionable life greeted her ears. So that a mighty

Cabinet Minister, or a duchess in great repute, or any special wonder of the season, could not fail of entering her precincts and being seen there for a few moments. It would, of course, happen that the doorway of her chamber would become blocked; but there were precautions taken to avoid this inconvenience as far as possible, and one man in livery was employed to go backwards and forwards between his mistress and the outer world, so as to keep the thread of a passage open.

But though Lady Monk was in this way enabled to rest herself during her labours, there was much in her night's work which was not altogether exhilarating. Ladies would come into her small room and sit there by the hour, with whom she had not the slightest wish to hold conversation. The Duchess of St. Bungay would always be there,—so that there was a special seat in one corner of the room which was called the Duchess' stool. "I shouldn't care a straw about her," Lady Monk had been heard to complain, "if she would talk to anybody. But nobody will talk to her, and then she listens to everything."

There had been another word or two between Burgo Fitzgerald and his aunt before the evening came, a word or two in the speaking of which she had found some difficulty. She was prepared with the money,—with that two hundred pounds for which he had asked,—obtained with what wiles, and lies, and baseness of subterfuge I need not stop here to describe. But she was by no means willing to give this over into her nephew's hands without security. She was willing to advance him this money; she had been willing even to go through unusual dirt to get it for him; but she was desirous that he should have it only for a certain purpose. How could she bind him down to spend it as she would have it spent? Could she undertake to hand it to him as soon as Lady Glencora should be in his power? Even though she could have brought herself to say as much,—and I think she might also have done so after what she had said,—she could not have carried out such a plan. In that case the want would be instant, and the action must be rapid. She therefore had no alternative but to entrust him with the bank-notes at once. "Burgo," she said, "if I find that you deceive me now, I will never trust you again." "All right," said Burgo, as he barely counted the money before he thrust it into his breast-pocket. "It is lent to you for a certain purpose, should you happen to want it," she said, solemnly. "I do happen to want it very much," he answered. She did not dare to say more; but as her nephew turned away from her with a step that was quite light in its gaiety, she almost felt that she was already cozened. Let Burgo's troubles be as heavy as they might be, there was something to him ecstatic in the touch of ready money which always cured them for the moment.

"All right," said Burgo, as he thrust the money into his breast-pocket

On the morning of Lady Monk's party a few very uncomfortable words passed between Mr. Palliser and his wife.

"Your cousin is not going, then?" said he.

"Alice is not going."

"Then you can give Mrs. Marsham a seat in your carriage?"

"Impossible, Plantagenet. I thought I had told you that I had promised my cousin Jane."

"But you can take three."

"Indeed I can't, — unless you would like me to sit out with the coachman."

There was something in this, — a tone of loudness, a touch of what he called to himself vulgarity, — which made him very angry. So he turned away from her, and looked as black as a thundercloud.

"You must know, Plantagenet," she went on, "that it is impossible for three women dressed to go out in one carriage. I am sure you wouldn't like to see me afterwards if I had been one of them."

"You need not have said anything to Lady Jane when Miss Vavasor refused. I had asked you before that."

"And I had told you that I liked going with young women, and not with old ones. That's the long and the short of it."

"Glencora, I wish you would not use such expressions."

"What! not the long and the short? It's good English. Quite as good as Mr. Bott's, when he said in the House the other night that the Government kept their accounts in a higgledy-piggledy way. You see, I have been studying the debates, and you shouldn't be angry with me."

"I am not angry with you. You speak like a child to say so. Then, I suppose, the carriage must go for Mrs. Marsham after it has taken you?"

"It shall go before. Jane will not be in a hurry, and I am sure I shall not."

"She will think you very uncivil; that is all. I told her that she could go with you when I heard that Miss Vavasor was not to be there."

"Then, Plantagenet, you shouldn't have told her so, and that's the long—; but I mustn't say that. The truth is this, if you give me any orders I'll obey them,—as far as I can. If I can't I'll say so. But if I'm left to go by my own judgement, it's not fair that I should be scolded afterwards."

"I have never scolded you."

"Yes, you have. You have told me that I was uncivil."

"I said that she would think you so."

"Then, if it's only what she thinks, I don't care two straws about it. She may have the carriage to herself if she likes, but she shan't have me in it,—not unless I'm ordered to go. I don't like her, and I won't pretend to like her. My belief is that she follows me about to tell you if she thinks that I do wrong."

"Glencora!"

"And that odious baboon with the red bristles does the same thing,— only he goes to her because he doesn't dare to go to you."

Plantagenet Palliser was struck wild with dismay. He understood well who it was whom his wife intended to describe; but that she should have spoken of any man as a baboon with red bristles, was terrible to his mind! He was beginning to think that he hardly knew how to manage his wife. And the picture she had drawn was very distressing to him. She had no mother; neither had he; and he had wished that Mrs. Marsham should give to her some of that matronly assistance and guidance which a mother does give to her young married daughter. It was true, too, as he knew, that a word or two as to some socially domestic matters had filtered through to him from Mr. Bott, down at Matching Priory, but only in such a way as to enable him to see what counsel it was needful that he should give. As for espionage over his wife,—no man could despise it more than he did! No man would be less willing to resort to it! And now his wife was accusing him of keeping spies, both male and female.

"Glencora!" he said again; and then he stopped, not knowing what to say to her.

"Well, my dear, it's better you should know at once what I feel about it. I don't suppose I'm very good; indeed I dare say I'm bad enough, but these people about me won't make me any better. The duennas don't make the Spanish ladies worth much."

"Duennas!" After that, Lady Glencora sat herself down, and Mr. Palliser stood for some moments looking at her.

It ended in his making her a long speech, in which he said a good deal of his own justice and forbearance, and something also of her frivolity and childishness. He told her that his only complaint of her was that she was too young, and, as he did so, she made a little grimace,—not to him, but to herself, as though saying to herself that that was all he knew about it. He did not notice it, or, if he did, his notice did not stop his eloquence. He assured her that he was far from keeping any watch over her, and declared that she had altogether mistaken Mrs. Marsham's character. Then there was another little grimace. "There's somebody has mistaken it worse than I have," the grimace said. Of the bristly baboon he condescended to say nothing, and he wound up by giving her a cold kiss, and saying that he would meet her at Lady Monk's.

When the evening came,—or rather the night,—the carriage went first for Mrs. Marsham, and having deposited her at Lady Monk's, went back to Park Lane for Lady Glencora. Then she had herself driven to St. James's Square, to pick up Lady Jane, so that altogether the coachman and horses did not have a good time of it. "I wish he'd keep a separate carriage for her," Lady Glencora said to her cousin Jane,—having perceived that her servants were not in a good humour. "That would be expensive," said Lady Jane. "Yes, it would be expensive," said Lady Glencora. She would not condescend to make any remark as to the non-importance of such expense to a man so wealthy as her husband, knowing that his wealth was, in fact, hers. Never to him or to any other,—not even to herself,—had she hinted that much was due to her because she had been magnificent as an heiress. There were many things about this woman that were not altogether what a husband might wish. She was not softly delicate in all her ways; but in disposition and temper she was altogether generous. I do not know that she was at all points a lady, but had Fate so willed it she would have been a thorough gentleman.

Mrs. Marsham was by no means satisfied with the way in which she was treated. She would not have cared to go at all to Lady Monk's party had she supposed that she would have to make her entry there alone. With Lady Glencora she would have seemed to receive some of that homage which would certainly have been paid to her companion. The carriage called, moreover, before she was fully ready, and the footman, as he stood at the door to hand her in, had been very sulky. She understood it all. She knew that Lady Glencora had positively declined her companionship; and if she resolved to be revenged, such resolution on her part was only natural. When she reached Lady Monk's house, she had to make her way up stairs all alone. The servants called her Mrs. Marsh, and under that name she got passed on into the front drawing-room. There she sat down, not having seen Lady Monk, and meditated over her injuries.

It was past eleven before Lady Glencora arrived, and Burgo Fitzgerald had begun to think that his evil stars intended that he should never see her again. He had been wickedly baulked at Monkshade, by what influence he had never yet ascertained; and now he thought that the same influence must be at work to keep her again away from his aunt's house. He had settled in his mind no accurate plan of a campaign; he had in his thoughts no fixed arrangement by which he might do the thing which he meditated. He had attempted to make some such plan; but, as is the case with all men to whom thinking is an unusual operation, concluded at last that he had better leave it to the course of events. It was, however, obviously necessary that he should see Lady Glencora before the course of events could be made to do anything for him. He had written to her, making his proposition in bold terms, and he felt that if she were utterly decided against him, her anger at his suggestion, or at least her refusal, would have been made known to him in some way. Silence did not absolutely give consent, but it seemed to show that consent was not impossible. From ten o'clock to past eleven he stood about on the staircase of his aunt's house, waiting for the name which he was desirous of hearing, and which he almost feared to hear. Men spoke to him, and women also, but he hardly answered. His aunt once called him into her room, and with a cautionary frown on her brow, bade him go dance. "Don't look so dreadfully preoccupied," she said to him in a whisper. But he shook his head at her, almost savagely, and went away, and did not dance. Dance! How was he to dance with such an enterprise as that upon his mind? Even to Burgo Fitzgerald the task of running away with another man's wife had in it something which prevented dancing. Lady Monk was older, and was able to regulate her feelings with more exactness. But Burgo, though he could not dance, went down into the dining-room and drank. He took a large beer-glass full of champagne and soon after that another. The drink did not flush his cheeks or make his forehead red, or bring out the sweat-drops on his brow, as it does with some men; but it added a peculiar brightness to his blue eyes. It was by the light of his eyes that men knew when Burgo had been drinking.

At last, while he was still in the supper room, he heard Lady Glencora's name announced. He had already seen Mr. Palliser come in and make his way up-stairs some quarter of an hour before; but as to that he was indifferent. He had known that the husband was to be there. When the long-expected name reached his ears, his heart seemed to jump within him. What, on the spur of the moment, should he do? As he had resolved that he would be doing, — that something should be done, let it be what it might, — he hurried to the dining-room door, and was just in time to see and be seen as Lady Glencora was passing up the stairs. She was just above him as he got himself out into the hall, so that he could not absolutely greet her with his hand; but he looked up at her, and caught her eye. He looked up, and moved his hand to her in token of salutation. She looked down at him, and the expression of her face altered visibly as her glance met his. She barely bowed to him, — with her eyes rather than with her head, but he flattered himself that there was, at any rate, no anger in her countenance. How beautiful he was as he gazed up at her, leaning against the wall as he stood, and watching her as she made her slow way up the stairs! She felt that his eyes were on her, and where the stairs turned she could not restrain herself from one other glance. As her eyes fell on his again, his mouth opened, and she fancied that she could hear the faint sigh that he uttered. It was a glorious mouth, such as the old sculptors gave to their marble gods! And Burgo, if it was so that he had not heart enough to love truly, could look as though he loved. It was not in him deceit,—or what men call acting. The expression came to him naturally, though it expressed so much more than there was within; as strong words come to some men who have no knowledge that they are speaking strongly. At this moment Burgo Fitzgerald looked as though it were possible that he might die of love.

Lady Glencora was met at the top of the stairs by Lady Monk, who came out to her, almost into the gallery, with her sweetest smile,—so that the newly-arrived guest, of course, entered into the small room. There sat the Duchess of St. Bungay on her stool in the corner, and there, next to the Duchess, but at the moment engaged in no conversation, stood Mr. Bott. There was another lady there, who stood very high in the world, and whom Lady Monk was very glad to welcome—the young Marchioness of Hartletop. She was in slight mourning; for her father-in-law, the late Marquis, had died not yet quite six months since. Very beautiful she was, and one whose presence at their houses ladies and gentlemen prized alike. She never said silly things, like the Duchess, never was troublesome as to people's conduct to her, was always gracious, yet was never led away into intimacies, was without peer the best-dressed woman in London, and yet gave herself no airs;—and then she was so exquisitely beautiful. Her smile was loveliness itself. There were, indeed, people who said that it meant nothing; but then, what should the smile of a young married woman mean? She had not been born in the purple, like Lady Glencora, her father being a country clergyman who had never reached a higher grade than that of an archdeacon; but she knew the ways of high life, and what an exigeant husband would demand of her, much better than poor Glencora. She would have spoken of no man as a baboon with a bristly beard. She never talked of the long and the short of it. She did not wander out o' nights in winter among the ruins. She made no fast friendship with ladies whom her lord did not like. She had once, indeed, been approached by a lover since she had been married,—Mr. Palliser himself having been the offender,—but she had turned the affair to infinite credit and profit, had gained her husband's closest confidence by telling him of it all, had yet not brought on any hostile collision, and had even dismissed her lover without annoying him. But then Lady Hartletop was a miracle of a woman!

Lady Glencora was no miracle. Though born in the purple, she was made of ordinary flesh and blood, and as she entered Lady Monk's little room, hardly knew how to recover herself sufficiently for the purposes of ordinary conversation. "Dear Lady Glencora, do come in for a moment to my den. We were so sorry not to have you at Monkshade. We heard such terrible things about your health." Lady Glencora said that it was only a cold,—a bad cold. "Oh, yes; we heard,—something about moonlight and ruins. So like you, you know. I love that sort of thing, above all people; but it doesn't do; does it? Circumstances are so exacting. I think you know Lady Hartletop;—and there's the Duchess of St. Bungay. Mr. Palliser was here five minutes since." Then Lady Monk was obliged to get to her door again and Lady Glencora found herself standing close to Lady Hartletop.

"We saw Mr. Palliser just pass through," said Lady Hartletop, who was able to meet and speak of the man who had dared to approach her with his love, without the slightest nervousness.

"Yes; he said he should be here," said Lady Glencora.

"There's a great crowd," said Lady Hartletop. "I didn't think London was so full."

"Very great." said Lady Glencora, and then they had said to each other all that society required. Lady Glencora, as we know, could talk with imprudent vehemence by the hour together if she liked her companion; but the other lady seldom committed herself by more words than she had uttered now,—unless it was to her tirewoman.

"How very well you are looking," said the Duchess. "And I heard you had been so ill." Of that midnight escapade among the ruins it was fated that Lady Glencora should never hear the last.

"How d'ye do, Lady Glencowrer?" sounded in her ear, and there was a great red paw stuck out for her to take. But after what had passed between Lady Glencora and her husband to-day about Mr. Bott, she was determined that she would not take Mr. Bott's hand.

"How are you, Mr. Bott?" she said. "I think I'll look for Mr. Palliser in the back room."

"Dear Lady Glencora," whispered the Duchess, in an ecstasy of agony. Lady Glencora turned and bowed her head to her stout friend. "Do let me go away with you. There's that woman, Mrs. Conway Sparkes, coming, and you know how I hate her." She had nothing to do but to take the Duchess under her wing, and they passed into the large room together. It is, I think, more than probable that Mrs. Conway Sparkes had been brought in by Lady Monk as the only way of removing the Duchess from her stool.

Just within the dancing-room Lady Glencora found her husband, standing in a corner, looking as though he were making calculations.

"I'm going away," said he, coming up to her. "I only just came because I said I would. Shall you be late?"

"Oh, no; I suppose not."

"Shall you dance?"

"Perhaps once,—just to show that I'm not an old woman."

"Don't heat yourself. Good-bye." Then he went, and in the crush of the doorway he passed Burgo Fitzgerald, whose eye was intently fixed upon his wife. He looked at Burgo, and some thought of that young man's former hopes flashed across his mind,—some remembrance, too, of a caution that had been whispered to him; but for no moment did a suspicion come to him that he ought to stop and watch by his wife.

CHAPTER L
HOW LADY GLENCORA CAME BACK
FROM LADY MONK'S PARTY

Burgo Fitzgerald remained for a minute or two leaning where we last saw him,—against the dining-room wall at the bottom of the staircase; and as he did so some thoughts that were almost solemn passed across his mind. This thing that he was about to do, or to attempt,—was it in itself a good thing, and would it be good for her whom he pretended to love? What would be her future if she consented now to go with him, and to divide herself from her husband? Of his own future he thought not at all. He had never done so. Even when he had first found himself attracted by the reputation of her wealth, he cannot be said to have looked forward in any prudential way to coming years. His desire to put himself in possession of so magnificent a fortune had simply prompted him, as he might have been prompted to play for a high stake at a gaming-table. But now, during these moments, he did think a little of her. Would she be happy, simply because he loved her, when all women should cease to acknowledge her; when men would regard her as one degraded and dishonoured; when society should be closed against her; when she would be driven to live loudly because the softness and graces of quiet life would be denied to her? Burgo knew well what must be the nature of such a woman's life in such circumstances. Would Glencora be happy with him while living such a life simply because he loved her? And, under such circumstances, was it likely that he would continue to love her? Did he not know himself to be the most inconstant of men, and the least trustworthy? Leaning thus against the wall at the bottom of the stairs he did ask himself all these questions with something of true feeling about his heart, and almost persuaded himself that he had better take his hat and wander forth anywhere into the streets. It mattered little what might become of himself. If he could drink himself out of the world, it might be an end of things that would be not altogether undesirable.

But then the remembrance of his aunt's two hundred pounds came upon him, which money he even now had about him on his person, and a certain idea of honour told him that he was bound to do that for which the money had been given to him. As to telling his aunt that he had changed his mind, and, therefore, refunding the money—no such thought as that was possible to him! To give back two hundred pounds entire,—two hundred pounds which were already within his clutches, was not within the compass of Burgo's generosity. Remembering the cash, he told himself that hesitation was no longer possible to him. So he gathered himself up, stretched his hands over his head, uttered a sigh that was audible to all around him, and took himself up-stairs.

He looked in at his aunt's room, and then he saw her and was seen by her. "Well, Burgo," she said, with her sweetest smile, "have you been dancing?" He turned away from her without answering her, muttering something between his teeth about a cold-blooded Jezebel,—which, if she had heard it, would have made her think him the most ungrateful of men. But she did not hear him, and smiled still as he went away, saying something to Mrs. Conway Sparkes as to the great change for the better which had taken place in her nephew's conduct.

"There's no knowing who may not reform," said Mrs. Sparkes, with an emphasis which seemed to Lady Monk to be almost uncourteous.

Burgo made his way first into the front room and then into the larger room where the dancing was in progress, and there he saw Lady Glencora standing up in a quadrille with the Marquis of Hartletop. Lord Hartletop was a man not much more given to conversation than his wife, and Lady Glencora seemed to go through her work with very little gratification either in the dancing or in the society of her partner. She was simply standing up to dance, because, as she had told Mr. Palliser, ladies of her age generally do stand up on such occasions. Burgo watched her as she crossed and re-crossed the room, and at last she was aware of his presence. It made no change in her, except that she became even somewhat less animated than she had been before. She would not seem to see him, nor would she allow herself to be driven into a pretence of a conversation with her partner because he was there. "I will go up to her at once, and ask her to waltz," Burgo said to himself, as soon as the last figure of the quadrille was in action. "Why should I not ask her as well as any other woman?" Then the music ceased, and after a minute's interval Lord Hartletop took away his partner on his arm into another room. Burgo, who had been standing near the door, followed them at once. The crowd was great, so that he could not get near them or even keep them in sight, but he was aware of the way in which they were going.

It was five minutes after this when he again saw her, and then she was seated on a cane bench in the gallery, and an old woman was standing close to her, talking to her. It was Mrs. Marsham cautioning her against some petty imprudence, and Lady Glencora was telling that lady that she needed no such advice, in words almost as curt as those I have used. Lord Hartletop had left her, feeling that, as far as that was concerned, he had done his duty for the night. Burgo knew nothing of Mrs. Marsham, — had never seen her before, and was quite unaware that she had any special connection with Mr. Palliser. It was impossible, he thought, to find Lady Glencora in a better position for his purpose, so he made his way up to her through the crowd, and muttering some slight inaudible word, offered her his hand.

"That will do very well thank you, Mrs. Marsham," Lady Glencora said at this moment. "Pray, do not trouble yourself," and then she gave her hand to Fitzgerald. Mrs. Marsham, though unknown to him, knew with quite sufficient accuracy who he was, and all his history, as far as it concerned her friend's wife. She had learned the whole story of the loves of Burgo and Lady Glencora. Though Mr. Palliser had never mentioned that man's name to her, she was well aware that her duty as a duenna would make it expedient that she should keep a doubly wary eye upon him should he come near the sheepfold. And there he was, close to them, almost leaning over them, with the hand of his late lady love, — the hand of Mr. Palliser's wife, — within his own! How Lady Glencora might have carried herself at this moment had Mrs. Marsham not been there, it is bootless now to surmise; but it may be well understood that under Mrs. Marsham's immediate eye all her resolution would be in Burgo's favour. She looked at him softly and kindly, and though she uttered no articulate word, her countenance seemed to show that the meeting was not unpleasant to her.

"Will you waltz?" said Burgo, — asking it not at all as though it were a special favour, — asking it exactly as he might have done had they been in the habit of dancing with each other every other night for the last three months.

"I don't think Lady Glencora will waltz to-night," said Mrs. Marsham, very stiffly. She certainly did not know her business as a duenna, or else the enormity of Burgo's proposition had struck her so forcibly as to take away from her all her presence of mind. Otherwise, she must have been aware that such an answer from her would surely drive her friend's wife into open hostility.

"And why not, Mrs. Marsham?" said Lady Glencora rising from her seat. "Why shouldn't I waltz to-night? I rather think I shall, the more especially as Mr. Fitzgerald waltzes very well." Thereupon she put her hand upon Burgo's arm.

Mrs. Marsham made still a little effort,—a little effort that was probably involuntary. She put out her hand, and laid it on Lady Glencora's left shoulder, looking into her face as she did so with all the severity of caution of which she was mistress. Lady Glencora shook her duenna off angrily. Whether she would put her fate into the hands of this man who was now touching her, or whether she would not, she had not as yet decided; but of this she was very sure, that nothing said or done by Mrs. Marsham should have any effect in restraining her.

What could Mrs. Marsham do? Mr. Palliser was gone. Some rumour of that proposed visit to Monkshade, and the way in which it had been prevented, had reached her ear. Some whispers had come to her that Fitzgerald still dared to love, as married, the woman whom he had loved before she was married. There was a rumour about that he still had some hope. Mrs. Marsham had never believed that Mr. Palliser's wife would really be false to her vows. It was not in fear of any such catastrophe as a positive elopement that she had taken upon herself the duty of duenna. Lady Glencora would, no doubt, require to be pressed down into that decent mould which it would become the wife of a Mr. Palliser to assume as her form; and this pressing down, and this moulding, Mrs. Marsham thought that she could accomplish. It had not hitherto occurred to her that she might be required to guard Mr. Palliser from positive dishonour; but now—now she hardly knew what to think about it. What should she do? To whom should she go? And then she saw Mr. Bott looming large before her on the top of the staircase.

Mr. Bott on the watch.

In the meantime Lady Glencora went off towards the dancers, leaning on Burgo's arm. "Who is that woman?" said Burgo. They were the first words he spoke to her, though since he had last seen her he had written to her that letter which even now she carried about her. His voice in her ears sounded as it used to sound when their intimacy had been close, and questions such as that he had asked were common between them. And her answer was of the same nature. "Oh, such an odious woman!" she said. "Her name is Mrs. Marsham; she is my bête noire." And then they were actually dancing, whirling round the room together, before a word had been said of that which was Burgo's settled purpose, and which at some moments was her settled purpose also.

Burgo waltzed excellently, and in old days, before her marriage, Lady Glencora had been passionately fond of dancing. She seemed to give herself up to it now as though the old days had come back to her. Lady Monk, creeping to the intermediate door between her den and the dancing-room, looked in on them, and then crept back again. Mrs. Marsham and Mr. Bott standing together just inside the other door, near to the staircase, looked on also—in horror.

"He shouldn't have gone away and left her," said Mr. Bott, almost hoarsely.

"But who could have thought it?" said Mrs. Marsham. "I'm sure I didn't."

"I suppose you'd better tell him?" said Mr. Bott.

"But I don't know where to find him," said Mrs. Marsham.

"I didn't mean now at once," said Mr. Bott;—and then he added, "Do you think it is as bad as that?"

"I don't know what to think," said Mrs. Marsham.

The waltzers went on till they were stopped by want of breath. "I am so much out of practice," said Lady Glencora; "I didn't think—I should have been able—to dance at all." Then she put up her face, and slightly opened her mouth, and stretched her nostrils,—as ladies do as well as horses when the running has been severe and they want air.

"You'll take another turn," said he.

"Presently," said she, beginning to have some thought in her mind as to whether Mrs. Marsham was watching her. Then there was a little pause, after which he spoke in an altered voice.

"Does it put you in mind of old days?" said he.

It was, of course, necessary for him that he should bring her to some thought of the truth. It was all very sweet, that dancing with her, as they used to dance, without any question as to the reason why it was so; that sudden falling into the old habits, as though everything between this night and the former nights had been a dream; but this would not further his views. The opportunity had come to him which he must use, if he intended ever to use such opportunity. There was the two hundred pounds in his pocket, which he did not intend to give back. "Does it put you in mind of 'old days?'" he said.

The words roused her from her sleep at once, and dissipated her dream. The facts all rushed upon her in an instant; the letter in her pocket; the request which she had made to Alice, that Alice might be induced to guard her from this danger; the words which her husband had spoken to her in the morning, and her anger against him in that he had subjected her to the eyes of a Mrs. Marsham; her own unsettled mind—quite unsettled whether it would be best for her to go or to stay! It all came upon her now at the first word of tenderness which Burgo spoke to her.

It has often been said of woman that she who doubts is lost,—so often that they who say it now, say it simply because others have said it before them, never thinking whether or no there be any truth in the proverb. But they who have said so, thinking of their words as they were uttered, have known but little of women. Women doubt every day, who solve their doubts at last on the right side, driven to do so, some by fear, more by conscience, but most of them by that half-prudential, half-unconscious knowledge of what is fitting, useful, and best under the cirumstances, which rarely deserts either men or women till they have brought themselves to the Burgo Fitzgerald state of recklessness. Men when they have fallen even to that, will still keep up some outward show towards the world; but women in this condition defy the world, and declare themselves to be children of perdition. Lady Glencora was doubting sorely; but, though doubting, she was not as yet lost.

"Does it put you in mind of old days?" said Burgo.

She was driven to answer, and she knew that much would be decided by the way in which she might now speak. "You must not talk of that," she said, very softly.

"May I not?" And now his tongue was unloosed, so that he began to speak quickly. "May I not? And why not? They were happy days,—so happy! Were not you happy when you thought—? Ah, dear! I suppose it is best not even to think of them?"

"Much the best."

"Only it is impossible. I wish I knew the inside of your heart, Cora, so that I could see what it is that you really wish."

In the old days he had always called her Cora, and now the name came from his lips upon her ears as a thing of custom, causing no surprise. They were standing back, behind the circle, almost in a corner, and Burgo knew well how to speak at such moments so that his words should be audible to none but her whom he addressed.

"You should not have come to me at all," she said.

"And why not? Who has a better right to come to you? Who has ever loved you as I have done? Cora, did you get my letter?"

"Come and dance," she said; "I see a pair of eyes looking at us." The pair of eyes which Lady Glencora saw were in the possession of Mr. Bott, who was standing alone, leaning against the side of the doorway, every now and then raising his heels from the ground, so that he might look down upon the sinners as from a vantage ground. He was quite alone. Mrs. Marsham had left him, and had gotten herself away in Lady Glencora's own carriage to Park Lane, in order that she might find Mr. Palliser there, if by chance he should be at home.

"Won't it be making mischief?" Mrs. Marsham had said when Mr. Bott had suggested this line of conduct.

"There'll be worse mischief if you don't," Mr. Bott had answered. "He can come back, and then he can do as he likes. I'll keep my eyes upon them." And so he did keep his eyes upon them.

Again they went round the room,—or that small portion of the room which the invading crowd had left to the dancers,—as though they were enjoying themselves thoroughly, and in all innocence. But there were others besides Mr. Bott who looked on and wondered. The Duchess of St. Bungay saw it, and shook her head sorrowing,—for the Duchess was good at heart. Mrs. Conway Sparkes saw it, and drank it down with keen appetite,—as a thirsty man with a longing for wine will drink champagne,—for Mrs. Conway Sparkes was not good at heart. Lady Hartletop saw it, and just raised her eyebrows. It was nothing to her. She liked to know what was going on, as such knowledge was sometimes useful; but, as for heart,—what she had was, in such a matter, neither good nor bad. Her blood circulated with its ordinary precision, and, in that respect, no woman ever had a better heart. Lady Monk saw it, and a frown gathered on her brow. "The fool!" she said to herself. She knew that Burgo would not help his success by drawing down the eyes of all her guests upon his attempt. In the meantime Mr. Bott stood there, mounting still higher on his toes, straightening his back against the wall.

"Did you get my letter?" Burgo said again, as soon as a moment's pause gave him breath to speak. She did not answer him. Perhaps her breath did not return to her as rapidly as his. But, of course, he knew that she had received it. She would have quickly signified to him that no letter from him had come to her hands had it not reached her. "Let us go out upon the stairs," he said, "for I must speak to you. Oh, if you could know what I suffered when you did not come to Monkshade! Why did you not come?"

"I wish I had not come here," she said.

"Because you have seen me? That, at any rate, is not kind of you."

They were now making their way slowly down the stairs, in the crowd, towards the supper-room. All the world was now intent on food and drink, and they were only doing as others did. Lady Glencora was not thinking where she went, but, glancing upwards, as she stood for a moment wedged upon the stairs, her eyes met those of Mr. Bott. "A man that can treat me like that deserves that I should leave him." That was the thought that crossed her mind at the moment.

"I'll get you some champagne with water in it," said Burgo. "I know that is what you like."

"Do not get me anything," she said. They had now got into the room, and had therefore escaped Mr. Bott's eyes for the moment. "Mr. Fitzgerald," — and now her words had become a whisper in his ear, — "do what I ask you. For the sake of the old days of which you spoke, the dear old days which can never come again—"

"By G——! they can," said he. "They can come back, and they shall."

"Never. But you can still do me a kindness. Go away, and leave me. Go to the sideboard, and then do not come back. You are doing me an injury while you remain with me."

"Cora," he said,

But she had now recovered her presence of mind, and understood what was going on. She was no longer in a dream, but words and things bore to her again their proper meaning. "I will not have it, Mr. Fitzgerald," she answered, speaking almost passionately. "I will not have it. Do as I bid you. Go and leave me, and do not return. I tell you that we are watched." This was still true, for Mr. Bott had now again got his eyes on them, round the supper-room door. Whatever was the reward for which he was working, private secretaryship or what else, it must be owned that he worked hard for it. But there are labours which are labours of love.

"Who is watching us?" said Burgo; "and what does it matter? If you are minded to do as I have asked you—"

"But I am not so minded. Do you not know that you insult me by proposing it?"

"Yes;—it is an insult, Cora,—unless such an offer be a joy to you. If you wish to be my wife instead of his, it is no insult."

"How can I be that?" Her face was not turned to him, and her words were half-pronounced, and in the lowest whisper, but, nevertheless, he heard them.

"Come with me,—abroad, and you shall yet be my wife. You got my letter? Do what I asked you, then. Come with me—to-night."

The pressing instance of the suggestion, the fixing of a present hour, startled her back to her propriety. "Mr. Fitzgerald," she said, "I asked you to go and leave me. If you do not do so, I must get up and leave you. It will be much more difficult."

"And is that to be all?"

"All;—at any rate, now." Oh, Glencora! how could you be so weak? Why did you add that word, "now"? In truth, she added it then, at that moment, simply feeling that she could thus best secure an immediate compliance with her request.

"I will not go," he said, looking at her sternly, and leaning before her, with earnest face, with utter indifference as to the eyes of any that might see them. "I will not go till you tell me that you will see me again."

"I will," she said in that low, all-but-unuttered whisper.

"When,—when,—when?" he asked.

Looking up again towards the doorway, in fear of Mr. Bott's eyes, she saw the face of Mr. Palliser as he entered the room. Mr. Bott had also seen him, and had tried to clutch him by the arm; but Mr. Palliser had shaken him off, apparently with indifference,—had got rid of him, as it were, without noticing him. Lady Glencora, when she saw her husband, immediately recovered her courage. She would not cower before him, or show herself ashamed of what she had done. For the matter of that, if he pressed her on the subject, she could bring herself to tell him that she loved Burgo Fitzgerald much more easily than she could whisper such a word to Burgo himself. Mr. Bott's eyes were odious to her as they watched her; but her husband's glance she could meet without quailing before it. "Here is Mr. Palliser," said she, speaking again in her ordinary clear-toned voice. Burgo immediately rose from his seat with a start, and turned quickly towards the door; but Lady Glencora kept her chair.

Mr. Palliser made his way as best he could through the crowd up to his wife. He, too, kept his countenance without betraying his secret. There was neither anger nor dismay in his face, nor was there any untoward hurry in his movement. Burgo stood aside as he came up, and Lady Glencora was the first to speak. "I thought you were gone home hours ago," she said.

"I did go home," he answered, "but I thought I might as well come back for you."

"What a model of a husband! Well; I am ready. Only, what shall we do about Jane? Mr. Fitzgerald, I left a scarf in your aunt's room,—a little black and yellow scarf,—would you mind getting it for me?"

"I will fetch it," said Mr. Palliser; "and I will tell your cousin that the carriage shall come back for her."

"If you will allow me—" said Burgo.

"I will do it," said Mr. Palliser; and away he went, making his slow progress up through the crowd, ordering his carriage as he passed through the hall, and leaving Mr. Bott still watching at the door.

Lady Glencora resolved that she would say nothing to Burgo while her husband was gone. There was a touch of chivalry in his leaving them again together, which so far conquered her. He might have bade her leave the scarf, and come at once. She had seen, moreover, that he had not spoken to Mr. Bott, and was thankful to him also for that. Burgo also seemed to have become aware that his chance for that time was over. "I will say good-night," he said. "Good-night, Mr. Fitzgerald," she answered, giving him her hand. He pressed it for a moment, and then turned and went. When Mr. Palliser came back he was no more to be seen.

Lady Glencora was at the dining-room door when her husband returned, standing close to Mr. Bott. Mr. Bott had spoken to her, but she made no reply. He spoke again, but her face remained as immovable as though she had been deaf. "And what shall we do about Mrs. Marsham?" she said, quite out loud, as soon as she put her hand on her husband's arm. "I had forgotten her."

"Mrs. Marsham has gone home," he replied.

"Have you seen her?"

"Yes."

"When did you see her?"

"She came to Park Lane."

"What made her do that?"

These questions were asked and answered as he was putting her into the carriage. She got in just as she asked the last, and he, as he took his seat, did not find it necessary to answer it. But that would not serve her turn. "What made Mrs. Marsham go to you at Park Lane after she left Lady Monk's?" she asked again. Mr. Palliser sat silent, not having made up his mind what he would say on the subject. "I suppose she went," continued Lady Glencora, "to tell you that I was dancing with Mr. Fitzgerald. Was that it?"

"I think, Glencora, we had better not discuss it now."

"I don't mean to discuss it now, or ever. If you did not wish me to see Mr. Fitzgerald you should not have sent me to Lady Monk's. But, Plantagenet, I hope you will forgive me if I say that no consideration shall induce me to receive again as a guest, in my own house, either Mrs. Marsham or Mr. Bott."

Mr. Palliser absolutely declined to say anything on the subject on that occasion, and the evening of Lady Monk's party in this way came to an end.

CHAPTER LI
BOLD SPECULATIONS ON MURDER

George Vavasor was not in a very happy mood when he left Queen Anne Street, after having flung his gift ring under the grate. Indeed there was much in his condition, as connected with the house which he was leaving, which could not but make him unhappy. Alice was engaged to be his wife, and had as yet said nothing to show that she meditated any breach of that engagement, but she had treated him in a way which made him long to throw her promise in her teeth. He was a man to whom any personal slight from a woman was unendurable. To slights from men, unless they were of a nature to provoke offence, he was indifferent. There was no man living for whose liking or disliking George Vavasor cared anything. But he did care much for the good opinion, or rather for the personal favour, of any woman to whom he had endeavoured to make himself agreeable. "I will marry you," Alice had said to him,—not in words, but in acts and looks, which were plainer than words,—"I will marry you for certain reasons of my own, which in my present condition make it seem that that arrangement will be more convenient to me than any other that I can make; but pray understand that there is no love mixed up with this. There is another man whom I love;—only, for those reasons above hinted, I do not care to marry him." It was thus that he read Alice's present treatment of him, and he was a man who could not endure this treatment with ease.

But though he could throw his ring under the grate in his passion, he could not so dispose of her. That he would have done so had his hands been free, we need not doubt. And he would have been clever enough to do so in some manner that would have been exquisitely painful to Alice, willing as she might be to be released from her engagement. But he could not do this to a woman whose money he had borrowed, and whose money he could not repay;—to a woman, more of whose money he intended to borrow immediately. As to that latter part of it, he did say to himself over and over again, that he would have no more of it. As he left the house in Queen Anne Street, on that occasion, he swore, that under no circumstances would he be indebted to her for another shilling. But before he had reached Great Marlborough Street, to which his steps took him, he had reminded himself that everything depended on a further advance. He was in Parliament, but Parliament would be dissolved within three months. Having sacrificed so much for his position, should he let it all fall from him now,—now, when success seemed to be within his reach? That wretched old man in Westmoreland, who seemed gifted almost with immortality,—why could he not die and surrender his paltry acres to one who could use them? He turned away from Regent Street into Hanover Square before he crossed to Great Marlborough Street, giving vent to his passion rather than arranging his thoughts. As he walked the four sides of the square he considered how good it would be if some accident should befall the old man. How he would rejoice were he to hear to-morrow that one of the trees of the "accursed place," had fallen on the "obstinate old idiot," and put an end to him! I will not say that he meditated the murder of his grandfather. There was a firm conviction on his mind, as he thought of all this, that such a deed as that would never come in his way. But he told himself, that if he chose to make the attempt, he would certainly be able to carry it through without detection. Then he remembered Rush and Palmer—the openly bold murderer and the secret poisoner. Both of them, in Vavasor's estimation, were great men. He had often said so in company. He had declared that the courage of Rush had never been surpassed. "Think of him," he would say with admiration, "walking into a man's house, with pistols sufficient to shoot every one there, and doing it as though he were killing rats! What was Nelson at Trafalgar to that? Nelson had nothing to fear!" And of Palmer he declared that he was a man of genius as well as courage. He had "looked the whole thing in the face," Vavasor would say, "and told himself that all scruples and squeamishness are bosh,—child's tales. And so they are. Who lives as though they fear either heaven or hell? And if we do live without such fear or respect, what is the use of telling lies to ourselves? To throw it all to the dogs, as Palmer did, is more manly." "And be hanged," some hearer of George's doctrine replied. "Yes, and be hanged,—if such is your destiny. But you hear of the one who is hanged, but hear nothing of the twenty who are not."

Vavasor walked round Hanover Square, nursing his hatred against the old Squire. He did not tell himself that he would like to murder his grandfather. But he suggested to himself, that if he desired to do so, he would have courage enough to make his way into the old man's room, and strangle him; and he explained to himself how he would be able to get down into Westmoreland without the world knowing that he had been there,— how he would find an entrance into the house by a window with which he was acquainted,—how he could cause the man to die as though, those around him should think, it was apoplexy,—he, George Vavasor, having read something on that subject lately. All this he considered very fully, walking rapidly round Hanover Square more than once or twice. If he were to become an active student in the Rush or Palmer school, he would so study the matter that he would not be the one that should be hung. He thought that he could, so far, trust his own ingenuity. But yet he did not meditate murder. "Beastly old idiot!" he said to himself, "he must have his chance as other men have, I suppose," And then he went across Regent Street to Mr. Scruby's office in Great Marlborough Street, not having, as yet, come to any positive conclusion as to what he would do in reference to Alice's money.

But he soon found himself talking to Mr. Scruby as though there were no doubts as to the forthcoming funds for the next elections. And Mr. Scruby talked to him very plainly, as though those funds must be forthcoming before long. "A stitch in time saves nine," said Mr. Scruby, meaning to insinuate that a pound in time might have the same effect. "And I'll tell you what, Mr. Vavasor,—of course I've my outstanding bills for the last affair. That's no fault of yours, for the things came so sharp one on another that my fellows haven't had time to make it out. But if you'll put me in funds for what I must be out of pocket in June—"

"Will it be so soon as June?"

"They are talking of June. Why, then, I'll lump the two bills together when it's all over."

In their discussion respecting money Mr. Scruby injudiciously mentioned the name of Mr. Tombe. No precise caution had been given to him, but he had become aware that the matter was being managed through an agency that was not recognized by his client; and as that agency was simply a vehicle of money which found its way into Mr. Scruby's pocket, he should have held his tongue. But Mr. Tombe's name escaped from him, and Vavasor immediately questioned him. Scruby, who did not often make such blunders, readily excused himself, shaking his head, and declaring that the name had fallen from his lips instead of that of another man. Vavasor accepted the excuse without further notice, and nothing more was said about Mr. Tombe while he was in Mr. Scruby's office. But he had not heard the name in vain, and had unfortunately heard it before. Mr. Tombe was a remarkable man in his way. He wore powder to his hair,—was very polite in his bearing,—was somewhat asthmatic, and wheezed in his talking,— and was, moreover, the most obedient of men, though it was said of him that he managed the whole income of the Ely Chapter just as he pleased. Being in these ways a man of note, John Grey had spoken of him to Alice, and his name had filtered through Alice and her cousin Kate to George Vavasor. George seldom forgot things or names, and when he heard Mr.

Tombe's name mentioned in connection with his own money matters, he remembered that Mr. Tombe was John Grey's lawyer.

As soon as he could escape out into the street he endeavoured to put all these things together, and after a while resolved that he would go to Mr. Tombe. What if there should be an understanding between John Grey and Alice, and Mr. Tombe should be arranging his money matters for him! Would not anything be better than this,—even that little tragedy down in Westmoreland, for which his ingenuity and courage would be required? He could endure to borrow money from Alice. He might even endure it still,— though that was very difficult after her treatment of him; but he could not endure to be the recipient of John Grey's money. By heavens, no! And as he got into a cab, and had himself driven off to the neighbourhood of Doctors' Commons, he gave himself credit for much fine manly feeling. Mr. Tombe's chambers were found without difficulty, and, as it happened, Mr. Tombe was there.

The lawyer rose from his chair as Vavasor entered, and bowed his powdered head very meekly as he asked his visitor to sit down. "Mr. Vavasor;—oh, yes. He had heard the name. Yes; he was in the habit of acting for his very old friend Mr. John Grey. He had acted for Mr. John Grey, and for Mr. John Grey's father,—he or his partner,—he believed he might say, for about half a century. There could not be a nicer gentleman than Mr. John Grey;—and such a pretty child as he used to be!" At every new sentence Mr. Tombe caught his poor asthmatic breath, and bowed his meek old head, and rubbed his hands together as though he hardly dared to keep his seat in Vavasor's presence without the support of some such motion; and wheezed apologetically, and seemed to ask pardon of his visitor for not knowing intuitively what was the nature of that visitor's business. But he was a sly old fox was Mr. Tombe, and was considering all this time how much it would be well that he should tell Mr. Vavasor, and how much it would be well that he should conceal. "The fat had got into the fire," as he told his old wife when he got home that evening. He told his old wife everything, and I don't know that any of his clients were the worse for his doing so. But while he was wheezing, and coughing, and apologizing, he made up his mind that if George Vavasor were to ask him certain questions, it would be best that he should answer them truly. If Vavasor did ask those questions, he would probably do so upon certain knowledge, and if so, why, in that case, lying would be of no use. Lying would not put the fat back into the frying pan. And even though such questions might be asked without any absolute knowledge, they would, at any rate, show that the questioner had the means of ascertaining the truth. He would tell as little as he could; but he decided during his last wheeze, that he could not lie in the matter with any chance of benefiting his client. "The prettiest child I ever saw, Mr. Vavasor!" said Mr. Tombe, and then he coughed violently. Some people who knew Mr. Tombe declared that he nursed his cough.

"I dare say," said George.

"Yes, indeed,—ugh—ugh—ugh."

"Can you tell me, Mr. Tombe, whether either you or he have anything to do with the payment of certain sums to my credit at Messrs. Hock and Block's?"

"Messrs. Hock and Block's, the bankers,—in Lom—bard Street?" said Mr. Tombe, taking a little more time.

"Yes; I bank there," said Vavasor, sharply.

"A most respectable house."

"Has any money been paid there to my credit, by you, Mr. Tombe?"

"May I ask you why you put the question to me, Mr. Vavasor?"

"Well, I don't think you may. That is to say, my reason for asking it can have nothing to do with yours for replying to it. If you have had no hand in any such payment, there is an end of it, and I need not take up your time by saying anything more on the subject."

"I am not prepared to go that length, Mr. Vavasor,—not altogether to go that length,—ugh—ugh—ugh."

"Then, will you tell me what you have done in the matter?"

"Well,—upon my word, you've taken me a little by surprise. Let me see. Pinkle,—Pinkle." Pinkle was a clerk who sat in an inner room, and Mr. Tombe's effort to call him seemed to be most ineffectual. But Pinkle understood the sound, and came. "Pinkle, didn't we pay some money into Hock and Block's a few weeks since, to the credit of Mr. George Vavasor?"

"Did we, sir?" said Pinkle, who probably knew that his employer was an old fox, and who, perhaps, had caught something of the fox nature himself.

"I think we did. Just look Pinkle;—and, Pinkle,—see the date, and let me know all about it. It's fine bright weather for this time of year, Mr. Vavasor; but these easterly winds!—ugh—ugh—ugh!"

Vavasor found himself sitting for an apparently interminable number of minutes in Mr. Tombe's dingy chamber, and was coughed at, and wheezed at, till he begun to be tired of his position; moreover, when tired, he showed his impatience. "Perhaps you'll let us write you a line when we have looked into the matter?" suggested Mr. Tombe.

"I'd rather know at once," said Vavasor. "I don't suppose it can take you very long to find out whether you have paid money to my account, by order of Mr. Grey. At any rate, I must know before I go away."

"Pinkle, Pinkle!" screamed the old man through his coughing; and again Pinkle came. "Well, Pinkle, was anything of the kind done, or is my memory deceiving me?" Mr. Tombe was, no doubt, lying shamefully, for, of course, he remembered all about it; and, indeed, George Vavasor had learned already quite enough for his own purposes.

"I was going to look," said Pinkle; and Pinkle again went away.

"I'm sorry to give your clerk so much trouble," said Vavasor, in an angry voice; "and I think it must be unnecessary. Surely you know whether Mr. Grey has commissioned you to pay money for me?"

"We have so many things to do, Mr. Vavasor; and so many clients. We have, indeed. You see, it isn't only one gentleman's affairs. But I think there was something done. I do, indeed."

"What is Mr. John Grey's address?" asked Vavasor, very sharply.

"Number 5, Suffolk Street, Pall Mall East," said Mr. Tombe. Herein Mr. Tombe somewhat committed himself. His client, Mr. Grey, was, in fact, in town, but Vavasor had not known or imagined that such was the case. Had Mr. Tombe given the usual address of Nethercoats, nothing further would have been demanded from him on that subject. But he had foolishly presumed that the question had been based on special information as to his client's visit to London, and he had told the plain truth in a very simple way.

"Number 5, Suffolk Street," said Vavasor, writing down the address. "Perhaps it will be better that I should go to him, as you do not seem inclined to give me any information." Then he took up his hat, and hardly bowing to Mr. Tombe, left the chambers. Mr. Tombe, as he did so, rose from his chair, and bent his head meekly down upon the table.

"Pinkle, Pinkle," wheezed Mr. Tombe. "Never mind; never mind." Pinkle didn't mind; and we may say that he had not minded; for up to that moment he had taken no steps towards a performance of the order which had been given him.

CHAPTER LII
WHAT OCCURRED IN SUFFOLK
STREET, PALL MALL

Mr. Tombe had gained nothing for the cause by his crafty silence. George Vavasor felt perfectly certain, as he walked out from the little street which runs at the back of Doctors' Commons, that the money which he had been using had come, in some shape, through the hands of John Grey. He did not care much to calculate whether the payments had been made from the personal funds of his rival, or whether that rival had been employed to dispense Alice's fortune. Under either view of the case his position was sufficiently bitter. The truth never for a moment occurred to him. He never dreamed that there might be a conspiracy in the matter, of which Alice was as ignorant as he himself had been. He never reflected that his uncle John, together with John, the lover, whom he so hated, might be the conspirators. To him it seemed to be certain that Alice and Mr. Grey were in league;—and if they were in league, what must he think of Alice, and of her engagement with himself!

There are men who rarely think well of women,—who hardly think well of any woman. They put their mothers and sisters into the background,—as though they belonged to some sex or race apart,—and then declare to themselves and to their friends that all women are false,—that no woman can be trusted unless her ugliness protect her; and that every woman may be attacked as fairly as may game in a cover, or deer on a mountain. What man does not know men who have so thought? I cannot say that such had been Vavasor's creed,—not entirely such. There had been periods of his life when he had believed implicitly in his cousin Alice;—but then there had been other moments in which he had ridiculed himself for his Quixotism in believing in any woman. And as he had grown older the moments of his Quixotism had become more rare. There would have been no such Quixotism left with him now, had not the various circumstances which I have attempted to describe, filled him, during the last twelve months, with a renewed desire to marry his cousin. Every man tries to believe in the honesty of his future wife; and, therefore, Vavasor had tried, and had in his way, believed. He had flattered himself, too, that Alice's heart had, in truth, been more prone to him than to that other suitor. Grey, as he thought, had been accepted by her cold prudence; but he thought, also, that she had found her prudence to be too cold, and had therefore returned where she had truly loved. Vavasor, though he did not love much himself, was willing enough to be the object of love.

This idea of his, however, had been greatly shaken by Alice's treatment of himself personally; but still he had not, hitherto, believed that she was false to him. Now, what could he believe of her? What was there within the compass of such a one to believe? As he walked out into St. Paul's Churchyard he called her by every name which is most offensive to a woman's ears. He hated her at this moment with even a more bitter hatred than that which he felt towards John Grey. She must have deceived him with unparalleled hypocrisy, and lied to him and to his sister Kate as hardly any woman had ever lied before. Or could it be that Kate, also, was lying to him? If so, Kate also should be included in the punishment.

But why should they have conspired to feed him with these moneys? There had been no deceit, at any rate, in reference to the pounds sterling which Scruby had already swallowed. They had been supplied, whatever had been the motives of the suppliers; and he had no doubt that more would be supplied if he would only keep himself quiet. He was still walking westward as he thought of this, down Ludgate Hill, on his direct line towards Suffolk Street; and he tried to persuade himself that it would be well that he should hide his wrath till after provision should have been made for this other election. They were his enemies,—Alice and Mr. Grey,—and why should he keep any terms with his enemies? It was still a trouble to him to think that he should have been in any way beholden to John Grey; but the terrible thing had been done, the evil had occurred. What would he gain by staying his hand now? Still, however, he walked on quickly along Fleet Street, and along the Strand, and was already crossing under the Picture Galleries towards Pall Mall East before he had definitely decided what steps he would take on this very day. Exactly at the corner of Suffolk Street he met John Grey.

"Mr. Grey," he said, stopping himself suddenly, "I was this moment going to call on you at your lodgings."

"At my lodgings, were you? Shall I return with you?"

"If you please," said Vavasor, leading the way up Suffolk Street. There had been no other greeting than this between them. Mr. Grey himself, though a man very courteous in his general demeanour, would probably have passed Vavasor in the street with no more than the barest salutation. Situated as they were towards each other there could hardly be any show of friendship between them; but when Vavasor had spoken to him, he had dressed his face in that guise of civility which men always use who do not intend to be offensive;—but Vavasor dressed his as men dress theirs who do mean to be offensive; and Mr. Grey had thoroughly appreciated the dressing.

"If you will allow me, I have the key," said Grey. Then they both entered the house, and Vavasor followed his host up-stairs. Mr. Grey, as he went up, felt almost angry with himself in having admitted his enemy into his lodgings. He was sure that no good could come of it, and remembered, when it was too late, that he might easily have saved himself from giving the invitation while he was still in the street. There they were, however, together in the sitting-room, and Grey had nothing to do but to listen. "Will you take a chair, Mr. Vavasor?" he said. "No," said Vavasor; "I will stand up." And he stood up, holding his hat behind his back with his left hand, with his right leg forward, and the thumb of his right hand in his waistcoat-pocket. He looked full into Grey's face, and Grey looked full into his; and as he looked the great cicatrice seemed to open itself and to become purple with fresh blood stains.

"I have come here from Mr. Tombe's office in the City," said Vavasor, "to ask you of what nature has been the interference which you have taken in my money matters?"

This was a question which Mr. Grey could not answer very quickly. In the first place it was altogether unexpected; in the next place he did not know what Mr. Tombe had told, and what he had not told; and then, before he replied, he must think how much of the truth he was bound to tell in answer to a question so put to him.

"Do you say that you have come from Mr. Tombe?" he asked.

"I think you heard me say so. I have come here direct from Mr. Tombe's chambers. He is your lawyer, I believe?"

"He is so."

"And I have come from him to ask you what interference you have lately taken in my money matters. When you have answered that, I shall have other questions to ask you."

"But, Mr. Vavasor, has it occurred to you that I may not be disposed to answer questions so asked?"

"It has not occurred to me to think that you will prevaricate. If there has been no such interference, I will ask your pardon, and go away; but if there has been such interference on your part, I have a right to demand that you shall explain to me its nature."

Grey had now made up his mind that it would be better that he should tell the whole story,—better not only for himself, but for all the Vavasors, including this angry man himself. The angry man evidently knew something, and it would be better that he should know the truth. "There has been such interference, Mr. Vavasor, if you choose to call it so. Money, to the extent of two thousand pounds, I think, has by my directions been paid to your credit by Mr. Tombe."

"Well," said Vavasor, taking his right hand away from his waistcoat, and tapping the round table with his fingers impatiently.

"I hardly know how to explain all the circumstances under which this has been done."

"I dare say not; but, nevertheless, you must explain them."

Grey was a man tranquil in temperament, very little prone to quarrelling, with perhaps an exaggerated idea of the evil results of a row,—a man who would take infinite trouble to avoid any such scene as that which now seemed to be imminent; but he was a man whose courage was quite as high as that of his opponent. To bully or be bullied were alike contrary to his nature. It was clear enough now that Vavasor intended to bully him, and he made up his mind at once that if the quarrel were forced upon him it should find him ready to take his own part. "My difficulty in explaining it comes from consideration for you," he said.

"Then I beg that your difficulty will cease, and that you will have no consideration for me. We are so circumstanced towards each other that any consideration must be humbug and nonsense. At any rate, I intend to have none for you. Now, let me know why you have meddled with my matters."

"I think I might, perhaps, better refer you to your uncle."

"No, sir; Mr. Tombe is not my uncle's lawyer. My uncle never heard his name, unless he heard of it from you."

"But it was by agreement with your uncle that I commissioned Mr. Tombe to raise for you the money you were desirous of borrowing from your cousin. We thought it better that her fortune should not be for the moment disturbed."

"But what had you to do with it? Why should you have done it? In the first place, I don't believe your story; it is altogether improbable. But why should he come to you of all men to raise money on his daughter's behalf?"

"Unless you can behave yourself with more discretion, Mr. Vavasor, you must leave the room," said Mr. Grey. Then, as Vavasor simply sneered at him, but spoke nothing, he went on. "It was I who suggested to your uncle that this arrangement should be made. I did not wish to see Miss Vavasor's fortune squandered."

"And what was her fortune to you, sir? Are you aware that she is engaged to me as my wife? I ask you, sir, whether you are aware that Miss Vavasor is to be my wife?"

"I must altogether decline to discuss with you Miss Vavasor's present or future position."

"By heavens, then, you shall hear me discuss it! She was engaged to you, and she has given you your dismissal. If you had understood anything of the conduct which is usual among gentlemen, or if you had had any particle of pride in you, sir, you would have left her and never mentioned her name again. I now find you meddling with her money matters, so as to get a hold upon her fortune."

"I have no hold upon her fortune."

"Yes, sir, you have. You do not advance two thousand pounds without knowing that you have security. She has rejected you; and in order that you may be revenged, or that you may have some further hold upon her,—that she may be in some sort within your power, you have contrived this rascally pettifogging way of obtaining power over her income. The money shall be repaid at once, with any interest that can be due; and if I find you interfering again, I will expose you."

"Mr. Vavasor," said Grey very slowly, in a low tone of voice, but with something in his eye which would have told any bystander that he was much in earnest, "you have used words in your anger which I cannot allow to pass. You must recall them."

"What were the words? I said that you were a pettifogging rascal. I now repeat them." As he spoke he put on his hat, so as to leave both his hands ready for action if action should be required.

Grey was much the larger man and much the stronger. It may be doubted whether he knew himself the extent of his own strength, but such as it was he resolved that he must now use it. "There is no help for it," he said, as he also prepared for action. The first thing he did was to open the door, and as he did so he became conscious that his mouth was full of blood from a sharp blow upon his face. Vavasor had struck him with his fist, and had cut his lip against his teeth. Then there came a scramble, and Grey was soon aware that he had his opponent in his hands. I doubt whether he had attempted to strike a blow, or whether he had so much as clenched his fist. Vavasor had struck him repeatedly, but the blows had fallen on his body or his head, and he was unconscious of them. He had but one object now in his mind, and that object was the kicking his assailant down the stairs. Then came a scramble, as I have said, and Grey had a hold of the smaller man by the nape of his neck. So holding him he forced him back through the door on to the landing, and there succeeded in pushing him down the first flight of steps. Grey kicked at him as he went, but the kick was impotent. He had, however, been so far successful that he had thrust his enemy out of the room, and had the satisfaction of seeing him sprawling on the landing-place.

Vavasor, when he raised himself, prepared to make another rush at the room, but before he could do so a man from below, hearing the noise, had come upon him and interrupted him. "Mr. Jones," said Grey, speaking from above, "if that gentleman does not leave the house, I must get you to search for a policeman."

Vavasor, though the lodging-house man had hold of the collar of his coat, made no attempt to turn upon his new enemy. When two dogs are fighting, any bystander may attempt to separate them with impunity. The brutes are so anxious to tear each other that they have no energies left for other purposes. It never occurs to them to turn their teeth upon newcomers in the quarrel. So it was with George Vavasor. Jones was sufficient to prevent his further attack upon the foe up-stairs, and therefore he had no alternative but to relinquish the fight.

"What's it all about, sir?" said Jones, who kept a tailor's establishment, and, as a tailor, was something of a fighting man himself. Of all tradesmen in London the tailors are, no doubt, the most combative, — as might be expected from the necessity which lies upon them of living down the general bad character in this respect which the world has wrongly given them. "What's it all about, sir?" said Jones, still holding Vavasor by his coat.

"That man has ill-used me, and I've punished him; that's all."

"I don't know much about punishing," said the tailor. "It seems to me he pitched you down pretty clean out of the room above. I think the best thing you can do now is to walk yourself off."

It was the only thing that Vavasor could do, and he did walk himself off. He walked himself off, and went home to his own lodgings in Cecil Street, that he might smooth his feathers after the late encounter before he went down to Westminster to take his seat in the House of Commons. I do not think that he was comfortable when he got there, or that he felt himself very well able to fight another battle that night on behalf of the River Bank. He had not been hurt, but he had been worsted. Grey had probably received more personal damage than had fallen to his share; but Grey had succeeded in expelling him from the room, and he knew that he had been found prostrate on the landing-place when the tailor first saw him.

But he might probably have got over the annoyance of this feeling had he not been overwhelmed by a consciousness that everything was going badly with him. He was already beginning to hate his seat in Parliament. What good had it done for him, or was it likely to do for him? He found himself to be associated there with Mr. Bott, and a few others of the same class,—men whom he despised; and even they did not admit him among them without a certain show of superiority on their part. Who has not ascertained by his own experience the different lights through which the same events may be seen, according to the success, or want of success, which pervades the atmosphere at the moment? At the present time everything was unsuccessful with George Vavasor; and though he told himself, almost from hour to hour, that he would go on with the thing which he had begun,—that he would persevere in Parliament till he had obtained a hearing there and created for himself success, he could not himself believe in the promises which he had made to himself. He had looked forward to his entrance into that Chamber as the hour of his triumph; but he had entered it with Mr. Bott, and there had been no triumph to him in doing so. He had sworn to himself that when there he would find men to hear him. Hitherto, indeed, he could not accuse himself of having missed his opportunities; his election had been so recent that he could hardly yet have made the attempt. But he had been there long enough to learn to fancy that there was no glory in attempting. This art of speaking in Parliament, which had appeared to him to be so grand, seemed already to be a humdrum, homely, dull affair. No one seemed to listen much to what was said. To such as himself,—Members without an acquired name,—men did not seem to listen at all. Mr. Palliser had once, in his hearing, spoken for two hours together, and all the House had treated his speech with respect,—had declared that it was useful, solid, conscientious, and what not; but more than half the House had been asleep more than half the time that he was on his legs. Vavasor had not as yet commenced his career as an orator; but night after night, as he sat there, the chance of commencing it with brilliance seemed to be further from him, and still further. Two thousand pounds of his own money, and two thousand more of Alice's money,—or of Mr. Grey's,—he had already spent to make his way into that assembly. He must spend, at any rate, two thousand more if he intended that his career should be prolonged beyond a three months' sitting;—and how was he to get this further sum after what had taken place to-day?

He would get it. That was his resolve as he walked in by the apple-woman's stall, under the shadow of the great policeman, and between the two august lamps. He would get it;—as long as Alice had a pound over which he could obtain mastery by any act or violence within his compass. He would get it; even though it should come through the hands of John Grey and Mr. Tombe. He would get it; though in doing so he might destroy his cousin Alice and ruin his sister Kate. He had gone too far to stick at any scruples. Had he not often declared how great had been that murderer who had been able to divest himself of all such scruples,—who had scoured his bosom free from all fears of the hereafter, and, as regarded the present, had dared to trust for everything to success? He would go to Alice and demand the money from her with threats, and with that violence in his eyes which he knew so well how to assume. He believed that when he so demanded it, the money would be forthcoming so as to satisfy, at any rate, his present emergencies.

That wretched old man in Westmoreland! If he would but die, there might yet be a hope remaining of permanent success! Even though the estate might be entailed so as to give him no more than a life-interest, still money might be raised on it. His life-interest in it would be worth ten or twelve years' purchase. He had an idea that his grandfather had not as yet made any such will when he left the place in Westmoreland. What a boon it would be if death could be made to overtake the old man before he did so! On this very night he walked about the lobbies of the House, thinking of all this. He went by himself from room to room, roaming along passages, sitting now for ten minutes in the gallery, and then again for a short space in the body of the House,—till he would get up and wander again out into the lobby, impatient of the neighbourhood of Mr. Bott. Certainly just at this time he felt no desire to bring before the House the subject of the River Embankment.

Nor was Mr. Grey much happier when he was left alone, than was his assailant. To give Vavasor his due, the memory of the affray itself did not long trouble him much. The success between the combatants had been nearly equal, and he had, at any rate, spoken his mind freely. His misery had come from other sources. But the reflection that he had been concerned in a row was in itself enough to make John Grey wretched for the time. Such a misfortune had never hitherto befallen him. In all his dealings with men words had been sufficient, and generally words of courtesy had sufficed. To have been personally engaged in a fighting scramble with such a man as George Vavasor was to him terrible. When ordering that his money might be expended with the possible object of saving Alice from her cousin, he had never felt a moment's regret; he had never thought that he was doing more than circumstances fairly demanded of him. But now he was almost driven to utter reproach. "Oh, Alice! that this thing should have come upon me through thy fault!"

When Vavasor was led away down stairs by the tailor, and Grey found that no more actual fighting would be required of him, he retired into his bedroom, that he might wash his mouth and free himself from the stains of the combat. He had heard the front door closed, and knew that the miscreant was gone,—the miscreant who had disturbed his quiet. Then he began to think what was the accusation with which Vavasor had charged him. He had been told that he had advanced money on behalf of Alice, in order that he might obtain some power over Alice's fortune, and thus revenge himself upon Alice for her treatment of him. Nothing could be more damnably false than this accusation. Of that he was well aware. But were not the circumstances of a nature to make it appear that the accusation was true? Security for the money advanced by him, of course, he had none;—of course he had desired none;—of course the money had been given out of his own pocket with the sole object of saving Alice, if that might be possible; but of all those who might hear of this affair, how many would know or even guess the truth?

While he was in this wretched state of mind, washing his mouth, and disturbing his spirit, Mr. Jones, his landlord, came up to him. Mr. Jones had known him for some years, and entertained a most profound respect for his character. A rather sporting man than otherwise was Mr. Jones. His father had been a tradesman at Cambridge, and in this way Jones had become known to Mr. Grey. But though given to sport, by which he meant modern prize-fighting and the Epsom course on the Derby day, Mr. Jones was a man who dearly loved respectable customers and respectable lodgers. Mr. Grey, with his property at Nethercoats, and his august manners, and his reputation at Cambridge, was a most respectable lodger, and Mr. Jones could hardly understand how any one could presume to raise his hand against such a man.

"Dear, dear, sir—this is a terrible affair!" he said, as he made his way into the room.

"It was very disagreeable, certainly," said Grey.

"Was the gentleman known to you?" asked the tailor.

"Yes; I know who he is."

"Any quarrel, sir?"

"Well, yes. I should not have pushed him down stairs had he not quarrelled with me."

"We can have the police after him if you wish it, sir?"

"I don't wish it at all."

"Or we might manage to polish him off in any other way, you know."

It was some time before Mr. Grey could get rid of the tailor, but he did so at last without having told any part of the story to that warlike, worthy, and very anxious individual.

CHAPTER LIII
THE LAST WILL OF THE OLD SQUIRE

In the meantime Kate Vavasor was living down in Westmoreland, with no other society than that of her grandfather, and did not altogether have a very pleasant life of it. George had been apt to represent the old man to himself as being as strong as an old tower, which, though it be but a ruin, shows no sign of falling. To his eyes the Squire had always seemed to be full of life and power. He could be violent on occasions, and was hardly ever without violence in his eyes and voice. But George's opinion was formed by his wish, or rather by the reverses of his wish. For years he had been longing that his grandfather should die,—had been accusing Fate of gross injustice in that she did not snap the thread; and with such thoughts in his mind he had grudged every ounce which the Squire's vigour had been able to sustain. He had almost taught himself to believe that it would be a good deed to squeeze what remained of life out of that violent old throat. But, indeed, the embers of life were burning low; and had George known all the truth, he would hardly have inclined his mind to thoughts of murder.

He was, indeed, very weak with age, and tottering with unsteady steps on the brink of his grave, though he would still come down early from his room, and would, if possible, creep out about the garden and into the farmyard. He would still sit down to dinner, and would drink his allotted portion of port wine, in the doctor's teeth. The doctor by no means desired to rob him of his last luxury, or even to stint his quantity; but he recommended certain changes in the mode and time of taking it. Against this, however, the old Squire indignantly rebelled, and scolded Kate almost off her legs when she attempted to enforce the doctor's orders. "What the mischief does it signify," the old man said to her one evening;—"what difference will it make whether I am dead or alive, unless it is that George would turn you out of the house directly he gets it."

"I was not thinking of any one but yourself, sir," said Kate, with a tear in her eye.

"You won't be troubled to think of me much longer," said the Squire; and then he gulped down the remaining half of his glass of wine.

Kate was, in truth, very good to him. Women always are good under such circumstances; and Kate Vavasor was one who would certainly stick to such duties as now fell to her lot. She was eminently true and loyal to her friends, though she could be as false on their behalf as most false people can be on their own. She was very good to the old man, tending all his wants, taking his violence with good-humour rather than with submission, not opposing him with direct contradiction when he abused his grandson, but saying little words to mitigate his wrath, if it were possible. At such times the Squire would tell her that she also would learn to know her brother's character some day. "You'll live to be robbed by him, and turned out as naked as you were born," he said to her one day. Then Kate fired up and declared that she fully trusted her brother's love. Whatever faults he might have, he had been staunch to her. So she said, and the old man sneered at her for saying so.

One morning, soon after this, when she brought him up to his bedroom some mixture of thin porridge, which he still endeavoured to swallow for his breakfast, he bade her sit down, and began to talk to her about the property. "I know you are a fool," he said, "about all matters of business;— more of a fool than even women generally are." To this Kate acceded with a little smile,—acknowledging that her understanding was limited. "I want to see Gogram," he said. "Do you write to him a line, telling him to come here to-day,—he or one of his men,—and send it at once by Peter." Gogram was an attorney who lived at Penrith, and who was never summoned to Vavasor Hall unless the Squire had something to say about his will. "Don't you think you'd better put it off till you are a little stronger?" said Kate. Whereupon the Squire fired at her such a volley of oaths that she sprang off the chair on which she was sitting, and darted across to a little table at which there was pen and ink, and wrote her note to Mr. Gogram, before she had recovered from the shaking which the battery had given her. She wrote the note, and ran away with it to Peter, and saw Peter on the pony on his way to Penrith, before she dared to return to her grandfather's bedside.

"What should you do with the estate if I left it you?" the Squire said to her the first moment she was again back with him.

This was a question she could not answer instantly. She stood by his bedside for a while thinking,—holding her grandfather's hand and looking down upon the bed. He, with his rough watery old eyes, was gazing up into her face, as though he were trying to read her thoughts. "I think I should give it to my brother," she said.

"Then I'm d—— if I'll leave it to you," said he.

She did not jump now, though he had sworn at her. She still stood, holding his hand softly, and looking down upon the bed. "If I were you, grandfather," she said almost in a whisper, "I would not trust myself to alter family arrangements whilst I was ill. I'm sure you would advise any one else against doing so."

"And if I were to leave it to Alice, she'd give it to him too," he said, speaking his thoughts out loud. "What it is you see in him, I never could even guess. He's as ugly as a baboon, with his scarred face. He has never done anything to show himself a clever fellow. Kate, give me some of that bottle the man sent." Kate handed him his medicine, and then stood again by his bedside.

"Where did he get the money to pay for his election?" the Squire asked, as soon as he had swallowed the draught. "They wouldn't give such a one as him credit a yard further than they could see him."

"I don't know where he got it," said Kate, lying.

"He has not had yours; has he?"

"He would not take it, sir."

"And you offered it to him?"

"Yes, sir."

"And he has not had it?"

"Not a penny of it, sir."

"And what made you offer it to him after what I said to you?"

"Because it was my own," said Kate, stoutly.

"You're the biggest idiot that ever I heard of, and you'll know it yourself some day. Go away now, and let me know when Gogram comes."

She went away, and for a time employed herself about her ordinary household work. Then she sat down alone in the dingy old dining-room, to think what had better be done in her present circumstances. The carpet of the room was worn out, as were also the covers of the old chairs and the horsehair sofa which was never moved from its accustomed place along the wall. It was not a comfortable Squire's residence, this old house at Vavasor. In the last twenty years no money had been spent on furniture or embellishments, and for the last ten years there had been no painting, either inside or out. Twenty years ago the Squire had been an embarrassed man, and had taken a turn in his life and had lived sparingly. It could not be said that he had become a miser. His table was kept plentifully, and there had never been want in his house. In some respects, too, he had behaved liberally to Kate and to others, and he had kept up the timber and fences on the property. But the house had become wretched in its dull, sombre, dirty darkness, and the gardens round it were as bad.

What ought she now to do? She believed that her grandfather's last days were coming, and she knew that others of the family should be with him besides herself. For their sakes, for his, and for her own, it would be proper that she should not be alone there when he died. But for whom should she send? Her brother was the natural heir, and would be the head of the family. Her duty to him was clear, and the more so as her grandfather was at this moment speaking of changes in his will. But it was a question to her whether George's presence at Vavasor, even if he would come, would not at this moment do more harm than good to his own interests. It would make some prejudicial change in the old man's will more probable instead of less so. George would not become soft and mild-spoken even by a death-bed side, and it would be likely enough that the Squire would curse his heir with his dying breath. She might send for her uncle John; but if she did so without telling George she would be treating George unfairly; and she knew that it was improbable that her uncle and her brother should act together in anything. Her aunt Greenow, she thought, would come to her, and her presence would not influence the Squire in any way with reference to the property. So she made up her mind at last that she would ask her aunt to come to Vavasor, and that she would tell her brother accurately all that she could tell,—leaving him to come or stay, as he might think. Alice would, no doubt, learn all the facts from him, and her uncle John would hear them from Alice. Then they could do as they pleased. As soon as Mr. Gogram had been there she would write her letters, and they should be sent over to Shap early on the following morning.

Mr. Gogram came and was closeted with the Squire, and the doctor also came. The doctor saw Kate, and, shaking his head, told her that her grandfather was sinking lower and lower every hour. It would be infinitely better for him if he would take that port wine at four doses in the day, or even at two, instead of taking it all together. Kate promised to try again, but stated her conviction that the trial would be useless. The doctor, when pressed on the matter, said that his patient might probably live a week, not improbably a fortnight,—perhaps a month, if he would be obedient,—and so forth. Gogram went away without seeing Kate; and Kate, who looked upon a will as an awful and somewhat tedious ceremony, was in doubt whether her grandfather would live to complete any new operation. But, in truth, the will had been made and signed and witnessed,—the parish clerk and one of the tenants having been had up into the room as witnesses. Kate knew that the men had been there, but still did not think that a new will had been perfected.

That evening when it was dusk the Squire came into the dining-room, having been shuffling about the grand sweep before the house for a quarter of an hour. The day was cold and the wind bleak, but still he would go out, and Kate had wrapped him up carefully in mufflers and great-coats. Now he came in to what he called dinner, and Kate sat down with him. He had drank no wine that day, although she had brought it to him twice during the morning. Now he attempted to swallow a little soup, but failed; and after that, while Kate was eating her bit of chicken, had the decanter put before him. "I can't eat, and I suppose it won't hurt you if I take my wine at once," he said. It went against the grain with him, even yet, that he could not wait till the cloth was gone from the table, but his impatience for the only sustenance that he could take was too much for him.

"But you should eat something, sir; will you have a bit of toast to sop in your wine?"

The word "sop" was badly chosen, and made the old Squire angry. "Sopped toast! why am I to spoil the only thing I can enjoy?"

"But the wine would do you more good if you would take something with it."

"Good! Nothing will do me any good any more. As for eating, you know I can't eat. What's the use of bothering me?" Then he filled his second glass, and paused awhile before he put it to his lips. He never exceeded four glasses, but the four he was determined that he would have, as long as he could lift them to his mouth.

Kate finished, or pretended to finish, her dinner within five minutes, in order that the table might be made to look comfortable for him. Then she poked the fire, and brushed up the hearth, and closed the old curtains with her own hands, moving about silently. As she moved his eye followed her, and when she came behind his chair, and pushed the decanter a little more within his reach, he put out his rough, hairy hand, and laid it upon one of hers which she had rested on the table, with a tenderness that was unusual with him. "You are a good girl, Kate. I wish you had been a boy, that's all."

"If I had, I shouldn't, perhaps, have been here to take care of you," she said, smiling.

"No; you'd have been like your brother, no doubt. Not that I think there could have been two so bad as he is."

"Oh, grandfather, if he has offended you, you should try to forgive him."

"Try to forgive him! How often have I forgiven him without any trying? Why did he come down here the other day, and insult me for the last time? Why didn't he keep away, as I had bidden him?"

"But you gave him leave to see you, sir."

"I didn't give him leave to treat me like that. Never mind; he will find that, old as I am, I can punish an insult."

"You haven't done anything, sir, to injure him?" said Kate.

"I have made another will, that's all. Do you suppose I had that man here all the way from Penrith for nothing?"

"But it isn't done yet?"

"I tell you it is done. If I left him the whole property it would be gone in two years' time. What's the use of doing it?"

"But for his life, sir! You had promised him that he should have it for his life."

"How dare you tell me that? I never promised him. As my heir, he would have had it all, if he would have behaved himself with common decency. Even though I disliked him, as I always have done, he should have had it."

"And you have taken it from him altogether?"

"I shall answer no questions about it, Kate." Then a fit of coughing came upon him, his four glasses of wine having been all taken, and there was no further talk about business. During the evening Kate read a chapter of the Bible out loud. But the Squire was very impatient under the reading, and positively refused permission for a second. "There isn't any good in so much of it, all at once," he said, using almost exactly the same words which Kate had used to him about the port wine. There may have been good produced by the small quantity to which he listened, as there is good from the physic which children take with wry faces, most unwillingly. Who can say?

For many weeks past Kate had begged her uncle to allow the clergyman of Vavasor to come to him; but he had positively declined. The vicar was a young man to whom the living had lately been given by the Chancellor, and he had commenced his career by giving instant offence to the Squire. This vicar's predecessor had been an old man, almost as old as the Squire himself, and had held the living for forty years. He had been a Westmoreland man, had read the prayers and preached his one Sunday sermon in a Westmoreland dialect, getting through the whole operation rather within an hour and a quarter. He had troubled none of his parishioners by much advice, and had been meek and obedient to the Squire. Knowing the country well, and being used to its habits, he had lived, and been charitable too, on the proceeds of his living, which had never reached two hundred a year. But the new comer was a close-fisted man, with higher ideas of personal comfort, who found it necessary to make every penny go as far as possible, who made up in preaching for what he could not give away in charity; who established an afternoon service, and who had rebuked the Squire for saying that the doing so was trash and nonsense. Since that the Squire had never been inside the church, except on the occasion of Christmas-day. For this, indeed, the state of his health gave ample excuse; but he had positively refused to see the vicar, though that gentleman had assiduously called, and had at last desired the servant to tell the clergyman not to come again unless he were sent for. Kate's task was, therefore, difficult, both as regarded the temporal and spiritual wants of her grandfather.

When the reading was finished, the old man dozed in his chair for half an hour. He would not go up to bed before the enjoyment of that luxury. He was daily implored to do so, because that sleep in the chair interfered so fatally with his chance of sleeping in bed. But sleep in his chair he would and did. Then he woke, and after a fit of coughing, was induced, with much ill-humour, to go up to his room. Kate had never seen him so weak. He was hardly able, even with her assistance and that of the old servant, to get up the broad stairs. But there was still some power left to him for violence of language after he got to his room, and he rated Kate and the old woman loudly, because his slippers were not in the proper place. "Grandfather," said Kate, "would you like me to stay in the room with you to-night?" He rated her again for this proposition, and then, with assistance from the nurse, he was gotten into bed and was left alone.

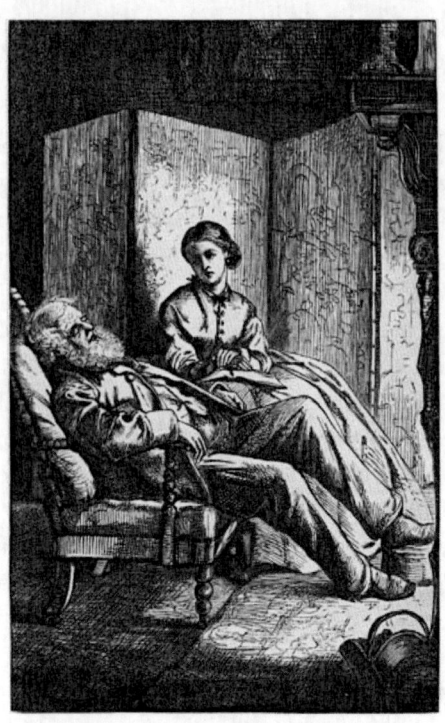

The last of the old squire.

After that Kate went to her own room and wrote her letters. The first she wrote was to her aunt Greenow. That was easily enough written. To Mrs. Greenow it was not necessary that she should say anything about money. She simply stated her belief that her grandfather's last day was near at hand, and begged her aunt to come and pay a last visit to the old man. "It will be a great comfort to me in my distress," she said; "and it will be a satisfaction to you to have seen your father again." She knew that her aunt would come, and that task was soon done.

But her letter to her brother was much more difficult. What should she tell him, and what should she not tell him? She began by describing her grandfather's state, and by saying to him, as she had done to Mrs. Greenow, that she believed the old man's hours were well-nigh come to a close. She told him that she had asked her aunt to come to her; "not," she said, "that I think her coming will be of material service, but I feel the loneliness of the house will be too much for me at such a time. I must leave it for you to decide," she said, "whether you had better be here. If anything should happen,"—people when writing such letters are always afraid to speak of death by its proper name,—"I will send you a message, and no doubt you would come at once."

Then came the question of the will. Had it not occurred to her that her own interests were involved she would have said nothing on the subject; but she feared her brother,—feared even his misconstruction of her motives, even though she was willing to sacrifice so much on his behalf,—and therefore she resolved to tell him all that she knew. He might turn upon her hereafter if she did not do so, and accuse her of a silence which had been prejudicial to him.

So she told it all, and the letter became long in the telling. "I write with a heavy heart," she said, "because I know it will be a great blow to you. He gave me to understand that in this will he left everything away from you. I cannot declare that he said so directly. Indeed I cannot remember his words; but that was the impression he left on me. The day before he had asked me what I should do if he gave me the estate; but of course I treated that as a joke. I have no idea what he put into his will. I have not even attempted to guess. But now I have told you all that I know." The letter was a very long one, and was not finished till late; but when it was completed she had the two taken out into the kitchen, as the boy was to start with them before daylight.

Early on the next morning she crept silently into her grandfather's room, as was her habit; but he was apparently sleeping, and then she crept back again. The old servant told her that the Squire had been awake at four, and at five, and at six, and had called for her. Then he had seemed to go to sleep. Four or five times in the course of the morning Kate went into the room, but her grandfather did not notice her. At last she feared he might already have passed away, and she put her hand upon his shoulder, and down his arm. He then gently touched her hand with his, showing her plainly that he was not only alive, but conscious. She then offered him food,—the thin porridge,—which he was wont to take, and the medicine. She offered him some wine too, but he would take nothing.

At twelve o'clock a letter was brought to her, which had come by the post. She saw that it was from Alice, and opening it found that it was very long. At that moment she could not read it, but she saw words in it that made her wish to know its contents as quickly as possible. But she could not leave her grandfather then. At two o'clock the doctor came to him, and remained there till the dusk of the evening had commenced. At eight o'clock the old man was dead.

CHAPTER LIV
SHOWING HOW ALICE WAS PUNISHED

Poor Kate's condition at the old Hall on that night was very sad. The presence of death is always a source of sorrow, even though the circumstances of the case are of a kind to create no agony of grief. The old man who had just passed away up-stairs was fully due to go. He had lived his span all out, and had himself known that to die was the one thing left for him to do. Kate also had expected his death, and had felt that the time had come in which it would be foolish even to wish that it should be arrested. But death close to one is always sad as it is solemn.

And she was quite alone at Vavasor Hall. She had no acquaintance within some miles of her. From the young vicar, though she herself had not quarrelled with him, she could receive no comfort, as she hardly knew him; nor was she of a temperament which would dispose her to turn to a clergyman at such a time for comfort, unless to one who might have been an old friend. Her aunt and brother would probably both come to her, but they could hardly be with her for a day or two, and during that day or two it would be needful that orders should be given which it is disagreeable for a woman to have to give. The servants, moreover, in the house were hardly fit to assist her much. There was an old butler, or footman, who had lived at the Hall for more than fifty years, but he was crippled with rheumatism, and so laden with maladies, that he rarely crept out of his own room. He was simply an additional burden on the others. There was a boy who had lately done all the work which the other should have done, and ever so much more beside. There is no knowing how much work such a boy will do when properly drilled, and he was now Kate's best minister in her distress. There was the old nurse,—but she had been simply good for nursing, and there were two rough Westmoreland girls who called themselves cook and housemaid.

On that first evening,—the very day on which her grandfather had died,—Kate would have been more comfortable had she really found something that she could do. But there was in truth nothing. She hovered for an hour or two in and out of the room, conscious of the letter which she had in her pocket, and very desirous in heart of reading it, but restrained by a feeling that at such a moment she ought to think only of the dead. In this she was wrong. Let the living think of the dead, when their thoughts will travel that way whether the thinker wish it or no. Grief taken up because grief is supposed to be proper, is only one degree better than pretended grief. When one sees it, one cannot but think of the lady who asked her friend, in confidence, whether hot roast fowl and bread-sauce were compatible with the earliest state of weeds; or of that other lady,—a royal lady she,—who was much comforted in the tedium of her trouble when assured by one of the lords about the Court that piquet was mourning.

It was late at night, near eleven, before Kate took out her letter and read it. As something of my story hangs upon it, I will give it at length, though it was a long letter. It had been written with great struggles, and with many tears, and Kate, as she read it to the end, almost forgot that her grandfather was lying dead in the room above her.

Queen Anne Street, April, 186—.

Dearest Kate,

I hardly know how to write to you—what I have to tell, and yet I must tell it. I must tell it to you, but I shall never repeat the story to any one else. I should have written yesterday, when it occurred, but I was so ill that I felt myself unable to make the exertion. Indeed, at one time, after your brother had left me, I almost doubted whether I should ever be able to collect my thoughts again. My dismay was at first so great that my reason for a time deserted me, and I could only sit and cry like an idiot.

Dear Kate, I hope you will not be angry with me for telling you. I have endeavoured to think about it as calmly as I can, and I believe that I have no alternative. The fact that your brother has quarrelled with me cannot be concealed from you, and I must not leave him to tell you of the manner of it. He came to me yesterday in great anger. His anger then was nothing to what it became afterwards; but even when he first came in he was full of wrath. He stood up before me, and asked me how it had come to pass that I had sent him the money which he had asked of me through the hands of Mr. Grey. Of course I had not done this, and so I told him at once. I had spoken of the matter to no one but papa, and he had managed it for me. Even now I know nothing of it, and as I have not yet spoken to papa I cannot understand it. George at once told me that he disbelieved me, and when I sat quiet under this insult, he used harsher words, and said that I had conspired to lower him before the world.

He then asked me whether I loved him. Oh, Kate, I must tell it you all, though it is dreadful to me that I should have to write it. You remember how it came to pass when we were in Westmoreland together at Christmas? Do not think that I am blaming you, but I was very rash then in the answers which I made to him. I thought that I could be useful to him as his wife, and I had told myself that it would be good that I should be of use in some way. When he asked me that question yesterday, I sat silent. Indeed, how could I have answered it in the affirmative, when he had just used such language to me,—while he was standing opposite to me, looking at me in that way which he has when he is enraged? Then he spoke again and demanded of me that I should at once send back to Mr. Grey all presents of his which I had kept, and at the same time took up and threw across the table on to the sofa near me, a little paper knife which Mr. Grey once gave me. I could not allow myself to be so ordered by him; so I said nothing, but put the knife back upon the table. He then took it again and threw it beneath the grate. "I have a right to look upon you as my wife," he said, "and, as such, I will not allow you to keep that man's things about you." I think I told him then that I should never become his wife, but though I remember many of his words, I remember none of my own. He swore, I know, with a great oath, that if I went back a second time from my word to him he would leave me no peace,—that he would punish me for my perfidy with some fearful punishment. Oh, Kate, I cannot tell you what he looked like. He had then come quite close to me, and I know that I trembled before him as though he were going to strike me. Of course I said nothing. What could I say to a man who behaved to me in such a manner? Then, as far as I can remember it, he sat down and began to talk about money. I forget what he said at first, but I know that I assured him that he might take what he wanted so long as enough was left to prevent my being absolutely a burden on papa. "That, madam, is a matter of course," he said. I remember those words so well. Then he explained that after what had passed between us, I had no right to ruin him by keeping back from him money which had been promised to him, and which was essential to his success.

In this, dear Kate, I think he was mainly right. But he could not have been right in putting it to me in that hard, cruel manner, especially as I had never refused anything that he had asked of me in respect of money. The money he may have while it lasts; but then there must be an end of it all between us, even though he should have the power of punishing me, as he says he will do. Punishing me, indeed! What punishment can be so hard as that which he has already inflicted?

He then desired me to write a letter to him which he might show to the lawyer,—to our own lawyer, I think he meant,—in order that money might be raised to pay back what Mr. Grey had advanced, and give him what he now required. I think he said it was to be five thousand pounds. When he asked this I did not move. Indeed, I was unable to move. Then he spoke very loud, and swore at me again, and brought me pen and ink, demanding that I should write the letter. I was so frightened that I thought of running to the door to escape, and I would have done so had I not distrusted my own power. Had it been to save my life I could not have written the letter. I believe I was now crying,—at any rate I threw myself back and covered my face with my hands. Then he came and sat by me, and took hold of my arms. Oh, Kate; I cannot tell it you all. He put his mouth close to my ear, and said words which were terrible, though I did not understand them. I do not know what it was he said, but he was threatening me with his anger if I did not obey him. Before he left me, I believe I found my voice to tell him that he should certainly have the money which he required. And so he shall. I will go to Mr. Round myself, and insist on its being done. My money is my own, and I may do with it as I please. But I hope,—I am obliged to hope, that I may never be made to see my cousin again.

I will not pretend to express any opinion as to the cause of all this. It is very possible that you will not believe all I say,—that you will think that I am mad and have deluded myself. Of course your heart will prompt you to accuse me rather than him. If it is so, and if there must therefore be a division between us, my grief will be greatly increased; but I do not know that I can help it. I cannot keep all this back from you. He has cruelly ill-used me and insulted me. He has treated me as I should have thought no man could have treated a woman. As regards money, I did all that I could do to show that I trusted him thoroughly, and my confidence has only led to suspicion. I do not know whether he understands that everything must be over between us; but, if not, I must ask you to tell him so. And I must ask you to explain to him that he must not come again to Queen Anne Street. If he does, nothing shall induce me to see him. Tell him also that the money that he wants shall assuredly be sent to him as soon as I can make Mr. Round get it.

Dearest Kate, good-bye. I hope you will feel for me. If you do not answer me I shall presume that you think yourself bound to support his side, and to believe me to have been wrong. It will make me very unhappy; but I shall remember that you are his sister, and I shall not be angry with you.

Yours always affectionately,
Alice Vavasor.

Kate, as she read her letter through, at first quickly, and then very slowly, came by degrees almost to forget that death was in the house. Her mind, and heart, and brain, were filled with thoughts and feelings that had exclusive reference to Alice and her brother, and at last she found herself walking the room with quick, impetuous steps, while her blood was hot with indignation.

All her sympathies in the matter were with Alice. It never occurred to her to disbelieve a word of the statement made to her, or to suggest to herself that it had been coloured by any fears or exaggerations on the part of her correspondent. She knew that Alice was true. And, moreover, much as she loved her brother,—willing as she had been and would still be to risk all that she possessed, and herself also, on his behalf,—she knew that it would be risking and not trusting. She loved her brother, such love having come to her by nature, and having remained with her from of old; and in his intellect she still believed. But she had ceased to have belief in his conduct. She feared everything that he might do, and lived with a consciousness that though she was willing to connect all her own fortunes with his, she had much reason to expect that she might encounter ruin in doing so. Her sin had been in this,—that she had been anxious to subject Alice to the same danger,—that she had intrigued, sometimes very meanly, to bring about the object which she had at heart,—that she had used all her craft to separate Alice from Mr. Grey. Perhaps it may be alleged in her excuse that she had thought,—had hoped rather than thought,—that the marriage which she contemplated would change much in her brother that was wrong, and bring him into a mode of life that would not be dangerous. Might not she and Alice together so work upon him, that he should cease to stand ever on the brink of some half-seen precipice? To risk herself for her brother was noble. But when she used her cunning in inducing her cousin to share that risk she was ignoble. Of this she had herself some consciousness, as she walked up and down the old dining-room at midnight, holding her cousin's letter in her hand.

Her cheeks became tinged with shame as she thought of the scene which Alice had described,—the toy thrown beneath the grate, the loud curses, the whispered threats, which had been more terrible than curses, the demand for money, made with something worse than a cut-throat's violence, the strong man's hand placed upon the woman's arm in anger and in rage, those eyes glaring, and the gaping horror of that still raw cicatrice, as he pressed his face close to that of his victim! Not for a moment did she think of defending him. She accused him to herself vehemently of a sin over and above those sins which had filled Alice with dismay. He had demanded money from the girl whom he intended to marry! According to Kate's idea, nothing could excuse or palliate this sin. Alice had accounted it as nothing,—had expressed her opinion that the demand was reasonable;—even now, after the ill-usage to which she had been subjected, she had declared that the money should be forthcoming, and given to the man who had treated her so shamefully. It might be well that Alice should so feel and so act, but it behoved Kate to feel and act very differently. She would tell her brother, even in the house of death, should he come there, that his conduct was mean and unmanly. Kate was no coward. She declared to herself that she would do this even though he should threaten her with all his fury,—though he should glare upon her with all the horrors of his countenance.

One o'clock, and two o'clock, still found her in the dark sombre parlour, every now and then pacing the floor of the room. The fire had gone out, and, though it was now the middle of April, she began to feel the cold. But she would not go to bed before she had written a line to Alice. To her brother a message by telegraph would of course be sent the next morning; as also would she send a message to her aunt. But to Alice she would write, though it might be but a line. Cold as she was, she found her pens and paper, and wrote her letter that night. It was very short. "Dear Alice, to-day I received your letter, and to-day our poor old grandfather died. Tell my uncle John, with my love, of his father's death. You will understand that I cannot write much now about that other matter; but I must tell you, even at such a moment as this, that there shall be no quarrel between you and me.

There shall be none at least on my side. I cannot say more till a few days shall have passed by. He is lying up-stairs, a corpse. I have telegraphed to George, and I suppose he will come down. I think my aunt Greenow will come also, as I had written to her before, seeing that I wanted the comfort of having her here. Uncle John will of course come or not as he thinks fitting. I don't know whether I am in a position to say that I shall be glad to see him; but I should be very glad. He and you will know that I can, as yet, tell you nothing further. The lawyer is to see the men about the funeral. Nothing, I suppose, will be done till George comes. Your own cousin and friend, Kate Vavasor." And then she added a line below, "My own Alice,—If you will let me, you shall be my sister, and be the nearest to me and the dearest."

Alice, when she received this, was at the first moment so much struck, and indeed surprised, by the tidings of her grandfather's death, that she was forced, in spite of the still existing violence of her own feelings, to think and act chiefly with reference to that event. Her father had not then left his room. She therefore went to him, and handed him Kate's letter. "Papa," she said, "there is news from Westmoreland; bad news, which you hardly expected yet." "My father is dead," said John Vavasor. Whereupon Alice gave him Kate's letter, that he might read it. "Of course I shall go down," he said, as he came to that part in which Kate had spoken of him. "Does she think I shall not follow my father to the grave, because I dislike her brother? What does she mean by saying that there shall be no quarrel between you and her?" "I will explain that at another time," said Alice. John Vavasor asked no further questions then, but declared at first that he should go to Westmoreland on the following day. Then he altered his purpose. "I'll go by the mail train to-night," he said. "It will be very disagreeable, but I ought to be there when the will is opened." There was very little more said in Queen Anne Street on the subject till the evening,—till a few moments before Mr. Vavasor left his house. He indeed had thought nothing more about that quarrelling, or rather that promise that there should be no quarrelling, between the girls. He still regarded his nephew George as the man who, unfortunately, was to be his son-in-law, and now, during this tedious sad day, in which he felt himself compelled to remain at home, he busied his mind in thinking of George and Alice, as living together at the old Hall. At six, the father and daughter dined, and soon after dinner Mr. Vavasor went up to his own room to prepare himself for his journey. After a while Alice followed him,—but she did not do so till she knew that if anything was to be told before the journey no further time could be lost. "Papa," she said, as soon as she had shut the door behind her, "I think I ought to tell you before you go that everything is over between me and George."

"Have you quarrelled with him too?" said her father, with uncontrolled surprise.

"I should perhaps say that he has quarrelled with me. But, dear papa, pray do not question me at present. I will tell you all when you come back, but I thought it right that you should know this before you went."

"It has been his doing then?"

"I cannot explain it to you in a hurry like this. Papa, you may understand something of the shame which I feel, and you should not question me now."

"And John Grey?"

"There is nothing different in regard to him."

"I'll be shot if I can understand you. George, you know, has had two thousand pounds of your money,—of yours or somebody else's. Well, we can't talk about it now, as I must be off. Thinking as I do of George, I'm glad of it,—that's all." Then he went, and Alice was left alone, to comfort herself as best she might by her own reflections.

George Vavasor had received the message on the day previous to that on which Alice's letter had reached her, but it had not come to him till late in the day. He might have gone down by the mail train of that night, but there were one or two persons, his own attorney especially, whom he wished to see before the reading of his grandfather's will. He remained in town, therefore, on the following day, and went down by the same train as that which took his uncle. Walking along the platform, looking for a seat, he peered into a carriage and met his uncle's eye. The two saw each other, but did not speak, and George passed on to another carriage. On the following morning, before the break of day, they met again in the refreshment room, at the station at Lancaster. "So my father has gone, George," said the uncle, speaking to the nephew. They must go to the same house, and Mr. Vavasor felt that it would be better that they should be on speaking terms when they reached it. "Yes," said George; "he has gone at last. I wonder what we shall find to have been his latest act of injustice." The reader will remember that he had received Kate's first letter, in which she had told him of the Squire's altered will. John Vavasor turned away disgusted. His finer feelings were perhaps not very strong, but he had no thoughts or hopes in reference to the matter which were mean. He expected nothing himself, and did not begrudge his nephew the inheritance. At this moment he was thinking of the old Squire as a father who had ever been kind to him. It might be natural that George should have no such old affection at his heart, but it was unnatural that he should express himself as he had done at such a moment.

The uncle turned away, but said nothing. George followed him with a little proposition of his own. "We shan't get any conveyance at Shap," he said. "Hadn't we better go over in a chaise from Kendal?" To this the uncle assented, and so they finished their journey together. George smoked all the time that they were in the carriage, and very few words were spoken. As they drove up to the old house, they found that another arrival had taken place before them,—Mrs. Greenow having reached the house in some vehicle from the Shap station. She had come across from Norwich to Manchester, where she had joined the train which had brought the uncle and nephew from London.

CHAPTER LV
THE WILL

The coming of Mrs. Greenow at this very moment was a great comfort to Kate. Without her she would hardly have known how to bear herself with her uncle and her brother. As it was, they were all restrained by something of the courtesy which strangers are bound to show to each other. George had never seen his aunt since he was a child, and some sort of introduction was necessary between them.

"So you are George," said Mrs. Greenow, putting out her hand and smiling.

"Yes; I'm George," said he.

"And a Member of Parliament!" said Mrs. Greenow. "It's quite an honour to the family. I felt so proud when I heard it!" She said this pleasantly, meaning it to be taken for truth, and then turned away to her brother. "Papa's time was fully come," she said, "though, to tell the truth, I had no idea that he was so weak as Kate describes him to have been."

"Nor I, either," said John Vavasor. "He went to church with us here on Christmas-day."

"Did he, indeed? Dear, dear! He seems at last to have gone off just like poor Greenow." Here she put her handkerchief up to her face. "I think you didn't know Greenow, John?"

"I met him once," said her brother.

"Ah! he wasn't to be known and understood in that way. I'm aware there was a little prejudice, because of his being in trade, but we won't talk of that now. Where should I have been without him, tradesman or no tradesman?"

"I've no doubt he was an excellent man."

"You may say that, John. Ah, well! we can't keep everything in this life for ever." It may, perhaps, be as well to explain now that Mrs. Greenow had told Captain Bellfield at their last meeting before she left Norwich, that, under certain circumstances, if he behaved himself well, there might possibly be ground of hope. Whereupon Captain Bellfield had immediately gone to the best tailor in that city, had told the man of his coming marriage, and had given an extensive order. But the tailor had not as yet supplied the goods, waiting for more credible evidence of the Captain's good fortune. "We're all grass of the field," said Mrs. Greenow, lightly brushing a tear from her eye, "and must be cut down and put into the oven in our turns." Her brother uttered a slight sympathetic groan, shaking his head in testimony of the uncertainty of human affairs, and then said that he would go out and look about the place. George, in the meantime, had asked his sister to show him his room, and the two were already together up-stairs.

Kate had made up her mind that she would say nothing about Alice at the present moment,—nothing, if it could be avoided, till after the funeral. She led the way up-stairs, almost trembling with fear, for she knew that that other subject of the will would also give rise to trouble and sorrow,— perhaps, also, to determined quarrelling.

"What has brought that woman here?" was the first question that George asked.

"I asked her to come," said Kate.

"And why did you ask her to come here?" said George, angrily. Kate immediately felt that he was speaking as though he were master of the house, and also as though he intended to be master of her. As regarded the former idea, she had no objection to it. She thoroughly and honestly wished that he might be the master; and though she feared that he might find himself mistaken in his assumption, she herself was not disposed to deny any appearance of right that he might take upon himself in that respect. But she had already begun to tell herself that she must not submit herself to his masterdom. She had gradually so taught herself since he had compelled her to write the first letter in which Alice had been asked to give her money.

"I asked her, George, before my poor grandfather's death, when I thought that he would linger perhaps for weeks. My life here alone with him, without any other woman in the house beside the servants, was very melancholy."

"Why did you not ask Alice to come to you?"

"Alice could not have come," said Kate, after a short pause.

"I don't know why she shouldn't have come. I won't have that woman about the place. She disgraced herself by marrying a blacksmith—."

"Why, George, it was you yourself who advised me to go and stay with her."

"That's a very different thing. Now that he's dead, and she's got his money, it's all very well that you should go to her occasionally; but I won't have her here."

"It's natural that she should come to her father's house at her father's death-bed."

"I hate to be told that things are natural. It always means humbug. I don't suppose she cared for the old man any more than I did,—or than she cared for the other old man who married her. People are such intense hypocrites. There's my uncle John, pulling a long face because he has come into this house, and he will pull it as long as the body lies up there; and yet for the last twenty years there's nothing on earth he has so much hated as going to see his father. When are they going to bury him?"

"On Saturday, the day after to-morrow."

"Why couldn't they do it to-morrow, so that we could get away before Sunday?"

"He only died on Monday, George," said Kate, solemnly.

"Psha! Who has got the will?"

"Mr. Gogram. He was here yesterday, and told me to tell you and uncle John that he would have it with him when he came back from the funeral."

"What has my uncle John to do with it?" said George, sharply. "I shall go over to Penrith this afternoon and make Gogram give it up to me."

"I don't think he'll do that, George."

"What right has he to keep it? What right has he to it at all? How do I know that he has really got the old man's last will? Where did my grandfather keep his papers?"

"In that old secretary, as he used to call it; the one that stands in the dining-room. It is sealed up."

"Who sealed it?"

"Mr. Gogram did,—Mr. Gogram and I together."

"What the deuce made you meddle with it?"

"I merely assisted him. But I believe he was quite right. I think it is usual in such cases."

"Balderdash! You are thinking of some old trumpery of former days. Till I know to the contrary, everything here belongs to me as heir-at-law, and I do not mean to allow of any interference till I know for certain that my rights have been taken from me. And I won't accept a death-bed will. What a man chooses to write when his fingers will hardly hold the pen, goes for nothing."

"You can't suppose that I wish to interfere with your rights?"

"I hope not."

"Oh, George!"

"Well; I say, I hope not. But I know there are those who would. Do you think my uncle John would not interfere with me if he could? By ——! if he does, he shall find that he does it to his cost. I'll lead him such a life through the courts, for the next two or three years, that he'll wish that he had remained in Chancery Lane, and had never left it."

A message was now brought up by the nurse, saying that Mrs. Greenow and Mr. Vavasor were going into the room where the old Squire was lying, "Would Miss Kate and Mr. George go with them?"

"Mr. Vavasor!" shouted out George, making the old woman jump. She did not understand his meaning in the least. "Yes, sir; the old Squire," she said.

"Will you come, George?" Kate asked.

"No; what should I go there for? Why should I pretend an interest in the dead body of a man whom I hated and who hated me;—whose very last act, as far as I know as yet, was an attempt to rob me? I won't go and see him."

Kate went, and was glad of an opportunity of getting away from her brother. Every hour the idea was becoming stronger in her mind that she must in some way separate herself from him. There had come upon him of late a hard ferocity which made him unendurable. And then he carried to such a pitch that hatred, as he called it, of conventional rules, that he allowed himself to be controlled by none of the ordinary bonds of society. She had felt this heretofore, with a nervous consciousness that she was doing wrong in endeavouring to bring about a marriage between him and Alice; but this demeanour and mode of talking had now so grown upon him that Kate began to feel herself thankful that Alice had been saved.

Kate went up with her uncle and aunt, and saw the face of her grandfather for the last time. "Poor, dear old man!" said Mrs. Greenow, as the easy tears ran down her face. "Do you remember, John, how he used to scold me, and say that I should never come to good. He has said the same thing to you, Kate, I dare say?"

"He has been very kind to me," said Kate, standing at the foot of the bed. She was not one of those whose tears stand near their eyes.

"He was a fine old gentleman," said John Vavasor;—"belonging to days that are now gone by, but by no means the less of a gentleman on that account. I don't know that he ever did an unjust or ungenerous act to any one. Come, Kate, we may as well go down." Mrs. Greenow lingered to say a word or two to the nurse, of the manner in which Greenow's body was treated when Greenow was lying dead, and then she followed her brother and niece.

George did not go into Penrith, nor did he see Mr. Gogram till that worthy attorney came out to Vavasor Hall on the morning of the funeral. He said nothing more on the subject, nor did he break the seals on the old upright desk that stood in the parlour. The two days before the funeral were very wretched for all the party, except, perhaps, for Mrs. Greenow, who affected not to understand that her nephew was in a bad humour. She called him "poor George," and treated all his incivility to herself as though it were the effect of his grief. She asked him questions about Parliament, which, of course, he didn't answer, and told him little stories about poor dear Greenow, not heeding his expressions of unmistakable disgust.

The two days at last went by, and the hour of the funeral came. There was the doctor and Gogram, and the uncle and the nephew, to follow the corpse,—the nephew taking upon himself ostentatiously the foremost place, as though he could thereby help to maintain his pretensions as heir. The clergyman met them at the little wicket-gate of the churchyard, having, by some reasoning, which we hope was satisfactory to himself, overcome a resolution which he at first formed, that he would not read the burial service over an unrepentant sinner. But he did read it, having mentioned his scruples to none but one confidential clerical friend in the same diocese.

"I'm told that you have got my grandfather's will," George said to the attorney as soon as he saw him.

"I have it in my pocket," said Mr. Gogram, "and purpose to read it as soon as we return from church."

"Is it usual to take a will away from a man's house in that way?" George asked.

"Quite usual," said the attorney; "and in this case it was done at the express desire of the testator."

"I think it is the common practice," said John Vavasor.

George upon this turned round at his uncle as though about to attack him, but he restrained himself and said nothing, though he showed his teeth.

The funeral was very plain, and not a word was spoken by George Vavasor during the journey there and back. John Vavasor asked a few questions of the doctor as to the last weeks of his father's life; and it was incidentally mentioned, both by the doctor and by the attorney, that the old Squire's intellect had remained unimpaired up to the last moment that he had been seen by either of them. When they returned to the hall Mrs. Greenow met them with an invitation to lunch. They all went to the dining-room, and drank each a glass of sherry. George took two or three glasses. The doctor then withdrew, and drove himself back to Penrith, where he lived.

"Shall we go into the other room now?" said the attorney.

The three gentlemen then rose up, and went across to the drawing-room, George leading the way. The attorney followed him, and John Vavasor closed the door behind them. Had any observer been there to watch them he might have seen by the faces of the two latter that they expected an unpleasant meeting. Mr. Gogram, as he had walked across the hall, had pulled a document out of his pocket, and held it in his hand as he took a chair. John Vavasor stood behind one of the chairs which had been placed at the table, and leaned upon it, looking across the room, up at the ceiling. George stood on the rug before the fire, with his hands in the pockets of his trousers, and his coat tails over his arms.

"Gentlemen, will you sit down?" said Mr. Gogram.

John Vavasor immediately sat down.

"I prefer to stand here," said George.

Mr. Gogram then opened the document before him.

"Before that paper is read," said George, "I think it right to say a few words. I don't know what it contains, but I believe it to have been executed by my grandfather only an hour or two before his death."

"On the day before he died,—early in the day," said the attorney.

"Well,—the day before he died; it is the same thing,—while he was dying, in fact. He never got out of bed afterwards."

"He was not in bed at the time, Mr. Vavasor. Not that it would have mattered if he had been. And he came down to dinner on that day. I don't understand, however, why you make these observations."

"If you'll listen to me you will understand. I make them because I deny my grandfather's fitness to make a will in the last moments of his existence, and at such an age. I saw him a few weeks ago, and he was not fit to be trusted with the management of property then."

"I do not think this is the time, George, to put forward such objections," said the uncle.

"I think it is," said George. "I believe that that paper purports to be an instrument by which I should be villanously defrauded if it were allowed to be held as good. Therefore I protest against it now, and shall question it at law if action be taken on it. You can read it now, if you please."

"Oh, yes, I shall read," said Mr. Gogram; "and I say that it is as valid a will as ever a man signed."

"And I say it's not. That's the difference between us."

The will was read amidst sundry interjections and expressions of anger from George, which it is not necessary to repeat. Nor need I trouble my readers with the will at length. It began by expressing the testator's great desire that his property might descend in his own family, and that the house might be held and inhabited by some one bearing the name of Vavasor. He then declared that he felt himself obliged to pass over his natural heir, believing that the property would not be safe in his hands; he therefore left it in trust to his son John Vavasor, whom he appointed to be sole executor of his will. He devised it to George's eldest son,—should George ever marry and have a son,—as soon as he might reach the age of twenty-five. In the meantime the property should remain in the hands of John Vavasor for his use and benefit, with a lien on it of five hundred a year to be paid annually to his granddaughter Kate. In the event of George having no son, the property was to go to the eldest son of Kate, or failing that to the eldest son of his other granddaughter who might take the name of Vavasor. All his personal property he left to his son, John Vavasor. "And, Mr. Vavasor," said the attorney, as he finished his reading, "you will, I fear, get very little by that latter clause. The estate now owes nothing; but I doubt whether the Squire had fifty pounds in his banker's hands when he died, and the value of the property about the place is very small. He has been unwilling to spend anything during the last ten years, but has paid off every shilling that the property owed."

"It is as I supposed," said George. His voice was very unpleasant, and so was the fire of his eyes and the ghastly rage of his scarred face. "The old man has endeavoured in his anger to rob me of everything because I would not obey him in his wickedness when I was here with him a short while before he died. Such a will as that can stand nowhere."

"As to that I have nothing to say at present," said the attorney.

"Where is his other will,—the one he made before that?"

"If I remember rightly we executed two before this."

"And where are they?"

"It is not my business to know, Mr. Vavasor. I believe that I saw him destroy one, but I have no absolute knowledge. As to the other, I can say nothing."

"And what do you mean to do?" said George, turning to his uncle.

"Do! I shall carry out the will. I have no alternative. Your sister is the person chiefly interested under it. She gets five hundred a year for her life; and if she marries and you don't, or if she has a son and you don't, her son will have the whole property."

George stood for a few moments thinking. Might it not be possible that by means of Alice and Kate together,—by marrying the former,—perhaps, he might still obtain possession of the property? But that which he wanted was the command of the property at once,—the power of raising money upon it instantly. The will had been so framed as to make that impossible in any way. Kate's share in it had not been left to her unconditionally, but was to be received even by her through the hands of her uncle John. Such a will shut him out from all his hopes. "It is a piece of d—— roguery," he said.

"What do you mean by that, sir?" said Gogram, turning round towards him.

"I mean exactly what I say. It is a piece of d—— roguery. Who was in the room when that thing was written?"

"The signature was witnessed by—"

"I don't ask as to the signature. Who was in the room when the thing was written?"

"I was here with your grandfather."

"And no one else?"

"No one else. The presence of any one else at such a time would be very unusual."

"Then I regard the document simply as waste paper." After saying this, George Vavasor left the room, and slammed the door after him.

"I never was insulted in such a way before," said the attorney, almost with tears in his eyes.

"He is a disappointed and I fear a ruined man," said John Vavasor. "I do not think you need regard what he says."

"But he should not on that account insult me. I have only done my duty. I did not even advise his grandfather. It is mean on his part and unmanly. If he comes in my way again I shall tell him so."

"He probably will not put himself in your way again, Mr. Gogram."

Then the attorney went, having suggested to Mr. Vavasor that he should instruct his attorney in London to take steps in reference to the proving of the will. "It's as good a will as ever was made," said Mr. Gogram. "If he can set that aside, I'll give up making wills altogether."

Who was to tell Kate? That was John Vavasor's first thought when he was left alone at the hall-door, after seeing the lawyer start away. And how was he to get himself back to London without further quarrelling with his nephew? And what was he to do at once with reference to the immediate duties of proprietorship which were entailed upon him as executor? It was by no means improbable, as he thought, that George might assume to himself the position of master of the house; that he might demand the keys, for instance, which no doubt were in Kate's hands at present, and that he would take possession with violence. What should he do under such circumstances? It was clear that he could not run away and get back to his club by the night mail train. He had duties there at the Hall, and these duties were of a nature to make him almost regret the position in which his father's will had placed him. Eventually he would gain some considerable increase to his means, but the immediate effect would be terribly troublesome. As he looked up at the melancholy pines which were slowly waving their heads in the wind before the door he declared to himself that he would sell his inheritance and his executorship very cheaply, if such a sale were possible.

In the dining-room he found his sister alone. "Well, John," said she; "well? How is it left?"

"Where is Kate?" he asked.

"She has gone out with her brother."

"Did he take his hat?"

"Oh, yes. He asked her to walk, and she went with him at once."

"Then, I suppose, he will tell her," said John Vavasor. After that he explained the circumstances of the will to Mrs. Greenow. "Bravo," exclaimed the widow. "I'm delighted. I love Kate dearly: and now she can marry almost whom she pleases."

CHAPTER LVI
ANOTHER WALK ON THE FELLS

George when he left the room in which he had insulted the lawyer, went immediately across to the parlour in which his aunt and sister were sitting. "Kate," said he, "put on your hat and come and walk with me. That business is over." Kate's hat and shawl were in the room, and they were out of the house together within a minute.

They walked down the carriage-road, through the desolate, untenanted grounds, to the gate, before either of them spoke a word. Kate was waiting for George to tell her of the will, but did not dare to ask any question. George intended to tell her of the will, but was not disposed to do so without some preparation. It was a thing not to be spoken of open-mouthed, as a piece of ordinary news. "Which way shall we go?" said Kate, as soon as they had passed through the old rickety gate, which swung at the entrance of the place. "Up across the fell," said George; "the day is fine, and I want to get away from my uncle for a time." She turned round, therefore, outside the hill of firs, and led the way back to the beacon wood through which she and Alice had walked across to Haweswater upon a memorable occasion. They had reached the top of the beacon hill, and were out upon the Fell, before George had begun his story. Kate was half beside herself with curiosity, but still she was afraid to ask. "Well," said George, when they paused a moment as they stepped over a plank that crossed the boundary ditch of the wood: "don't you want to know what that dear old man has done for you?" Then he looked into her face very steadfastly. "But perhaps you know already," he added. He had come out determined not to quarrel with his sister. He had resolved, in that moment of thought which had been allowed to him, that his best hope for the present required that he should keep himself on good terms with her, at any rate till he had settled what line of conduct he would pursue. But he was, in truth, so sore with anger and disappointment,—he had become so nearly mad with that continued, unappeased wrath in which he now indulged against all the world, that he could not refrain himself from bitter words. He was as one driven by the Furies, and was no longer able to control them in their driving of him.

"I know nothing of it," said Kate. "Had I known I should have told you. Your question is unjust to me."

"I am beginning to doubt," said he, "whether a man can be safe in trusting any one. My grandfather has done his best to rob me of the property altogether."

"I told you that I feared he would do so."

"And he has made you his heir."

"Me?"

"Yes; you."

"He told me distinctly that he would not do that."

"But he has, I tell you."

"Then, George, I shall do that which I told him I should do in the event of his making such a will; for he asked me the question. I told him I should restore the estate to you, and upon that he swore that he would not leave it to me."

"And what a fool you were," said he, stopping her in the pathway. "What an ass! Why did you tell him that? You knew that he would not, on that account, do justice to me."

"He asked me, George."

"Psha! now you have ruined me, and you might have saved me."

"But I will save you still, if he has left the estate to me. I do not desire to take it from you. As God in heaven sees me, I have never ceased to endeavour to protect your interests here at Vavasor. I will sign anything necessary to make over my right in the property to you." Then they walked on over the Fell for some minutes without speaking. They were still on the same path,—that path which Kate and Alice had taken in the winter,—and now poor Kate could not but think of all that she had said that day on George's behalf;—how had she mingled truth and falsehood in her efforts to raise her brother's character in her cousin's eyes! It had all been done in vain. At this very moment of her own trouble Kate thought of John Grey, and repented of what she had done. Her hopes in that direction were altogether blasted. She knew that her brother had ill-treated Alice, and that she must tell him so if Alice's name were mentioned between them. She could no longer worship her brother, and hold herself at his command in all things. But, as regarded the property to which he was naturally the heir, if any act of hers could give it to him, that act would be done. "If the will is as you say, George, I will make over my right to you."

"You can make over nothing," he answered. "The old robber has been too cunning for that; he has left it all in the hands of my uncle John. D—— him. D—— them both."

"George! George! he is dead now."

"Dead; of course he is dead. What of that? I wish he had been dead ten years ago,—or twenty. Do you suppose I am to forgive him because he is dead? I'll heap his grave with curses, if that can be of avail to punish him."

"You can only punish the living that way."

"And I will punish them;—but not by cursing them. My uncle John shall have such a life of it for the next year or two that he shall bitterly regret the hour in which he has stepped between me and my rights."

"I do not believe that he has done so."

"Not done so! What was he down here for at Christmas? Do you pretend to think that that make-believe will was concocted without his knowledge?"

"I'm sure that he knew nothing of it. I don't think my grandfather's mind was made up a week before he died."

"You'll have to swear that, remember, in a court. I'm not going to let the matter rest, I can tell you. You'll have to prove that. How long is it since he asked you what you would do with the estate if he left it to you?"

Kate thought for a moment before she answered. "It was only two days before he died, if I remember rightly."

"But you must remember rightly. You'll have to swear to it. And now tell me this honestly; do you believe, in your heart, that he was in a condition fit for making a will?"

"I advised him not to make it."

"Why? why? What reason did you give?"

"I told him that I thought no man should alter family arrangements when he was so ill."

"Exactly. You told him that. And what did he say?"

"He was very angry, and made me send for Mr. Gogram."

"Now, Kate, think a little before you answer me again. If ever you are to do me a good turn, you must do it now. And remember this, I don't at all want to take anything away from you. Whatever you think is fair you shall have."

He was a fool not to have known her better than that.

"I want nothing," she said, stopping, and stamping with her foot upon the crushed heather. "George, you don't understand what it is to be honest."

He smiled,—with a slight provoking smile that passed very rapidly from his face. The meaning of the smile was to be read, had Kate been calm enough to read it. "I can't say that I do." That was the meaning of the smile. "Well, never mind about that," said he; "you advised my grandfather not to make his will,—thinking, no doubt, that his mind was not clear enough?"

She paused a moment again before she answered him. "His mind was clear," she said; "but I thought that he should not trust his judgement while he was so weak."

"Look here, Kate; I do believe that you at any rate have no mind to assist in this robbery. That it is a robbery you can't have any doubt. I said he had left the estate to you. That is not what he has done. He has left the estate to my uncle John."

"Why tell me, then, what was untrue?"

"Are you disappointed?"

"Of course I am; uncle John won't give it you. George, I don't understand you; I don't, indeed."

"Never mind about that, but listen to me. The estate is left in the hands of John Vavasor; but he has left you five hundred a year out of it till somebody is twenty-five years old who is not yet born, and probably never will be born. The will itself shows the old fool to have been mad."

"He was no more mad than you are, George."

"Listen to me, I tell you. I don't mean that he was a raging maniac. Now, you had advised him not to make any new will because you thought he was not in a fit condition?"

"Yes; I did."

"You can swear to that?"

"I hope I may not be called on to do so. I hope there may be no swearing about it. But if I am asked the question I must swear it."

"Exactly. Now listen till you understand what it is I mean. That will, if it stands, gives all the power over the estate to John Vavasor. It renders you quite powerless as regards any help or assistance that you might be disposed to give to me. But, nevertheless, your interest under the will is greater than his,—or than that of any one else,—for your son would inherit if I have none. Do you understand?"

"Yes; I think so."

"And your testimony as to the invalidity of the will would be conclusive against all the world."

"I would say in a court what I have told you, if that will do any good."

"It will not be enough. Look here, Kate; you must be steadfast here; everything depends on you. How often have you told me that you will stick to me throughout life? Now you will be tried."

Kate felt that her repugnance towards him,—towards all that he was doing and wished her to do,—was growing stronger within her at every word he spoke. She was becoming gradually aware that he desired from her something which she could not and would not do, and she was aware also that in refusing him she would have to encounter him in all his wrath. She set her teeth firmly together, and clenched her little fist. If a fight was necessary, she would fight with him. As he looked at her closely with his sinister eyes, her love towards him was almost turned to hatred.

"But that was what you meant when you advised him not to make the will because you thought his intellect was impaired!"

"No; not so."

"Stop, Kate, stop. If you will think of it, it was so. What is the meaning of his judgement being weak?"

"I didn't say his judgement was weak."

"But that was what you meant when you advised him not to trust it!"

"Look here, George; I think I know now what you mean. If anybody asks me if his mind was gone, or his intellect deranged, I cannot say that there was anything of the kind."

"You will not?"

"Certainly not. It would be untrue."

"Then you are determined to throw me over and claim the property for yourself." Again he turned towards and looked at her as though he were resolved to frighten her. "And I am to count you also among my enemies? You had better take care, Kate."

They were now upon the fell side, more than three miles away from the Hall; and Kate, as she looked round, saw that they were all alone. Not a cottage,—not a sign of humanity was within sight. Kate saw that it was so, and was aware that the fact pressed itself upon her as being of importance. Then she thought again of her resolution to fight with him, if any fight were necessary; to tell him, in so many words, that she would separate herself from him and defy him. She would not fear him, let his words and face be ever so terrible! Surely her own brother would do her no bodily harm. And even though he should do so,—though he should take her roughly by the arm as he had done to Alice,—though he should do worse than that, still she would fight him. Her blood was the same as his, and he should know that her courage was, at any rate, as high.

And, indeed, when she looked at him, she had cause to fear. He intended that she should fear. He intended that she should dread what he might do to her at that moment. As to what he would do he had no resolve made. Neither had he resolved on anything when he had gone to Alice and had shaken her rudely as she sat beside him. He had been guided by no fixed intent when he had attacked John Grey, or when he insulted the attorney; but a Fury was driving him, and he was conscious of being so driven. He almost wished to be driven to some act of frenzy. Everything in the world had gone against him, and he desired to expend his rage on some one.

"Kate," said he, stopping her, "we will have this out here, if you please. So much, at any rate, shall be settled to-day. You have made many promises to me, and I have believed them. You can now keep them all, by simply saying what you know to be the truth,—that that old man was a drivelling idiot when he made this will. Are you prepared to do me that justice? Think before you answer me, for, by G——, if I cannot have justice among you, I will have revenge." And he put his hand upon her breast up near to her throat.

"Take your hand down, George," said she. "I'm not such a fool that you can frighten me in that way."

"Answer me!" he said, and shook her, having some part of her raiment within his clutch.

"Oh, George, that I should live to be so ashamed of my brother!"

"Answer me," he said again; and again he shook her.

"I have answered you. I will say nothing of the kind that you want me to say. My grandfather, up to the latest moment that I saw him, knew what he was about. He was not an idiot. He was, I believe, only carrying out a purpose fixed long before. You will not make me change what I say by looking at me like that, nor get it by shaking me. You don't know me, George, if you think you can frighten me like a child."

He heard her to the last word, still keeping his hand upon her, and holding her by the cloak she wore; but the violence of his grasp had relaxed itself, and he let her finish her words, as though his object had simply been to make her speak out to him what she had to say. "Oh," said he, when she had done, "That's to be it; is it? That's your idea of honesty. The very name of the money being your own has been too much for you. I wonder whether you and my uncle had contrived it all between you beforehand?"

"You will not dare to ask him, because he is a man," said Kate, her eyes brimming with tears, not through fear, but in very vexation at the nature of the charge he had brought against her.

"Shall I not? You will see what I dare do. As for you, with all your promises—. Kate, you know that I keep my word. Say that you will do as I desire you, or I will be the death of you."

"Do you mean that you will murder me?" said she.

"Murder you! yes; why not? Treated as I have been among you, do you suppose that I shall stick at anything? Why should I not murder you—you and Alice, too, seeing how you have betrayed me?"

"Poor Alice!" As she spoke the words she looked straight into his eyes, as though defying him, as far as she herself were concerned.

"Poor Alice, indeed! D—— hypocrite! There's a pair of you; cursed, whining, false, intriguing hypocrites. There; go down and tell your uncle and that old woman there that I threatened to murder you. Tell the judge so, when you're brought into court to swear me out of my property. You false liar!" Then he pushed her from him with great violence, so that she fell heavily upon the stony ground.

He did not stop to help her up, or even to look at her as she lay, but walked away across the heath, neither taking the track on towards Haweswater, nor returning by the path which had brought them thither. He went away northwards across the wild fell; and Kate, having risen up and seated herself on a small cairn of stones which stood there, watched him as he descended the slope of the hill till he was out of sight. He did not run, but he seemed to move rapidly, and he never once turned round to look at her. He went away, down the hill northwards, and presently the curving of the ground hid him from her view.

When she first seated herself her thoughts had been altogether of him. She had feared no personal injury, even when she had asked him whether he would murder her. Her blood had been hot within her veins, and her heart had been full of defiance. Even yet she feared nothing, but continued to think of him and his misery, and his disgrace. That he was gone for ever, utterly and irretrievably ruined, thrown out, as it were, beyond the pale of men, was now certain to her. And this was the brother in whom she had believed; for whom she had not only been willing to sacrifice herself, but for whose purposes she had striven to sacrifice her cousin! What would he do now? As he passed from out of her sight down the hill, it seemed to her as though he were rushing straight into some hell from which there could be no escape.

Kate.

She knew that her arm had been hurt in the fall, but for a while she would not move it or feel it, being resolved to take no account of what might have happened to herself. But when he had been gone some ten minutes, she rose to her feet, and finding that the movement pained her greatly, and that her right arm was powerless, she put up her left hand and became aware that the bone of her arm was broken below the elbow. Her first thought was given to the telling him of this, or the not telling, when she should meet him below at the house. How should she mention the accident to him? Should she lie, and say that she had fallen as she came down the hill alone? Of course he would not believe her, but still some such excuse as that might make the matter easier for them all. It did not occur to her that she might not see him again at all that day; and that, as far as he was concerned, there might be need for no lie.

She started off to walk down home, holding her right arm steadily against her body with her left hand. Of course she must give some account of herself when she got to the house; but it was of the account to be given to him that she thought. As to the others she cared little for them. "Here I am; my arm is broken; and you had better send for a doctor." That would be sufficient for them.

When she got into the wood the path was very dark. The heavens were overcast with clouds, and a few drops began to fall. Then the rain fell faster and faster, and before she had gone a quarter of a mile down the beacon hill, the clouds had opened themselves, and the shower had become a storm of water. Suffering as she was she stood up for a few moments under a large tree, taking the excuse of the rain for some minutes of delay, that she might make up her mind as to what she would say. Then it occurred to her that she might possibly meet him again before she reached the house; and, as she thought of it, she began for the first time to fear him. Would he come out upon her from the trees and really kill her? Had he made his way round, when he got out of her sight, that he might fall upon her suddenly and do as he had threatened? As the idea came upon her, she made a little attempt to run, but she found that running was impracticable from the pain the movement caused her. Then she walked on through the hard rain, steadily holding her arm against her side, but still looking every moment through the trees on the side from which George might be expected to reach her. But no one came near her on her way homewards. Had she been calm enough to think of the nature of the ground, she might have known that he could not have returned upon her so quickly. He must have come back up the steep hill-side which she had seen him descend. No;—he had gone away altogether, across the fells towards Bampton, and was at this moment vainly buttoning his coat across his breast, in his unconscious attempt to keep out the wet. The Fury was driving him on, and he himself was not aware whither he was driven.

Dinner at the Hall had been ordered at five, the old hour; or rather that had been assumed to be the hour for dinner without any ordering. It was just five when Kate reached the front door. This she opened with her left hand, and turning at once into the dining-room, found her uncle and her aunt standing before the fire.

"Dinner is ready," said John Vavasor; "where is George?"

"You are wet, Kate," said aunt Greenow.

"Yes, I am very wet," said Kate. "I must go up-stairs. Perhaps you'll come with me, aunt?"

"Come with you,—of course I will." Aunt Greenow had seen at once that something was amiss.

"Where's George?" said John Vavasor. "Has he come back with you, or are we to wait for him?"

Kate seated herself in her chair. "I don't quite know where he is," she said. In the meantime her aunt had hastened up to her side just in time to catch her as she was falling from her chair. "My arm," said Kate, very gently; "my arm!" Then she slipped down against her aunt, and had fainted.

"He has done her a mischief," said Mrs. Greenow, looking up at her brother. "This is his doing."

John Vavasor stood confounded, wishing himself back in Queen Anne Street.

CHAPTER LVII
SHOWING HOW THE WILD BEAST GOT HIMSELF BACK FROM THE MOUNTAINS

About eleven o'clock on that night,—the night of the day on which Kate Vavasor's arm had been broken,—there came a gentle knock at Kate's bedroom door. There was nothing surprising in this, as of all the household Kate only was in bed. Her aunt was sitting at this time by her bedside, and the doctor, who had been summoned from Penrith and who had set her broken arm, was still in the house, talking over the accident with John Vavasor in the dining-room, before he proceeded back on his journey home.

"She will do very well," said the doctor. "It's only a simple fracture. I'll see her the day after to-morrow."

"Is it not odd that such an accident should come from a fall whilst walking?" asked Mr. Vavasor.

The doctor shrugged his shoulders. "One never can say how anything may occur," said he. "I know a young woman who broke the os femoris by just kicking her cat;—at least, she said she did."

"Indeed! I suppose you didn't take any trouble to inquire?"

"Not much. My business was with the injury, not with the way she got it. Somebody did make inquiry, but she stuck to her story and nothing came of it. Good night, Mr. Vavasor. Don't trouble her with questions till she has had some hours' sleep, at any rate." Then the doctor went, and John Vavasor was left alone, standing with his back to the dining-room fire.

There had been so much trouble and confusion in the house since Kate had fainted, almost immediately upon her reaching home, that Mr. Vavasor had not yet had time to make up his mind as to the nature of the accident which had occurred. Mrs. Greenow had at once ascertained that the bone was broken, and the doctor had been sent for. Luckily he had been found at home, and had reached the Hall a little before ten o'clock. In the meantime, as soon as Kate recovered her senses, she volunteered her account of what had occurred.

Her brother had quarrelled with her about the will, she said, and had left her abruptly on the mountain. She had fallen, she went on to say, as she turned from him, and had at once found that she had hurt herself. But she had been too angry with him to let him know it; and, indeed, she had not known the extent herself till he had passed out of her sight. This was her story; and there was nothing in it that was false by the letter, though there was much that was false in the spirit. It was certainly true that George had not known that she was injured. It was true that she had asked him for no help. It was true, in one sense, that she had fallen, and it was true that she had not herself known how severe had been the injury done to her till he had gone beyond the reach of her voice. But she repressed all mention of his violence, and when she was pressed as to the nature of the quarrel, she declined to speak further on that matter.

Neither her uncle nor her aunt believed her. That was a matter of course, and she knew that they did not believe her. George's absence, their recent experience of his moods, and the violence by which her arm must have been broken, made them certain that Kate had more to tell if she chose to tell it. But in her present condition they could not question her. Mrs. Greenow did ask as to the probability of her nephew's return.

"I can only tell you," said Kate, "that he went away across the Fell in the direction of Bampton. Perhaps he has gone on to Penrith. He was very angry with us all; and as the house is not his own, he has probably resolved that he will not stay another night under the roof. But, who can say? He is not in his senses when he is angered."

John Vavasor, as he stood alone after the doctor's departure, endeavoured to ascertain the truth by thinking of it. "I am sure," he said to himself, "that the doctor suspects that there has been violence. I know it from his tone, and I can see it in his eye. But how to prove it? and would there be good in proving it? Poor girl! Will it not be better for her to let it pass as though we believed her story?" He made up his mind that it would be better. Why should he take upon himself the terrible task of calling this insane relation to account for an act which he could not prove? The will itself, without that trouble, would give him trouble enough. Then he began to long that he was back at his club, and to think that the signing-room in Chancery Lane was not so bad. And so he went up to his bed, calling at Kate's door to ask after the patient.

In the meantime there had come a messenger to Mrs. Greenow, who had stationed herself with her niece. One of the girls of the house brought up a scrap of paper to the door, saying that a boy had brought it over with a cart from Shap, and that it was intended for Miss Vavasor, and it was she who knocked at the sickroom door. The note was open and was not addressed; indeed, the words were written on a scrap of paper that was crumpled up rather than folded, and were as follows: "Send me my clothes by the bearer. I shall not return to the house." Mrs. Greenow took it in to Kate, and then went away to see her nephew's things duly put into his portmanteau. This was sent away in the cart, and Mr. Vavasor, as he went up-stairs, was told what had been done.

Neither on that night or on the following day did Mrs. Greenow ask any further questions; but on the morning after that, when the doctor had left them with a good account of the broken limb, her curiosity would brook no further delay. And, indeed, indignation as well as curiosity urged her on. In disposition she was less easy, and, perhaps, less selfish, than her brother. If it were the case that that man had ill-treated his sister, she would have sacrificed much to bring him to punishment. "Kate," she said, when the doctor was gone, "I expect that you will tell me the whole truth as to what occurred between you and your brother when you had this accident."

"I have told you the truth."

"But not the whole truth."

"All the truth I mean to tell, aunt. He has quarrelled with me, as I think, most unnecessarily, but you don't suppose that I am going to give an exact account of the quarrel? We were both wrong, probably, and so let there be an end of it."

"Was he violent to you when he quarrelled with you?"

"When he is angry he is always violent in his language."

"But, did he strike you?"

"Dear aunt, don't be angry with me if I say that I won't be cross-examined. I would rather answer no more questions about it. I know that questioning can do no good."

Mrs. Greenow knew her niece well enough to be aware that nothing more would be told her, but she was quite sure now that Kate had not broken her arm by a simple fall. She was certain that the injury had come from positive violence. Had it not been so, Kate would not have contented herself with refusing to answer the last question that had been asked, but would also have repelled the charge made against her brother with indignation.

"You must have it your own way," said Mrs. Greenow; "but let me just tell you this, that your brother George had better keep out of my way."

"It is probable that he will," said Kate. "Especially if you remain here to nurse me."

Kate's conduct in answering all the questions made to her was not difficult, but she found that there was much difficulty in planning her own future behaviour towards her own brother. Must she abandon him altogether from henceforth; divide herself from him, as it were; have perfectly separate interests, and interests that were indeed hostile? and must she see him ruined and overwhelmed by want of money, while she had been made a rich woman by her grandfather's will? It will be remembered that her life had hitherto been devoted to him; that all her schemes and plans had had his success as their object; that she had taught herself to consider it to be her duty to sacrifice everything to his welfare. It is very sad to abandon the only object of a life! It is very hard to tear out from one's heart and fling away from it the only love that one has cherished! What was she to say to Alice about all this—to Alice whom she had cheated of a husband worthy of her, that she might allure her into the arms of one so utterly unworthy? Luckily for Kate, her accident was of such a nature that any writing to Alice was now out of the question.

But a blow! What woman can bear a blow from a man, and afterwards return to him with love? A wife may have to bear it and to return. And she may return with that sort of love which is a thing of custom. The man is the father of her children, and earns the bread which they eat and which she eats. Habit and the ways of the world require that she should be careful in his interests, and that she should live with him in what amity is possible to them. But as for love,—all that we mean by love when we speak of it and write of it,—a blow given by the defender to the defenceless crushes it all! A woman may forgive deceit, treachery, desertion,—even the preference given to a rival. She may forgive them and forget them; but I do not think that a woman can forget a blow. And as for forgiveness,—it is not the blow that she cannot forgive, but the meanness of spirit that made it possible.

Kate, as she thought of it, told herself that everything in life was over for her. She had long feared her brother's nature,—had feared that he was hard and heartless; but still there had been some hope with her fear. Success, if he could be made to achieve it, would soften him, and then all might be right. But now all was wrong, and she knew that it was so. When he had compelled her to write to Alice for money, her faith in him had almost succumbed. That had been very mean, and the meanness had shocked her. But now he had asked her to perjure herself that he might have his own way, and had threatened to murder her, and had raised his hand against her because she had refused to obey him. And he had accused her of treachery to himself,—had accused her of premeditated deceit in obtaining this property for herself!

"But he does not believe it," said Kate to herself. "He said that because he thought it would vex me; but I know he does not think it." Kate had watched her brother longing for money all his life,—had thoroughly understood the intensity of his wish for it,—the agony of his desire. But so far removed was she from any such longing on her own account, that she could not believe that her brother would in his heart accuse her of it. How often had she offered to give him, on the instant, every shilling that she had in the world! At this moment she resolved, in her mind, that she never wished to see him more; but even now, had it been practicable, she would have made over to him, without any drawback, all her interest in the Vavasor estate.

But any such making over was impossible. John Vavasor remained in Westmoreland for a week, and during that time many discussions were, of course, held about the property. Mr. Round came down from London, and met Mr. Gogram at Penrith. As to the validity of the will Mr. Round said that there was no shadow of a doubt. So an agent was appointed for receiving the rents, and it was agreed that the old Hall should be let in six months from that date. In the meantime Kate was to remain there till her arm should become strong, and she could make her plans for the future. Aunt Greenow promised to remain at the Hall for the present, and offered, indeed, indefinite services for the future, as though she were quite forgetful of Captain Bellfield. Of Mr. Cheesacre she was not forgetful, for she still continued to speak of that gentleman to Kate, as though he were Kate's suitor. But she did not now press upon her niece the acceptance of Mr. Cheesacre's hand as an absolute duty. Kate was mistress of a considerable fortune, and though such a marriage might be comfortable, it was no longer necessary. Mrs. Greenow called him poor Cheesacre, pointing out how easily he might be managed, and how indubitable were his possessions; but she no longer spoke of Kate's chances in the marriage market as desperate, even though she should decline the Cheesacre alliance.

"A young woman, with six hundred a year, my dear, may do pretty nearly what she pleases," said aunt Greenow. "It's better than having ten years' grace given you."

"And will last longer, certainly," said Kate.

Kate's desire was that Alice should come down to her for a while in Westmoreland, before the six months were over, and this desire she mentioned to her uncle. He promised to carry the message up to Alice, but could not be got to say more than that upon the subject. Then Mr. Vavasor went away, leaving the aunt and niece together at the Hall.

"What on earth shall we do if that wild beast shows himself suddenly among us women?" asked Mrs. Greenow of her brother.

The brother could only say, "that he hoped the wild beast would keep his distance."

And the wild beast did keep his distance, at any rate as long as Mrs. Greenow remained at the Hall. We will now go back to the wild beast, and tell how he walked across the mountains, in the rain, to Bampton, a little village at the foot of Haweswater. It will be remembered that after he had struck his sister, he turned away from her, and walked with quick steps down the mountain-side, never turning back to look at her. He had found himself to be without any power of persuasion over her, as regarded her evidence to be given, if the will were questioned. The more he threatened her the steadier she had been in asserting her belief in her grandfather's capacity. She had looked into his eye and defied him, and he had felt himself to be worsted. What was he to do? In truth, there was nothing for him to do. He had told her that he would murder her; and in the state of mind to which his fury had driven him, murder had suggested itself to him as a resource to which he might apply himself. But what could he gain by murdering her,—or, at any rate, by murdering her then, out on the mountain-side? Nothing but a hanging! There would be no gratification even to his revenge. If, indeed, he had murdered that old man, who was now, unfortunately, gone beyond the reach of murder;—if he could have poisoned the old man's cup before that last will had been made—there might have been something in such a deed! But he had merely thought of it, letting "I dare not wait upon I would"—as he now told himself, with much self-reproach. Nothing was to be got by killing his sister. So he restrained himself in his passion, and walked away from her, solitary, down the mountain.

The rain soon came on, and found him exposed on the hill-side. He thought little about it, but buttoned his coat, as I have said before, and strode on. It was a storm of rain, so that he was forced to hold his head to one side, as it hit him from the north. But with his hand to his hat, and his head bent against the wind, he went on till he had reached the valley at the foot, and found that the track by which he had been led thither had become a road. He had never known the mountains round the Hall as Kate had known them, and was not aware whither he was going. On one thing only had he made up his mind since he had left his sister, and that was that he would not return to the house. He knew that he could do nothing there to serve his purpose; his threats would be vain impotence; he had no longer any friend in the house. He could hardly tell himself what line of conduct he would pursue, but he thought that he would hurry back to London, and grasp at whatever money he could get from Alice. He was still, at this moment, a Member of Parliament; and as the rain drenched him through and through, he endeavoured to get consolation from the remembrance of that fact in his favour.

As he got near the village he overtook a shepherd boy coming down from the hills, and learned his whereabouts from him. "Baampton," said the boy, with an accent that was almost Scotch, when he was asked the name of the place. When Vavasor further asked whether a gig were kept there, the boy simply stared at him, not knowing a gig by that name. At last, however, he was made to understand the nature of his companion's want, and expressed his belief that "John Applethwaite, up at the Craigs yon, had got a mickle cart." But the Craigs was a farm-house, which now came in view about a mile off, up across the valley; and Vavasor, hoping that he might still find a speedier conveyance than John Applethwaite's mickle cart, went on to the public-house in the village. But, in truth, neither there, nor yet from John Applethwaite, to whom at last an application was sent, could he get any vehicle; and between six and seven he started off again, through the rain, to make his weary way on foot to Shap. The distance was about five miles, and the little byways, lying between walls, were sticky, and almost glutinous with light-coloured, chalky mud. Before he started he took a glass of hot rum-and-water, but the effect of that soon passed away from him, and then he became colder and weaker than he had been before.

Wearily and wretchedly he plodded on. A man may be very weary in such a walk as that, and yet be by no means wretched. Tired, hungry, cold, wet, and nearly penniless, I have sat me down and slept among those mountain tracks,—have slept because nature refused to allow longer wakefulness. But my heart has been as light as my purse, and there has been something in the air of the hills that made me buoyant and happy in the midst of my weariness. But George Vavasor was wretched as well as weary, and every step that he took, plodding through the mud, was a new misfortune to him. What are five miles of a walk to a young man, even though the rain be falling and the ways be dirty? what, though they may come after some other ten that he has already traversed on his feet? His sister Kate would have thought nothing of the distance. But George stopped on his way from time to time, leaning on the loose walls, and cursing the misfortune that had brought him to such a pass. He cursed his grandfather, his uncle, his sister, his cousin, and himself. He cursed the place in which his forefathers had lived, and he cursed the whole county. He cursed the rain, and the wind, and his town-made boots, which would not keep out the wet slush. He cursed the light as it faded, and the darkness as it came. Over and over again he cursed the will that had robbed him, and the attorney that had made it. He cursed the mother that had borne him and the father that had left him poor. He thought of Scruby, and cursed him, thinking how that money would be again required of him by that stern agent. He cursed the House of Commons, which had cost him so much, and the greedy electors who would not send him there without his paying for it. He cursed John Grey, as he thought of those two thousand pounds, with double curses. He cursed this world, and all worlds beyond; and thus, cursing everything, he made his way at last up to the inn at Shap.

It was nearly nine when he got there. He had wasted over an hour at Bampton in his endeavour to get John Applethwaite's cart to carry him on, and he had been two hours on his walk from Bampton to Shap,—two hours amidst his cursing. He ordered supper and brandy-and-water, and, as we know, sent off a Mercury for his clothes. But the Mercuries of Westmoreland do not move on quick wings, and it was past midnight before he got his possessions. During all this time he had, by no means, ceased from cursing, but continued it over his broiled ham and while he swallowed his brandy-and-water. He swore aloud, so that the red-armed servant at the inn could not but hear him, that those thieves at the Hall intended to rob him of his clothes;—that they would not send him his property. He could not restrain himself, though he knew that every word he uttered would injure his cause, as regarded the property in Westmoreland, if ever he could make a cause. He knew that he had been mad to strike his sister, and cursed himself for his madness. Yet he could not restrain himself. He told himself that the battle for him was over, and he thought of poison for himself. He thought of poison, and a pistol,—of the pistols he had ever loaded at home, each with six shots, good for a life apiece. He thought of an express train, rushing along at its full career, and of the instant annihilation which it would produce. But if that was to be the end of him, he would not go alone. No, indeed! why should he go alone, leaving those pistols ready loaded in his desk? Among them they had brought him to ruin and to death. Was he a man to pardon his enemies when it was within his power to take them with him, down, down, down—? What were the last words upon his impious lips, as with bloodshot eyes, half drunk, and driven by the Fury, he took himself off to the bed prepared for him, cursing aloud the poor red-haired girl as he went, I may not utter here.

CHAPTER LVIII
THE PALLISERS AT BREAKFAST

Gentle reader, do you remember Lady Monk's party, and how it ended,—how it ended, at least as regards those special guests with whom we are concerned? Mr. Palliser went away early, Mrs. Marsham followed him to his house in Park Lane, caught him at home, and told her tale. He returned to his wife, found her sitting with Burgo in the dining-room, under the Argus eyes of the constant Bott, and bore her away home. Burgo disappeared utterly from the scene, and Mr. Bott, complaining inwardly that virtue was too frequently allowed to be its own reward, comforted himself with champagne, and then walked off to his lodgings. Lady Monk, when Mr. Palliser made his way into her room up-stairs, seeking his wife's scarf,—which little incident, also, the reader may perhaps remember,—saw that the game was up, and thought with regret of the loss of her two hundred pounds. Such was the ending of Lady Monk's party.

Lady Glencora, on her journey home in the carriage with her husband, had openly suggested that Mrs. Marsham had gone to Park Lane to tell of her doings with Burgo, and had declared her resolution never again to see either that lady or Mr. Bott in her own house. This she said with more of defiance in her tone than Mr. Palliser had ever hitherto heard. He was by nature less ready than her, and knowing his own deficiency in that respect, abstained from all answer on the subject. Indeed, during that drive home very few further words were spoken between them. "I will breakfast with you to-morrow," he said to her, as she prepared to go up-stairs. "I have work still to do to-night, and I will not disturb you by coming to your room."

"You won't want me to be very early?" said his wife.

"No," said he, with more of anger in his voice than he had yet shown. "What hour will suit you? I must say something of what has occurred to-night before I leave you to-morrow."

"I don't know what you can have got to say about to-night, but I'll be down by half-past eleven, if that will do?" Mr. Palliser said that he would make it do, and then they parted.

Lady Glencora had played her part very well before her husband. She had declined to be frightened by him; had been the first to mention Burgo's name, and had done so with no tremor in her voice, and had boldly declared her irreconcilable enmity to the male and female duennas who had dared to take her in charge. While she was in the carriage with her husband she felt some triumph in her own strength; and as she wished him good night on the staircase, and slowly walked up to her room, without having once lowered her eyes before his, something of this consciousness of triumph still supported her. And even while her maid remained with her she held herself up, as it were, inwardly, telling herself that she would not yield, — that she would not be cowed either by her husband or by his spies. But when she was left alone all her triumph departed from her.

She bade her maid go while she was still sitting in her dressing-gown; and when the girl was gone she got close over the fire, sitting with her slippers on the fender, with her elbows on her knees, and her face resting on her hands. In this position she remained for an hour, with her eyes fixed on the altering shapes of the hot coals. During this hour her spirit was by no means defiant, and her thoughts of herself anything but triumphant. Mr. Bott and Mrs. Marsham she had forgotten altogether. After all, they were but buzzing flies, who annoyed her by their presence. Should she choose to leave her husband, they could not prevent her leaving him. It was of her husband and of Burgo that she was thinking, — weighing them one against the other, and connecting her own existence with theirs, not as expecting joy or the comfort of love from either of them, but with an assured conviction that on either side there must be misery for her. But of that shame before all the world which must be hers for ever, should she break her vows and consent to live with a man who was not her husband, she thought hardly at all. That which in the estimation of Alice was everything, to her, at this moment, was almost nothing. For herself, she had been sacrificed; and, — as she told herself with bitter denunciations against herself, — had been sacrificed through her own weakness. But that was done. Whatever way she might go, she was lost. They had married her to a man who cared nothing for a wife, nothing for any woman, — so at least she declared to herself, — but who had wanted a wife that he might have an heir. Had it been given to her to have a child, she thought that she might have been happy, — sufficiently happy in sharing her husband's joy in that respect. But everything had gone against her. There was nothing in her home to give her comfort. "He looks at me every time he sees me as the cause of his misfortune," she said to herself. Of her husband's rank, of the future possession of his title and his estates, she thought much. But of her own wealth she thought nothing. It did not occur to her that she had given him enough in that respect to make his marriage with her a comfort to him. She took it for granted that that marriage was now one distasteful to him, as it was to herself, and that he would eventually be the gainer if she should so conduct herself that her marriage might be dissolved.

Lady Glencora

As to Burgo, I doubt whether she deceived herself much as to his character. She knew well enough that he was a man infinitely less worthy than her husband. She knew that he was a spendthrift, idle, given to bad courses,—that he drank, that he gambled, that he lived the life of the loosest man about the town. She knew also that whatever chance she might have had to redeem him, had she married him honestly before all the world, there could be no such chance if she went to him as his mistress, abandoning her husband and all her duties, and making herself vile in the eyes of all women. Burgo Fitzgerald would not be influenced for good by such a woman as she would then be. She knew much of the world and its ways, and told herself no lies about this. But, as I have said before, she did not count herself for much. What though she were ruined? What though Burgo were false, mean, and untrustworthy? She loved him, and he was the only man she ever had loved! Lower and lower she crouched before the fire; and then, when the coals were no longer red, and the shapes altered themselves no more, she crept into bed. As to what she should say to her husband on the following morning,—she had not yet begun to think of that.

Exactly at half-past eleven she entered the little breakfast parlour which looked out over the park. It was the prettiest room in the house, and now, at this springtide, when the town trees were putting out their earliest greens, and were fresh and bright almost as country trees, it might be hard to find a prettier chamber. Mr. Palliser was there already, sitting with the morning paper in his hand. He rose when she entered, and, coming up to her, just touched her with his lips. She put her cheek up to him, and then took her place at the breakfast table.

"Have you any headache this morning?" he asked.

"Oh, no," she said. Then he took his tea and his toast, spoke some word to her about the fineness of the weather, told her some scraps of news, and soon returned to the absorbing interest of a speech made by the leader of the Opposition in the House of Lords. The speech was very interesting to Mr. Palliser, because in it the noble lord alluded to a break-up in the present Cabinet, as to which the rumours were, he said, so rife through the country as to have destroyed all that feeling of security in the existing Government which the country so much valued and desired. Mr. Palliser had as yet heard no official tidings of such a rupture; but if such rupture were to take place, it must be in his favour. He felt himself at this moment to be full of politics,—to be near the object of his ambition, to have affairs upon his hands which required all his attention. Was it absolutely incumbent on him to refer again to the incidents of last night? The doing so would be odious to him. The remembrance of the task now immediately before him destroyed all his political satisfaction. He did not believe that his wife was in any serious danger. Might it not yet be possible for him to escape from the annoyance, and to wash his mind clean of all suspicion? He was not jealous; he was indeed incapable of jealousy. He knew what it would be to be dishonoured, and he knew that under certain circumstances the world would expect him to exert himself in a certain way. But the thing that he had now to do was a great trouble to him. He would rather have to address the House of Commons with ten columns of figures than utter a word of remonstrance to his wife. But she had defied him,—defied him by saying that she would see his friends no more; and it was the remembrance of this, as he sat behind his newspaper, that made him ultimately feel that he could not pass in silence over what had been done.

Nevertheless, he went on reading, or pretending to read, as long as the continuance of the breakfast made it certain that his wife would remain with him. Every now and then he said some word to her of what he was reading, endeavouring to use the tone of voice that was customary to him in his domestic teachings of politics. But through it all there was a certain hesitation,—there were the sure signs of an attempt being made, of which he was himself conscious, and which she understood with the most perfect accuracy. He was deferring the evil moment, and vainly endeavouring to make himself believe that he was comfortably employed the while. She had no newspaper, and made no endeavour to deceive herself. She, therefore, was the first to begin the conversation.

"Plantagenet," she said, "you told me last night, as I was going to bed, that you had something to say about Lady Monk's party."

He put down the newspaper slowly, and turned towards her. "Yes, my dear. After what happened, I believe that I must say something."

"If you think anything, pray say it," said Glencora.

"It is not always easy for a man to show what he thinks by what he says," he replied. "My fear is that you should suppose me to think more than I do. And it was for that reason that I determined to sleep on it before I spoke to you."

"If anybody is angry with me I'd much rather they should have it out with me while their anger is hot. I hate cold anger."

"But I am not angry."

"That's what husbands always say when they're going to scold."

"But I am not going to scold. I am only going to advise you."

"I'd sooner be scolded. Advice is to anger just what cold anger is to hot."

"But, my dear Glencora, surely if I find it necessary to speak—"

"I don't want to stop you, Plantagenet. Pray, go on. Only it will be so nice to have it over."

He was now more than ever averse to the task before him. Husbands, when they give their wives a talking, should do it out of hand, uttering their words hard, sharp, and quick,—and should then go. There are some works that won't bear a preface, and this work of marital fault-finding is one of them. Mr. Palliser was already beginning to find out the truth of this. "Glencora," he said, "I wish you to be serious with me."

"I am very serious," she replied, as she settled herself in her chair with an air of mockery, while her eyes and mouth were bright and eloquent with a spirit which her husband did not love to see. Poor girl! There was seriousness enough in store for her before she would be able to leave the room.

"You ought to be serious. Do you know why Mrs. Marsham came here from Lady Monk's last night?"

"Of course I do. She came to tell you that I was waltzing with Burgo Fitzgerald. You might as well ask me whether I knew why Mr. Bott was standing at all the doors, glaring at me."

"I don't know anything about Mr. Bott."

"I know something about him though," she said, again moving herself in her chair.

"I am speaking now of Mrs. Marsham."

"You should speak of them both together as they hunt in couples."

"Glencora, will you listen to me, or will you not? If you say that you will not, I shall know what to do."

"I don't think you would, Plantagenet." And she nodded her little head at him, as she spoke. "I'm sure I don't know what you would do. But I will listen to you. Only, as I said before, it will be very nice when it's over."

"Mrs. Marsham came here, not simply to tell me that you were waltzing with Mr. Fitzgerald,—and I wish that when you mention his name you would call him Mr. Fitzgerald."

"So I do."

"You generally prefix his Christian name, which it would be much better that you should omit."

"I will try," she said, very gently; "but it's hard to drop an old habit. Before you married me you knew that I had learned to call him Burgo."

"Let me go on," said Mr. Palliser.

"Oh, certainly."

"It was not simply to tell me that you were waltzing that Mrs. Marsham came here."

"And it was not simply to see me waltzing that Mr. Bott stood in the doorways, for he followed me about, and came down after me to the supper-room."

"Glencora, will you oblige me by not speaking of Mr. Bott?"

"I wish you would oblige me by not speaking of Mrs. Marsham." Mr. Palliser rose quickly from his chair with a gesture of anger, stood upright for half a minute, and then sat down again. "I beg your pardon, Plantagenet," she said. "I think I know what you want, and I'll hold my tongue till you bid me speak."

"Mrs. Marsham came here because she saw that every one in the room was regarding you with wonder." Lady Glencora twisted herself about in her chair, but she said nothing. "She saw that you were not only dancing with Mr. Fitzgerald, but that you were dancing with him,—what shall I say?"

"Upon my word I can't tell you."

"Recklessly."

"Oh! recklessly, was I? What was I reckless of?"

"Reckless of what people might say; reckless of what I might feel about it; reckless of your own position."

"Am I to speak now?"

"Perhaps you had better let me go on. I think she was right to come to me."

"That's of course. What's the good of having spies, if they don't run and tell as soon as they see anything, especially anything—reckless."

"Glencora, you are determined to make me angry. I am angry now,— very angry. I have employed no spies. When rumours have reached me, not from spies, as you choose to call them, but through your dearest friends and mine—"

"What do you mean by rumours from my dearest friends?"

"Never mind. Let me go on."

"No; not when you say my dear friends have spread rumours about me. Tell me who they are. I have no dear friends. Do you mean Alice Vavasor?"

"It does not signify. But when I was warned that you had better not go to any house in which you could meet that man, I would not listen to it. I said that you were my wife, and that as such I could trust you anywhere, everywhere, with any person. Others might distrust you, but I would not do so. When I wished you to go to Monkshade, were there to be any spies there? When I left you last night at Lady Monk's, do you believe in your heart that I trusted to Mrs. Marsham's eyes rather than to your own truth? Do you think that I have lived in fear of Mr. Fitzgerald?"

"No, Plantagenet; I do not think so."

"Do you believe that I have commissioned Mr. Bott to watch your conduct? Answer me, Glencora."

She paused a moment, thinking what actually was her true belief on that subject. "He does watch me, certainly," she said.

"That does not answer my question. Do you believe that I have commissioned him to do so?"

"No; I do not."

"Then it is ignoble in you to talk to me of spies. I have employed no spies. If it were ever to come to that, that I thought spies necessary, it would be all over with me."

There was something of feeling in his voice as he said this,—something that almost approached to passion which touched his wife's heart. Whether or not spies would be of any avail, she knew that she had in truth done that of which he had declared that he had never suspected her. She had listened to words of love from her former lover. She had received, and now carried about with her a letter from this man, in which he asked her to elope with him. She had by no means resolved that she would not do this thing. She had been false to her husband; and as her husband spoke of his confidence in her, her own spirit rebelled against the deceit which she herself was practising.

"I know that I have never made you happy," she said. "I know that I never can make you happy."

He looked at her, struck by her altered tone, and saw that her whole manner and demeanour were changed. "I do not understand what you mean," he said. "I have never complained. You have not made me unhappy."

He was one of those men to whom this was enough. If his wife caused him no uneasiness, what more was he to expect from her? No doubt she might have done much more for him. She might have given him an heir. But he was a just man, and knew that the blank he had drawn was his misfortune, and not her fault.

But now her heart was loosed and she spoke out, at first slowly, but after a while with all the quietness of strong passion. "No, Plantagenet; I shall never make you happy. You have never loved me, nor I you. We have never loved each other for a single moment. I have been wrong to talk to you about spies; I was wrong to go to Lady Monk's; I have been wrong in everything that I have done; but never so wrong as when I let them persuade me to be your wife!"

"Glencora!"

"Let me speak now, Plantagenet. It is better that I should tell you everything; and I will. I will tell you everything;—everything! I do love Burgo Fitzgerald. I do! I do! I do! How can I help loving him? Have I not loved him from the first,—before I had seen you? Did you not know that it was so? I do love Burgo Fitzgerald, and when I went to Lady Monk's last night, I had almost made up my mind that I must tell him so, and that I must go away with him and hide myself. But when he came to speak to me—"

"He has asked you to go with him, then?" said the husband, in whose bosom the poison was beginning to take effect, thereby showing that he was neither above nor below humanity.

Glencora was immediately reminded that though she might, if she pleased, tell her own secrets, she ought not, in accordance with her ideas of honour, tell those of her lover. "What need is there of asking, do you think, when people have loved each other as we have done?"

"You wanted to go with him, then?"

"Would it not have been the best for you? Plantagenet, I do not love you;—not as women love their husbands when they do love them. But, before God, my first wish is to free you from the misfortune that I have brought on you." As she made this attestation she started up from her chair, and coming close to him, took him by the coat. He was startled, and stepped back a pace, but did not speak; and then stood looking at her as she went on.

**"Before God, my first wish is to free you from
the misfortune that I have brought on you."**

"What matters it whether I drown myself, or throw myself away by going with such a one as him, so that you might marry again, and have a child? I'd die;—I'd die willingly. How I wish I could die! Plantagenet, I would kill myself if I dared."

He was a tall man and she was short of stature, so that he stood over her and looked upon her, and now she was looking up into his face with all her eyes. "I would," she said. "I would—I would! What is there left for me that I should wish to live?"

Softly, slowly, very gradually, as though he were afraid of what he was doing, he put his arm round her waist. "You are wrong in one thing," he said. "I do love you."

She shook her head, touching his breast with her hair as she did so.

"I do love you," he repeated. "If you mean that I am not apt at telling you so, it is true, I know. My mind is running on other things."

"Yes," she said; "your mind is running on other things."

"But I do love you. If you cannot love me, it is a great misfortune to us both. But we need not therefore be disgraced. As for that other thing of which you spoke,—of our having, as yet, no child"—and in saying this he pressed her somewhat closer with his arm—"you allow yourself to think too much of it;—much more of it than I do. I have made no complaints on that head, even within my own breast."

"I know what your thoughts are, Plantagenet."

"Believe me that you wrong my thoughts. Of course I have been anxious, and have, perhaps, shown my anxiety by the struggle I have made to hide it. I have never told you what is false, Glencora."

"No; you are not false!"

"I would rather have you for my wife, childless,—if you will try to love me,—than any other woman, though another might give me an heir. Will you try to love me?"

She was silent. At this moment, after the confession that she had made, she could not bring herself to say that she would even try. Had she said so, she would have seemed to have accepted his forgiveness too easily.

"I think, dear," he said, still holding her by her waist, "that we had better leave England for a while. I will give up politics for this season. Should you like to go to Switzerland for the summer, or perhaps to some of the German baths, and then on to Italy when the weather is cold enough?" Still she was silent. "Perhaps your friend, Miss Vavasor, would go with us?"

He was killing her by his goodness. She could not speak to him yet; but now, as he mentioned Alice's name, she gently put up her hand and rested it on the back of his.

At that moment there came a knock at the door;—a sharp knock, which was quickly repeated.

"Come in," said Mr. Palliser, dropping his arm from his wife's waist, and standing away from her a few yards.

CHAPTER LIX
THE DUKE OF ST. BUNGAY IN SEARCH OF A MINISTER

It was the butler who had knocked,—showing that the knock was of more importance than it would have been had it been struck by the knuckles of the footman in livery. "If you please, sir, the Duke of St. Bungay is here."

"The Duke of St. Bungay!" said Mr. Palliser, becoming rather red as he heard the announcement.

"Yes, sir, his grace is in the library. He bade me tell you that he particularly wanted to see you; so I told him that you were with my lady."

"Quite right; tell his grace that I will be with him in two minutes." Then the butler retired, and Mr. Palliser was again alone with his wife.

"I must go now, my dear," he said; "and perhaps I shall not see you again till the evening."

"Don't let me put you out in any way," she answered.

"Oh no;—you won't put me out. You will be dressing, I suppose, about nine."

"I did not mean as to that," she answered. "You must not think more of Italy. He has come to tell you that you are wanted in the Cabinet."

Again he turned very red. "It may be so," he answered, "but though I am wanted, I need not go. But I must not keep the duke waiting. Good-bye." And he turned to the door.

She followed him and took hold of him as he went, so that he was forced to turn to her once again. She managed to get hold of both his hands, and pressed them closely, looking up into his face with her eyes laden with tears. He smiled at her gently, returned the pressure of the hands, and then left her,—without kissing her. It was not that he was minded not to kiss her. He would have kissed her willingly enough had he thought that the occasion required it. "He says that he loves me," said Lady Glencora to herself, "but he does not know what love means."

But she was quite aware that he had behaved to her with genuine, true nobility. As soon as she was alone and certain of her solitude, she took out that letter from her pocket, and tearing it into very small fragments, without reading it, threw the pieces on the fire. As she did so, her mind seemed to be fixed, at any rate, to one thing,—that she would think no more of Burgo Fitzgerald as her future master. I think, however, that she had arrived at so much certainty as this, at that moment in which she had been parting with Burgo Fitzgerald, in Lady Monk's dining-room. She had had courage enough,—or shall we rather say sin enough,—to think of going with him,—to tell herself that she would do so; to put herself in the way of doing it; nay, she had had enough of both to enable her to tell her husband that she had resolved that it would be good for her to do so. But she was neither bold enough nor wicked enough to do the thing. As she had said of her own idea of destroying herself,—she did not dare to take the plunge. Therefore, knowing now that it was so, she tore up the letter that she had carried so long, and burnt it in the fire.

She had in truth told him everything, believing that in doing so she was delivering her own death-warrant as regarded her future position in his house. She had done this, not hoping thereby for any escape; not with any purpose as regarded herself, but simply because deceit had been grievous to her, and had become unendurable as soon as his words and manner had in them any feeling of kindness. But her confession had no sooner been made than her fault had been forgiven. She had told him that she did not love him. She had told him, even, that she had thought of leaving him. She had justified by her own words any treatment of his, however harsh, which he might choose to practise. But the result had been—the immediate result—that he had been more tender to her than she had ever remembered him to be before. She knew that he had conquered her. However cold and heartless his home might be to her, it must be her home now. There could be no further thought of leaving him. She had gone out into the tiltyard and had tilted with him, and he had been the victor.

Mr. Palliser himself had not time for much thought before he found himself closeted with the Duke; but as he crossed the hall and went up the stairs, a thought or two did pass quickly across his mind. She had confessed to him, and he had forgiven her. He did not feel quite sure that he had been right, but he did feel quite sure that the thing had been done. He recognized it for a fact that, as regarded the past, no more was to be said. There were to be no reproaches, and there must be some tacit abandoning of Mrs. Marsham's close attendance. As to Mr. Bott;—he had begun to hate Mr. Bott, and had felt cruelly ungrateful, when that gentleman endeavoured to whisper a word into his ear as he passed through the doorway into Lady Monk's dining-room. And he had offered to go abroad,—to go abroad and leave his politics, and his ambition, and his coming honours. He had persisted in his offer, even after his wife had suggested to him that the Duke of St. Bungay was now in the house with the object of offering him that very thing for which he had so longed! As he thought of this his heart became heavy within him. Such chances,—so he told himself,—do not come twice in a man's way. When returning from a twelvemonth's residence abroad he would be nobody in politics. He would have lost everything for which he had been working all his life. But he was a man of his word, and as he opened the library door he was resolute,—he thought that he could be resolute in adhering to his promise.

"Duke," he said, "I'm afraid I have kept you waiting." And the two political allies shook each other by the hand.

The Duke was in a glow of delight. There had been no waiting. He was only too glad to find his friend at home. He had been prepared to wait, even if Mr. Palliser had been out. "And I suppose you guess why I'm come?" said the Duke.

"I would rather be told than have to guess," said Mr. Palliser, smiling for a moment. But the smile quickly passed off his face as he remembered his pledge to his wife.

"He has resigned at last. What was said in the Lords last night made it necessary that he should do so, or that Lord Brock should declare himself able to support him through thick and thin. Of course, I can tell you everything now. He must have gone, or I must have done so. You know that I don't like him in the Cabinet. I admire his character and his genius, but I think him the most dangerous man in England as a statesman. He has high principles,—the very highest; but they are so high as to be out of sight to ordinary eyes. They are too exalted to be of any use for everyday purposes. He is honest as the sun, I'm sure; but it's just like the sun's honesty,—of a kind which we men below can't quite understand or appreciate. He has no instinct in politics, but reaches his conclusions by philosophical deduction. Now, in politics, I would a deal sooner trust to instinct than to calculation.

I think he may probably know how England ought to be governed three centuries hence better than any man living, but of the proper way to govern it now, I think he knows less. Brock half likes him and half fears him. He likes the support of his eloquence, and he likes the power of the man; but he fears his restless activity, and thoroughly dislikes his philosophy. At any rate, he has left us, and I am here to ask you to take his place."

The Duke, as he concluded his speech, was quite contented, and almost jovial. He was thoroughly satisfied with the new political arrangement which he was proposing. He regarded Mr. Palliser as a steady, practical man of business, luckily young, and therefore with a deal of work in him, belonging to the race from which English ministers ought, in his opinion, to be taken, and as being, in some respects, his own pupil. He had been the first to declare aloud that Plantagenet Palliser was the coming Chancellor of the Exchequer; and it had been long known, though no such declaration had been made aloud, that the Duke did not sit comfortably in the same Cabinet with the gentleman who had now resigned. Everything had now gone as the Duke wished; and he was prepared to celebrate some little ovation with his young friend before he left the house in Park Lane.

"And who goes out with him?" asked Mr. Palliser, putting off the evil moment of his own decision; but before the Duke could answer him, he had reminded himself that under his present circumstances he had no right to ask such a question. His own decision could not rest upon that point. "But it does not matter," he said; "I am afraid I must decline the offer you bring me."

"Decline it!" said the Duke, who could not have been more surprised had his friend talked of declining heaven.

"I fear I must." The Duke had now risen from his chair, and was standing, with both his hands upon the table. All his contentment, all his joviality, had vanished. His fine round face had become almost ludicrously long; his eyes and mouth were struggling to convey reproach, and the reproach was almost drowned in vexation. Ever since Parliament had met he had been whispering Mr. Palliser's name into the Prime Minister's ear, and now —. But he could not, and would not, believe it. "Nonsense, Palliser," he said. "You must have got some false notion into your head. There can be no possible reason why you should not join us. Finespun himself will support us, at any rate for a time." Mr. Finespun was the gentleman whose retirement from the ministry the Duke of St. Bungay had now announced.

"It is nothing of that kind," said Mr. Palliser, who perhaps felt himself quite equal to the duties proposed to him, even though Mr. Finespun should not support him. "It is nothing of that kind;—it is no fear of that sort that hinders me."

"Then, for mercy's sake, what is it? My dear Palliser, I looked upon you as being as sure in this matter as myself; and I had a right to do so. You certainly intended to join us a month ago, if the opportunity offered. You certainly did."

"It is true, Duke. I must ask you to listen to me now, and I must tell you what I would not willingly tell to any man." As Mr. Palliser said this a look of agony came over his face. There are men who can talk easily of all their most inmost matters, but he was not such a man. It went sorely against the grain with him to speak of the sorrow of his home, even to such a friend as the Duke; but it was essentially necessary to him that he should justify himself.

"Upon my word," said the Duke, "I can't understand that there should be any reason strong enough to make you throw your party over."

"I have promised to take my wife abroad."

"Is that it?" said the Duke, looking at him with surprise, but at the same time with something of returning joviality in his face. "Nobody thinks of going abroad at this time of the year. Of course, you can get away for a time when Parliament breaks up."

"But I have promised to go at once."

"Then, considering your position, you have made a promise which it behoves you to break. I am sure Lady Glencora will see it in that light."

"You do not quite understand me, and I am afraid I must trouble you to listen to matters which, under other circumstances, it would be impertinent in me to obtrude upon you." A certain stiffness of demeanour, and measured propriety of voice, much at variance with his former manner, came upon him as he said this.

"Of course, Palliser, I don't want to interfere for a moment."

"If you will allow me, Duke. My wife has told me that, this morning, which makes me feel that absence from England is requisite for her present comfort. I was with her when you came, and had just promised her that she should go."

"But, Palliser, think of it. If this were a small matter, I would not press you; but a man in your position has public duties. He owes his services to his country. He has no right to go back, if it be possible that he should so do."

"When a man has given his word, it cannot be right that he should go back from that."

"Of course not. But a man may be absolved from a promise. Lady Glencora—"

"My wife would, of course, absolve me. It is not that. Her happiness demands it, and it is partly my fault that it is so. I cannot explain to you more fully why it is that I must give up the great object for which I have striven with all my strength."

"Oh, no!" said the Duke. "If you are sure that it is imperative—"

"It is imperative."

"I could give you twenty-four hours, you know." Mr. Palliser did not answer at once, and the Duke thought that he saw some sign of hesitation. "I suppose it would not be possible that I should speak to Lady Glencora?"

"It could be of no avail, Duke. She would only declare, at the first word, that she would remain in London; but it would not be the less my duty on that account to take her abroad."

"Well; I can't say. Of course, I can't say. Such an opportunity may not come twice in a man's life. And at your age too! You are throwing away from you the finest political position that the world can offer to the ambition of any man. No one at your time of life has had such a chance within my memory. That a man under thirty should be thought fit to be Chancellor of the Exchequer, and should refuse it,—because he wants to take his wife abroad! Palliser, if she were dying, you should remain under such an emergency as this. She might go, but you should remain."

Mr. Palliser remained silent for a moment or two in his chair; he then rose and walked towards the window, as he spoke. "There are things worse than death," he said, when his back was turned. His voice was very low, and there was a tear in his eye as he spoke them; the words were indeed whispered, but the Duke heard them, and felt that he could not press him any more on the subject of his wife.

"And must this be final?" said the Duke.

"I think it must. But your visit here has come so quickly on my resolution to go abroad,—which, in truth, was only made ten minutes before your name was brought to me,—that I believe I ought to ask for a portion of those twenty-four hours which you have offered me. A small portion will be enough. Will you see me, if I come to you this evening, say at eight? If the House is up in the Lords I will go to you in St. James's Square."

"We shall be sitting after eight, I think."

"Then I will see you there. And, Duke, I must ask you to think of me in this matter as a friend should think, and not as though we were bound together only by party feeling."

"I will,—I will."

"I have told you what I shall never whisper to any one else."

"I think you know that you are safe with me."

"I am sure of it. And, Duke, I can tell you that the sacrifice to me will be almost more than I can bear. This thing that you have offered me to-day is the only thing that I have ever coveted. I have thought of it and worked for it, have hoped and despaired, have for moments been vain enough to think that it was within my strength, and have been wretched for weeks together because I have told myself that it was utterly beyond me."

"As to that, neither Brock nor I, nor any of us, have any doubt. Finespun himself says that you are the man."

"I am much obliged to them. But I say all this simply that you may understand how imperative is the duty which, as I think, requires me to refuse the offer."

"But you haven't refused as yet," said the Duke. "I shall wait at the House for you, whether they are sitting or not. And endeavour to join us. Do the best you can. I will say nothing as to that duty of which you speak; but if it can be made compatible with your public service, pray—pray let it be done. Remember how much such a one as you owes to his country." Then the Duke went, and Mr. Palliser was alone.

He had not been alone before since the revelation which had been made to him by his wife, and the words she had spoken were still sounding in his ears. "I do love Burgo Fitzgerald;—I do! I do! I do!" They were not pleasant words for a young husband to hear. Men there are, no doubt, whose nature would make them more miserable under the infliction than it had made Plantagenet Palliser. He was calm, without strong passion, not prone to give to words a stronger significance than they should bear;—and he was essentially unsuspicious. Never for a moment had he thought, even while those words were hissing in his ears, that his wife had betrayed his honour. Nevertheless, there was that at his heart, as he remembered those words, which made him feel that the world was almost too heavy for him. For the first quarter of an hour after the Duke's departure he thought more of his wife and of Burgo Fitzgerald than he did of Lord Brock and Mr. Finespun. But of this he was aware,—that he had forgiven his wife; that he had put his arm round her and embraced her after hearing her confession,—and that she, mutely, with her eyes, had promised him that she would do her best for him. Then something of an idea of love came across his heart, and he acknowledged to himself that he had married without loving or without requiring love. Much of all this had been his own fault. Indeed, had not the whole of it come from his own wrong-doing? He acknowledged that it was so. But now,—now he loved her. He felt that he could not bear to part with her, even if there were no question of public scandal, or of disgrace. He had been torn inwardly by that assertion that she loved another man. She had got at his heart-strings at last. There are men who may love their wives, though they never can have been in love before their marriage.

When the Duke had been gone about an hour, and when, under ordinary circumstances, it would have been his time to go down to the House, he took his hat and walked into the Park. He made his way across Hyde Park, and into Kensington Gardens, and there he remained for an hour, walking up and down beneath the elms. The quidnuncs of the town, who chanced to see him, and who had heard something of the political movements of the day, thought, no doubt, that he was meditating his future ministerial career. But he had not been there long before he had resolved that no ministerial career was at present open to him. "It has been my own fault," he said, as he returned to his house, "and with God's help I will mend it, if it be possible."

But he was a slow man, and he did not go off instantly to the Duke. He had given himself to eight o'clock, and he took the full time. He could not go down to the House of Commons because men would make inquiries of him which he would find it difficult to answer. So he dined at home, alone. He had told his wife that he would see her at nine, and before that hour he would not go to her. He sat alone till it was time for him to get into his brougham, and thought it all over. That seat in the Cabinet and Chancellorship of the Exchequer, which he had so infinitely desired, were already done with. There was no doubt about that. It might have been better for him not to have married; but now that he was married, and that things had brought him untowardly to this pass, he knew that his wife's safety was his first duty. "We will go through Switzerland," he said to himself, "to Baden, and then we will get on to Florence and to Rome. She has seen nothing of all these things yet, and the new life will make a change in her. She shall have her own friend with her." Then he went down to the House of Lords, and saw the Duke.

"Well, Palliser," said the Duke, when he had listened to him, "of course I cannot argue it with you any more. I can only say that I am very sorry;— more sorry than perhaps you will believe. Indeed, it half breaks my heart." The Duke's voice was very sad, and it might almost have been thought that he was going to shed a tear. In truth he disliked Mr. Finespun with the strongest political feeling of which he was capable, and had attached himself to Mr. Palliser almost as strongly. It was a thousand pities! How hard had he not worked to bring about this arrangement, which was now to be upset because a woman had been foolish! "I never above half liked her," said the Duke to himself, thinking perhaps a little of the Duchess's complaints of her. "I must go to Brock at once," he said aloud, "and tell him. God knows what we must do now. Goodbye! good-bye! No; I'm not angry. There shall be no quarrel. But I am very sorry." In this way the two politicians parted.

We may as well follow this political movement to its end. The Duke saw Lord Brock that night, and then those two ministers sent for another minister,—another noble Lord, a man of great experience in Cabinets. These three discussed the matter together, and on the following day Lord Brock got up in the House, and made a strong speech in defence of his colleague, Mr. Finespun. To the end of the Session, at any rate, Mr. Finespun kept his position, and held the seals of the Exchequer while all the quidnuncs of the nation, shaking their heads, spoke of the wonderful power of Mr. Finespun, and declared that Lord Brock did not dare to face the Opposition without him.

In the meantime Mr. Palliser had returned to his wife, and told her of his resolution with reference to their tour abroad. "We may as well make up our minds to start at once," said he. "At any rate, there is nothing on my side to hinder us."

CHAPTER LX
ALICE VAVASOR'S NAME GETS INTO THE MONEY MARKET

Some ten or twelve days after George Vavasor's return to London from Westmoreland he appeared at Mr. Scruby's offices with four small slips of paper in his hand. Mr. Scruby, as usual, was pressing for money. The third election was coming on, and money was already being spent very freely among the men of the River Bank. So, at least, Mr. Scruby declared. Mr. Grimes, of the "Handsome Man," had shown signs of returning allegiance. But Mr. Grimes could not afford to be loyal without money. He had his little family to protect. Mr. Scruby, too, had his little family, and was not ashamed to use it on this occasion. "I'm a family man, Mr. Vavasor, and therefore I never run any risks. I never go a yard further than I can see my way back." This he had said in answer to a proposition that he should take George's note of hand for the expenses of the next election, payable in three months' time. "It is so very hard to realize," said George, "immediately upon a death, when all the property left is real property." "Very hard indeed," said Mr. Scruby, who had heard with accuracy all the particulars of the old Squire's will. Vavasor understood the lawyer, cursed him inwardly, and suggested to himself that some day he might murder Mr. Scruby as well as John Grey,—and perhaps also a few more of his enemies. Two days after the interview in which his own note of hand had been refused, he again called in Great Marlborough Street. Upon this occasion he tendered to Mr. Scruby for his approval the four slips of paper which have been mentioned. Mr. Scruby regarded them with attention, looking first at one side horizontally, and then at the other side perpendicularly. But before we learn the judgement pronounced by Mr. Scruby as to these four slips of paper, we must go back to their earlier history. As they were still in their infancy, we shall not have to go back far.

One morning, at about eleven o'clock the parlour-maid came up to Alice, as she sat alone in the drawing-room in Queen Anne Street, and told her there was a "gentleman" in the hall waiting to be seen by her. We all know the tone in which servants announce a gentleman when they know that the gentleman is not a gentleman.

"A gentleman wanting to see me! What sort of a gentleman?"

"Well, miss, I don't think he's just of our sort; but he's decent to look at."

Alice Vavasor had no desire to deny herself to any person but one. She was well aware that the gentleman in the hall could not be her cousin George, and therefore she did not refuse to see him.

"Let him come up," she said. "But I think, Jane, you ought to ask him his name." Jane did ask him his name, and came back immediately, announcing Mr. Levy.

This occurred immediately after the return of Mr. John Vavasor from Westmoreland. He had reached home late on the preceding evening, and at the moment of Mr. Levy's call was in his dressing-room.

Alice got up to receive her visitor, and at once understood the tone of her maid's voice. Mr. Levy was certainly not a gentleman of the sort to which she had been most accustomed. He was a little dark man, with sharp eyes, set very near to each other in his head, with a beaked nose, thick at the bridge, and a black moustache, but no other beard. Alice did not at all like the look of Mr. Levy, but she stood up to receive him, made him a little bow, and asked him to sit down.

"Is papa dressed yet?" Alice asked the servant.

"Well, miss, I don't think he is, —not to say dressed."

Alice had thought it might be as well that Mr. Levy should know that there was a gentleman in the house with her.

"I've called about a little bit of business, miss," said Mr. Levy, when they were alone. "Nothing as you need disturb yourself about. You'll find it all square, I think." Then he took a case out of his breast-pocket, and produced a note, which he handed to her. Alice took the note, and saw immediately that it was addressed to her by her cousin George. "Yes, Mr. George Vavasor," said Mr. Levy. "I dare say you never saw me before, miss?"

"No, sir; I think not," said Alice.

"I am your cousin's clerk."

"Oh, you're Mr. Vavasor's clerk. I'll read his letter, if you please, sir."

"If you please, miss."

George Vavasor's letter to his cousin was as follows:—

Dear Alice,

After what passed between us when I last saw you I thought that on my return from Westmoreland I should learn that you had paid in at my bankers' the money that I require. But I find that this is not so; and of course I excuse you, because women so seldom know when or how to do that which business demands of them. You have, no doubt, heard the injustice which my grandfather has done me, and will probably feel as indignant as I do. I only mention this now, because the nature of his will makes it more than ever incumbent on you that you should be true to your pledge to me.

Till there shall be some ground for a better understanding between us,—and this I do not doubt will come,—I think it wiser not to call, myself, at Queen Anne Street. I therefore send my confidential clerk with four bills, each of five hundred pounds, drawn at fourteen days' date, across which I will get you to write your name. Mr. Levy will show you the way in which this should be done. Your name must come under the word "accepted," and just above the name of Messrs. Drummonds, where the money must be lying ready, at any rate, not later than Monday fortnight. Indeed, the money must be there some time on the Saturday. They know you so well at Drummonds' that you will not object to call on the Saturday afternoon, and ask if it is all right.

I have certainly been inconvenienced by not finding the money as I expected on my return to town. If these bills are not properly provided for, the result will be very disastrous to me. I feel, however, sure that this will be done, both for your own sake and for mine.

Affectionately yours,
George Vavasor.

The unparalleled impudence of this letter had the effect which the writer had intended. It made Alice think immediately of her own remissness,—if she had been remiss,—rather than of the enormity of his claim upon her. The decision with which he asked for her money, without any pretence at an excuse on his part, did for the time induce her to believe that she had no alternative but to give it to him, and that she had been wrong in delaying it. She had told him that he should have it, and she ought to have been as good as her word. She should not have forced upon him the necessity of demanding it.

But the idea of signing four bills was terrible to her, and she felt sure that she ought not to put her name to orders for so large an amount and then intrust them to such a man as Mr. Levy. Her father was in the house, and she might have asked him. The thought that she would do so of course occurred to her. But then it occurred to her also that were she to speak to her father as to this advancing of money to her cousin,—to this giving of money, for she now well understood that it would be a gift;—were she to consult her father in any way about it, he would hinder her, not only from signing the bills for Mr. Levy, but, as far as he could do so, from keeping the promise made to her cousin. She was resolved that George should have the money, and she knew that she could give it to him in spite of her father. But her father might probably be able to delay the gift, and thus rob it of its chief value. If she were to sign the bills, the money must be made to be forthcoming. So much she understood.

Mr. Levy had taken out the four bills from the same case, and had placed them on the table before him. "Mr. Vavasor has explained, I believe, miss, what it is you have to do?" he said.

"Yes, sir; my cousin has explained."

"And there is nothing else to trouble you with, I believe. If you will just write your name across them, here, I need not detain you by staying any longer." Mr. Levy was very anxious to make his visit as short as possible, since he had heard that Mr. John Vavasor was in the house.

But Alice hesitated. Two thousand pounds is a very serious sum of money. She had heard much of sharpers, and thought that she ought to be cautious. What if this man, of whom she had never before heard, should steal the bills after she had signed them? She looked again at her cousin's letter, chiefly with the object of gaining time.

"It's all right, miss," said Mr. Levy.

"Could you not leave them with me, sir?" said Alice.

"Well; not very well, miss. No doubt Mr. Vavasor has explained it all; but the fact is, he must have them this afternoon. He has got a heavy sum to put down on the nail about this here election, and if it ain't down to-day, them on whom he has to depend will be all abroad."

"But, sir, the money will not be payable to-day. If I understand it, they are not cheques."

"No, miss, no; they are not cheques. But your name, miss, at fourteen days, is the same as ready money;—just the same."

She paused, and while she paused, he reached a pen for her from the writing-table, and then she signed the four bills as he held them before her. She was quick enough at doing this when she had once commenced the work. Her object, then, was that the man should be gone from the house before her father could meet him.

These were the four bits of paper which George Vavasor tendered to Mr. Scruby's notice on the occasion which we have now in hand. In doing so, he made use of them after the manner of a grand capitalist, who knows that he may assume certain airs as he allows the odours of the sweetness of his wealth to drop from him.

"You insisted on ready money, with your d—— suspicions," said he; "and there it is. You're not afraid of fourteen days, I dare say."

"Fourteen days is neither here nor there," said Mr. Scruby. "We can let our payments stand over as long as that, without doing any harm. I'll send one of my men down to Grimes, and tell him I can't see him, till,—let me see," and he looked at one of the bills, "till the 15th."

But this was not exactly what George Vavasor wanted. He was desirous that the bills should be immediately turned into money, so that the necessity of forcing payments from Alice, should due provision for the bills not be made, might fall into other hands than his.

"We can wait till the 15th," said Scruby, as he handed the bits of paper back to his customer.

"You will want a thousand, you say?" said George.

"A thousand to begin with. Certainly not less."

"Then you had better keep two of them."

"Well—no! I don't see the use of that. You had better collect them through your own banker, and let me have a cheque on the 15th or 16th."

"How cursed suspicious you are, Scruby."

"No, I ain't. I'm not a bit suspicious. I don't deal in such articles; that's all!"

"What doubt can there be about such bills as those? Everybody knows that my cousin has a considerable fortune, altogether at her own disposal."

"The truth is, Mr. Vavasor, that bills with ladies' names on them,— ladies who are no way connected with business,—ain't just the paper that people like."

"Nothing on earth can be surer."

"You take them into the City for discount, and see if the bankers don't tell you the same. They may be done, of course, upon your name. I say nothing about that."

"I can explain to you the nature of the family arrangement, but I can't do that to a stranger. However, I don't mind."

"Of course not. The time is so short that it does not signify. Have them collected through your own bankers, and then, if it don't suit you to call, send me a cheque for a thousand pounds when the time is up." Then Mr. Scruby turned to some papers on his right hand, as though the interview had been long enough. Vavasor looked at him angrily, opening his wound at him and cursing him inwardly. Mr. Scruby went on with his paper, by no means regarding either the wound or the unspoken curses. Thereupon Vavasor got up and went away without any word of farewell.

As he walked along Great Marlborough Street, and through those unalluring streets which surround the Soho district, and so on to the Strand and his own lodgings, he still continued to think of some wide scheme of revenge,—of some scheme in which Mr. Scruby might be included. There had appeared something latterly in Mr. Scruby's manner to him, something of mingled impatience and familiarity, which made him feel that he had fallen in the attorney's estimation. It was not that the lawyer thought him to be less honourable, or less clever, than he had before thought him; but that the man was like a rat, and knew a falling house by the instinct that was in him. So George Vavasor cursed Mr. Scruby, and calculated some method of murdering him without detection.

The reader is not to suppose that the Member for the Chelsea Districts had, in truth, resolved to gratify his revenge by murder,—by murdering any of those persons whom he hated so vigorously. He did not, himself, think it probable that he would become a murderer. But he received some secret satisfaction in allowing his mind to dwell upon the subject, and in making those calculations. He reflected that it would not do to take off Scruby and John Grey at the same time, as it would be known that he was connected with both of them; unless, indeed, he was to take off a third person at the same time,—a third person, as to the expediency of ending whose career he made his calculations quite as often as he did in regard to any of those persons whom he cursed so often. It need hardly be explained to the reader that this third person was the sitting Member for the Chelsea Districts.

As he was himself in want of instant ready money Mr. Scruby's proposition that he should leave the four bills at his own bankers', to be collected when they came to maturity, did not suit him. He doubted much, also, whether at the end of the fourteen days the money would be forthcoming. Alice would be driven to tell her father, in order that the money might be procured, and John Vavasor would probably succeed in putting impediments in the way of the payment. He must take the bills into the City, and do the best there that he could with them. He was too late for this to-day, and therefore he went to his lodgings, and then down to the House. In the House he sat all the night with his hat over his eyes, making those little calculations of which I have spoken.

"You have heard the news; haven't you?" said Mr. Bott to him, whispering in his ear.

"News; no. I haven't heard any news."

"Finespun has resigned, and Palliser is at this moment with the Duke of St. Bungay in the Lords' library."

"They may both be at the bottom of the Lords' fishpond, for what I care," said Vavasor.

"That's nonsense, you know," said Bott. "Still, you know Palliser is Chancellor of the Exchequer at this moment. What a lucky fellow you are to have such a chance come to you directly you get in. As soon as he takes his seat down there, of course we shall go up behind him."

"We shall have another election in a month's time," said George. "I'm safe enough," said Bott. "It never hurts a man at elections to be closely connected with the Government."

George Vavasor was in the City by times the next morning, but he found that the City did not look with favourable eyes on his four bills. The City took them up, first horizontally, and then, with a twist of its hand, perpendicularly, and looked at them with distrustful eyes. The City repeated the name, Alice Vavasor, as though it were not esteemed a good name on Change. The City suggested that as the time was so short, the holder of the bills would be wise to hold them till he could collect the amount. It was very clear that the City suspected something wrong in the transaction. The City, by one of its mouths, asserted plainly that ladies' bills never meant business. George Vavasor cursed the City, and made his calculation about murdering it. Might not a river of strychnine be turned on round the Exchange about luncheon time? Three of the bills he left at last with his own bankers for collection, and retained the fourth in his breast-pocket, intending on the morrow to descend with it into those lower depths of the money market which he had not as yet visited. Again, on the next day, he went to work and succeeded to some extent. Among those lower depths he found a capitalist who was willing to advance him two hundred pounds, keeping that fourth bill in his possession as security. The capitalist was to have forty pounds for the transaction, and George cursed him as he took his cheque. George Vavasor knew quite enough of the commercial world to enable him to understand that a man must be in a very bad condition when he consents to pay forty pounds for the use of two hundred for fourteen days. He cursed the City. He cursed the House of Commons. He cursed his cousin Alice and his sister Kate. He cursed the memory of his grandfather. And he cursed himself.

Mr. Levy had hardly left the house in Queen Anne Street, before Alice had told her father what she had done. "The money must be forthcoming," said Alice. To this her father made no immediate reply, but turning himself in his chair away from her with a sudden start, sat looking at the fire and shaking his head. "The money must be made to be forthcoming," said Alice. "Papa, will you see that it is done?" This was very hard upon poor John Vavasor, and so he felt it to be. "Papa, if you will not promise, I must go to Mr. Round about it myself, and must find out a broker to sell out for me. You would not wish that my name should be dishonoured."

"You will be ruined," said he, "and for such a rascal as that!"

"Never mind whether he is a rascal or not, papa. You must acknowledge that he has been treated harshly by his grandfather."

"I think that will was the wisest thing my father ever did. Had he left the estate to George, there wouldn't have been an acre of it left in the family in six months' time."

"But the life interest, papa!"

"He would have raised all he could upon that, and it would have done him no good."

"At any rate, papa, he must have this two thousand pounds. You must promise me that."

"And then he will want more."

"No; I do not think he will ask for more. At any rate, I do not think that I am bound to give him all that I have."

"I should think not. I should like to know how you can be bound to give him anything?"

"Because I promised it. I have signed the bills now, and it must be done." Still Mr. Vavasor made no promise. "Papa, if you will not say that you will do it, I must go down to Mr. Round at once."

"I don't know that I can do it. I don't know that Mr. Round can do it. Your money is chiefly on mortgage." Then there was a pause for a moment in the conversation. "Upon my word, I never heard of such a thing in my life," said Mr. Vavasor; "I never did. Four thousand pounds given away to such a man as that, in three months! Four thousand pounds! And you say you do not intend to marry him."

"Certainly not; all that is over."

"And does he know that it is over?"

"I suppose he does."

"You suppose so! Things of that sort are so often over with you!" This was very cruel. Perhaps she had deserved the reproach, but still it was very cruel. The blow struck her with such force that she staggered under it. Tears came into her eyes, and she could hardly speak lest she should betray herself by sobbing.

"I know that I have behaved badly," she said at last; "but I am punished, and you might spare me now!"

"I didn't want to punish you," he said, getting up from his chair and walking about the room. "I don't want to punish you. But, I don't want to see you ruined!"

"I must go to Mr. Round then, myself."

Mr. Vavasor went on walking about the room, jingling the money in his trousers-pockets, and pushing the chairs about as he chanced to meet them. At last, he made a compromise with her. He would take a day to think whether he would assist her in getting the money, and communicate his decision to her on the following morning.

CHAPTER LXI
THE BILLS ARE MADE ALL RIGHT

Mr. Vavasor was at his wits' end about his daughter. She had put her name to four bills for five hundred pounds each, and had demanded from him, almost without an apology, his aid in obtaining money to meet them. And she might put her name to any other number of bills, and for any amount! There was no knowing how a man ought to behave to such a daughter. "I don't want her money," the father said to himself; "and if she had got none of her own, I would make her as comfortable as I could with my own income. But to see her throw her money away in such a fashion as this is enough to break a man's heart."

Mr. Vavasor went to his office in Chancery Lane, but he did not go to the chambers of Mr. Round, the lawyer. Instead of calling on Mr. Round he sent a note by a messenger to Suffolk Street, and the answer to the note came in the person of Mr. Grey. John Grey was living in town in these days, and was in the habit of seeing Mr. Vavasor frequently. Indeed, he had not left London since the memorable occasion on which he had pitched his rival down the tailor's stairs at his lodgings. He had made himself pretty well conversant with George Vavasor's career, and had often shuddered as he thought what might be the fate of any girl who might trust herself to marry such a man as that.

He had been at home when Mr. Vavasor's note had reached his lodgings, and had instantly walked off towards Chancery Lane. He knew his way to Mr. Vavasor's signing-office very accurately, for he had acquired a habit of calling there, and of talking to the father about his daughter. He was a patient, persevering man, confident in himself, and apt to trust that he would accomplish those things which he attempted, though he was hardly himself aware of any such aptitude. He had never despaired as to Alice. And though he had openly acknowledged to himself that she had been very foolish,—or rather, that her judgement had failed her,—he had never in truth been angry with her. He had looked upon her rejection of himself, and her subsequent promise to her cousin, as the effects of a mental hallucination, very much to be lamented,—to be wept for, perhaps, through a whole life, as a source of terrible sorrow to himself and to her. But he regarded it all as a disease, of which the cure was yet possible, — as a disease which, though it might never leave the patient as strong as she was before, might still leave her altogether. And as he would still have clung to his love had she been attacked by any of those illnesses for which doctors have well-known names, so would he cling to her now that she was attacked by a malady for which no name was known. He had already heard from Mr. Vavasor that Alice had discovered how impossible it was that she should marry her cousin, and, in his quiet, patient, enduring way, was beginning to feel confident that he would, at last, carry his mistress off with him to Nethercoats.

It was certainly a melancholy place, that signing-office, in which Mr. John Vavasor was doomed to spend twelve hours a week, during every term time, of his existence. Whether any man could really pass an existence of work in such a workshop, and not have gone mad, — could have endured to work there for seven hours a day, every week-day of his life, I am not prepared to say. I doubt much whether any victims are so doomed. I have so often wandered through those gloomy passages without finding a sign of humanity there, — without hearing any slightest tick of the hammer of labour, that I am disposed to think that Lord Chancellors have been anxious to save their subordinates from suicide, and have mercifully decreed that the whole staff of labourers, down to the very message boys of the office, should be sent away to green fields or palatial clubs during, at any rate, a moiety of their existence.

The dismal set of chambers, in which the most dismal room had been assigned to Mr. Vavasor, was not actually in Chancery Lane. Opening off from Chancery Lane are various other small lanes, quiet, dingy nooks, some of them in the guise of streets going no whither, some being thoroughfares to other dingy streets beyond, in which sponging-houses abound, and others existing as the entrances to so-called Inns of Court, — inns of which all knowledge has for years been lost to the outer world of the laity, and, as I believe, lost almost equally to the inner world of the legal profession. Who has ever heard of Symonds' Inn? But an ancestral Symonds, celebrated, no doubt, in his time, did found an inn, and there it is to this day. Of Staples' Inn, who knows the purposes or use? Who are its members, and what do they do as such? And Staples' Inn is an inn with pretensions, having a chapel of its own, or, at any rate, a building which, in its external dimensions, is ecclesiastical, having a garden and architectural proportions; and a façade towards Holborn, somewhat dingy, but respectable, with an old gateway, and with a decided character of its own.

The building in which Mr. John Vavasor had a room and a desk was located in one of these side streets, and had, in its infantine days, been regarded with complacency by its founder. It was stone-faced, and strong, and though very ugly, had about it that air of importance which justifies a building in assuming a special name of itself. This building was called the Accountant-General's Record Office, and very probably, in the gloom of its dark cellars, may lie to this day the records of the expenditure of many a fair property which has gotten itself into Chancery, and has never gotten itself out again. It was entered by a dark hall, the door of which was never closed; and which, having another door at its further end leading into another lane, had become itself a thoroughfare. But the passers through it were few in number. Now and then a boy might be seen there carrying on his head or shoulders a huge mass of papers which you would presume to be accounts, or some clerk employed in the purlieus of Chancery Lane who would know the shortest possible way from the chambers of some one attorney to those of some other. But this hall, though open at both ends, was as dark as Erebus; and any who lingered in it would soon find themselves to be growing damp, and would smell mildew, and would become naturally affected by the exhalations arising from those Chancery records beneath their feet.

Up the stone stairs, from this hall, John Grey passed to Mr. Vavasor's signing-room. The stairs were broad, and almost of noble proportions, but the darkness and gloom which hung about the hall, hung also about them,—a melancholy set of stairs, up and down which no man can walk with cheerful feet. Here he came upon a long, broad passage, in which no sound was, at first, to be heard. There was no busy noise of doors slamming, no rapid sound of shoes, no passing to and fro of men intent on their daily bread. Pausing for a moment, that he might look round about him and realize the deathlike stillness of the whole, John Grey could just distinguish the heavy breathing of a man, thereby learning that there was a captive in, at any rate, one of those prisons on each side of him. As he drew near to the door of Mr. Vavasor's chamber he knew that the breathing came from thence.

On the door there were words inscribed, which were just legible in the gloom—"Signing Room. Mr. Vavasor."

How John Vavasor did hate those words! It seemed to him that they had been placed there with the express object of declaring his degradation aloud to the world. Since his grandfather's will had been read to him he had almost made up his mind to go down those melancholy stairs for the last time, to shake the dust off his feet as he left the Accountant-General's Record Office for ever, and content himself with half his official income. But how could he give up so many hundreds a year while his daughter was persisting in throwing away thousands as fast as, or faster than, she could lay her hands on them?

John Grey entered the room and found Mr. Vavasor sitting all alone in an arm-chair over the fire. I rather think that that breathing had been the breathing of a man asleep. He was resting himself amidst the labours of his signing. It was a large, dull room, which could not have been painted, I should think, within the memory of man, looking out backwards into some court. The black wall of another building seemed to stand up close to the window,—so close that no direct ray of the sun ever interrupted the signing-clerk at his work. In the middle of the room there was a large mahogany-table, on which lay a pile of huge papers. Across the top of them there was placed a bit of blotting-paper, with a quill pen, the two only tools which were necessary to the performance of the signing-clerk's work. On the table there stood a row of official books, placed lengthways on their edges: the "Post-Office Directory," the "Court Circular," a "Directory to the Inns of Court," a dusty volume of Acts of Parliament, which had reference to Chancery accounts,—a volume which Mr. Vavasor never opened; and there were some others; but there was no book there in which any Christian man or woman could take delight, either for amusement or for recreation. There were three or four chairs round the wall, and there was the one arm-chair which the occupant of the chamber had dragged away from its sacred place to the hearth-rug. There was also an old Turkey carpet on the floor. Other furniture there was none. Can it be a matter of surprise to any one that Mr. Vavasor preferred his club to his place of business? He was not left quite alone in this deathlike dungeon. Attached to his own large room there was a small closet, in which sat the signing-clerk's clerk,—a lad of perhaps seventeen years of age, who spent the greatest part of his time playing tit-tat-to by himself upon official blotting-paper. Had I been Mr. Vavasor I should have sworn a bosom friendship with that lad, have told him all my secrets, and joined his youthful games.

"Come in!" Mr. Vavasor had cried when John Grey disturbed his slumber by knocking at the door. "I'm glad to see you,—very. Sit down; won't you? Did you ever see such a wretched fire? The coals they give you in this place are the worst in all London. Did you ever see such coals?" And he gave a wicked poke at the fire.

It was now the 1st of May, and Grey, who had walked from Suffolk Street, was quite warm. "One hardly wants a fire at all, such weather as this," he said.

"Oh; don't you?" said the signing-clerk. "If you had to sit here all day, you'd see if you didn't want a fire. It's the coldest building I ever put my foot in. Sometimes in winter I have to sit here the whole day in a great-coat. I only wish I could shut old Sugden up here for a week or two, after Christmas." The great lawyer whom he had named was the man whom he supposed to have inflicted on him the terrible injury of his life, and he was continually invoking small misfortunes on the head of that tyrant.

"How is Alice?" said Grey, desiring to turn the subject from the ten-times-told tale of his friend's wrongs.

Mr. Vavasor sighed. "She is well enough, I believe," he said.

"Is anything the matter in Queen Anne Street?"

"You'll hardly believe it when I tell you; and, indeed, I hardly know whether I ought to tell you or not."

"As you and I have gone so far together, I think that you ought to tell me anything that concerns her nearly."

"That's just it. It's about her money. Do you know, Grey, I'm beginning to think that I've been wrong in allowing you to advance what you have done on her account?"

"Why wrong?"

"Because I foresee there'll be a difficulty about it. How are we to manage about the repayment?"

"If she becomes my wife there will be no management wanted."

"But how if she never becomes your wife? I'm beginning to think she'll never do anything like any other woman."

"I'm not quite sure that you understand her," said Grey; "though of course you ought to do so better than any one else."

"Nobody can understand her," said the angry father. "She told me the other day, as you know, that she was going to have nothing more to do with her cousin—"

"Has she—has she become friends with him again?" said Grey. As he asked the question there came a red spot on each cheek, showing the strong mental anxiety which had prompted it.

"No; I believe not;—that is, certainly not in the way you mean. I think that she is beginning to know that he is a rascal."

"It is a great blessing that she has learned the truth before it was too late."

"But would you believe it;—she has given him her name to bills for two thousand pounds, payable at two weeks' sight? He sent to her only this morning a fellow that he called his clerk, and she has been fool enough to accept them. Two thousand pounds! That comes of leaving money at a young woman's own disposal."

"But we expected that, you know," said Grey, who seemed to take the news with much composure.

"Expected it?"

"Of course we did. You yourself did not suppose that what he had before would have been the last."

"But after she had quarrelled with him!"

"That would make no difference with her. She had promised him her money, and as it seems that he will be content with that, let her keep her promise."

"And give him everything! Not if I can help it. I'll expose him. I will indeed. Such a pitiful rascal as he is!"

"You will do nothing, Mr. Vavasor, that will injure your daughter. I'm very sure of that."

"But, by heavens—. Such sheer robbery as that! Two thousand pounds more in fourteen days!" The shortness of the date at which the bills were drawn seemed to afflict Mr. Vavasor almost as keenly as the amount. Then he described the whole transaction as accurately as he could do so, and also told how Alice had declared her purpose of going to Mr. Round the lawyer, if her father would not undertake to procure the money for her by the time the bills should become due. "Mr. Round, you know, has heard nothing about it," he continued. "He doesn't dream of any such thing. If she would take my advice, she would leave the bills, and let them be dishonoured. As it is, I think I shall call at Drummonds', and explain the whole transaction."

"You must not do that," said Grey. "I will call at Drummonds', instead, and see that the money is all right for the bills. As far as they go, let him have his plunder."

"And if she won't take you, at last, Grey? Upon my word, I don't think she ever will. My belief is she'll never get married. She'll never do anything like any other woman."

"The money won't be missed by me if I never get married," said Grey, with a smile. "If she does marry me, of course I shall make her pay me."

"No, by George! that won't do," said Vavasor. "If she were your daughter you'd know that she could not take a man's money in that way."

"And I know it now, though she is not my daughter. I was only joking. As soon as I am certain,—finally certain,—that she can never become my wife, I will take back my money. You need not be afraid. The nature of the arrangement we have made shall then be explained to her."

In this way it was settled; and on the following morning the father informed the daughter that he had done her bidding, and that the money would be placed to her credit at the bankers' before the bills came due. On that Saturday, the day which her cousin had named in his letter, she trudged down to Drummonds', and was informed by a very courteous senior clerk in that establishment, that due preparation for the bills had been made.

So far, I think we may say that Mr. George Vavasor was not unfortunate.

CHAPTER LXII
GOING ABROAD

One morning, early in May, a full week before Alice's visit to the bankers' at Charing Cross, a servant in grand livery, six feet high, got out of a cab at the door in Queen Anne Street, and sent up a note for Miss Vavasor, declaring that he would wait in the cab for her answer. He had come from Lady Glencora, and had been specially ordered to go in a cab and come back in a cab, and make himself as like a Mercury, with wings to his feet, as may be possible to a London footman. Mr. Palliser had arranged his plans with his wife that morning,—or, I should more correctly say, had given her his orders, and she, in consequence, had sent away her Mercury in hot pressing haste to Queen Anne Street. "Do come;—instantly if you can," the note said. "I have so much to tell you, and so much to ask of you. If you can't come, when shall I find you, and where?" Alice sent back a note, saying that she would be in Park Lane as soon as she could put on her bonnet and walk down; and then the Mercury went home in his cab.

Alice found her friend in the small breakfast-room up-stairs, sitting close by the window. They had not as yet met since the evening of Lady Monk's party, nor had Lady Glencora seen Alice in the mourning which she now wore for her grandfather. "Oh, dear, what a change it makes in you," she said. "I never thought of your being in black."

"I don't know what it is you want, but shan't I do in mourning as well as I would in colours?"

"You'll do in anything, dear. But I have so much to tell you, and I don't know how to begin. And I've so much to ask of you, and I'm so afraid you won't do it."

"You generally find me very complaisant."

"No I don't, dear. It is very seldom you will do anything for me. But I must tell you everything first. Do take your bonnet off, for I shall be hours in doing it."

"Hours in telling me!"

"Yes; and in getting your consent to what I want you to do. But I think I'll tell you that first. I'm to be taken abroad immediately."

"Who is to take you?"

"Ah, you may well ask that. If you could know what questions I have asked myself on that head! I sometimes say things to myself as though they were the most proper and reasonable things in the world, and then within an hour or two I hate myself for having thought of them."

"But why don't you answer me? Who is going abroad with you?"

"Well; you are to be one of the party."

"I!"

"Yes; you. When I have named so very respectable a chaperon for my youth, of course you will understand that my husband is to take us."

"But Mr. Palliser can't leave London at this time of the year?"

"That's just it. He is to leave London at this time of the year. Don't look in that way, for it's all settled. Whether you go with me or not, I've got to go. To-day is Tuesday. We are to be off next Tuesday night, if you can make yourself ready. We shall breakfast in Paris on Wednesday morning, and then it will be to us all just as if we were in a new world. Mr. Palliser will walk up and down the new court of the Louvre, and you will be on his left arm, and I shall be on his right,—just like English people,—and it will be the most proper thing that ever was seen in life. Then we shall go on to Basle"— Alice shuddered as Basle was mentioned, thinking of the balcony over the river—"and so to Lucerne—. But no; that was the first plan, and Mr. Palliser altered it. He spent a whole day up here with maps and Bradshaw's and Murray's guide-books, and he scolded me so because I didn't care whether we went first to Baden or to some other place. How could I care? I told him I would go anywhere he chose to take me. Then he told me I was heartless;— and I acknowledged that I was heartless. 'I am heartless,' I said. 'Tell me something I don't know.'"

"Oh, Cora, why did you say that?"

"I didn't choose to contradict my husband. Besides, it's true. Then he threw the Bradshaw away, and all the maps flew about. So I picked them up again, and said we'd go to Switzerland first. I knew that would settle it, and of course he decided on stopping at Baden. If he had said Jericho, it would have been the same thing to me. Wouldn't you like to go to Jericho?"

"I should have no special objection to Jericho."

"But you are to go to Baden instead."

"I've said nothing about that yet. But you have not told me half your story. Why is Mr. Palliser going abroad in the middle of Parliament in this way?"

"Ah; now I must go back to the beginning. And indeed, Alice, I hardly know how to tell you; not that I mind you knowing it, only there are some things that won't get themselves told. You can hardly guess what it is that he is giving up. You must swear that you won't repeat what I'm going to tell you now?"

"I'm not a person apt to tell secrets, but I shan't swear anything."

"What a woman you are for discretion! it is you that ought to be Chancellor of the Exchequer; you are so wise. Only you haven't brought your own pigs to the best market, after all."

"Never mind my own pigs now, Cora."

"I do mind them, very much. But the secret is this. They have asked Mr. Palliser to be Chancellor of the Exchequer, and he has—refused. Think of that!"

"But why?"

"Because of me,—of me, and my folly, and wickedness, and abominations. Because he has been fool enough to plague himself with a wife—he who of all men ought to have kept himself free from such troubles. Oh, he has been so good! It is almost impossible to make any one understand it. If you could know how he has longed for this office;—how he has worked for it day and night, wearing his eyes out with figures when everybody else has been asleep, shutting himself up with such creatures as Mr. Bott when other men have been shooting and hunting and flirting and spending their money. He has been a slave to it for years,—all his life I believe,—in order that he might sit in the Cabinet, and be a minister and a Chancellor of the Exchequer. He has hoped and feared, and has been, I believe, sometimes half-mad with expectation. This has been his excitement,—what racing and gambling are to other men. At last, the place was there, ready for him, and they offered it to him. They begged him to take it, almost on their knees. The Duke of St. Bungay was here all one morning about it; but Mr. Palliser sent him away, and refused the place. It's all over now, and the other man, whom they all hate so much, is to remain in."

"But why did he refuse it?"

"I keep on telling you—because of me. He found that I wanted looking after, and that Mrs. Marsham and Mr. Bott between them couldn't do it."

"Oh, Cora! how can you talk in that way?"

"If you knew all, you might well ask how I could. You remember about Lady Monk's ball, that you would not go to,—as you ought to have done. If you had gone, Mr. Palliser would have been Chancellor of the Exchequer at this minute; he would, indeed. Only think of that! But though you did not go, other people did who ought to have remained at home. I went for one,—and you know who was there for another."

"What difference could that make to you?" said Alice, angrily.

"It might have made a great deal of difference. And, for the matter of that, so it did. Mr. Palliser was there too, but, of course, he went away immediately. I can't tell you all the trouble there had been about Mrs. Marsham,—whether I was to take her with me or not. However, I wouldn't take her, and didn't take her. The carriage went for her first, and there she was when we got there; and Mr. Bott was there too. I wonder whether I shall ever make you understand it all."

"There are some things I don't want to understand."

"There they both were watching me,—looking at me the whole evening; and, of course, I resolved that I would not be put down by them."

"I think, if I had been you, I would not have allowed their presence to make any difference to me."

"That is very easily said, my dear, but by no means so easily done. You can't make yourself unconscious of eyes that are always looking at you. I dared them, at any rate, to do their worst, for I stood up to dance with Burgo Fitzgerald."

"Oh, Cora!"

"Why shouldn't I? At any rate I did; and I waltzed with him for half an hour. Alice, I never will waltz again;—never. I have done with dancing now. I don't think, even in my maddest days, I ever kept it up so long as I did then. And I knew that everybody was looking at me. It was not only Mrs. Marsham and Mr. Bott, but everybody there. I felt myself to be desperate,—mad, like a wild woman. There I was, going round and round and round with the only man for whom I ever cared two straws. It seemed as though everything had been a dream since the old days. Ah! how well I remember the first time I danced with him,—at his aunt's house in Cavendish Square. They had only just brought me out in London then, and I thought that he was a god."

"Cora! I cannot bear to hear you talk like that."

"I know well enough that he is no god now; some people say that he is a devil, but he was like Apollo to me then. Did you ever see anyone so beautiful as he is?"

"I never saw him at all."

"I wish you could have seen him; but you will some day. I don't know whether you care for men being handsome." Alice thought of John Grey, who was the handsomest man that she knew, but she made no answer. "I do; or, rather, I used to do," continued Lady Glencora. "I don't think I care much about anything now; but I don't see why handsome men should not be run after as much as handsome women."

"But you wouldn't have a girl run after any man, would you; whether handsome or ugly?"

"But they do, you know. When I saw him the other night he was just as handsome as ever;—the same look, half wild and half tame, like an animal you cannot catch, but which you think would love you so if you could catch him. In a little while it was just like the old time, and I had made up my mind to care nothing for the people looking at me."

"And you think that was right?"

"No, I don't. Yes, I do; that is. It wasn't right to care about dancing with him, but it was right to disregard all the people gaping round. What was it to them? Why should they care who I danced with?"

"That is nonsense, dear, and you must know that it is so. If you were to see a woman misbehaving herself in public, would not you look on and make your comments? Could you help doing so if you were to try?"

"You are very severe, Alice. Misbehaving in public!"

"Yes, Cora. I am only taking your own story. According to that, you were misbehaving in public."

Lady Glencora got up from her chair near the window, on which she had been crouching close to Alice's knees, and walked away towards the fireplace. "What am I to say to you, or how am I to talk to you?" said Alice. "You would not have me tell you a lie?"

"Of all things in the world, I hate a prude the most," said Lady Glencora.

"Cora, look here. If you consider it prudery on my part to disapprove of your waltzing with Mr. Fitzgerald in the manner you have described,—or, indeed, in any other manner,—you and I must differ so totally about the meaning of words and the nature of things that we had better part."

"Alice, you are the unkindest creature that ever lived. You are as cold as stone. I sometimes think that you can have no heart."

"I don't mind your saying that. Whether I have a heart or not I will leave you to find out for yourself; but I won't be called a prude by you. You know you were wrong to dance with that man. What has come of it? What have you told me yourself this morning? In order to preserve you from misery and destruction, Mr. Palliser has given up all his dearest hopes. He has had to sacrifice himself that he might save you. That, I take it, is about the truth of it,—and yet you tell me that you have done no wrong."

"I never said so." Now she had come back to her chair by the window, and was again sitting in that crouching form. "I never said that I was not wrong. Of course I was wrong. I have been so wrong throughout that I have never been right yet. Let me tell it on to the end, and then you can go away if you like, and tell me that I am too wicked for your friendship."

"Have I ever said anything like that, Cora?"

"But you will, I dare say, when I have done. Well; what do you think my senior duenna did,—the female one, I mean? She took my own carriage, and posted off after Mr. Palliser as hard as ever she could, leaving the male duenna on the watch. I was dancing as hard as I could, but I knew what was going on all the time as well as though I had heard them talking. Of course Mr. Palliser came after me. I don't know what else he could do, unless, indeed, he had left me to my fate. He came there, and behaved so well,—so much like a perfect gentleman. Of course I went home, and I was prepared to tell him everything, if he spoke a word to me,—that I intended to leave him, and that cart-ropes should not hold me!"

"To leave him, Cora!"

"Yes, and go with that other man whose name you won't let me mention. I had a letter from him in my pocket asking me to go. He asked me a dozen times that night. I cannot think how it was that I did not consent."

"That you did not consent to your own ruin and disgrace?"

"That I did not consent to go off with him,—anywhere. Of course it would have been my own destruction. I'm not such a fool as not to know that. Do you suppose I have never thought of it;—what it would be to be a man's mistress instead of his wife. If I had not I should be a thing to be hated and despised. When once I had done it I should hate and despise myself. I should feel myself to be loathsome, and, as it were, a beast among women. But why did they not let me marry him, instead of driving me to this? And though I might have destroyed myself, I should have saved the man who is still my husband. Do you know, I told him all that,—told him that if I had gone away with Burgo Fitzgerald he would have another wife, and would have children, and would—?"

"You told your husband that you had thought of leaving him?"

"Yes; I told him everything. I told him that I dearly loved that poor fellow, for whom, as I believe, nobody else on earth cares a single straw."

"And what did he say?"

"I cannot tell you what he said, only that we are all to go to Baden together, and then to Italy. But he did not seem a bit angry; he very seldom is angry, unless at some trumpery thing, as when he threw the book away. And when I told him that he might have another wife and a child, he put his arm round me and whispered to me that he did not care so much about it as I had imagined. I felt more like loving him at that moment than I had ever done before."

"He must be fit to be an angel."

"He's fit to be a cabinet minister, which, I'm quite sure, he'd like much better. And now you know everything; but no,—there is one thing you don't know yet. When I tell you that, you'll want to make him an archangel or a prime minister. 'We'll go abroad,' he said,—and remember, this was his own proposition, made long before I was able to speak a word;—'We'll go abroad, and you shall get your cousin Alice to go with us.' That touched me more than anything. Only think if he had proposed Mrs. Marsham!"

"But yet he does not like me."

"You're wrong there, Alice. There has been no question of liking or of disliking. He thought you would be a kind of Mrs. Marsham, and when you were not, but went out flirting among the ruins with Jeffrey Palliser, instead—"

"I never went out flirting with Jeffrey Palliser."

"He did with you, which is all the same thing. And when Plantagenet knew of that,—for, of course, Mr. Bott told him—"

"Mr. Bott can't see everything."

"Those men do. The worst is, they see more than everything. But, at any rate, Mr. Palliser has got over all that now. Come, Alice; the fact of the offer having come from himself should disarm you of any such objection as that. As he has held out his hand to you, you have no alternative but to take it."

"I will take his hand willingly."

"And for my sake you will go with us? He understands himself that I am not fit to be his companion, and to have no companion but him. Now there is a spirit of wisdom about you that will do for him, and a spirit of folly that will suit me. I can manage to put myself on a par with a girl who has played such a wild game with her lovers as you have done."

Alice would give no promise then. Her first objection was that she had undertaken to go down to Westmoreland and comfort Kate in the affliction of her broken arm. "And I must go," said Alice, remembering how necessary it was that she should plead her own cause with George Vavasor's sister. But she acknowledged that she had not intended to stay long in Westmoreland, probably not more than a week, and it was at last decided that the Pallisers should postpone their journey for four or five days, and that Alice should go with them immediately upon her return from Vavasor Hall.

"I have no objection;" said her father, speaking with that voice of resignation which men use when they are resolved to consider themselves injured whatever may be done. "I can get along in lodgings. I suppose we had better leave the house, as you have given away so much of your own fortune?" Alice did not think it worth her while to point out to him, in answer to this, that her contribution to their joint housekeeping should still remain the same as ever. Such, however, she knew would be the fact, and she knew also that she would find her father in the old house when she returned from her travels. To her, in her own great troubles, the absence from London would be as serviceable as it could be to Lady Glencora. Indeed, she had already begun to feel the impossibility of staying quietly at home. She could lecture her cousin, whose faults were open, easy to be defined, and almost loud in their nature; but she was not on that account the less aware of her own. She knew that she too had cause to be ashamed of herself. She was half afraid to show her face among her friends, and wept grievously over her own follies. Those cruel words of her father rang in her ears constantly:— "Things of that sort are so often over with you." The reproach, though cruel, was true, and what reproach more galling could be uttered to an unmarried girl such as was Alice Vavasor? She had felt from the first moment in which the proposition was made to her, that it would be well that she should for a while leave her home, and especially that drawing-room in Queen Anne Street, which told her so many tales that she would fain forget, if it were possible.

Mr. Palliser would not allow his wife to remain in London for the ten or twelve days which must yet elapse before they started, nor could he send her into the country alone. He took her down to Matching Priory, having obtained leave to be absent from the House for the remainder of the Session, and remained with her there till within two days of their departure. That week down at Matching, as she afterwards told Alice, was very terrible. He never spoke a word to rebuke her. He never hinted that there had been aught in her conduct of which he had cause to complain. He treated her with a respect that was perfect, and indeed with more outward signs of affection than had ever been customary with him. "But," as Lady Glencora afterwards expressed it, "he was always looking after me. I believe he thought that Burgo Fitzgerald had hidden himself among the ruins," she said once to Alice. "He never suspected me, I am sure of that; but he thought that he ought to look after me." And Lady Glencora in this had very nearly hit the truth. Mr. Palliser had resolved, from that hour in which he had walked out among the elms in Kensington Gardens, that he would neither suspect his wife, nor treat her as though he suspected her. The blame had been his, perhaps, more than it had been hers. So much he had acknowledged to himself, thinking of the confession she had made to him before their marriage. But it was manifestly his imperative duty,—his duty of duties,— to save her from that pitfall into which, as she herself had told him, she had been so ready to fall. For her sake and for his this must be done. It was a duty so imperative, that in its performance he had found himself forced to abandon his ambition. To have his wife taken from him would be terrible, but the having it said all over the world that such a misfortune had come upon him would be almost more terrible even than that.

So he went with his wife hither and thither, down at Matching, allowing himself to be driven about behind Dandy and Flirt. He himself proposed these little excursions. They were tedious to him, but doubly tedious to his wife, who now found it more difficult than ever to talk to him. She struggled to talk, and he struggled to talk, but the very struggles themselves made the thing impossible. He sat with her in the mornings, and he sat with her in the evenings; he breakfasted with her, lunched with her, and dined with her. He went to bed early, having no figures which now claimed his attention. And so the week at last wore itself away. "I saw him yawning sometimes," Lady Glencora said afterwards, "as though he would fall in pieces."

CHAPTER LXIII
MR. JOHN GREY IN QUEEN ANNE STREET

Alice was resolved that she would keep her promise to Kate, and pay her visit to Westmoreland before she started with the Pallisers. Kate had written to her three lines with her left hand, begging her to come, and those three lines had been more eloquent than anything she could have written had her right arm been uninjured. Alice had learned something of the truth as to the accident from her father; or, rather, had heard her father's surmises on the subject. She had heard, too, how her cousin George had borne himself when the will was read, and how he had afterwards disappeared, never showing himself again at the hall. After all that had passed she felt that she owed Kate some sympathy. Sympathy may, no doubt, be conveyed by letter; but there are things on which it is almost impossible for any writer to express himself with adequate feeling; and there are things, too, which can be spoken, but which cannot be written. Therefore, though the journey must be a hurried one, Alice sent word down to Westmoreland that she was to be expected there in a day or two. On her return she was to go at once to Park Lane, and sleep there for the two nights which would intervene before the departure of the Pallisers.

On the day before she started for Westmoreland her father came to her in the middle of the day, and told her that John Grey was going to dine with him in Queen Anne Street on that evening.

"To-day, papa?" she asked.

"Yes, to-day. Why not? No man is less particular as to what he eats than Grey."

"I was not thinking of that, papa," she said.

To this Mr. Vavasor made no reply, but stood for some minutes looking out of the window. Then he prepared to leave the room, getting himself first as far as the table, where he lifted a book, and then on half-way to the door before Alice arrested him.

"Perhaps, papa, you and Mr. Grey had better dine alone."

"What do you mean by alone?"

"I meant without me,—as two men generally like to do."

"If I wanted that I should have asked him to dine at the club," said Mr. Vavasor, and then he again attempted to go.

"But, papa—"

"Well, my dear! If you mean to say that because of what has passed you object to meet Mr. Grey, I can only tell you it's nonsense,—confounded nonsense. If he chooses to come there can be no reason why you shouldn't receive him."

"It will look as though—"

"Look what?"

"As though he were asked as my guest."

"That's nonsense. I saw him yesterday, and I asked him to come. I saw him again to-day, and he said he would come. He's not such a fool as to suppose after that, that you asked him."

"No; not that I asked him."

"And if you run away you'll only make more of the thing than it's worth. Of course I can't make you dine with me if you don't like."

Alice did not like it, but, after some consideration, she thought that she might be open to the imputation of having made more of the thing than it was worth if she ran away, as her father called it. She was going to leave the country for some six or eight months,—perhaps for a longer time than that, and it might be as well that she should have an opportunity of telling her plans to Mr. Grey. She could do it, she thought, in such a way as to make him understand that her last quarrel with George Vavasor was not supposed to alter the footing on which she stood with him. She did not doubt that her father had told everything to Mr. Grey. She knew well enough what her father's wishes still were. It was not odd that he should be asking John Grey to his house, though such exercises of domestic hospitality were very unusual with him. But,—so she declared to herself,—such little attempts on his part would be altogether thrown away. It was a pity that he had not yet learned to know her better. She would receive Mr. Grey as the mistress of her father's house now, for the last time; and then, on her return in the following year, he would be at Nethercoats, and the whole thing would be over.

She dressed herself very plainly, simply changing one black frock for another, and then sat herself in her drawing-room awaiting the two gentlemen. It was already past the hour of dinner before her father came up-stairs. She knew that he was in the house, and in her heart she accused him of keeping out of the way, in order that John Grey might be alone with her. Whether or no she were right in her suspicions John Grey did not take advantage of the opportunity offered to him. Her father came up first, and had seated himself silently in his arm-chair before the visitor was announced.

As Mr. Grey entered the room Alice knew that she was flurried, but still she managed to carry herself with some dignity. His bearing was perfect. But then, as she declared to herself afterwards, no possible position in life would put him beside himself. He came up to her with his usual quiet smile,—a smile that was genial even in its quietness, and took her hand. He took it fairly and fully into his; but there was no squeezing, no special pressure, no love-making. And when he spoke to her he called her Alice, as though his doing so was of all things the most simply a matter of course. There was no tell-tale hesitation in his voice. When did he ever hesitate at anything? "I hear you are going abroad," he said, "with your cousin, Lady Glencora Palliser."

She managed to carry herself with some dignity.

"Yes," said Alice; "I am going with them for a long tour. We shall not return, I fancy, till the end of next winter."

"Plans of that sort are as easily broken as they are made," said her father. "You won't be your own mistress; and I advise you not to count too surely upon getting further than Baden."

"If Mr. Palliser changes his mind of course I shall come home," said Alice, with a little attempt at a smile.

"I should think him a man not prone to changes," said Grey. "But all London is talking about his change of mind at this moment. They say at the clubs that he might have been in the Cabinet if he would, but that he has taken up this idea of going abroad at the moment when he was wanted."

"It's his wife's doing, I take it," said Mr. Vavasor.

"That's the worst of being in Parliament," said Grey. "A man can't do anything without giving a reason for it. There must be men for public life, of course; but, upon my word, I think we ought to be very much obliged to them."

Alice, as she took her old lover's arm, and walked down with him to dinner, thought of all her former quarrels with him on this very subject. On this very point she had left him. He had never argued the matter with her. He had never asked her to argue with him. He had not condescended so far as that. Had he done so, she thought that she would have brought herself to think as he thought. She would have striven, at any rate, to do so. But she could not become unambitious, tranquil, fond of retirement, and philosophic, without an argument on the matter,—without being allowed even the poor grace of owning herself to be convinced. If a man takes a dog with him from the country up to town, the dog must live a town life without knowing the reason why;—must live a town life or die a town death. But a woman should not be treated like a dog. "Had he deigned to discuss it with me!" Alice had so often said. "But, no; he will read his books, and I am to go there to fetch him his slippers, and make his tea for him." All this came upon her again as she walked down-stairs by his side; and with it there came a consciousness that she had been driven by this usage into the terrible engagement which she had made with her cousin. That, no doubt, was now over. There was no longer to her any question of her marrying George Vavasor. But the fact that she had been mad enough to think and talk of such a marriage, had of itself been enough to ruin her. "Things of that sort are so often over with you!" After such a speech as that to her from her father, Alice told herself that there could be no more "things of that sort" for her. But all her misery had been brought about by this scornful superiority to the ordinary pursuits of the world,—this looking down upon humanity.

"It seems to me," she said, very quietly, while her hand was yet upon his arm, "that your pity is hardly needed. I should think that no persons can be happier than those whom you call our public men."

"Ah!" said he, "that is our old quarrel." He said it as though the quarrel had simply been an argument between them, or a dozen arguments,—as arguments do come up between friends; not as though it had served to separate for life two persons who had loved each other dearly. "It's the old story of the town mouse and the country mouse,—as old as the hills. Mice may be civil for a while, and compliment each other; but when they come to speak their minds freely, each likes his own life best." She said nothing more at the moment, and the three sat down to their small dinner-table. It was astonishing to Alice that he should be able to talk in this way, to hint at such things, to allude to their former hopes and present condition, without a quiver in his voice, or, as far as she could perceive, without any feeling in his heart.

"Alice," said her father, "I can't compliment your cook upon her soup."

"You don't encourage her, papa, by eating it often enough. And then you only told me at two o'clock to-day."

"If a cook can't make soup between two and seven, she can't make it in a week."

"I hope Mr. Grey will excuse it," said Alice.

"Isn't it good?" said he. "I won't say that it is, because I should be pretending to have an opinion; but I should not have found out anything against it of myself."

"Where do you dine usually, now you are in London?" Mr. Vavasor asked.

"At the old club, at the corner of Suffolk Street. It's the oldest club in London, I believe. I never belonged to any other, and therefore can't compare them; but I can't imagine anything much nicer."

"They give you better soup than ours?" said Alice.

"You've an excellent cook," said Mr. Vavasor, with great gravity; "one of the best second-class cooks in London. We were very nearly getting him, but you nicked him just in time. I know him well."

"It's a great deal more than I do, or hope to do. There's another branch of public life for which I'm quite unfitted. I'd as soon be called on to choose a Prime Minister for the country, as I would a cook for a club."

"Of course you would," said Mr. Vavasor. "There may be as many as a dozen cooks about London to be looked up, but there are never more than two possible Prime Ministers about. And as one of them must be going out when the other is coming in, I don't see that there can be any difficulty. Moreover, now-a-days, people do their politics for themselves, but they expect to have their dinners cooked for them."

The little dinner went on quietly and very easily. Mr. Vavasor found fault with nearly everything. But as, on this occasion, the meat and the drink, with the manner of the eating and drinking, did not constitute the difficulty, Alice was indifferent to her father's censures. The thing needed was that she and Mr. Grey should be able to sit together at the same table without apparent consciousness of their former ties. Alice felt that she was succeeding indifferently well while she was putting in little mock defences for the cook. And as for John Grey, he succeeded so well that his success almost made Alice angry with him. It required no effort with him at all to be successful in this matter. "If he can forget all that has passed, so much the better," said Alice to herself when she got up into the drawing-room. Then she sat herself down on the sofa, and cried. Oh! what had she not lost! Had any woman ever been so mad, so reckless, so heartless as she had been! And she had done it, knowing that she loved him! She cried bitterly, and then went away to wash her eyes, that she might be ready to give him his coffee when he should come up-stairs.

"She does not look well," said Grey as soon as she had left the room.

"Well;—no: how can she look well after what she has gone through? I sometimes think, that of all the people I ever knew, she has been the most foolish. But, of course, it is not for me to say anything against my own child; and, of all people, not to you."

"Nothing that you could say against her would make any difference to me. I sometimes fancy that I know her better than you do."

"And you think that she'll still come round again?"

"I cannot say that I think so. No one can venture to say whether or not such wounds as hers may be cured. There are hearts and bodies so organized, that in them severe wounds are incurable, whereas in others no injury seems to be fatal. But I can say that if she be not cured it shall not be from want of perseverance on my part."

"Upon my word, Grey, I don't know how to thank you enough. I don't, indeed."

"It doesn't seem to me to be a case for thanking."

"Of course it isn't. I know that well enough. And in the ordinary way of the world no father would think of thanking a man for wanting to marry his daughter. But things have come to such a pass with us, that, by George! I don't feel like any other father. I don't mind saying anything to you, you know. That claret isn't very good, but you might as well take another glass."

"Thank you, I will. I should have said that that was rather good wine, now."

"It's not just the thing. What's the use of my having good wine here, when nobody comes to drink it? But, as I was saying about Alice, of course I've felt all this thing very much. I feel as though I were responsible, and yet what could I do? She's her own mistress through it all. When she told me she was going to marry that horrible miscreant, my nephew, what could I do?"

"That's over now, and we need not talk about it."

"It's very kind of you to say so,—very. I believe she's a good girl. I do, indeed, in spite of it all."

"I've no doubt of her being what you call a good girl,—none in the least. What she has done to me does not impair her goodness. I don't think you have ever understood how much all this has been a matter of conscience with her."

"Conscience!" said the angry father. "I hate such conscience. I like the conscience that makes a girl keep her word, and not bring disgrace upon those she belongs to."

"I shall not think that I am disgraced," said Grey, quietly, "if she will come and be my wife. She has meant to do right, and has endeavoured to take care of the happiness of other people rather than her own."

"She has taken very little care of mine," said Mr. Vavasor.

"I shall not be at all afraid to trust mine to her,—if she will let me do so. But she has been wounded sorely, and it must take time."

"And, in the meantime, what are we to do when she tells us that Mr. George Vavasor wants another remittance? Two thousand pounds a quarter comes heavy, you know!"

"Let us hope that he has had enough."

"Enough! Did such a man ever have enough?"

"Let us hope, then, that she thinks he has had enough. Come;—may I go up-stairs?"

"Oh, yes. I'll follow you. She'll think that I mean something if I leave you together."

From all this it will be seen that Alice's father and her lover still stood together on confidential terms. Not easily had Mr. Vavasor brought himself to speak of his daughter to John Grey, in such language as he had now used; but he had been forced by adverse circumstances to pass the Rubicon of parental delicacy; he had been driven to tell his wished-for son-in-law that he did wish to have him as a son-in-law; he had been compelled to lay aside those little airs of reserve with which a father generally speaks of his daughter,—and now all was open between them.

"And you really start to-morrow?" said Grey, as he stood close over Alice's work-table. Mr. Vavasor had followed him into the drawing-room, but had seated himself in an easy-chair on the other side of the fire. There was no tone of whispering in Grey's voice, but yet he spoke in a manner which showed that he did not intend to be audible on the other side of the room.

"I start for Westmoreland to-morrow. We do not leave London for the continent till the latter end of next week."

"But you will not be here again?"

"No; I shall not come back to Queen Anne Street."

"And you will be away for many months?"

"Mr. Palliser talked of next Easter as the term of his return. He mentioned Easter to Lady Glencora. I have not seen him myself since I agreed to go with him."

"What should you say if you met me somewhere in your travels?" He had now gently seated himself on the sofa beside her;—not so close to her as to give her just cause to move away, but yet so near as to make his conversation with her quite private.

"I don't think that will be very likely," she replied, not knowing what to say.

"I think it is very likely. For myself, I hate surprises. I could not bring myself to fall in upon your track unawares. I shall go abroad, but it will not be till the late autumn, when the summer heats are gone,—and I shall endeavour to find you."

"To find me, Mr. Grey!" There was a quivering in her voice, as she spoke, which she could not prevent, though she would have given worlds to prevent it. "I do not think that will be quite fair."

"It will not be unfair, I think, if I give you notice of my approach. I will not fall upon you and your friends unawares."

"I was not thinking of them. They would be glad to know you, of course."

"And equally, of course! or, rather, much more of course, you will not be glad to see me? That's what you mean?"

"I mean that we had better not meet more than we can help."

"I think differently, Alice,—quite differently. The more we meet the better,—that is what I think. But I will not stop to trouble you now. Good night!" Then he got up and went away, and her father went with him. Mr. Vavasor, as he rose from his chair, declared that he would just walk through a couple of streets; but Alice knew that he was gone to his club.

CHAPTER LXIV
THE ROCKS AND VALLEYS

During these days Mrs. Greenow was mistress of the old Hall down in Westmoreland, and was nursing Kate assiduously through the calamity of her broken arm. There had come to be a considerable amount of confidence between the aunt and the niece. Kate had acknowledged to her aunt that her brother had behaved badly,—very badly; and the aunt had confessed to the niece that she regarded Captain Bellfield as a fit subject for compassion.

"And he was violent to you, and broke your arm? I always knew it was so," Mrs. Greenow had said, speaking with reference to her nephew. But this Kate had denied. "No," said she; "that was an accident. When he went away and left me, he knew nothing about it. And if he had broken both my arms I should not have cared much. I could have forgiven him that." But that which Kate could not forgive him was the fault which she had herself committed. For his sake she had done her best to separate Alice and John Grey, and George had shown himself to be unworthy of the kindness of her treachery. "I would give all I have in the world to bring them together again," Kate said. "They'll come together fast enough if they like each other," said Mrs. Greenow. "Alice is young still, and they tell me she's as good looking as ever. A girl with her money won't have far to seek for a husband, even if this paragon from Cambridgeshire should not turn up again."

"You don't know Alice, aunt."

"No, I don't. But I know what young women are, and I know what young men are. All this nonsense about her cousin George,—what difference will it make? A man like Mr. Grey won't care about that,—especially not if she tells him all about it. My belief is that a girl can have anything forgiven her, if she'll only tell it herself."

But Kate preferred the other subject, and so, I think, did Mrs. Greenow herself. "Of course, my dear," she would say, "marriage with me, if I should marry again, would be a very different thing to your marriage, or that of any other young person. As for love, that has been all over for me since poor Greenow died. I have known nothing of the softness of affection since I laid him in his cold grave, and never can again. 'Captain Bellfield,' I said to him, 'if you were to kneel at my feet for years, it would not make me care for you in the way of love.'"

"And what did he say to that?"

"How am I to tell you what he said? He talked nonsense about my beauty, as all the men do. If a woman were hump-backed, and had only one eye, they wouldn't be ashamed to tell her she was a Venus."

"But, aunt, you are a handsome woman, you know."

"Laws, my dear, as if I didn't understand all about it; as if I didn't know what makes a woman run after? It isn't beauty,—and it isn't money altogether. I've seen women who had plenty of both, and not a man would come nigh them. They didn't dare. There are some of them, a man would as soon think of putting his arm round a poplar tree, they are so hard and so stiff. You know you're a little that way yourself, Kate, and I've always told you it won't do."

"I'm afraid I'm too old to mend, aunt."

"Not at all, if you'll only set your wits to work and try. You've plenty of money now, and you're good-looking enough, too, when you take the trouble to get yourself up. But, as I said before, it isn't that that's wanted. There's a stand-off about some women,—what the men call a 'nollimy tangere,' that a man must be quite a furious Orlando to attempt to get the better of it. They look as though matrimony itself were improper, and as if they believed that little babies were found about in the hedges and ditches. They talk of women being forward! There are some of them a deal too backward, according to my way of thinking."

"Yours is a comfortable doctrine, aunt."

"That's just what I want it to be. I want things to be comfortable. Why shouldn't things be nice about one when one's got the means? Nobody can say it's a pleasant thing to live alone. I always thought that man in the song hit it off properly. You remember what he says? 'The poker and tongs to each other belongs.' So they do, and that should be the way with men and women."

"But the poker and tongs have but a bad life of it sometimes."

"Not so often as the people say, my dear. Men and women ain't like lumps of sugar. They don't melt because the water is sometimes warm. Now, if I do take Bellfield,—and I really think I shall; but if I do he'll give me a deal of trouble. I know he will. He'll always be wanting my money, and, of course, he'll get more than he ought. I'm not a Solomon, nor yet a Queen of Sheba, no more than anybody else. And he'll smoke too many cigars, and perhaps drink more brandy-and-water than he ought. And he'll be making eyes, too, at some of the girls who'll be fools enough to let him."

"Dear me, aunt, if I thought all that ill of him, I'm sure I wouldn't marry him;—especially as you say you don't love him."

"As for love, my dear, that's gone,—clear gone!" Whereupon Mrs. Greenow put up her handkerchief to her eyes. "Some women can love twice, but I am not one of them. I wish I could,—I wish I could!" These last words were spoken in a tone of solemn regret, which, however, she contrived to change as quickly as she had adopted it. "But my dear, marriage is a comfortable thing. And then, though the Captain may be a little free, I don't doubt but what I shall get the upper hand with him at last. I shan't stop his cigars and brandy-and-water you know. Why shouldn't a man smoke and have a glass, if he don't make a beast of himself? I like to see a man enjoy himself. And then," she added, speaking tenderly of her absent lover, "I do think he's fond of me,—I do, indeed."

"So is Mr. Cheesacre for the matter of that."

"Poor Cheesy! I believe he was, though he did talk so much about money. I always like to believe the best I can of them. But then there was no poetry about Cheesy. I don't care about saying it now, as you've quite made up your mind not to have him."

"Quite, aunt."

"Your grandfather's will does make a difference, you know. But, as I was saying, I do like a little romance about them,—just a sniff, as I call it, of the rocks and valleys. One knows that it doesn't mean much; but it's like artificial flowers,—it gives a little colour, and takes off the dowdiness. Of course, bread-and-cheese is the real thing. The rocks and valleys are no good at all, if you haven't got that, But enough is as good as a feast. Thanks to dear Greenow,"—here the handkerchief was again used—"Thanks to dear Greenow, I shall never want. Of course I shan't let any of the money go into his hands,—the Captain's, I mean. I know a trick worth two of that, my dear. But, lord love you! I've enough for him and me. What's the good of a woman's wanting to keep it all to herself?"

A sniff of the rocks and valleys.

"And you think you'll really take him, aunt, and pay his washerwoman's bills for him? You remember what you told me when I first saw him?"

"Oh, yes; I remember. And if he can't pay his own washerwoman, isn't that so much more of a reason that I should do it for him? Well; yes; I think I will take him. That is, if he lets me take him just as I choose. Beggars mustn't be choosers, my dear."

In this way the aunt and niece became very confidential, and Mrs. Greenow whispered into Kate's ears her belief that Captain Bellfield might possibly make his way across the country to Westmoreland. "There would be no harm in offering him a bed, would there?" Mrs. Greenow asked. "You see the inn at Shap is a long way off for morning calls." Kate could not take upon herself to say that there would be any harm, but she did not like the idea of having Captain Bellfield as a visitor. "After all, perhaps he mayn't come," said the widow. "I don't see where he is to raise the money for such a journey, now that he has quarrelled with Mr. Cheesacre."

"If Captain Bellfield must come to Vavasor Hall, at any rate let him not come till Alice's visit had been completed." That was Kate's present wish, and so much she ventured to confide to her aunt. But there seemed to be no way of stopping him. "I don't in the least know where he is, my dear, and as for writing to him, I never did such a thing in my life, and I shouldn't know how to begin." Mrs. Greenow declared that she had not positively invited the Captain; but on this point Kate hardly gave full credit to her aunt's statement.

Alice arrived, and, for a day or two, the three ladies lived very pleasantly together. Kate still wore her arm in a sling; but she was able to walk out, and would take long walks in spite of the doctor's prohibition. Of course, they went up on the mountains. Indeed, all the walks from Vavasor Hall led to the mountains, unless one chose to take the road to Shap. But they went up, across the beacon hill, as though by mutual consent. There were no questions asked between them as to the route to be taken; and though they did not reach the stone on which they had once sat looking over upon Haweswater, they did reach the spot upon which Kate had encountered her accident. "It was here I fell," she said; "and the last I saw of him was his back, as he made his way down into the valley, there. When I got upon my legs I could still see him. It was one of those evenings when the clouds are dark, but you can see all objects with a peculiar clearness through the air. I stood here ever so long, holding my arm, and watching him; but he never once turned to look back at me. Do you know, Alice, I fancy that I shall never see him again."

"Do you suppose that he means to quarrel with you altogether?"

"I can hardly tell you what I mean! He seemed to me to be going away from me, as though he went into another world. His figure against the light was quite clear, and he walked quickly, and on he went, till the slope of the hill hid him from me. Of course, I thought that he would return to the Hall. At one time I almost feared that he would come upon me through the woods, as I went back myself. But yet, I had a feeling,—what people call a presentiment, that I should never see him again."

"He has never written?"

"No; not a word. You must remember that he did not know that I had hurt myself. I am sure he will not write, and I am sure, also, that I shall not. If he wanted money I would send it to him, but I would not write to him."

"I fear he will always want money, Kate."

"I fear he will. If you could know what I suffered when he made me write that letter to you! But, of course, I was a beast. Of course, I ought not to have written it."

"I thought it a very proper letter."

"It was a mean letter. The whole thing was mean! He should have starved in the street before he had taken your money. He should have given up Parliament, and everything else! I had doubted much about him before, but it was that which first turned my heart against him. I had begun to fear that he was not such a man as I had always thought him,—as I had spoken of him to you."

"I had judged of him for myself," said Alice.

"Of course you did. But I had endeavoured to make you judge kindly. Alice, dear! we have both suffered for him; you more than I, perhaps; but I, too, have given up everything for him. My whole life has been at his service. I have been his creature, to do his bidding, just as he might tell me. He made me do things that I knew to be wrong,—things that were foreign to my own nature; and yet I almost worshipped him. Even now, if he were to come back, I believe that I should forgive him everything."

"I should forgive him, but I could never do more."

"But he will never come back. He will never ask us to forgive him, or even wish it. He has no heart."

"He has longed for money till the Devil has hardened his heart," said Alice.

"And yet how tender he could be in his manner when he chose it;— how soft he could make his words and his looks! Do you remember how he behaved to us in Switzerland? Do you remember that balcony at Basle, and the night we sat there, when the boys were swimming down the river?"

"Yes;—I remember."

"So do I! So do I! Alice, I would give all I have in the world, if I could recall that journey to Switzerland."

"If you mean for my sake, Kate—"

"I do mean for your sake. It made no difference to me. Whether I stayed in Westmoreland or went abroad, I must have found out that my god was made of bricks and clay instead of gold. But there was no need for you to be crushed in the ruins."

"I am not crushed, Kate!"

"Of course, you are too proud to own it?"

"If you mean about Mr. Grey, that would have happened just the same, whether I had gone abroad or remained at home."

"Would it, dear?"

"Just the same."

There was nothing more than this said between them about Mr. Grey. Even to her cousin, Alice could not bring herself to talk freely on that subject. She would never allow herself to think, for a moment, that she had been persuaded by others to treat him as she had treated him. She was sure that she had acted on her own convictions of what was right and wrong; and now, though she had begun to feel that she had been wrong, she would hardly confess as much even to herself.

They walked back, down the hill, to the Hall in silence for the greater part of the way. Once or twice Kate repeated her conviction that she should never again see her brother. "I do not know what may happen to him," she said in answer to her cousin's questions; "but when he was passing out of my sight into the valley, I felt that I was looking at him for the last time."

"That is simply what people call a presentiment," Alice replied.

"Exactly so; and presentiments, of course, mean nothing," said Kate.

Then they walked on towards the house without further speech; but when they reached the end of the little path which led out of the wood, on to the gravelled sweep before the front door, they were both arrested by a sight that met their eyes. There was a man standing, with a cigar in his mouth, before them, swinging a little cane, and looking about him up at the wood. He had on his head a jaunty little straw-hat, and he wore a jacket with brass buttons, and white trousers. It was now nearly the middle of May, but the summer does not come to Westmoreland so early as that, and the man, as he stood there looking about him, seemed to be cold and almost uncomfortable. He had not as yet seen the two girls, who stood at the end of the walk, arrested by the sight of him. "Who is it?" asked Alice, in a whisper.

"Captain Bellfield," said Kate, speaking with something very like dismay in her voice.

"What! aunt Greenow's Captain?"

"Yes; aunt Greenow's Captain. I have been fearing this, and now, what on earth are we to do with him? Look at him. That's what aunt Greenow calls a sniff of the rocks and valleys."

The Captain began to move,—just to move, as though it were necessary to do something to keep the life in his limbs. He had finished his cigar, and looked at the end of it with manifest regret. As he threw it away among a tuft of shrubs his eye fell upon the two ladies, and he uttered a little exclamation.

Then he came forward, waving his little straw-hat in his hand, and made his salutation. "Miss Vavasor, I am delighted," he said. "Miss Alice Vavasor, if I am not mistaken? I have been commissioned by my dear friend Mrs. Greenow to go out and seek you, but, upon my word, the woods looked so black that I did not dare to venture;—and then, of course, I shouldn't have found you."

Kate put out her left hand, and then introduced her cousin to the Captain. Again he waved his little straw-hat, and strove to bear himself as though he were at home and comfortable. But he failed, and it was manifest that he failed. He was not the Bellfield who had conquered Mr. Cheesacre on the sands at Yarmouth, though he wore the same jacket and waistcoat, and must now have enjoyed the internal satisfaction of feeling that his future maintenance in life was assured to him. But he was not at his ease. His courage had sufficed to enable him to follow his quarry into Westmoreland, but it did not suffice to make him comfortable while he was there. Kate instantly perceived his condition, and wickedly resolved that she would make no effort to assist him. She went through some ceremony of introduction, and then expressed her surprise at seeing him so far north.

"Well," said he; "I am a little surprised myself;—I am, indeed! But I had nothing to do in Norwich,—literally nothing; and your aunt had so often talked to me of the beauties of this place,"—and he waved his hand round at the old house and the dark trees,—"that I thought I'd take the liberty of paying you a flying visit. I didn't mean to intrude in the way of sleeping; I didn't indeed, Miss Vavasor; only Mrs. Greenow has been so kind as to say—"

"We are so very far out of the world, Captain Bellfield, that we always give our visitors beds."

"I didn't intend it; I didn't indeed, miss!" Poor Captain Bellfield was becoming very uneasy in his agitation. "I did just put my bag, with a change of things, into the gig, which brought me over, not knowing quite where I might go on to."

"We won't send you any further to-day, at any rate," said Kate.

"Mrs. Greenow has been very kind,—very kind, indeed. She has asked me to stay till—Saturday!"

Kate bit her lips in a momentary fit of anger. The house was her house, and not her aunt's. But she remembered that her aunt had been kind to her at Norwich and at Yarmouth, and she allowed this feeling to die away. "We shall be very glad to see you," she said. "We are three women together here, and I'm afraid you will find us rather dull."

"Oh dear, no,—dull with you! That would be impossible!"

"And how have you left your friend, Mr. Cheesacre?"

"Quite well;—very well, thank you. That is to say, I haven't seen him much lately. He and I did have a bit of a breeze, you know."

"I can't say that I did know, Captain Bellfield."

"I thought, perhaps, you had heard. He seemed to think that I was too particular in a certain quarter! Ha—ha—ha—ha! That's only my joke, you know, ladies."

They then went into the house, and the Captain straggled in after them. Mrs. Greenow was in neither of the two sitting-rooms which they usually occupied. She, too, had been driven somewhat out of the ordinary composure of her manner by the arrival of her lover,—even though she had expected it, and had retired to her room, thinking that she had better see Kate in private before they met in the presence of the Captain. "I suppose you have seen my aunt since you have been here?" said Kate.

"Oh dear, yes. I saw her, and she suggested that I had better walk out and find you. I did find you, you know, though I didn't walk very far."

"And have you seen your room?"

"Yes;—yes. She was kind enough to show me my room. Very nice indeed, thank you;—looking out into the front, and all that kind of thing." The poor fellow was no doubt thinking how much better was his lot at Vavasor Hall than it had been at Oileymead. "I shan't stay long, Miss Vavasor,—only just a night or so; but I did want to see your aunt again,—and you, too, upon my word."

"My aunt is the attraction, Captain Bellfield. We all know that."

He actually simpered,—simpered like a young girl who is half elated and half ashamed when her lover is thrown in her teeth. He fidgeted with the things on the table, and moved himself about uneasily from one leg to the other. Perhaps he was remembering that though he had contrived to bring himself to Vavasor Hall he had not money enough left to take him back to Norwich. The two girls left him and went to their rooms. "I will go to my aunt at once," said Kate, "and find out what is to be done."

"I suppose she means to marry him?"

"Oh, yes; she means to marry him, and the sooner the better now. I knew this was coming, but I did so hope it would not be while you were here. It makes me feel so ashamed of myself that you should see it."

Kate boldly knocked at her aunt's door, and her aunt received her with a conscious smile. "I was waiting for you to come," said Mrs. Greenow.

"Here I am, aunt; and, what is more to the purpose, there is Captain Bellfield in the drawing-room."

"Stupid man! I told him to take himself away about the place till dinner-time. I've half a mind to send him back to Shap at once;—upon my word I have."

"Don't do that, aunt; it would be inhospitable."

"But he is such an oaf. I hope you understand, my dear, that I couldn't help it?"

"But you do mean to—to marry him, aunt; don't you?"

"Well, Kate, I really think I do. Why shouldn't I? It's a lonely sort of life being by myself; and, upon my word, I don't think there's very much harm in him."

"I am not saying anything against him; only in that case you can't very well turn him out of the house."

"Could not I, though? I could in a minute; and, if you wish it, you shall see if I can't do it."

"The rocks and valleys would not allow that, aunt."

"It's all very well for you to laugh, my dear. If laughing would break my bones I shouldn't be as whole as I am now. I might have had Cheesacre if I liked, who is a substantial man, and could have kept a carriage for me; but it was the rocks and valleys that prevented that;—and perhaps a little feeling that I might do some good to a poor fellow who has nobody in the world to look after him." Mrs. Greenow, as she said this, put her handkerchief up to her eyes, and wiped away the springing moisture. Tears were always easy with her, but on this occasion Kate almost respected her tears. "I'm sure I hope you'll be happy, aunt."

"If he makes me unhappy he shall pay for it;" and Mrs. Greenow, having done with the tears, shook her head, as though upon this occasion she quite meant all that she said.

At dinner they were not very comfortable. Either the gloomy air of the place and the neighbourhood of the black pines had depressed the Captain, or else the glorious richness of the prospects before him had made him thoughtful. He had laid aside the jacket with the brass buttons, and had dressed himself for dinner very soberly. And he behaved himself at dinner and after dinner with a wonderful sobriety, being very unlike the Captain who had sat at the head of the table at Mrs. Greenow's picnic. When left to himself after dinner he barely swallowed two glasses of the old Squire's port wine before he sauntered out into the garden to join the ladies, whom he had seen there; and when pressed by Kate to light a cigar he positively declined.

On the following morning Mrs. Greenow had recovered her composure, but Captain Bellfield was still in a rather disturbed state of mind. He knew that his efforts were to be crowned with success, and that he was sure of his wife, but he did not know how the preliminary difficulties were to be overcome, and he did not know what to do with himself at the Hall. After breakfast he fidgeted about in the parlour, being unable to contrive for himself a mode of escape, and was absolutely thrown upon his beam-ends when the widow asked him what he meant to do with himself between that and dinner.

"I suppose I'd better take a walk," he said; "and perhaps the young ladies—"

"If you mean my two nieces," said Mrs. Greenow, "I'm afraid you'll find they are engaged. But if I'm not too old to walk with—" The Captain assured her that she was just of the proper age for a walking companion, as far as his taste went, and then attempted some apology for the awkwardness of his expression, at which the three women laughed heartily. "Never mind, Captain," said Mrs. Greenow. "We'll have our walk all the same, and won't mind those young girls. Come along." They started, not up towards the mountains, as Kate always did when she walked in Westmoreland, but mildly, and at a gentle pace, as beseemed their years, along the road towards Shap. The Captain politely opened the old gate for the widow, and then carefully closed it again,—not allowing it to swing, as he would have done at Yarmouth. Then he tripped up to his place beside her, suggested his arm, which she declined, and walked on for some paces in silence. What on earth was he to say to her? He had done his love-making successfully, and what was he to do next?

"Well, Captain Bellfield," said she. They were walking very slowly, and he was cutting the weeds by the roadside with his cane. He knew by her voice that something special was coming, so he left the weeds and ranged himself close up alongside of her. "Well, Captain Bellfield,—so I suppose I'm to be good-natured; am I?"

"Arabella, you'll make me the happiest man in the world."

"That's all fudge." She would have said, "all rocks and valleys," only he would not have understood her.

"Upon my word, you will."

"I hope I shall make you respectable?"

"Oh, yes; certainly. I quite intend that."

"It is the great thing that you should intend. Of course I am going to make a fool of myself."

"No, no; don't say that."

"If I don't say it, all my friends will say it for me. It's lucky for you that I don't much care what people say."

"It is lucky;—I know that I'm lucky. The very first day I saw you I thought what a happy fellow I was to meet you. Then, of course, I was only thinking of your beauty."

"Get along with you!"

"Upon my word, yes. Come, Arabella, as we are to be man and wife, you might as well." At this moment he had got very close to her, and had recovered something of his usual elasticity; but she would not allow him even to put his arm round her waist. "Out in the high road!" she said. "How can you be so impertinent,—and so foolish?"

"You might as well, you know,—just once."

"Captain Bellfield, I brought you out here not for such fooling as that, but in order that we might have a little chat about business. If we are to be man and wife, as you say, we ought to understand on what footing we are to begin together. I'm afraid your own private means are not considerable?"

"Well, no; they are not, Mrs. Greenow."

"Have you anything?" The Captain hesitated, and poked the ground with his cane. "Come, Captain Bellfield, let us have the truth at once, and then we shall understand each other." The Captain still hesitated, and said nothing. "You must have had something to live upon, I suppose?" suggested the widow. Then the Captain, by degrees, told his story. He had a married sister by whom a guinea a week was allowed to him. That was all. He had been obliged to sell out of the army, because he was unable to live on his pay as a lieutenant. The price of his commission had gone to pay his debts, and now,—yes, it was too true,—now he was in debt again. He owed ninety pounds to Cheesacre, thirty-two pounds ten to a tailor at Yarmouth, over seventeen pounds at his lodgings in Norwich. At the present moment he had something under thirty shillings in his pocket. The tailor at Yarmouth had lent him three pounds in order that he might make his journey into Westmoreland, and perhaps be enabled to pay his debts by getting a rich wife. In the course of the cross-examination Mrs. Greenow got much information out of him; and then, when she was satisfied that she had learned, not exactly all the truth, but certain indications of the truth, she forgave him all his offences.

"And now you will give a fellow a kiss,—just one kiss," said the ecstatic Captain, in the height of his bliss.

"Hush!" said the widow, "there's a carriage coming on the road—close to us."

CHAPTER LXV
THE FIRST KISS

"Hush!" said the widow, "there's a carriage coming on the road—close to us." Mrs. Greenow, as she spoke these words, drew back from the Captain's arms before the first kiss of permitted ante-nuptial love had been exchanged. The scene was on the high road from Shap to Vavasor, and as she was still dressed in all the sombre habiliments of early widowhood, and as neither he nor his sweetheart were under forty, perhaps it was as well that they were not caught toying together in so very public a place. But they were only just in time to escape the vigilant eyes of a new visitor. Round the corner of the road, at a sharp trot, came the Shap post-horse, with the Shap gig behind him,—the same gig which had brought Bellfield to Vavasor on the previous day,—and seated in the gig, looming large, with his eyes wide awake to everything round him, was—Mr. Cheesacre.

It was a sight terrible to the eyes of Captain Bellfield, and by no means welcome to those of Mrs. Greenow. As regarded her, her annoyance had chiefly reference to her two nieces, and especially to Alice. How was she to account for this second lover? Kate, of course, knew all about it; but how could Alice be made to understand that she, Mrs. Greenow, was not to blame,—that she had, in sober truth, told this ardent gentleman that there was no hope for him? And even as to Kate,—Kate, whom her aunt had absurdly chosen to regard as the object of Mr. Cheesacre's pursuit,—what sort of a welcome would she extend to the owner of Oileymead? Before the wheels had stopped, Mrs. Greenow had begun to reflect whether it might be possible that she should send Mr. Cheesacre back without letting him go on to the Hall; but if Mrs. Greenow was dismayed, what were the feelings of the Captain? For he was aware that Cheesacre knew that of him which he had not told. How ardently did he now wish that he had sailed nearer to the truth in giving in the schedule of his debts to Mrs. Greenow.

"That man's wanted by the police," said Cheesacre, speaking while the gig was still in motion. "He's wanted by the police, Mrs. Greenow," and in his ardour he stood up in the gig and pointed at Bellfield. Then the gig stopped suddenly, and he fell back into his seat in his effort to prevent his falling forward. "He's wanted by the police," he shouted out again, as soon as he was able to recover his voice.

Mrs. Greenow turned pale beneath the widow's veil which she had dropped. What might not her Captain have done? He might have procured things, to be sent to him, out of shops on false pretences; or, urged on by want and famine, he might have committed—forgery. "Oh, my!" she said, and dropped her hand from his arm, which she had taken.

"It's false," said Bellfield.

"It's true," said Cheesacre.

"I'll indict you for slander, my friend," said Bellfield.

"Pay me the money you owe me," said Cheesacre. "You're a swindler!"

Mrs. Greenow cared little as to her lover being a swindler in Mr. Cheesacre's estimation. Such accusations from him she had heard before. But she did care very much as to this mission of the police against her Captain. If that were true, the Captain could be her Captain no longer. "What is this I hear, Captain Bellfield?" she said.

"It's a lie and a slander. He merely wants to make a quarrel between us. What police are after me, Mr. Cheesacre?"

"It's the police, or the sheriff's officer, or something of the kind," said Cheesacre.

"Oh, the sheriff's officers!" exclaimed Mrs. Greenow, in a tone of voice which showed how great had been her relief. "Mr. Cheesacre, you shouldn't come and say such things;—you shouldn't, indeed. Sheriff's officers can be paid, and there's an end of them."

"I'll indict him for the libel—I will, as sure as I'm alive," said Bellfield.

"Nonsense," said the widow. "Don't you make a fool of yourself. When men can't pay their way they must put up with having things like that said of them. Mr. Cheesacre, where were you going?"

"I was going to Vavasor Hall, on purpose to caution you."

"It's too late," said Mrs. Greenow, sinking behind her veil.

"Why, you haven't been and married him since yesterday? He only had twenty-four hours' start of me, I know. Or, perhaps, you had it done clandestine in Norwich? Oh, Mrs. Greenow!"

He got out of the gig, and the three walked back towards the Hall together, while the boy drove on with Mr. Cheesacre's carpetbag. "I hardly know," said Mrs. Greenow, "whether we can welcome you. There are other visitors, and the house is full."

"I'm not one to intrude where I'm not wanted. You may be sure of that. If I can't get my supper for love, I can get at for money. That's more than some people can say. I wonder when you're going to pay me what you owe me, Lieutenant Bellfield?"

"I wonder when you're going to pay me
what you owe me, Lieutenant Bellfield?"

Nevertheless, the widow had contrived to reconcile the two men before she reached the Hall. They had actually shaken hands, and the lamb Cheesacre had agreed to lie down with the wolf Bellfield. Cheesacre, moreover, had contrived to whisper into the widow's ears the true extent of his errand into Westmoreland. This, however, he did not do altogether in Bellfield's hearing. When Mrs. Greenow ascertained that there was something to be said, she made no scruple in sending her betrothed away from her "You won't throw a fellow over, will you, now?" whispered Bellfield into her ear as he went. She merely frowned at him, and bade him begone, so that the walk which Mrs. Greenow began with one lover she ended in company with the other.

Bellfield, who was sent on to the house, found Alice and Kate surveying the newly arrived carpet bag. "He knows 'un," said the boy who had driven the gig, pointing to the Captain.

"It belongs to your old friend, Mr. Cheesacre," said Bellfield to Kate.

"And has he come too?" said Kate.

The Captain shrugged his shoulders, and admitted that it was hard. "And it's not the slightest use," said he, "not the least in the world. He never had a chance in that quarter."

"Not enough of the rocks and valleys about him, was there, Captain Bellfield?" said Kate. But Captain Bellfield understood nothing about the rocks and valleys, though he was regarded by certain eyes as being both a rock and a valley himself.

In the meantime Cheesacre was telling his story. He first asked, in a melancholy tone, whether it was really necessary that he must abandon all his hopes. "He wasn't going to say anything against the Captain," he said, "if things were really fixed. He never begrudged any man his chance."

"Things are really fixed," said Mrs. Greenow.

He could, however, not keep himself from hinting that Oileymead was a substantial home, and that Bellfield had not as much as a straw mattress to lie upon. In answer to this Mrs. Greenow told him that there was so much more reason why some one should provide the poor man with a mattress. "If you look at it in that light, of course it's true," said Cheesacre. Mrs. Greenow told him that she did look at it in that light. "Then I've done about that," said Cheesacre; "and as to the little bit of money he owes me, I must give him his time about it, I suppose." Mrs. Greenow assured him that it should be paid as soon as possible after the nuptial benediction had been said over them. She offered, indeed, to pay it at once if he was in distress for it, but he answered contemptuously that he never was in distress for money. He liked to have his own,—that was all.

After this he did not get away to his next subject quite so easily as he wished; and it must be admitted that there was a difficulty. As he could not have Mrs. Greenow he would be content to put up with Kate for his wife. That was his next subject. Rumours as to the old Squire's will had no doubt reached him, and he was now willing to take advantage of that assistance which Mrs. Greenow had before offered him in this matter. The time had come in which he ought to marry; of that he was aware. He had told many of his friends in Norfolk that Kate Vavasor had thrown herself at his head, and very probably he had thought it true. In answer to all his love speeches to herself, the aunt had always told him what an excellent wife her niece would make him. So now he had come to Westmoreland with this second string to his bow. "You know you put it into my head your own self," pleaded Mr. Cheesacre. "Didn't you, now?"

"But things are so different since that," said the widow.

"How different? I ain't different. There's Oileymead just where it always was, and the owner of it don't owe a shilling to any man. How are things different?"

"My niece has inherited property."

"And is that to make a change? Oh! Mrs. Greenow, who would have thought to find you mercenary like that? Inherited property! Is she going to fling a man over because of that?"

Mrs. Greenow endeavoured to explain to him that her niece could hardly be said to have flung him over, and at last pretended to become angry when he attempted to assert his position. "Why, Mr. Cheesacre, I am quite sure she never gave you a word of encouragement in her life."

"But you always told me I might have her for the asking."

"And now I tell you that you mayn't. It's of no use your going on there to ask her, for she will only send you away with an answer you won't like. Look here, Mr. Cheesacre; you want to get married, and it's quite time you should. There's my dear friend Charlie Fairstairs. How could you get a better wife than Charlie?"

"Charlie Fairstairs!" said Cheesacre, turning up his nose in disgust. "She hasn't got a penny, nor any one belonging to her. The man who marries her will have to find the money for the smock she stands up in."

"Who's mercenary now, Mr. Cheesacre? Do you go home and think of it; and if you'll marry Charlie, I'll go to your wedding. You shan't be ashamed of her clothing. I'll see to that."

They were now close to the gate, and Cheesacre paused before he entered. "Do you think there's no chance at all for me, then?" said he.

"I know there's none. I've heard her speak about it."

"Somebody else, perhaps, is the happy man?"

"I can't say anything about that, but I know that she wouldn't take you. I like farming, you know, but she doesn't."

"I might give that up," said Cheesacre readily,—"at any rate, for a time."

"No, no, no; it would do no good. Believe me, my friend, that it is of no use."

He still paused at the gate. "I don't see what's the use of my going in," said he. To this she made him no answer. "There's a pride about me," he continued, "that I don't choose to go where I'm not wanted."

"I can't tell you, Mr. Cheesacre, that you are wanted in that light, certainly."

"Then I'll go. Perhaps you'll be so good as to tell the boy with the gig to come after me? That's six pound ten it will have cost me to come here and go back. Bellfield did it cheaper, of course; he travelled second class. I heard of him as I came along."

"The expense does not matter to you, Mr. Cheesacre."

To this he assented, and then took his leave, at first offering his hand to Mrs. Greenow with an air of offended dignity, but falling back almost into humility during the performance of his adieu. Before he was gone he had invited her to bring the Captain to Oileymead when she was married, and had begged her to tell Miss Vavasor how happy he should be to receive her. "And Mr. Cheesacre," said the widow, as he walked back along the road, "don't forget dear Charlie Fairstairs."

They were all standing at the front door of the house when Mrs. Greenow re-appeared,—Alice, Kate, Captain Bellfield, the Shap boy, and the Shap horse and gig. "Where is he?" Kate asked in a low voice, and everyone there felt how important was the question. "He has gone," said the widow. Bellfield was so relieved that he could not restrain his joy, but took off his little straw hat and threw it up into the air. Kate's satisfaction was almost as intense. "I am so glad," said she. "What on earth should we have done with him?" "I never was so disappointed in my life," said Alice. "I have heard so much of Mr. Cheesacre, but have never seen him." Kate suggested that she should get into the gig and drive after him. "He ain't a been and took hisself off?" suggested the boy, whose face became very dismal as the terrible idea struck him. But, with juvenile craft, he put his hand on the carpet-bag, and finding that it did not contain stones, was comforted. "You drive after him, young gentleman, and you'll find him on the road to Shap," said Mrs. Greenow. "Mind you give him my love," said the Captain in his glee, "and say I hope he'll get his turnips in well."

This little episode went far to break the day, and did more than anything else could have done to put Captain Bellfield at his ease. It created a little joint-stock fund of merriment between the whole party, which was very much needed. The absence of such joint-stock fund is always felt when a small party is thrown together without such assistance. Some bond is necessary on these occasions, and no other bond is so easy or so pleasant. Now, when the Captain found himself alone for a quarter of an hour with Alice, he had plenty of subjects for small-talk. "Yes, indeed. Old Cheesacre, in spite of his absurdities, is not a bad sort of fellow at bottom;—awfully fond of his money, you know, Miss Vavasor, and always boasting about it." "That's not pleasant," said Alice. "No, the most unpleasant thing in the world. There's nothing I hate so much, Miss Vavasor, as that kind of talking. My idea is this,—when a man has lots of money, let him make the best use he can of it, and say nothing about it. Nobody ever heard me talking about my money." He knew that Alice knew that he was a pauper; but, nevertheless, he had the satisfaction of speaking of himself as though he were not a pauper.

In this way the afternoon went very pleasantly. For an hour before dinner Captain Bellfield was had into the drawing-room and was talked to by his widow on matters of business; but he had of course known that this was necessary. She scolded him soundly about those sheriff's officers. Why had he not told her? "As long as there's anything kept back, I won't have you," said she. "I won't become your wife till I'm quite sure there's not a penny owing that is not shown in the list." Then I think he did tell her all,—or nearly all. When all was counted it was not so very much. Three or four hundred pounds would make him a new man, and what was such a sum as that to his wealthy widow! Indeed, for a woman wanting a husband of that sort, Captain Bellfield was a safer venture than would be a man of a higher standing among his creditors. It is true Bellfield might have been a forger, or a thief, or a returned convict,—but then his debts could not be large. Let him have done his best, he could not have obtained credit for a thousand pounds; whereas, no one could tell the liabilities of a gentleman of high standing. Burgo Fitzgerald was a gentleman of high standing, and his creditors would have swallowed up every shilling that Mrs. Greenow possessed; but with Captain Bellfield she was comparatively safe.

Upon the whole I think that she was lucky in her choice; or, perhaps, I might more truly say, that she had chosen with prudence. He was no forger, or thief—in the ordinary sense of the word; nor was he a returned convict. He was simply an idle scamp, who had hung about the world for forty years, doing nothing, without principle, shameless, accustomed to eat dirty puddings, and to be kicked—morally kicked—by such men as Cheesacre. But he was moderate in his greediness, and possessed of a certain appreciation of the comfort of a daily dinner, which might possibly suffice to keep him from straying very wide as long as his intended wife should be able to keep the purse-strings altogether in her own hands. Therefore, I say that Mrs. Greenow had been lucky in her choice, and not altogether without prudence.

"I think of taking this house," said she, "and of living here."

"What, in Westmoreland!" said the Captain, with something of dismay in his tone. What on earth would he do with himself all his life in that gloomy place!

"Yes, in Westmoreland. Why not in Westmoreland as well as anywhere else? If you don't like Westmoreland, it's not too late yet, you know." In answer to this the poor Captain was obliged to declare that he had no objection whatever to Westmoreland.

"I've been talking to my niece about it," continued Mrs. Greenow, "and I find that such an arrangement can be made very conveniently. The property is left between her and her uncle,—the father of my other niece, and neither of them want to live here."

"But won't you be rather dull, my dear?"

"We could go to Yarmouth, you know, in the autumn." Then the Captain's visage became somewhat bright again. "And perhaps, if you are not extravagant, we could manage a month or so in London during the winter, just to see the plays and do a little shopping." Then the Captain's face became very bright. "That will be delightful," said he. "And as for being dull," said the widow, "when people grow old they must be dull. Dancing can't go on for ever." In answer to this the widow's Captain assured the widow that she was not at all old; and now, on this occasion, that ceremony came off successfully which had been interrupted on the Shap road by the noise of Mr. Cheesacre's wheels. "There goes my cap," said she. "What a goose you are! What will Jeannette say?" "Bother Jeannette," said the Captain in his bliss. "She can do another cap, and many more won't be wanted." Then I think the ceremony was repeated.

Upon the whole the Captain's visit was satisfactory—at any rate to the Captain. Everything was settled. He was to go away on Saturday morning, and remain in lodgings at Penrith till the wedding, which they agreed to have celebrated at Vavasor Church. Kate promised to be the solitary bridesmaid. There was some talk of sending for Charlie Fairstairs, but the idea was abandoned. "We'll have her afterwards," said the widow to Kate, "when you are gone, and we shall want her more. And I'll get Cheesacre here, and make him marry her. There's no good in paying for two journeys." The Captain was to be allowed to come over from Penrith twice a week previous to his marriage; or perhaps, I might more fairly say, that he was commanded to do so. I wonder how he felt when Mrs. Greenow gave him his first five-pound note, and told him that he must make it do for a fortnight?—whether it was all joy, or whether there was about his heart any touch of manly regret?

"Captain Bellfield, of Vavasor Hall, Westmoreland. It don't sound badly," he said to himself, as he travelled away on his first journey to Penrith.

CHAPTER LXVI
LADY MONK'S PLAN

On the night of Lady Monk's party, Burgo Fitzgerald disappeared; and when the guests were gone and the rooms were empty, his aunt inquired for him in vain. The old butler and factotum of the house, who was employed by Sir Cosmo to put out the lamps and to see that he was not robbed beyond a certain point on these occasions of his wife's triumphs, was interrogated by his mistress, and said that he thought Mr. Burgo had left the house. Lady Monk herself knocked at her nephew's door, when she went up-stairs, ascending an additional flight of stairs with her weary old limbs in order that she might do so; she even opened the door and saw the careless debris of his toilet about the room. But he was gone. "Perhaps, after all, he has arranged it," she said to herself, as she went down to her own room.

But Burgo, as we know, had not "arranged it." It may be remembered that when Mr. Palliser came back to his wife in the supper-room at Lady Monk's, bringing with him the scarf which Lady Glencora had left up-stairs, Burgo was no longer with her. He had become well aware that he had no chance left, at any rate for that night. The poor fool, acting upon his aunt's implied advice rather than his own hopes, had secured a post-chaise, and stationed it in Bruton Street, some five minutes' walk from his aunt's house. And he had purchased feminine wrappings, cloaks, &c.—things that he thought might be necessary for his companion. He had, too, ordered rooms at the new hotel near the Dover Station,—the London Bridge Station,—from whence was to start on the following morning a train to catch the tidal boat for Boulogne. There was a dressing-bag there for which he had paid twenty-five guineas out of his aunt's money, not having been able to induce the tradesman to grant it to him on credit; and there were other things,—slippers, collars, stockings, handkerchiefs, and what else might, as he thought, under such circumstances be most necessary. Poor thoughtful, thoughtless fool!

The butler was right. He did leave the house. He saw Lady Glencora taken to her carriage from some back hiding-place in the hall, and then slipped out, unmindful of his shining boots, and dress coat and jewelled studs. He took a Gibus hat,—his own, or that of some other unfortunate,—

and slowly made his way down to the place in Bruton Street. There was the carriage and pair of horses, all in readiness; and the driver, when he had placed himself by the door of the vehicle, was not long in emerging from the neighbouring public-house. "All ready, your honour," said the man. "I shan't want you to-night," said Burgo, hoarsely;—"go away." "And about the things, your honour?" "Take them to the devil. No; stop. Take them back with you, and ask somebody to keep them till I send for them. I shall want them and another carriage in a day or two." Then he gave the man half a sovereign, and went away, not looking at the little treasures which he had spent so much of his money in selecting for his love. When he was gone, the waterman and the driver turned them over with careful hands and gloating eyes. "It's a 'eiress, I'll go bail," said the waterman. "Pretty dear! I suppose her parints was too many for her," said the driver. But neither of them imagined the enormity which the hirer of the chaise had in truth contemplated.

Burgo from thence took his way back into Grosvenor Square, and from thence down Park Street, and through a narrow passage and a mews which there are in those parts, into Park Lane. He had now passed the position of Mr. Palliser's house, having come out on Park Lane at a spot nearer to Piccadilly; but he retraced his steps, walking along by the rails of the Park, till he found himself opposite to the house. Then he stood there, leaning back upon the railings, and looking up at Lady Glencora's windows. What did he expect to see? Or was he, in truth, moved by love of that kind which can take joy in watching the slightest shadow that is made by the one loved object,—that may be made by her, or, by some violent conjecture of the mind, may be supposed to have been so made? Such love as that is, I think, always innocent. Burgo Fitzgerald did not love like that. I almost doubt whether he can be said to have loved at all. There was in his breast a mixed, feverish desire, which he took no trouble to analyse. He wanted money. He wanted the thing of which this Palliser had robbed him. He wanted revenge,—though his desire for that was not a burning desire. And among other things, he wanted the woman's beauty of the woman whom he coveted. He wanted to kiss her again as he had once kissed her, and to feel that she was soft, and lovely, and loving for him. But as for seeing her shadow, unless its movement indicated some purpose in his favour,—I do not think that he cared much about that.

And why then was he there? Because in his unreasoning folly he did not know what step to take, or what step not to take. There are men whose energies hardly ever carry them beyond looking for the thing they want. She might see him from the window, and come to him. I do not say that he thought that it would be so. I fancy that he never thought at all about that or about anything. If you lie under a tree, and open your mouth, a plum may fall into it. It was probably an undefined idea of some such chance as this which brought him against the railings in the front of Mr. Palliser's house; that, and a feeling made up partly of despair and partly of lingering romance that he was better there, out in the night air, under the gas-lamps, than he could be elsewhere. There he stood and looked, and cursed his ill-luck. But his curses had none of the bitterness of those which George Vavasor was always uttering. Through it all there remained about Burgo one honest feeling,—one conviction that was true,—a feeling that it all served him right, and that he had better, perhaps, go to the devil at once, and give nobody any more trouble. If he loved no one sincerely, neither did he hate any one; and whenever he made any self-inquiry into his own circumstances, he always told himself that it was all his own fault. When he cursed his fate, he only did so because cursing is so easy. George Vavasor would have ground his victims up to powder if he knew how; but Burgo Fitzgerald desired to hurt no one.

There he stood till he was cold, and then, as the plum did not drop into his mouth, he moved on. He went up into Oxford Street, and walked along it the whole distance to the corner of Bond Street, passing by Grosvenor Square, to which he intended to return. At the corner of Bond Street, a girl took hold of him, and looked up into his face. "Ah!" she said, "I saw you once before."—"Then you saw the most miserable devil alive," said Burgo. "You can't be miserable," said the girl. "What makes you miserable? You've plenty of money."—"I wish I had," said Burgo. "And plenty to eat and drink," exclaimed the girl; "and you are so handsome! I remember you. You gave me supper one night when I was starving. I ain't hungry now. Will you give me a kiss?"—"I'll give you a shilling, and that's better," said Burgo. "But give me a kiss too," said the girl. He gave her first the kiss, and then the shilling, and after that he left her and passed on. "I'm d——d if I wouldn't change with her!" he said to himself. "I wonder whether anything really ails him?" thought the girl. "He said he was wretched before. Shouldn't I like to be good to such a one as him!"

Burgo went on, and made his way into the house in Grosvenor Square, by some means probably unknown to his aunt, and certainly unknown to his uncle. He emptied his pockets as he got into bed, and counted a roll of notes which he had kept in one of them. There were still a hundred and thirty pounds left. Lady Glencora had promised that she would see him again. She had said as much as that quite distinctly. But what use would there be in that if all his money should then be gone? He knew that the keeping of money in his pocket was to him quite an impossibility. Then he thought of his aunt. What should he say to his aunt if he saw her in the course of the coming day? Might it not be as well for him to avoid his aunt altogether?

He breakfasted up-stairs in his bedroom,—in the bed, indeed, eating a small paté de foie gras from the supper-table, as he read a French novel. There he was still reading his French novel in bed when his aunt's maid came to him, saying that his aunt wished to see him before she went out. "Tell me, Lucy," said he, "how is the old girl?"

"She's as cross as cross, Mr. Burgo. Indeed, I shan't;—not a minute longer. Don't, now; will you? I tell you she's waiting for me." From which it may be seen that Lucy shared the general feminine feeling in favour of poor Burgo.

Thus summoned Burgo applied himself to his toilet; but as he did so, he recruited his energies from time to time by a few pages of the French novel, and also by small doses from a bottle of curaçoa which he had in his bedroom. He was utterly a pauper. There was no pauper poorer than he in London that day. But, nevertheless, he breakfasted on paté de foie gras and curaçoa, and regarded those dainties very much as other men regard bread and cheese and beer.

But though he was dressing at the summons of his aunt, he had by no means made up his mind that he would go to her. Why should he go to her? What good would it do him? She would not give him more money. She would only scold him for his misconduct. She might, perhaps, turn him out of the house if he did not obey her,—or attempt to do so; but she would be much more likely to do this when he had made her angry by contradicting her. In neither case would he leave the house, even though its further use were positively forbidden him, because his remaining there was convenient; but as he could gain nothing by seeing "the old girl," as he had called her, he resolved to escape to his club without attending to her summons.

But his aunt, who was a better general than he, out-manœuvred him. He crept down the back stairs; but as he could not quite condescend to escape through the area, he was forced to emerge upon the hall, and here his aunt pounced upon him, coming out of the breakfast-parlour. "Did not Lucy tell you that I wanted to see you?" Lady Monk asked, with severity in her voice.

Burgo replied, with perfect ease, that he was going out just to have his hair washed and brushed. He would have been back in twenty minutes. There was no energy about the poor fellow, unless, perhaps, when he was hunting; but he possessed a readiness which enabled him to lie at a moment's notice with the most perfect ease. Lady Monk did not believe him; but she could not confute him, and therefore she let the lie pass.

"Never mind your hair now," she said. "I want to speak to you. Come in here for a few minutes."

As there was no way of escape left to him, he followed his aunt into the breakfast-parlour.

"Burgo," she said, when she had seated herself, and had made him sit in a chair opposite to her, "I don't think you will ever do any good."

"I don't much think I shall, aunt."

"What do you mean, then, to do with yourself?"

"Oh,—I don't know. I haven't thought much about it."

"You can't stay here in this house. Sir Cosmo was speaking to me about you only yesterday morning."

"I shall be quite willing to go down to Monkshade, if Sir Cosmo likes it better;—that is, when the season is a little more through."

"He won't have you at Monkshade. He won't let you go there again. And he won't have you here. You know that you are turning what I say into joke."

"No, indeed, aunt,"

"Yes, you are;—you know you are. You are the most ungrateful, heartless creature I ever met. You must make up your mind to leave this house at once."

"Where does Sir Cosmo mean that I should go, then?"

"To the workhouse, if you like. He doesn't care."

"I don't suppose he does;—the least in the world," said Burgo, opening his eyes, and stretching his nostrils, and looking into his aunt's face as though he had great ground for indignation.

But the turning of Burgo out of the house was not Lady Monk's immediate purpose. She knew that he would hang on there till the season was over. After that he must not be allowed to return again, unless he should have succeeded in a certain enterprise. She had now caught him in order that she might learn whether there was any possible remaining chance of success as to that enterprise. So she received his indignation in silence, and began upon another subject. "What a fool you made of yourself last night, Burgo!"

"Did I;—more of a fool than usual?"

"I believe that you will never be serious about anything. Why did you go on waltzing in that way when every pair of eyes in the room was watching you?"

"I couldn't help going on, if she liked it."

"Oh, yes,—say it was her fault. That's so like a man!"

"Look here, aunt, I'm not going to sit here and be abused. I couldn't take her in my arms, and fly away with her out of a crowd."

"Who wants you to fly away with her?"

"For the matter of that, I suppose that you do."

"No, I don't."

"Well, then, I do."

"You! you haven't spirit to do that, or anything else. You are like a child that is just able to amuse itself for the moment, and never can think of anything further. You simply disgraced yourself last night, and me too,— and her; but, of course, you care nothing about that."

"I had a plan all ready;—only he came back."

"Of course he came back. Of course he came back, when they sent him word how you and she were going on. And now he will have forgiven her, and after that, of course, the thing will be all over."

"I tell you what, aunt; she would go if she knew how. When I was forced to leave her last night, she promised to see me again. And as for being idle, and not doing anything;—why, I was out in Park Lane last night, after you were in bed."

"What good did that do?"

"It didn't do any good, as it happened. But a fellow can only try. I believe, after all, it would be easier down in the country,—especially now that he has taken it into his head to look after her."

Lady Monk sat silent for a few moments, and then she said in a low voice, "What did she say to you when you were parting? What were her exact words?" She, at any rate, was not deficient in energy. She was anxious enough to see her purpose accomplished. She would have conducted the matter with discretion, if the running away with Mr. Palliser's wife could, in very fact, have been done by herself.

"She said she would see me again. She promised it twice."

"And was that all?"

"What could she say more, when she was forced to go away?"

"Had she said that she would go with you?"

"I had asked her,—half a dozen times, and she did not once refuse. I know she means it, if she knew how to get away. She hates him;—I'm sure of it. A woman, you know, wouldn't absolutely say that she would go, till she was gone."

"If she really meant it, she would tell you."

"I don't think she could have told me plainer. She said she would see me again. She said that twice over."

Again Lady Monk sat silent. She had a plan in her head,—a plan that might, as she thought, give to her nephew one more chance. But she hesitated before she could bring herself to explain it in detail. At first she had lent a little aid to this desired abduction of Mr. Palliser's wife, but in lending it had said no word upon the subject. During the last season she had succeeded in getting Lady Glencora to her house in London, and had taken care that Burgo should meet her there. Then a hint or two had been spoken, and Lady Glencora had been asked to Monkshade. Lady Glencora, as we know, did not go to Monkshade, and Lady Monk had then been baffled. But she did not therefore give up the game. Having now thought of it so much, she began to speak of it more boldly, and had procured money for her nephew that he might thereby be enabled to carry off the woman. But though this had been well understood between them, though words had been spoken which were sufficiently explicit, the plan had not been openly discussed. Lady Monk had known nothing of the mode in which Lady Glencora was to have been carried off after her party, nor whither she was to have been taken. But now,—now she must arrange it herself, and have a scheme of her own, or else the thing must fail absolutely. Even she was almost reluctant to speak out plainly to her nephew on such a subject. What if he should be false to her, and tell of her? But when a woman has made such schemes, nothing distresses her so sadly as their failure. She would risk all rather than that Mr. Palliser should keep his wife.

"I will try and help you," she said at last, speaking hoarsely, almost in a whisper, "if you have courage to make an attempt yourself."

"Courage!" said he "What is it you think I am afraid of? Mr. Palliser? I'd fight him,—or all the Pallisers, one after another, if it would do any good."

"Fighting! There's no fighting wanted, as you know well enough. Men don't fight nowadays. Look here! If you can get her to call here some day,— say on Thursday, at three o'clock,—I will be here to receive her; and instead of going back into her carriage, you can have a cab for her somewhere near. She can come, as it were, to make a morning call."

"A cab!"

"Yes; a cab won't kill her, and it is less easily followed than a carriage."

"And where shall we go?"

"There is a train to Southampton at four, and the boat sails for Jersey at half-past six; you will be in Jersey the next morning, and there is a boat goes on to St. Malo, almost at once. You can go direct from one boat to the other,—that is, if she has strength and courage." After that, who will say that Lady Monk was not a devoted aunt?

"That would do excellently well," said the enraptured Burgo.

"She will have difficulty in getting away from me, out of the house. Of course I shall say nothing about it, and shall know nothing about it. She had better tell her coachman to drive somewhere to pick some one up, and to return;—out somewhere to Tyburnia, or down to Pimlico. Then she can leave me, and go out on foot, to where you have the cab. She can tell the hall-porter that she will walk to her carriage. Do you understand?" Burgo declared that he did understand.

"You must call on her, and make your way in, and see her, and arrange all this. It must be a Thursday, because of the boats." Then she made inquiry about his money, and took from him the notes which he had, promising to return them, with something added, on the Thursday morning; but he asked, with a little whine, for a five-pound note, and got it. Burgo then told her about the travelling-bags and the stockings, and they were quite pleasant and confidential. "Bid her come in a stout travelling-dress," said Lady Monk. "She can wear some lace or something over it, so that the servants won't observe it. I will take no notice of it." Was there ever such an aunt?

After this, Burgo left his aunt, and went away to his club, in a state of most happy excitement.

CHAPTER LXVII
THE LAST KISS

Alice, on her return from Westmoreland, went direct to Park Lane, whither Lady Glencora and Mr. Palliser had also returned before her. She was to remain with them in London one entire day, and on the morning after that they were to start for Paris. She found Mr. Palliser in close attendance upon his wife. Not that there was anything in his manner which at all implied that he was keeping watch over her, or that he was more with her, or closer to her than a loving husband might wish to be with a young wife; but the mode of life was very different from that which Alice had seen at Matching Priory!

On her arrival Mr. Palliser himself received her in the hall, and took her up to his wife before she had taken off her travelling hat. "We are so much obliged to you, Miss Vavasor," he said. "I feel it quite as deeply as Glencora."

"Oh, no," she said; "it is I that am under obligation to you for taking me."

He merely smiled, and shook his head, and then took her up-stairs. On the stairs he said one other word to her: "You must forgive me if I was cross to you that night she went out among the ruins." Alice muttered something, — some little fib of courtesy as to the matter having been forgotten, or never borne in mind; and then they went on to Lady Glencora's room. It seemed to Alice that he was not so big or so much to be dreaded as when she had seen him at Matching. His descent from an expectant, or more than an expectant, Chancellor of the Exchequer, down to a simple, attentive husband, seemed to affect his gait, his voice, and all his demeanour. When he received Alice at the Priory he certainly loomed before her as something great, whereas now his greatness seemed to have fallen from him. We must own that this was hard upon him, seeing that the deed by which he had divested himself of his greatness had been so pure and good!

"Dear Alice, this is so good of you! I am all in the midst of packing, and Plantagenet is helping me." Plantagenet winced a little under this, as the hero of old must have winced when he was found with the distaff. Mr. Palliser had relinquished his sword of state for the distaff which he had assumed, and could take no glory in the change. There was, too, in his wife's voice the slightest hint of mockery, which, slight as it was, he perhaps thought she might have spared. "You have nothing left to pack," continued Glencora, "and I don't know what you can do to amuse yourself."

"I will help you," said Alice.

"But we have so very nearly done. I think we shall have to pull all the things out, and put them up again, or we shall never get through to-morrow. We couldn't start to-morrow;—could we, Plantagenet?"

"Not very well, as your rooms are ordered in Paris for the next day."

"As if we couldn't find rooms at every inn on the road. Men are so particular. Now in travelling I should like never to order rooms,—never to know where I was going or when I was going, and to carry everything I wanted in a market-basket." Alice, who by this time had followed her friend along the passage to her bedroom, and had seen how widely the packages were spread about, bethought herself that the market-basket should be a large one. "And I would never travel among Christians. Christians are so slow, and they wear chimney-pot hats everywhere. The further one goes from London among Christians, the more they wear chimney-pot hats. I want Plantagenet to take us to see the Kurds, but he won't."

"I don't think that would be fair to Miss Vavasor," said Mr. Palliser, who had followed them.

"Don't put the blame on her head," said Lady Glencora. "Women have always pluck for anything. Wouldn't you like to see a live Kurd, Alice?"

"I don't exactly know where they live," said Alice.

"Nor I. I have not the remotest idea of the way to the Kurds. You see my joke, don't you, though Plantagenet doesn't? But one knows that they are Eastern, and the East is such a grand idea!"

"I think we'll content ourselves with Rome, or perhaps Naples, on this occasion," said Mr. Palliser.

The notion of Lady Glencora packing anything for herself was as good a joke as that other one of the Kurds and whey. But she went flitting about from room to room, declaring that this thing must be taken, and that other, till the market-basket would have become very large indeed. Alice was astonished at the extent of the preparations, and the sort of equipage with which they were about to travel. Lady Glencora was taking her own carriage. "Not that I shall ever use it," she said to Alice, "but he insists upon it, to show that I am not supposed to be taken away in disgrace. He is so good;—isn't he?"

"Very good," said Alice. "I know no one better."

"And so dull!" said Lady Glencora. "But I fancy that all husbands are dull from the nature of their position. If I were a young woman's husband, I shouldn't know what to say to her that wasn't dull."

Two women and two men servants were to be taken. Alice had received permission to bring her own maid—"or a dozen, if you want them," Lady Glencora had said. "Mr. Palliser in his present mood would think nothing too much to do for you. If you were to ask him to go among the Kurds, he'd go at once;—or on to Crim Tartary, if you made a point of it." But as both Lady Glencora's servants spoke French, and as her own did not, Alice trusted herself in that respect to her cousin. "You shall have one all to yourself," said Lady Glencora. "I only take two for the same reason that I take the carriage,—just as you let a child go out in her best frock, for a treat, after you've scolded her."

When Alice asked why it was supposed that Mr. Palliser was so specially devoted to her, the thing was explained to her. "You see, my dear, I have told him everything. I always do tell everything. Nobody can say I am not candid. He knows about your not letting me come to your house in the old days. Oh, Alice!—you were wrong then; I shall always say that. But it's done and gone; and things that are done and gone shall be done and gone for me. And I told him all that you said,—about you know what. I have had nothing else to do but make confessions for the last ten days, and when a woman once begins, the more she confesses the better. And I told him that you refused Jeffrey."

"You didn't?"

"I did indeed, and he likes you the better for that. I think he'd let Jeffrey marry you now if you both wished it;—and then, oh dear!—supposing that you had a son and that we adopted it?"

"Cora, if you go on in that way I will not remain with you."

"But you must, my dear. You can't escape now. At any rate, you can't when we once get to Paris. Oh dear! you shouldn't grudge me my little naughtinesses. I have been so proper for the last ten days. Do you know I got into a way of driving Dandy and Flirt at the rate of six miles an hour, till I'm sure the poor beasts thought they were always going to a funeral. Poor Dandy and poor Flirt! I shan't see them now for another year."

On the following morning they breakfasted early, because Mr. Palliser had got into an early habit. He had said that early hours would be good for them. "But he never tells me why," said Lady Glencora. "I think it is pleasant when people are travelling," said Alice. "It isn't that," her cousin answered; "but we are all to be such particularly good children. It's hardly fair, because he went to sleep last night after dinner while you and I kept ourselves awake: but we needn't do that another night, to be sure." After breakfast they all three went to work to do nothing. It was ludicrous and almost painful to see Mr. Palliser wandering about and counting the boxes, as though he could do any good by that. At this special crisis of his life he hated his papers and figures and statistics, and could not apply himself to them. He, whose application had been so unremitting, could apply himself now to nothing. His world had been brought to an abrupt end, and he was awkward at making a new beginning. I believe that they all three were reading novels before one o'clock. Lady Glencora and Alice had determined that they would not leave the house throughout the day. "Nothing has been said about it, but I regard it as part of the bond that I'm not to go out anywhere. Who knows but what I might be found in Gloucester Square?" There was, however, no absolute necessity that Mr. Palliser should remain with them; and, at about three, he prepared himself for a solitary walk. He would not go down to the House. All interest in the House was over with him for the present. He had the Speaker's leave to absent himself for the season. Nor would he call on anyone. All his friends knew, or believed they knew, that he had left town. His death and burial had been already chronicled, and were he now to reappear, he could reappear only as a ghost. He was being talked of as the departed one;—or rather, such talk on all sides had now come nearly to an end. The poor Duke of St. Bungay still thought of him with regret when more than ordinarily annoyed by some special grievance coming to him from Mr. Finespun; but even the Duke had become almost reconciled to the present order of things. Mr. Palliser knew better than to disturb all this by showing himself again in public; and prepared himself, therefore, to take another walk under the elms in Kensington Gardens.

He had his hat on his head in the hall, and was in the act of putting on his gloves, when there came a knock at the front door. The hall-porter was there, a stout, plethoric personage, not given to many words, who was at this moment standing with his master's umbrella in his hand, looking as though he would fain be of some use to somebody, if any such utility were compatible with the purposes of his existence. Now had come this knock at the door, while the umbrella was still in his hand, and the nature of his visage changed, and it was easy to see that he was oppressed by the temporary multiplicity of his duties. "Give me the umbrella, John," said Mr. Palliser. John gave up the umbrella, and opening the door disclosed Burgo Fitzgerald standing upon the door-step. "Is Lady Glencora at home?" asked Burgo, before he had seen the husband. John turned a dismayed face upon his master, as though he knew that the comer ought not to be making a morning call at that house,—as no doubt he did know very well,—and made no instant reply. "I am not sure," said Mr. Palliser, making his way out as he had originally purposed. "The servant will find out for you." Then he went on his way across Park Lane and into the Park, never once turning back his face to see whether Burgo had effected an entrance into the house. Nor did he return a minute earlier than he would otherwise have done. After all, there was something chivalrous about the man.

"Yes; Lady Glencora was at home," said the porter, not stirring to make any further inquiry. It was no business of his if Mr. Palliser chose to receive such a guest. He had not been desired to say that her ladyship was not at home. Burgo was therefore admitted and shown direct up into the room in which Lady Glencora was sitting. As chance would have it, she was alone. Alice had left her and was in her own chamber, and Lady Glencora was sitting at the window of the small room up-stairs that overlooked the Park. She was seated on a footstool with her face between her hands when Burgo was admitted, thinking of him, and of what the world might have been to her had "they left her alone," as she was in the habit of saying to Alice and to herself.

She rose quickly, so that he saw her only as she was rising. "Ask Miss Vavasor to come to me," she said, as the servant left the room; and then she came forward to greet her lover.

"Cora," he said, dashing at once into his subject—hopelessly, but still with a resolve to do as he had said that he would do. "Cora, I have come to you, to ask you to go with me."

"I will not go with you," said she.

"Do not answer me in that way, without a moment's thought. Everything is arranged—"

"Yes, everything is arranged," she said. "Mr. Fitzgerald, let me ask you to leave me alone, and to behave to me with generosity. Everything is arranged. You can see that my boxes are all prepared for going. Mr. Palliser and I, and my friend, are starting to-morrow. Wish me God-speed and go, and be generous."

"And is this to be the end of everything?" He was standing close to her, but hitherto he had only touched her hand at greeting her. "Give me your hand, Cora," he said.

"No;—I will never give you my hand again. You should be generous to me and go. This is to be the end of everything,—of everything that is common to you and to me. Go, when I ask you."

· "Cora; did you ever love me?"

"Yes; I did love you. But we were separated, and there was no room for love left between us."

"You are as dear to me now,—dearer than ever you were. Do not look at me like that. Did you not tell me when we last parted that I might come to you again? Are we children, that others should come between us and separate us like that?"

"Yes, Burgo; we are children. Here is my cousin coming. You must leave me now." As she spoke the door was opened and Alice entered the room. "Miss Vavasor, Mr. Fitzgerald," said Lady Glencora. "I have told him to go and leave me. Now that you have come, Alice, he will perhaps obey me."

Alice was dumbfounded, and knew not how to speak either to him or to her; but she stood with her eyes riveted on the face of the man of whom she had heard so much. Yes; certainly he was very beautiful. She had never before seen man's beauty such as that. She found it quite impossible to speak a word to him then—at the spur of the moment, but she acknowledged the introduction with a slight inclination of the head, and then stood silent, as though she were waiting for him to go.

"Mr. Fitzgerald, why do you not leave me and go?" said Lady Glencora.

Poor Burgo also found it difficult enough to speak. What could he say? His cause was one which certainly did not admit of being pleaded in the presence of a strange lady; and he might have known from the moment in which he heard Glencora's request that a third person should be summoned to their meeting—and probably did know, that there was no longer any hope for him. It was not on the cards that he should win. But there remained one thing that he must do. He must get himself out of that room; and how was he to effect that?

"I had hoped," said he, looking at Alice, though he addressed Lady Glencora—"I had hoped to be allowed to speak to you alone for a few minutes."

"No, Mr. Fitzgerald; it cannot be so. Alice do not go. I sent for my cousin when I saw you, because I did not choose to be alone with you. I have asked you to go—"

"You perhaps have not understood me?"

"I understand you well enough."

"Then, Mr. Fitzgerald," said Alice, "why do you not do as Lady Glencora has asked you? You know—you must know, that you ought not to be here."

"I know nothing of the kind," said he, still standing his ground.

"Alice," said Lady Glencora, "we will leave Mr. Fitzgerald here, since he drives us from the room."

In such contests, a woman has ever the best of it at all points. The man plays with a button to his foil, while the woman uses a weapon that can really wound. Burgo knew that he must go,—felt that he must skulk away as best he might, and perhaps hear a low titter of half-suppressed laughter as he went. Even that might be possible. "No, Lady Glencora," he said, "I will not drive you from the room. As one must be driven out, it shall be I. I own I did think that you would at any rate have been—less hard to me." He then turned to go, bowing again very slightly to Miss Vavasor.

He was on the threshold of the door before Glencora's voice recalled him. "Oh my God!" she said, "I am hard,—harder than flint. I am cruel. Burgo!" And he was back with her in a moment, and had taken her by the hand.

"Glencora," said Alice, "pray,—pray let him go. Mr. Fitzgerald, if you are a man, do not take advantage of her folly."

"I will speak to him," said Lady Glencora. "I will speak to him, and then he shall leave me." She was holding him by the hand now and turning to him, away from Alice, who had taken her by the arm. "Burgo," she said, repeating his name twice again, with all the passion that she could throw into the word,—"Burgo, no good can come of this. Now, you must leave me. You must go. I shall stay with my husband as I am bound to do. Because I have wronged you, I will not wrong him also. I loved you;—you know I loved you." She still held him by the hand, and was now gazing up into his face, while the tears were streaming from her eyes.

"Sir," said Alice, "you have heard from her all that you can care to hear. If you have any feeling of honour in you, you will leave her."

"I will never leave her, while she tells me that she loves me!"

"Yes, Burgo, you will;—you must! I shall never tell you that again, never. Do as she bids you. Go, and leave us;—but I could not bear that you should tell me that I was hard."

"You are hard;—hard and cruel, as you said, yourself."

"Am I? May God forgive you for saying that of me!"

"Then why do you send me away?"

"Because I am a man's wife, and because I care for his honour, if not for my own. Alice, let us go."

He still held her, but she would have been gone from him had he not stooped over her, and put his arm round her waist. In doing this, I doubt whether he was quicker than she would have been had she chosen to resist him. As it was, he pressed her to his bosom, and, stooping over her, kissed her lips. Then he left her, and making his way out of the room, and down the stairs, got himself out into the street.

"Thank God, that he is gone!" said Alice.

"You may say so," said Lady Glencora, "for you have lost nothing!"

"And you have gained everything!"

"Have I? I did not know that I had ever gained anything, as yet. The only human being to whom I have ever yet given my whole heart,—the only thing that I have ever really loved, has just gone from me for ever, and you bid me thank God that I have lost him. There is no room for thankfulness in any of it;—either in the love or in the loss. It is all wretchedness from first to last!"

"At any rate, he understands now that you meant it when you told him to leave you."

"Of course I meant it. I am beginning to know myself by degrees. As for running away with him, I have not the courage to do it. I can think of it, scheme for it, wish for it;—but as for doing it, that is beyond me. Mr. Palliser is quite safe. He need not try to coax me to remain."

Alice knew that it was useless to argue with her, so she came and sat over her,—for Lady Glencora had again placed herself on the stool by the window,—and tried to sooth her by smoothing her hair, and nursing her like a child.

"Of course I know that I ought to stay where I am," she said, breaking out, almost with rage, and speaking with quick, eager voice. "I am not such a fool as to mistake what I should be if I left my husband, and went to live with that man as his mistress. You don't suppose that I should think that sort of life very blessed. But why have I been brought to such a pass as this? And, as for female purity! Ah! What was their idea of purity when they forced me, like ogres, to marry a man for whom they knew I never cared? Had I gone with him,—had I now eloped with that man who ought to have been my husband,—whom would a just God have punished worst,—me, or those two old women and my uncle, who tortured me into this marriage?"

"Come, Cora,—be silent."

"I won't be silent! You have had the making of your own lot. You have done what you liked, and no one has interfered with you. You have suffered, too; but you, at any rate, can respect yourself."

"And so can you, Cora,—thoroughly, now."

"How;—when he kissed me, and I could hardly restrain myself from giving him back his kiss tenfold, could I respect myself? But it is all sin. I sin towards my husband, feigning that I love him; and I sin in loving that other man, who should have been my husband. There;—I hear Mr. Palliser at the door. Come away with me; or rather, stay, for he will come up here, and you can keep him in talk while I try to recover myself."

Mr. Palliser did at once as his wife had said, and came up-stairs to the little front room, as soon as he had deposited his hat in the hall. Alice was, in fact, in doubt what she should do, as to mentioning, or omitting to mention, Mr. Fitzgerald's name. In an ordinary way, it would be natural that she should name any visitor who had called, and she specially disliked the idea of remaining silent because that visitor had come as the lover of her host's wife. But, on the other hand, she owed much to Lady Glencora; and there was no imperative reason, as things had gone, why she should make mischief. There was no further danger to be apprehended. But Mr. Palliser at once put an end to her doubts. "You have had a visitor here?" said he.

"Yes," said Alice.

"I saw him as I went out," said Mr. Palliser. "Indeed, I met him at the hall door. He, of course, was wrong to come here;—so wrong, that he deserves punishment, if there were any punishment for such offences."

"He has been punished, I think," said Alice.

"But as for Glencora," continued Mr. Palliser, without any apparent notice of what Alice had said, "I thought it better that she should see him or not, as she should herself decide."

"She had no choice in the matter. As it turned out, he was shown up here at once. She sent for me, and I think she was right to do that."

"Glencora was alone when he came in?"

"For a minute or two,—till I could get to her."

"I have no questions to ask about it," said Mr. Palliser, after waiting for a few moments. He had probably thought that Alice would say something further. "I am very glad that you were within reach of her, as otherwise her position might have been painful. For her, and for me perhaps, it may be as well that he has been here. As for him, I can only say, that I am forced to suppose him to be a villain. What a man does when driven by passion, I can forgive; but that he should deliberately plan schemes to ruin both her and me, is what I can hardly understand." As he made this little speech I wonder whether his conscience said anything to him about Lady Dumbello, and a certain evening in his own life, on which he had ventured to call that lady, Griselda.

The little party of three dined together very quietly, and after dinner they all went to work with their novels. Before long Alice saw that Mr. Palliser was yawning, and she began to understand how much he had given up in order that his wife might be secure. It was then, when he had left the room for a few minutes, in order that he might wake himself by walking about the house, that Glencora told Alice of his yawning down at Matching. "I used to think that he would fall in pieces. What are we to do about it?"

"Don't seem to notice it," said Alice.

"That's all very well," said the other; "but he'll set us off yawning as bad as himself, and then he'll notice it. He has given himself up to politics, till nothing else has any salt in it left for him. I cannot think why such a man as that wanted a wife at all."

"You are very hard upon him, Cora."

"I wish you were his wife, with all my heart. But, of course, I know why he got married. And I ought to feel for him as he has been so grievously disappointed." Then Mr. Palliser having walked off his sleep, returned to the room, and the remainder of the evening was passed in absolute tranquillity.

Burgo Fitzgerald, when he left the house, turned back into Grosvenor Square, not knowing, at first, whither he was going. He took himself as far as his uncle's door, and then, having paused there for a moment, hurried on. For half an hour, or thereabouts, something like true feeling was at work within his heart. He had once more pressed to his bosom the woman he had, at any rate, thought that he had loved. He had had his arm round her, and had kissed her, and the tone with which she had called him by his name was still ringing in his ears, "Burgo!" He repeated his own name audibly to himself, as though in this way he could recall her voice. He comforted himself for a minute with the conviction that she loved him. He felt,—for a moment,—that he could live on such consolation as that! But among mortals there could, in truth, hardly be one with whom such consolation would go a shorter way. He was a man who required to have such comfort backed by patés and curaçoa to a very large extent, and now it might be doubted whether the amount of patés and curaçoa at his command would last him much longer.

He would not go in and tell his aunt at once of his failure, as he could gain nothing by doing so. Indeed, he thought that he would not tell his aunt at all. So he turned back from Grosvenor Square, and went down to his club in St. James's Street, feeling that billiards and brandy-and-water might, for the present, be the best restorative. But, as he went back, he blamed himself very greatly in the matter of those bank-notes which he had allowed Lady Monk to take from him. How had it come to pass that he had been such a dupe in her hands? When he entered his club in St. James's Street his mind had left Lady Glencora, and was hard at work considering how he might best contrive to get that spoil out of his aunt's possession.

CHAPTER LXVIII
FROM LONDON TO BADEN

On the following morning everybody was stirring by times at Mr. Palliser's house in Park Lane, and the master of that house yawned no more. There is some life in starting for a long journey, and the life is the stronger and the fuller if the things and people to be carried are numerous and troublesome. Lady Glencora was a little troublesome, and would not come down to breakfast in time. When rebuked on account of this manifest breach of engagement, she asserted that the next train would do just as well; and when Mr. Palliser proved to her, with much trouble, that the next train could not enable them to reach Paris on that day, she declared that it would be much more comfortable to take a week in going than to hurry over the ground in one day. There was nothing she wanted so much as to see Folkestone.

"If that is the case, why did not you tell me so before?" said Mr. Palliser, in his gravest voice. "Richard and the carriage went down yesterday, and are already on board the packet."

"If Richard and the carriage are already on board the packet," said Lady Glencora, "of course we must follow them, and we must put off the glories of Folkestone till we come back. Alice, haven't you observed that, in travelling, you are always driven on by some Richard or some carriage, till you feel that you are a slave?"

All this was trying to Mr. Palliser; but I think that he enjoyed it, nevertheless, and that he was happy when he found that he did get his freight off from the Pimlico Station in the proper train.

Of course Lady Glencora and Alice were very ill crossing the Channel; of course the two maids were worse than their mistresses; of course the men kept out of their master's way when they were wanted, and drank brandy-and-water with the steward down-stairs; and of course Lady Glencora declared that she would not allow herself to be carried beyond Boulogne that day;—but, nevertheless, they did get on to Paris. Had Mr. Palliser become Chancellor of the Exchequer, as he had once hoped, he could hardly have worked harder than he did work. It was he who found out which carriage had been taken for them, and who put, with his own hands, the ladies' dressing-cases and cloaks on to the seats,—who laid out the novels, which, of course, were not read by the road,—and made preparations as though this stage of their journey was to take them a week, instead of five hours and a half.

"Oh, dear! how I have slept!" said Lady Glencora, as they came near to Paris.

"I think you've been tolerably comfortable," said Mr. Palliser, joyfully.

"Since we got out of that horrid boat I have done pretty well. Why do they make the boats so nasty? I'm sure they do it on purpose."

"It would be difficult to make them nice, I suppose?" said Alice.

"It is the sea that makes them uncomfortable," said Mr. Palliser.

"Never mind; we shan't have any more of it for twelve months, at any rate. We can get to the Kurds, Alice, without getting into a packet again. That, to my way of thinking, is the great comfort of the Continent. One can go everywhere without being seasick."

Mr. Palliser said nothing, but he sighed as he thought of being absent for a whole year. He had said that such was his intention, and would not at once go back from what he himself had said. But how was he to live for twelve months out of the House of Commons? What was he to do with himself, with his intellect and his energy, during all these coming dreary days? And then,—he might have been Chancellor of the Exchequer! He might even now, at this very moment, have been upon his legs, making a financial statement of six hours' duration, to the delight of one-half of the House, and bewilderment of the other, instead of dragging cloaks across that dingy, dull, dirty waiting-room at the Paris Station, in which British subjects are kept in prison while their boxes are being tumbled out of the carriages.

"But we are not to stop here;—are we?" said Lady Glencora, mournfully.

"No, dear;—I have given the keys to Richard. We will go on at once."

"But can't we have our things?"

"In about half an hour," pleaded Mr. Palliser.

"I suppose we must bear it, Alice?" said Lady Glencora as she got into the carriage that was waiting for her.

Alice thought of the last time in which she had been in that room,— when George and Kate had been with her,—and the two girls had been quite content to wait patiently while their trunks were being examined. But Alice was now travelling with great people,—with people who never spoke of their wealth, or seemed ever to think of it, but who showed their consciousness of it at every turn of their lives. "After all," Alice had said to herself more than once, "I doubt whether the burden is not greater than the pleasure."

They stayed in Paris for a week, and during that time Alice found that she became very intimate with Mr. Palliser. At Matching she had, in truth, seen but little of him, and had known nothing. Now she began to understand his character, and learned how to talk to him, She allowed him to tell her of things in which Lady Glencora resolutely persisted in taking no interest. She delighted him by writing down in a little pocket-book the number of eggs that were consumed in Paris every day, whereas Glencora protested that the information was worth nothing unless her husband could tell her how many of the eggs were good, and how many bad. And Alice was glad to find that a hundred and fifty thousand female operatives were employed in Paris, while Lady Glencora said it was a great shame, and that they ought all to have husbands. When Mr. Palliser explained that that was impossible, because of the redundancy of the female population, she angered him very much by asserting that she saw a great many men walking about who, she was quite sure, had not wives of their own.

"I do so wish you had married him!" Glencora said to Alice that evening. "You would always have had a pocket-book ready to write down the figures, and you would have pretended to care about the eggs, and the bottles of wine, and the rest of it. As for me, I can't do it. If I see an hungry woman, I can give her my money; or if she be a sick woman, I can nurse her; or if I hear of a very wicked man, I can hate him;—but I cannot take up poverty and crime in the lump. I never believe it all. My mind isn't big enough."

They went into no society at Paris, and at the end of a week were all glad to leave it.

"I don't know that Baden will be any better," Lady Glencora said; "but, you know, we can leave that again after a bit,—and so we shall go on getting nearer to the Kurds."

To this, Mr. Palliser demurred. "I think we had better make up our mind to stay a month at Baden."

"But why should we make up our minds at all?" his wife pleaded.

"I like to have a plan," said Mr. Palliser.

"And so do I," said his wife,—"if only for the sake of not keeping it."

"There's nothing I hate so much as not carrying out my intentions," said Mr. Palliser.

Upon this, Lady Glencora shrugged her shoulders, and made a mock grimace to her cousin. All this her husband bore for a while meekly, and it must be acknowledged that he behaved very well. But, then, he had his own way in everything. Lady Glencora did not behave very well,—contradicting her husband, and not considering, as, perhaps, she ought to have done, the sacrifice he was making on her behalf. But, then, she had her own way in nothing.

She had her own way in almost nothing; but on one point she did conquer her husband. He was minded to go from Paris back to Cologne, and so down the Rhine to Baden. Lady Glencora declared that she hated the Rhine,—that, of all rivers, it was the most distasteful to her; that, of all scenery, the scenery of the Rhine was the most over-praised; and that she would be wretched all the time if she were carried that way. Upon this, Mr. Palliser referred the matter to Alice; and she, who had last been upon the Rhine with her cousins Kate and George Vavasor, voted for going to Baden by way of Strasbourg.

"We will go by Strasbourg, then," said Mr. Palliser, gallantly.

"Not that I want to see that horrid church again," said Glencora.

"Everything is alike horrid to you, I think," said her husband. "You are determined not to be contented, so that it matters very little which way we go."

"That's the truth," said his wife. "It does matter very little."

They got on to Baden,—with very little delay at Strasbourg, and found half an hotel prepared for their reception. Here the carriage was brought into use for the first time, and the mistress of the carriage talked of sending home for Dandy and Flirt. Mr. Palliser, when he heard the proposition, calmly assured his wife that the horses would not bear the journey. "They would be so out of condition," he said, "as not to be worth anything for two or three months."

"I only meant to ask for them if they could come in a balloon," said Lady Glencora.

This angered Mr. Palliser, who had really, for a few minutes, thought of pacifying his wife by sending for the horses.

"Alice," she asked, one morning, "how many eggs are eaten in Baden every morning before ten o'clock?"

Mr. Palliser, who at the moment was in the act of eating one, threw down his spoon, and pushed his plate from him.

"What's the matter, Plantagenet?" she asked.

"The matter!" he said. "But never mind; I am a fool to care for it."

"I declare I didn't know that I had done anything wrong," said Lady Glencora. "Alice, do you understand what it is?"

Alice said that she did understand very well.

"Of course she understands," said Mr. Palliser. "How can she help it? And, indeed, Miss Vavasor, I am more unhappy than I can express myself, to think that your comfort should be disturbed in this way."

"Upon my word I think Alice is doing very well," said Lady Glencora. "What is there to hurt her comfort? Nobody scolds her. Nobody tells her that she is a fool. She never jokes, or does anything wicked, and, of course, she isn't punished."

Mr. Palliser, as he wandered that day alone through the gambling-rooms at the great Assembly House, thought that, after all, it might have been better for him to have remained in London, to have become Chancellor of the Exchequer, and to have run all risks.

"I wonder whether it would be any harm if I were to put a few pieces of money on the table, just once?" Lady Glencora said to her cousin, on the evening of the same day, in one of those gambling salons. There had been some music on that evening in one side of the building, and the Pallisers had gone to the rooms. But as neither of the two ladies would dance, they had strayed away into the other apartments.

"The greatest harm in the world!" said Alice; "and what on earth could you gain by it? You don't really want any of those horrid people's money?"

"I'll tell you what I want,—something to live for,—some excitement. Is it not a shame that I see around me so many people getting amusement, and that I can get none? I'd go and sit out there, and drink beer and hear the music, only Plantagenet wouldn't let me. I think I'll throw one piece on to the table to see what becomes of it."

"I shall leave you if you do," said Alice.

"You are such a prude! It seems to me as if it must have been my special fate,—my good fate, I mean,—that has thrown me so much with you. You look after me quite as carefully as Mr. Bott and Mrs. Marsham ever did; but as I chose you myself, I can't very well complain, and I can't very well get rid of you."

"Do you want to get rid of me, Cora?"

"Sometimes. Do you know, there are moments when I almost make up my mind to go headlong to the devil,—when I think it is the best thing to be done. It's a hard thing for a woman to do, because she has to undergo so much obloquy before she gets used to it. A man can take to drinking, and gambling and all the rest of it, and nobody despises him a bit. The domestic old fogies give him lectures if they can catch him, but he isn't fool enough for that. All he wants is money, and he goes away and has his fling. Now I have plenty of money,—or, at any rate, I had,—and I never got my fling yet. I do feel so tempted to rebel, and go ahead, and care for nothing."

"Throwing one piece on to the table wouldn't satisfy that longing."

"You think I should be like the wild beast that has tasted blood, and can't be controlled. Look at all these people here. There are husbands gambling, and their wives don't know it; and wives gambling, and their husbands don't know it. I wonder whether Plantagenet ever has a fling? What a joke it would be to come and catch him!"

"I don't think you need be afraid."

"Afraid! I should like him all the better for it. If he came to me, some morning, and told me that he had lost a hundred thousand pounds, I should be so much more at my ease with him."

"You have no chance in that direction, I'm quite sure."

"None the least. He'd make a calculation that the chances were nine to seven against him, and then the speculation would seem to him to be madness."

"I don't suppose he'd wish to try, even though he were sure of winning."

"Of course not. It would be a very vulgar kind of thing then. Look,— there's an opening there. I'll just put on one napoleon."

"You shall not. If you do, I'll leave you at once. Look at the women who are playing. Is there one there whom it would not disgrace you to touch? Look what they are. Look at their cheeks, and their eyes, and their hands. Those men who rake about the money are bad enough, but the women look like fiends."

"You're not going to frighten me in that hobgoblin sort of way, you know. I don't see anything the matter with any of the people."

"What do you think of that young woman who has just got a handful of money from the man next to her?"

"I think she is very happy. I never get money given to me by handfuls, and the man to whom I belong gives me no encouragement when I want to amuse myself." They were now standing near to one end of the table, and suddenly there came to be an opening through the crowd up to the table itself. Lady Glencora, leaving Alice's side, at once stepped up and deposited a piece of gold on one of the marked compartments. As soon as she placed it she retreated again with flushed face, and took hold of Alice's arm. "There," she said, "I have done it." Alice, in her dismay, did not know what step to take. She could not scold her friend now, as the eyes of many were turned upon them, nor could she, of course, leave her, as she had threatened. Lady Glencora laughed with her peculiar little low laughter, and stood her ground. "I was determined you shouldn't frighten me out of it," she said.

Lady Glencora at Baden

One of the ministers at the table had in the meantime gone on with the cards, and had called the game; and another minister had gently pushed three or four more pieces of gold up to that which Lady Glencora had flung down, and had then cunningly caught her eye, and, with all the courtesy of which he was master, had pushed them further on towards her. She had supposed herself to be unknown there in the salon, but no doubt all the croupiers and half the company knew well enough who was the new customer at the table. There was still the space open, near to which she stood, and then someone motioned to her to come and take up the money which she had won. She hesitated, and then the croupier asked her, in that low, indifferent voice which these men always use, whether she desired that her money should remain. She nodded her head to him, and he at once drew the money back again to the spot on which she had placed the first napoleon. Again the cards were turned up softly, again the game was called, and again she won. The money was dealt out to her,—on this occasion with a full hand. There were lying there between twenty and thirty napoleons, of which she was the mistress. Her face had flushed before, but now it became very red. She caught hold of Alice, who was literally trembling beside her, and tried to laugh again. But there was that in her eye which told Alice that she was really frightened. Some one then placed a chair for her at the table, and in her confusion, not knowing what she was to do, she seated herself. "Come away," said Alice, taking hold of her, and disregarding everything but her own purpose, in the agony of the moment. "You must come away! You shall not sit there!" "I must get rid of that money," said Glencora, trying to whisper her words, "and then I will come away." The croupier again asked her if the money was to remain, and she again nodded her head. Everybody at the table was now looking at her. The women especially were staring at her,—those horrid women with vermilion cheeks, and loud bonnets half off their heads, and hard, shameless eyes, and white gloves, which, when taken off in the ardour of the game, disclosed dirty hands. They stared at her with that fixed stare which such women have, and Alice saw it all, and trembled.

Again she won. "Leave it," said Alice, "and come away." "I can't leave it," said Glencora. "If I do, there'll be a fuss. I'll go the next time." What she said was, of course, in English, and was probably understood by no one near her; but it was easy to be seen that she was troubled, and, of course, those around her looked at her the more because of her trouble. Again that little question and answer went on between her and the croupier, and on this occasion the money was piled up on the compartment—a heap of gold which made envious the hearts of many who stood around there. Alice had now both her hands on the back of the chair, needing support. If the devil should persist, and increase that stock of gold again, she must go and seek for Mr. Palliser. She knew not what else to do. She understood nothing of the table, or of its laws; but she supposed all those ministers of the game to be thieves, and believed that all villainous contrivances were within their capacity. She thought that they might go on adding to that heap so long as Lady Glencora would sit there, presuming that they might thus get her into their clutches. Of course, she did not sift her suspicions. Who does at such moments? "Come away at once, and leave it," she said, "or I shall go." At that moment the croupier raked it all up, and carried it all away; but Alice did not see that this had been done. A hand had been placed on her shoulder, and as she turned round her face her eyes met those of Mr. Palliser. "It is all gone," said Glencora, laughing. And now she, turning round, also saw her husband. "I am so glad that you are come," said Alice. "Why did you bring her here?" said Mr. Palliser. There was anger in his tone, and anger in his eye. He took his wife's arm upon his own, and walked away quickly, while Alice followed them alone. He went off at once, down the front steps of the building, towards the hotel. What he said to his wife, Alice did not hear; but her heart was swelling with the ill-usage to which she herself was subjected. Though she might have to go back alone to England, she would tell him that he was ill-treating her. She followed him on, up into their drawing-room, and there he stood with the door open in his hand for her, while Lady Glencora threw herself upon a sofa, and burst out into affected laughter. "Here's a piece of work," she said, "about a little accident."

"An accident!" said Mr. Palliser.

"Yes, an accident. You don't suppose that I sat down there meaning to win all that money?" Whereupon he looked at her with scorn.

"Mr. Palliser," said Alice, "you have treated me this evening in a manner I did not expect from you. It is clear that you blame me."

"I have not said a word, Miss Vavasor."

"No; you have not said a word. You know well how to show your anger without speaking. As I do not choose to undergo your displeasure, I will return to England by myself."

"Alice! Alice!" said Glencora, jumping up, "that is nonsense! What is all this trumpery thing about? Leave me, because he chooses to be angry about nothing?"

"Is it nothing that I find my wife playing at a common gambling-table, surrounded by all that is wretched and vile,—established there, seated, with heaps of gold before her?"

"You wrong me, Plantagenet," said Glencora. "There was only one heap, and that did not remain long. Did it, Alice?"

"It is impossible to make you ashamed of anything," he said.

"I certainly don't like being ashamed," she answered; "and don't feel any necessity on this occasion."

"If you don't object, Mr. Palliser," said Alice, "I will go to bed. You can think over all this at night,—and so can I. Good night, Glencora." Then Alice took her candle, and marched off to her own room, with all the dignity of which she was mistress.

CHAPTER LXIX
FROM BADEN TO LUCERNE

The second week in July saw Mr. Palliser's party, carriage and all, established at Lucerne, in Switzerland, safe beyond the reach of the German gambling tables. Alice Vavasor was still with them; and the reader will therefore understand that that quarrel about Lady Glencora's wickedness had been settled without any rupture. It had been settled amicably, and by the time that they had reached Lucerne, Alice was inclined to acknowledge that the whole thing was not worth notice; but for many days her anger against Mr. Palliser had not been removed, and her intimacy with him had been much checked. It was now a month since the occurrence of that little scene in the salon at Baden, which was described in the last chapter,—since Mr. Palliser had marched off with his wife, leaving Alice to follow as she best could by herself. After that, as the reader may remember, he had almost told her that she was to be blamed because of his wife's indiscretion; and when she had declared her intention of leaving him, and making her way home to England by herself, he had answered her not at all, and had allowed her to go off to her own room under the full ban of his displeasure. Since that he had made no apology to her; he had not, in so many words, acknowledged that he had wronged her; but Alice had become aware that he intended to apologize by his conduct, and she had been content so far to indulge his obstinacy as to accept this conduct on his part in lieu of any outspoken petition for pardon. The acknowledgement of a mistake and the asking for grace is almost too much for any woman to expect from such a man as Mr. Palliser.

Early on the morning after the scene in question, Lady Glencora had gone into Alice's bedroom, and had found her cousin in her dressing-gown, packing up her things, or looking as though she intended to do so. "You are not such a fool," she said, "as to think anything of what occurred yesterday?" Alice assured her that, whether fool or not, she did think a great deal of it. "In point of fact," said Alice, "I can't stand it. He expects me to take care of you, and chooses to show himself offended if you don't do just what he thinks proper; whereas, as you know well enough, I have not the slightest influence over you." All these positions Lady Glencora contradicted vigorously. Of course, Mr. Palliser had been wrong in walking out of the Assembly Rooms as he had done, leaving Alice behind him. So much Lady Glencora admitted. But this had come of his intense anxiety. "And you know what a man he is," said his wife—"how stiff, and hard, and unpleasant he can be without meaning it."—"There is no reason why I should bear his unpleasantness," said Alice. "Yes, there is,—great reason. You are to do it for the sake of friendship. And as for my not doing what you tell me, you know that's not true."

"Did I not beg you to keep away from the table?"

"Of course you did, and of course I was naughty; but that was only once. Alice, I want you more than I ever wanted you before. I cannot tell you more now, but you must stay with me."

Alice consented to come down to breakfast without any immediate continuance of her active preparations for going, and at last, of course, she stayed. When she entered the breakfast-room Mr. Palliser came up to her, and offered her his hand. She had no alternative but to take it, and then seated herself. That there was an intended apology in the manner in which he offered her toast and butter, she was convinced; and the special courtesy with which he handed her to the carriage, when she and Lady Glencora went out for their drive, after dinner, was almost as good as a petition for pardon. So the thing went on, and by degrees Mr. Palliser and Miss Vavasor were again friends.

But Alice never knew in what way the matter was settled between Mr. Palliser and his wife, or whether there was any such settling. Probably there was none. "Of course, he understands that it didn't mean anything," Lady Glencora had said. "He knows that I don't want to gamble." But let that be as it might, their sojourn at Baden was curtailed, and none of the party went up again to the Assembly Rooms before their departure.

Before establishing themselves at Lucerne they made a little tour round by the Falls of the Rhine and Zurich. In their preparations for this journey, Alice made a struggle, but a struggle in vain, to avoid a passage through Basle. It was only too clear to her that Mr. Palliser was determined to go by Basle. She could not bring herself to say that she had recollections connected with that place which would make a return to it unpleasant to her. If she could have said as much, even to Glencora, Mr. Palliser would no doubt have gone round,—round by any more distant route that might have been necessary to avoid that eternal gateway into Switzerland. But she could not say it. She was very averse to talking about herself and her own affairs, even with her cousin. Of course Lady Glencora knew the whole story of Mr. John Grey and his rejection,—and knew much also of that other story of Mr. George Vavasor. And, of course, like all Alice's friends, she hated George Vavasor, and was prepared to receive Mr. John Grey with open arms, if there were any possibility that her cousin would open her arms to him also. But Alice was so stubborn about her own affairs that her friend found it almost impossible to speak of them. "It is not that you trouble me," Alice once said, "but that you trouble yourself about that which is of no use. It is all done and over; and though I know that I have behaved badly,—very badly,—yet I believe that everything has been done for the best. I am inclined to think that I can live alone, or perhaps with my cousin Kate, more happily than I could with any husband."

"That is such nonsense."

"Perhaps so; but, at any rate, I mean to try. We Vavasors don't seem to be good at marrying."

"You want some one to break your heart for you; that's what you want," said Lady Glencora. In saying this she knew but little of the state of her friend's heart, and perhaps was hardly capable of understanding it. With all the fuss that Lady Glencora made to herself,—with all the tears that she had shed about her lost lover, and was so often shedding,—with all her continual thinking of the matter, she had never loved Burgo Fitzgerald as Alice Vavasor had loved Mr. Grey. But her nature was altogether different to that of Alice. Love with her had in it a gleam of poetry, a spice of fun, a touch of self-devotion, something even of hero-worship; but with it all there was a dash of devilry, and an aptitude almost for wickedness. She knew Burgo Fitzgerald to be a scapegrace, and she liked him the better on that account. She despised her husband because he had no vices. She would have given everything she had to Burgo,—pouring her wealth upon him with a total disregard of herself, had she been allowed to do so. She would have forgiven him sin after sin, and might perhaps have brought him round, at last, to some life not absolutely reckless and wretched. But in all that she might have done, there would have been no thoughtfulness,—no true care either for him or for herself. And now that she was married there was no thoughtfulness, or care either for herself or for her husband. She was ready to sacrifice herself for him, if any sacrifice might be required of her. She believed herself to be unfit for him, and would have submitted to be divorced,—or smothered out of the way, for the matter of that,—if the laws of the land would have permitted it. But she had never for a moment given to herself the task of thinking what conduct on her part might be the best for his welfare.

But Alice's love had been altogether of another kind,—and I am by no means sure that it was better suited for the work of this work-a-day world than that of her cousin. It was too thoughtful. I will not say that there was no poetry in it, but I will say that it lacked romance. Its poetry was too hard for romance. There was certainly in it neither fun nor wickedness; nor was there, I fear, so large a proportion of hero-worship as there always should be in a girl's heart when she gives it away. But there was in it an amount of self-devotion which none of those near to her had hitherto understood,—unless it were that one to whom the understanding of it was of the most importance. In all the troubles of her love, of her engagements, and her broken promises, she had thought more of others than of herself,—and, indeed, those troubles had chiefly come from that self-devotion. She had left John Grey because she feared that she would do him no good as his wife,—that she would not make him happy; and she had afterwards betrothed herself for a second time to her cousin, because she believed that she could serve him by marrying him. Of course she had been wrong. She had been very wrong to give up the man she did love, and more wrong again in suggesting to herself the possibility of marrying the man she did not love. She knew that she had been wrong in both, and was undergoing repentance with very bitter inward sackcloth. But she said little of all this even to her cousin.

They went to Lucerne by Basle, and put up at the big hotel with the balcony over the Rhine, which Alice remembered so well. On the first evening of her arrival she found herself again looking down upon the river, as though it might have been from the same spot which she had occupied together with George and Kate. But, in truth, that house is very large, and has many bedrooms over the water. Who has ever been through Basle, and not stood in one of them, looking down upon the father of waters? Here, on this very spot, in one of these balconies, was brought to her a letter from her cousin Kate, which was filled with tidings respecting her cousin George. Mr. Palliser brought it to her with his own hands, and she had no other alternative but to read it in his presence. "George has lost his election," the letter began. For one moment Alice thought of her money, and the vain struggle in which it had been wasted. For one moment, something like regret for the futility of the effort she had made came upon her. But it passed away at once. "It was worth our while to try it," she said to herself, and then went on with her letter. "I and Aunt Greenow are up in London," the letter went on to say, "and have just heard the news. Though I have been here for three days, and have twice sent word to him to say so, he has not been near me. Perhaps it is best that he should stay away, as I do not know how any words could pass between us that would be pleasant. The poll was finished this afternoon, and he lost his election by a large majority. There were five candidates altogether for the two seats—three Liberals, and two Conservatives. The other two Liberals were seated, and he was the last of the five. I continue to hear tidings about him from day to day,—or rather, my aunt hears them and tells them to me, which fill me full of fears as to his future career. I believe that he has abandoned his business, and that he has now no source of income. I would willingly share what I have with him; or I would do more than that. After keeping back enough to repay you gradually what he owes you, I would give him all my share of the income out of the estate. But I cannot do this while we are presumed to be enemies. I am up here to see a lawyer as to some steps which he is taking to upset grandpapa's will. The lawyer says that it is all nonsense, and that George's lawyer is not really in earnest; but I cannot do anything till the matter is settled. Dear Alice, though so much of your money is for a time gone, I am bound to congratulate you on your safety,—on what I may more truly call your escape. You will understand what my own feelings must be in writing this, after all that I did to bring you and him together,—after all my hopes and ambition respecting him. As for the money, it shall be repaid. I do not think I shall ever dare to indulge in any strong desire again. I think you will forgive me the injury I have done you;—and I know that you will pity me.

"I am here to see the London lawyer,—but not only for that. Aunt Greenow is buying her wedding clothes, and Captain Bellfield is in lodgings near to us, also buying his trousseau; or, as I should more properly say, having it bought for him. I am hardly in a mood for much mirth, but it is impossible not to laugh inwardly when she discusses before me the state of his wardrobe, and proposes economical arrangements—greatly to his disgust. At present, she holds him very tightly in hand, and makes him account for all his hours as well as all his money. 'Of course, he'll run wild directly he's married,' she said to me, yesterday; 'and, of course, there'll always be a fight about it; but the more I do to tame him now, the less wild he'll be by-and-by. And though I dare say, I shall scold him sometimes, I shall never quarrel with him.' I have no doubt all that is true; but what a fool she is to trouble herself with such a man. She says she does it for an occupation. I took courage to tell her once that a caged tiger would give her as much to do, and be less dangerous. She was angry at this, and answered me very sharply. I had tried my hand on a tiger, she said, and had felt his claws. She chose to sacrifice herself,—if a sacrifice it were to be,—when some good result might be possible. I had nothing further to say; and from that time to this we have been on the pleasantest terms possible as to the Captain. They have settled with your father to take Vavasor Hall for three years, and I suppose I shall stay with them till your return. What I may do then will depend entirely upon your doings. I feel myself to be a desolate, solitary being, without any tie to any person, or to any place. I never thought that I should feel the death of my grandfather to be such a loss to me as it has been. Except you, I have nothing left to me; and, as regards you, I have the unpleasant feeling that I have for years been endeavouring to do you the worst possible injury, and that you must regard me as an enemy from whom you have escaped indeed, but not without terrible wounds."

Alice was always angered by any assumption that her conduct to Mr. Grey had been affected by the advice or influence of her cousin Kate. But this very feeling seemed to preserve Kate from the worse anger, which might have been aroused against her, had Alice acknowledged the injury which her cousin had in truth done to her. It was undoubtedly true that had Alice neither seen nor heard from Kate during the progress of John Grey's courtship, John Grey would not have lost his wife. But against this truth Alice was always protesting within her own breast. She had been weak, foolish, irresolute,—and had finally acted with false judgement. So much she now admitted to herself. But she would not admit that any other woman had persuaded her to such weakness. "She mistakes me," Alice thought, as she put up her letter. "She is not the enemy who has wounded me."

Mr. Palliser, who had brought her the letter, was seated in the same balcony, and while Alice had been reading, had almost buried himself in newspapers which conveyed intelligence as to the general elections then in progress. He was now seated with a sheet of *The Times* in his hand, opened to its full extent,—for he had been too impatient to cut the paper,—and as he held it up in his hands before his eyes, was completely hidden beneath it. Five or six other open papers were around him, and he had not spoken a word since he had commenced his present occupation. Lady Glencora was standing on the other side of him, and she also had received letters. "Sophy tells me that you are returned for Silverbridge," she said at last.

"Who? I! yes; I'm returned," said Mr. Palliser, speaking with something like disdain in his voice as to the possibility of anybody having stood with a chance of success against him in his own family borough. For a full appreciation of the advantages of a private seat in the House of Commons let us always go to those great Whig families who were mainly instrumental in carrying the Reform Bill. The house of Omnium had been very great on that occasion. It had given up much, and had retained for family use simply the single seat at Silverbridge. But that that seat should be seriously disputed hardly suggested itself as possible to the mind of any Palliser. The Pallisers and the other great Whig families have been right in this. They have kept in their hands, as rewards for their own services to the country, no more than the country is manifestly willing to give them. "Yes; I have been returned," said Mr. Palliser. "I'm sorry to see, Miss Vavasor, that your cousin has not been so fortunate."

"So I find," said Alice. "It will be a great misfortune to him."

"Ah! I suppose so. Those Metropolitan elections cost so much trouble and so much money, and under the most favourable circumstances, are so doubtful. A man is never sure there till he has fought for his seat three or four times."

"This has been the third time with him," said Alice, "and he is a poor man."

"Dear, dear," said Mr. Palliser, who himself knew nothing of such misfortunes. "I have always thought that those seats should be left to rich commercial men who can afford to spend money upon them. Instead of that, they are generally contested by men of moderate means. Another of my friends in the House has been thrown out."

"Who is that unfortunate?" asked Lady Glencora.

"Mr. Bott," said the unthinking husband.

"Mr. Bott out!" exclaimed Lady Glencora. "Mr. Bott thrown out! I am so glad. Alice, are you not glad? The red-haired man, that used to stand about, you know, at Matching;—he has lost his seat in Parliament. I suppose he'll go and stand about somewhere in Lancashire, now."

A very indiscreet woman was poor Lady Glencora. Mr. Palliser's face became black beneath *The Times* newspaper. "I did not know," said he, "that my friend Mr. Bott and Miss Vavasor were enemies."

"Enemies! I don't suppose they were enemies," said Glencora. "But he was a man whom no one could help observing,—and disliking."

"He was a man I specially disliked," said Alice, with great courage. "He may be very well in Parliament; but I never met a man who could make himself so disagreeable in society. I really did feel myself constrained to be his enemy."

"Bravo, Alice!" said Lady Glencora.

"I hope he did nothing at Matching, to—to—to—," began Mr. Palliser, apologetically.

"Nothing especially to offend me, Mr. Palliser,—except that he had a way that I especially dislike of trying to make little secret confidences."

"And then he was so ugly," said Lady Glencora.

"I felt certain that he endeavoured to do mischief," said Alice.

"Of course he did," said Lady Glencora; "and he had a habit of rubbing his head against the papers in the rooms, and leaving a mark behind him that was quite unpardonable."

Mr. Palliser was effectually talked down, and felt himself constrained to abandon his political ally. Perhaps he did this the easier as the loss which Mr. Bott had just suffered would materially interfere with his political utility. "I suppose he will remain now among his own people," said Mr. Palliser.

"Let us hope he will," said Lady Glencora,—"and that his own people will appreciate the advantage of his presence." Then there was nothing more said about Mr. Bott.

It was evening, and while they were still sitting among their letters and newspapers, there came a shout along the water, and the noise of many voices from the bridge. Suddenly, there shot down before them in the swift running stream the heads of many swimmers in the river, and with the swimmers came boats carrying their clothes. They went by almost like a glance of light upon the waters, so rapid was the course of the current. There was the shout of voices,—the quick passage of the boats,—the uprising, some half a dozen times, of the men's hands above the surface; and then they were gone down the river, out of sight,—like morsels of wood thrown into a cataract, which are borne away instantly.

"Oh, how I wish I could do that!" said Lady Glencora.

"It seems to be very dangerous," said Mr. Palliser. "I don't know how they can stop themselves."

"Why should they want to stop themselves?" said Lady Glencora. "Think how cool the water must be, and how beautiful to be carried along so quickly, and to go on, and on, and on! I suppose we couldn't try it?"

As no encouragement was given to this proposition, Lady Glencora did not repeat it; but stood leaning on the rail of the balcony, and looking enviously down upon the water. Alice was, of course, thinking of that other evening, when perhaps the same swimmers had come down under the bridge and before the balcony, and where George Vavasor was sitting in her presence. It was, I think, on that evening, that she made up her mind to separate herself from Mr. Grey.

On the day after that, Mr. Palliser and his party went on to Lucerne, making that journey, as I have said, by slow stages; taking Schaffhausen and Zurich in their way. At Lucerne, they established themselves for some time, occupying nearly a dozen rooms in the great hotel which overlooks the lake. Here there came to them a visitor, of whose arrival I will speak in the next chapter.

CHAPTER LXX
AT LUCERNE

I am inclined to think that Mr. Palliser did not much enjoy this part of his tour abroad. When he first reached Lucerne there was no one there with whom he could associate pleasantly, nor had he any occupation capable of making his time run easily. He did not care for scenery. Close at his elbow was the finest to be had in Europe; but it was nothing to him. Had he been simply journeying through Lucerne at the proper time of the year for such a journey, when the business of the Session was over, and a little change of air needed, he could have enjoyed the thing in a moderate way, looking about him, passing on, and knowing that it was good for him to be there at that moment. But he had none of that passion for mountains and lakes, none of that positive joy in the heather, which would have compensated many another man for the loss of all that Mr. Palliser was losing. His mind was ever at home in the House of Commons, or in that august assembly which men call the Cabinet, and of the meetings of which he read from week to week the simple records. Therein were mentioned the names of those heroes to whom Fortune had been so much kinder than she had been to him; and he envied them. He took short, solitary walks, about the town, over the bridges, and along the rivers, making to himself the speeches which he would have made to full houses, had not his wife brought ruin upon all his hopes. And as he pictured to himself the glorious successes which probably never would have been his had he remained in London, so did he prophesy to himself an absolute and irremediable downfall from all political power as the result of his absence,—having, in truth, no sufficient cause for such despair. As yet, he was barely thirty, and had he been able to judge his own case as keenly as he could have judged the case of another, he would have known that a short absence might probably raise his value in the estimation of others rather than lower it. But his personal annoyance was too great to allow of his making such calculations aright. So he became fretful and unhappy; and though he spoke no word of rebuke to his wife, though he never hinted that she had robbed him of his glories, he made her conscious by his manner that she had brought him to this miserable condition.

Lady Glencora herself had a love for the mountains and lakes, but it was a love of that kind which requires to be stimulated by society, and which is keenest among cold chickens, picnic-pies, and the flying of champagne corks. When they first entered Switzerland she was very enthusiastic, and declared her intention of climbing up all the mountains, and going through all the passes. She endeavoured to induce her husband to promise that she should be taken up Mont Blanc. And I think she would have carried this on, and would have been taken up Mont Blanc, had Mr. Palliser's aspirations been congenial. But they were not congenial, and Lady Glencora soon lost all her enthusiasm. By the time that they were settled at Lucerne she had voted the mountains to be bores, and had almost learned to hate the lake, which she declared always made her wet through when she got into a small boat, and sea-sick when she put her foot in a large one. At Lucerne they made no acquaintances, Mr. Palliser being a man not apt to new friendships. They did not even dine at the public table, though Lady Glencora had expressed a wish to do so. Mr. Palliser did not like it, and of course Lady Glencora gave way. There were, moreover, some marital passages which were not pleasant to a third person. They did not scold each other; but Lady Glencora would make little speeches of which her husband disapproved. She would purposely irritate him by continuing her tone of badinage, and then Mr. Palliser would become fretful, and would look as though the cares of the world were too many for him. I cannot, therefore, say that Alice had much to make the first period of her sojourn at Lucerne a period of enjoyment.

But when they had been there about a fortnight, a stranger arrived, whose coming at any rate lent the grace of some excitement to their lives. Their custom was to breakfast at nine,—or as near nine as Lady Glencora could be induced to appear,—and then Mr. Palliser would read till three. At that hour he would walk forth by himself, after having handed the two ladies into their carriage, and they would be driven about for two hours. "How I do hate this carriage," Lady Glencora said one day. "I do so wish it would come to grief, and be broken to pieces. I wonder whether the Swiss people think that we are going to be driven about here for ever." There were moments, however, which seemed to indicate that Lady Glencora had something to tell her cousin, which, if told, would alter the monotony of their lives. Alice, however, would not press her for her secret.

"If you have anything to tell, why don't you tell it?" Alice once said.

"You are so hard," said Lady Glencora.

"So you tell me very often," Alice replied; "and it is not complimentary. But hard or soft, I won't make a petition for your confidence." Then Lady Glencora said something savage, and the subject was dropped for a while.

But we must go back to the stranger. Mr. Palliser had put the ladies into their carriage, and was standing between the front door of the hotel and the lake on a certain day, doubting whether he would walk up the hill to the left or turn into the town on the right, when he was accosted by an English gentleman, who, raising his hat, said that he believed that he spoke to Mr. Palliser.

"I am Mr. Palliser," said our friend, very courteously, returning the salute, and smiling as he spoke. But though he smiled, and though he was courteous, and though he raised his hat, there was something in his look and voice which would not have encouraged any ordinary stranger to persevere. Mr. Palliser was not a man with whom it was easy to open an acquaintance.

"My name is John Grey," said the stranger.

Then the smile was dropped, the look of extreme courtesy disappeared, the tone of Mr. Palliser's voice was altered, and he put out his hand. He knew enough of Mr. John Grey's history to be aware that Mr. John Grey was a man with whom he might permit himself to become acquainted. After the interchange of a very few words, the two men started off for a walk together.

"Perhaps you don't wish to meet the carriage?" said Mr. Palliser. "If so, we had better go through the town and up the river."

They went through the town, and up the river, and when Mr. Palliser, on his return, was seen by Alice and Lady Glencora, he was alone. They dined together, and nothing was said. Together they sauntered out in the evening, and together came in and drank their tea; but still nothing was said. At last, Alice and her cousin took their candles from Mr. Palliser's hands and left the sitting-room for the night.

"Alice," said Lady Glencora, as soon as they were in the passage together, "I have been dying for this time to come. I could not speak before, or I should have made blunders, and so would you. Let us go into your room at once. Who do you think is here, at Lucerne, in this house, at this very moment?"

Alice knew at once who it was. She knew, immediately, that Mr. Grey had followed her, though no word had been written to her or spoken to her on the subject since that day on which he himself had told her that they would meet abroad. But though she was quite sure, she did not mention his name. "Who is it, Glencora?" she asked, very calmly.

"Whom in all the world would you best like to see?" said Glencora.

"My cousin Kate, certainly," said Alice.

"Then it is not your cousin Kate. And I don't believe you;—or else you're a fool."

Alice was accustomed to Lady Glencora's mode of talking, and therefore did not think much of this. "Perhaps I am a fool," she said.

"Only I know you are not. But I am not at all so sure as to your being no hypocrite. The person I mean is a gentleman, of course. Why don't you show a little excitement, at any rate? When Plantagenet told me, just before dinner, I almost jumped out of my shoes. He was going to tell you himself after dinner, in the politest way in the world, no doubt, and just as the servants were carrying away the apples. I thought it best to save you from that; but, I declare, I believe I might have left him to do it; it would have had no effect upon you. Who is it that has come, do you suppose?"

"Of course I know now," said Alice, very calmly, "that Mr. John Grey has come."

"Yes, Mr. John Grey has come. He is here in this house at this minute;— or, more probably, waiting outside by the lake till he shall see a light in your bedroom." Then Lady Glencora paused for a moment, waiting that Alice might say something. But Alice said nothing. "Well?" said Lady Glencora, rising up from her chair. "Well?"

"Well?" said Alice.

"Have you nothing to say? Is it the same to you as though Mr. Smith had come?"

"No; not exactly the same. I am quite alive to the importance of Mr. Grey's arrival, and shall probably lie awake all night thinking about it,—if it will do you any good to know that; but I don't feel that I have much to say about it."

"I wish I had let Mr. Palliser tell you, in an ordinary way, before all the servants. I do indeed."

"It would not have made much difference."

"Not the least, I believe. I wonder whether you ever did care for anybody in your life,—for him, or for that other one, or for anybody. For nobody, I believe;—except your cousin Kate. Still waters, they say, run deep; and sometimes I think your waters run too deep for me to fathom. I suppose I may go now, if you have got nothing more to say?"

"What do you want me to say? Of course I know why he has come here. He told me he should come."

"And you have never said a word about it."

"He told me he should come, and I thought it better not to say a word about it. He might change his mind, or anything might happen. I told him not to come; and it would have been much better that he should have remained away."

"Why;—why;—why would it be better?"

"Because his being here will do no good to any one."

"No good! It seems to me impossible but that it should do all the good in the world. Look here, Alice. If you do not altogether make it up with him before to-morrow evening, I shall believe you to be utterly heartless. Had I been you I should have been in his arms before this. I'll go now, and leave you to lie awake, as you say you will." Then she left the room, but returned in a moment to ask another question. "What is Plantagenet to say to him about seeing you to-morrow? Of course he has asked permission to come and call."

"He may come if he pleases. You don't think I have quarrelled with him, or would refuse to see him!"

"And may we ask him to dine with us?"

"Oh, yes."

"And make up a picnic, and all the rest of it. In fact, he is to be regarded as only an ordinary person. Well;—good night. I don't understand you, that's all."

It may be doubted whether Alice understood herself. As soon as her friend was gone, she put out her candle and seated herself at the open window of her room, looking out upon the moonlight as it played upon the lake. Would he be there, thinking of her, looking up, perhaps, as Glencora had hinted, to see if he could distinguish her light among the hundred that would be flickering across the long front of the house. If it were so, at any rate he should not see her, so she drew the curtain, and sat there watching the lake. It was a pity that he should have come, and yet she loved him dearly for coming. It was a pity that he should have come, as his coming could lead to no good result. Of this she assured herself over and over again, and yet she hardly knew why she was so sure of it. Glencora had called her hard; but her conviction on that matter had not come from hardness. Now that she was alone, her heart was full of love, of the soft romance of love towards this man; and yet she felt that she ought not to marry him, even though he might still be willing to take her. That he was still willing to take her, that he desired to have her for his wife in spite of all the injury she had done him, there could be no doubt. Why else had he followed her to Switzerland? And she remembered, now at this moment, how he had told her at Cheltenham that he would never consider her to be lost to him, unless she should, in truth, become the wife of another man. Why, then, should it not be as he wished it?

Alice.

She asked herself the question, and did not answer it; but still she felt that it might not be so. She had no right to such happiness after the evil that she had done. She had been driven by a frenzy to do that which she herself could not pardon; and having done it, she could not bring herself to accept the position which should have been the reward of good conduct. She could not analyse the causes which made her feel that she must still refuse the love that was proffered to her; she could not clearly read her own thoughts; but the causes were as I have said, and such was the true reading of her thoughts. Had she simply refused his hand after she had once accepted it,—had she refused it, and then again changed her mind, she could have brought herself to ask him to forgive her. But she had done so much more than this, and so much worse! She had affianced herself to another man since she had belonged to him,—since she had been his, as his future wife. What must he not think of her, and what not suspect? Then she remembered those interviews which she had had with her cousin since she had written to him, accepting his offer. When he had been with her in Queen Anne Street she had shrunk from all outward signs of a love which she did not feel. There had been no caress between them. She had not allowed him to touch her with his lips. But it was impossible that the nature of that mad engagement between her and her cousin George should ever be made known to Mr. Grey. She sat there wiping the tears from her eyes as she looked for his figure among the figures by the lake-side; but, as she sat there, she promised herself no happiness from his coming. Oh! reader, can you forgive her in that she had sinned against the softness of her feminine nature? I think that she may be forgiven, in that she had never brought herself to think lightly of her own fault.

If he were there, by the lake-side, she did not see him. I think we may say that John Grey was not a man to console himself in his love by looking up at his lady's candle. He was one who was capable of doing as much as most men in the pursuit of his love,—as he proved to be the case when he followed Alice to Cheltenham, and again to London, and now again to Lucerne; but I doubt whether a glimmer from her bedroom-window, had it been unmistakably her own glimmer, and not that of some ugly old French woman who might chance to sleep next to her, would have done him much good. He had come to Lucerne with a purpose, which purpose, if it might be possible, he meant to carry out; but I think he was already in bed, being tired with long travel, before Lady Glencora had left Alice's room.

At breakfast the next morning nothing was said for a while about the new arrival. At last Mr. Palliser ventured to speak. "Glencora has told you, I think, that Mr. Grey is here? Mr. Grey is an old friend of yours, I believe?"

Alice, keeping her countenance as well as she was able, said Mr. Grey had been, and, indeed, was, a very dear friend of hers. Mr. Palliser knew the whole story, and what was the use of any little attempt at dissimulation? "I shall be glad to see him,—if you will allow me?" she went on to say.

"Glencora suggests that we should ask him to dinner," said Mr. Palliser; and then that matter was settled.

But Mr. Grey did not wait till dinner-time to see Alice. Early in the morning his card was brought up, and Lady Glencora, as soon as she saw the name, immediately ran away.

"Indeed you need not go," said Alice.

"Indeed I shall go," said her ladyship. "I know what's proper on these occasions, if you don't."

So she went, whisking herself along the passages with a little run; and Mr. Grey, as he was shown into her ladyship's usual sitting-room, saw the skirt of her ladyship's dress as she whisked herself off towards her husband.

"I told you I should come," he said, with his ordinary sweet smile. "I told you that I should follow you, and here I am."

He took her hand, and held it, pressing it warmly. She hardly knew with what words first to address him, or how to get her hand back from him.

"I am very glad to see you,—as an old friend," she said; "but I hope—"

"Well;—you hope what?"

"I hope you have had some better cause for travelling than a desire to see me?"

"No, dearest; no. I have had no better cause, and, indeed, none other. I have come on purpose to see you; and had Mr. Palliser taken you off to Asia or Africa, I think I should have felt myself compelled to follow him. You know why I follow you?"

"Hardly," said she,—not finding at the moment any other word that she could say.

"Because I love you. You see what a plain-spoken John Bull I am, and how I come to the point at once. I want you to be my wife; and they say that perseverance is the best way when a man has such a want as that."

"You ought not to want it," she said, whispering the words as though she were unable to speak them out loud.

"But I do, you see. And why should I not want it?"

"I am not fit to be your wife."

"I am the best judge of that, Alice. You have to make up your mind whether I am fit to be your husband."

"You would be disgraced if you were to take me, after all that has passed;—after what I have done. What would other men say of you when they knew the story?"

"Other men, I hope, would be just enough to say, that when I had made up my mind, I was tolerably constant in keeping to it. I do not think they could say much worse of me than that."

"They would say that you had been jilted, and had forgiven the jilt."

"As far as the forgiveness goes, they would tell the truth. But, indeed, Alice, I don't very much care what men do say of me."

"But I care, Mr. Grey;—and though you may forgive me, I cannot forgive myself. Indeed I know now, as I have known all along, that I am not fit to be your wife. I am not good enough. And I have done that which makes me feel that I have no right to marry anyone." These words she said, jerking out the different sentences almost in convulsions; and when she had come to the end of them, the tears were streaming down her cheeks. "I have thought about it, and I will not. I will not. After what has passed, I know that it will be better,—more seemly, that I should remain as I am."

Soon after that she left him, not, however, till she had told him that she would meet him again at dinner, and had begged him to treat her simply as a friend. "In spite of everything, I hope that we may always be friends,—dear friends," she said.

"I hope we may," he answered;—"the very dearest." And then he left her.

In the afternoon he again encountered Mr. Palliser, and having thought over the matter since his interview with Alice, he resolved to tell his whole story to his new acquaintance,—not in order that he might ask for counsel from him, for in this matter he wanted no man's advice,—but that he might get some assistance. So the two men walked off together, up the banks of the clear-flowing Reuss, and Mr. Palliser felt the comfort of having a companion.

"I have always liked her," said Mr. Palliser, "though, to tell the truth, I have twice been very angry with her."

"I have never been angry with her," said the lover.

"And my anger was in both instances unjust. You may imagine how great is my confidence in her, when I have thought she was the best companion my wife could have for a long journey, taken under circumstances that were—that were—; but I need not trouble you with that."

So great had been the desolation of Mr. Palliser's life since his banishment from London that he almost felt tempted to tell the story of his troubles to this absolute stranger. But he bethought himself of the blood of the Pallisers, and refrained. There are comforts which royalty may never enjoy, and luxuries in which such men as Plantagenet Palliser may not permit themselves to indulge.

"About her and her character I have no doubt in the world," said Grey. "In all that she has done I think that I have seen her motives; and though I have not approved of them, I have always known them to be pure and unselfish. She has done nothing that I did not forgive as soon as it was done. Had she married that man, I should have forgiven her even that,—though I should have known that all her future life was destroyed, and much of mine also. I think I can make her happy if she will marry me, but she must first be taught to forgive herself. Living as she is with you, and with your wife, she may, perhaps, just now be more under your influence and your wife's than she can possibly be under mine." Whereupon, Mr. Palliser promised that he would do what he could. "I think she loves me," said Mr. Grey.

Mr. Palliser said that he was sure she did, though what ground he had for such assurance I am quite unable to surmise. He was probably desirous of saying the most civil thing which occurred to him.

The little dinner-party that evening was pleasant enough, and nothing more was said about love. Lady Glencora talked nonsense to Mr. Grey, and Mr. Palliser contradicted all the nonsense which his wife talked. But this was all done in such a way that the evening passed away pleasantly. It was tacitly admitted among them that Mr. Grey was to be allowed to come among them as a friend, and Lady Glencora managed to say one word to him aside, in which she promised to give him her most cordial cooperation.

CHAPTER LXXI
SHOWING HOW GEORGE VAVASOR RECEIVED A VISIT

We must go back for a few pages to scenes which happened in London during this summer, so that the reader may understand Mr. Grey's position when he reached Lucerne. He had undergone another quarrel with George Vavasor, and something of the circumstances of that quarrel must be told.

It has been already said that George Vavasor lost his election for the Chelsea Districts, after all the money which he had spent,—money which he had been so ill able to spend, and on which he had laid his hands in a manner so disreputable! He had received two thousand pounds from the bills which Alice had executed on his behalf,—or rather, had received the full value of three out of the four bills, and a part of the value of the fourth, on which he had been driven to raise what immediate money he had wanted by means of a Jew bill-discounter. One thousand pounds he had paid over at once into the hands of Mr. Scruby, his Parliamentary election agent, towards the expenses of his election; and when the day of polling arrived had exactly in his hands the sum of five hundred pounds. Where he was to get more when this was gone he did not know. If he were successful,—if the enlightened constituents of the Chelsea Districts, contented with his efforts on behalf of the River Bank, should again send him to Parliament, he thought that he might still carry on the war. A sum of ready money he would have in hand; and, as to his debts, he would be grandly indifferent to any consideration of them. Then there might be pickings in the way of a Member of Parliament of his calibre. Companies,—mercantile companies,—would be glad to have him as a director, paying him a guinea a day, or perhaps more, for his hour's attendance. Railways in want of vice-chairmen might bid for his services; and in the City he might turn that "M.P." which belonged to him to good account in various ways. With such a knowledge of the City world as he possessed, he thought that he could pick up a living in London, if only he could retain his seat in Parliament.

But what was he to do if he could not retain it? No sooner had Mr. Scruby got the thousand pounds into his clutches than he pressed for still more money. George Vavasor, with some show of justice on his side, pointed out to this all-devouring agent that the sum demanded had already been paid. This Mr. Scruby admitted, declaring that he was quite prepared to go on without any further immediate remittance, although by doing so might subject himself to considerable risk. But another five hundred pounds, paid at once, would add greatly to the safety of the seat; whereas eight hundred judiciously thrown in at the present moment would make the thing quite secure. But Vavasor swore to himself that he would not part with another shilling. Never had he felt such love for money as he did for that five hundred pounds which he now held in his pocket. "It's no use," he said to Mr. Scruby. "I have done what you asked, and would have done more had you asked for more at that time. As it is, I cannot make another payment before the election." Mr. Scruby shrugged his shoulders, and said that he would do his best. But George Vavasor soon knew that the man was not doing his best,—that the man had, in truth, abandoned his cause. The landlord of the "Handsome Man" jeered him when he went there canvassing. "Laws, Mr. Vavasor!" said the landlord of the "Handsome Man," "you're not at all the fellow for us chaps along the river,—you ain't. You're afraid to come down with the stumpy,—that's what you are." George put his hand upon his purse, and acknowledged to himself that he had been afraid to come down with the stumpy.

For the last five days of the affair George Vavasor knew that his chance was gone. Mr. Scruby's face, manner, and words, told the result of the election as plainly as any subsequent figures could do. He would be absent when Vavasor called, or the clerk would say that he was absent. He would answer in very few words, constantly shrugging his shoulders. He would even go away and leave the anxious candidate while he was in the middle of some discussion as to his plans. It was easy to see that Mr. Scruby no longer regarded him as a successful man, and the day of the poll showed very plainly how right Mr. Scruby had been.

George Vavasor was rejected, but he still had his five hundred pounds in his pocket. Of course he was subject to that mortification which a man feels when he reflects that some little additional outlay would have secured his object. Whether it might have been so, or not, who can say? But there he was, with the gateway between the lamps barred against him, ex-Member of Parliament for the Chelsea Districts, with five hundred pounds in his pocket, and little or nothing else that he could call his own. What was he to do with himself?

After trying to make himself heard upon the hustings when he was rejected, and pledging himself to stand again at the next election, he went home to his lodgings in Cecil Street, and endeavoured to consider calmly his position in the world. He had lost his inheritance. He had abandoned one profession after another, and was now beyond the pale of another chance in that direction. His ambition had betrayed him, and there were no longer possible to him any hopes of political activity. He had estranged from himself every friend that he had ever possessed. He had driven from him with violence the devotion even of his sister. He had robbed the girl whom he intended to marry of her money, and had so insulted her that no feeling of amity between them was any longer possible. He had nothing now but himself and that five hundred pounds, which he still held in his pocket. What should he do with himself and his money? He thought over it all with outer calmness for awhile, as he sat there in his arm-chair.

From the moment in which he had first become convinced that the election would go against him, and that he was therefore ruined on all sides, he had resolved that he would be calm amidst his ruin. Sometimes he assumed a little smile, as though he were laughing at his own position. Mr. Bott's day of rejection had come before his own, and he had written to Mr. Bott a drolling note of consolation and mock sympathy. He had shaken hands with Mr. Scruby, and had poked his fun at the agent, bidding him be sure to send in his little bill soon. To all who accosted him, he replied in a subrisive tone; and he bantered Calder Jones, whose seat was quite sure, till Calder Jones began to have fears that were quite unnecessary. And now, as he sat himself down, intending to come to some final decision as to what he would do, he maintained the same calmness. He smiled in the same way, though there was no one there to see the smile. He laughed even audibly once or twice, as he vainly endeavoured to persuade himself that he was able to regard the world and all that belonged to it as a bubble.

There came to him a moment in which he laughed out very audibly. "Ha! ha!" he shouted, rising up from his chair, and he walked about the room, holding a large paper-knife in his hand. "Ha! ha!" Then he threw the knife away from him, and thrusting his hands into his trousers-pockets, laughed again—"Ha! ha!" He stood still in the centre of the room, and the laughter was very plainly visible on his face, had there been anybody there to see it.

But suddenly there was a change upon his face, as he stood there all alone, and his eyes became fierce, and the cicatrice that marred his countenance grew to be red and ghastly, and he grinned with his teeth, and he clenched his fists as he still held them within his pockets. "Curse him!" he said out loud. "Curse him, now and for ever!" He had broken down in his calmness, when he thought of that old man who had opposed him during his life, and had ruined him at his death. "May all the evils which the dead can feel cling to him for ever and ever!" His laughter was all gone, and his assumed tranquillity had deserted him. Walking across the room, he struck his foot against a chair; upon this, he took the chair in his hands, and threw it across the room. But he hardly arrested the torrent of his maledictions as he did so. What good was it that he should lie to himself by that mock tranquillity, or that false laughter? He lied to himself no longer, but uttered a song of despair that was true enough. What should he do? Where should he go? From what fountain should he attempt to draw such small draughts of the water of comfort as might support him at the present moment? Unless a man have some such fountain to which he can turn, the burden of life cannot be borne. For the moment, Vavasor tried to find such fountain in a bottle of brandy which stood near him. He half filled a tumbler, and then, dashing some water on it, swallowed it greedily. "By ——!" he said, "I believe it is the best thing a man can do."

But where was he to go? to whom was he to turn himself? He went to a high desk which stood in one corner of the room, and unlocking it, took out a revolving pistol, and for a while carried it about with him in his hand. He turned it up, and looked at it, and tried the lock, and snapped it without caps, to see that the barrel went round fairly. "It's a beggarly thing to do," he said, and then he turned the pistol down again; "and if I do do it, I'll use it first for another purpose." Then he poured out for himself more brandy-and-water, and having drunk it, he threw himself upon the sofa, and seemed to sleep.

But he did not sleep, and by-and-by there came a slight single knock at the door, which he instantly answered. But he did not answer it in the usual way by bidding the comer to come in. "Who's there?" he said. Then the comer attempted to enter, turning the handle of the door. But the door had been locked, and the key was on Vavasor's side. "Who's there?" he asked again, speaking out loudly, but in an angry voice. "It is I," said a woman's voice. "D——ation!" said George Vavasor.

The woman heard him, but she made no sign of having heard him. She simply remained standing where she was till something further should be done within. She knew the man well, and knew that she must bide his time. She was very patient,—and for the time was meek, though it might be that there would come an end to her meekness. Vavasor, when he had heard her voice, and knew who was there, had again thrown himself on the sofa. There flashed across his mind another thought or two as to his future career,—another idea about the pistol, which still lay upon the table. Why should he let the intruder in, and undergo the nuisance of a disagreeable interview, if the end of all things might come in time to save him from such trouble? There he lay for ten minutes thinking, and then the low single knock was heard again. He jumped upon his feet, and his eyes were full of fire. He knew that it was useless to bid her go and leave him. She would sit there, if it were through the whole night. Should he open the door and strangle her, and pass out over her with the pistol in his hand, so that he might make that other reckoning which he desired to accomplish, and then never come back any more?

He took a turn through the room, and then walked gently up to the door, and undid the lock. He did not open the door, nor did he bid his visitor enter, but having made the way easy for her if she chose to come in, he walked back to the sofa and threw himself on it again. As he did so, he passed his hand across the table so as to bring the pistol near to himself at the place where he would be lying. She paused a moment after she had heard the sound of the key, and then she made her way into the room. He did not at first speak to her. She closed the door very gently, and then, looking around, came up to the foot of the sofa. She paused a moment, waiting for him to address her; but as he said nothing, but lay there looking at her, she was the first to speak. "George," she said, "what am I to do?"

She was a woman of about thirty years of age, dressed poorly, in old garments, but still with decency, and with some attempt at feminine prettiness. There were flowers in the bonnet on her head, though the bonnet had that unmistakable look of age which is quite as distressing to bonnets as it is to women, and the flowers themselves were battered and faded. She had long black ringlets on each cheek, hanging down much below her face, and brought forward so as to hide in some degree the hollowness of her jaws. Her eyes had a peculiar brightness, but now they left on those who looked at her cursorily no special impression as to their colour. They had been blue,—that dark violet blue, which is so rare, but is sometimes so lovely. Her forehead was narrow, her mouth was small, and her lips were thin; but her nose was perfect in its shape, and, by the delicacy of its modelling, had given a peculiar grace to her face in the days when things had gone well with her, when her cheeks had been full with youth and good living, and had been dimpled by the softness of love and mirth. There were no dimples there now, and all the softness which still remained was that softness which sorrow and continual melancholy give to suffering women. On her shoulders she wore a light shawl, which was fastened to her bosom with a large clasp brooch. Her faded dress was supported by a wide crinoline, but the under garment had lost all the grace of its ancient shape, and now told that woman's tale of poverty and taste for dress which is to be read in the outward garb of so many of Eve's daughters. The whole story was told so that those who ran might read it. When she had left her home this afternoon, she had struggled hard to dress herself so that something of the charm of apparel might be left to her; but she had known of her own failure at every twist that she had given to her gown, and at every jerk with which she had settled her shawl. She had despaired at every push she had given to her old flowers, vainly striving to bring them back to their old forms; but still she had persevered. With long tedious care she had mended the old gloves which would hardly hold her fingers. She had carefully hidden the rags of her sleeves. She had washed her little shrivelled collar, and had smoothed it out painfully. It had been a separate grief to her that she could find no cuffs to put round her wrists;—and yet she knew that no cuffs could have availed her anything. Nothing could avail her now. She expected nothing from her visit; yet she had come forth anxiously, and would have waited there throughout the whole night had access to his room been debarred to her. "George," she said, standing at the bottom of the sofa, "what am I to do?"

As he lay there with his face turned towards her, the windows were at her back, and he could see her very plainly. He saw and appreciated the little struggles she had made to create by her appearance some reminiscence of her former self. He saw the shining coarseness of the long ringlets which had once been softer than silk. He saw the sixpenny brooch on her bosom where he had once placed a jewel, the price of which would now have been important to him. He saw it all, and lay there for a while, silently reading it.

"Don't let me stand here," she said, "without speaking a word to me."

"I don't want you to stand there," he said.

"That's all very well, George. I know you don't want me to stand here. I know you don't want to see me ever again."

"Never."

"I know it. Of course I know it. But what am I to do? Where am I to go for money? Even you would not wish that I should starve?"

"That's true, too. I certainly would not wish it. I should be delighted to hear that you had plenty to eat and plenty to drink, and plenty of clothes to wear. I believe that's what you care for the most, after all."

"It was only for your sake,—because you liked it."

"Well;—I did like it; but that has come to an end, as have all my other likings. You know very well that I can do nothing more for you. What good do you do yourself by coming here to annoy me? Have I not told you over and over again that you were never to look for me here? Is it likely that I should give you money now, simply because you have disobeyed me!"

"Where else was I to find you?"

"Why should you have found me at all? I don't want you to find me. I shall give you nothing;—not a penny. You know very well that we've had all that out before. When I put you into business I told you that we were to see no more of each other."

"Business!" she said. "I never could make enough out of the shop to feed a bird."

"That wasn't my fault. Putting you there cost me over a hundred pounds, and you consented to take the place."

"I didn't consent. I was obliged to go there because you took my other home away from me."

"Have it as you like, my dear. That was all I could do for you;—and more than most men would have done, when all things are considered." Then he got up from the sofa, and stood himself on the hearthrug, with his back to the fireplace. "At any rate, you may be sure of this, Jane;—that I shall do nothing more. You have come here to torment me, but you shall get nothing by it."

"I have come here because I am starving."

"I have nothing for you. Now go;" and he pointed to the door. Nevertheless, for more than three years of his life this woman had been his closest companion, his nearest friend, the being with whom he was most familiar. He had loved her according to his fashion of loving, and certainly she had loved him. "Go," he said repeating the word very angrily. "Do as I bid you, or it will be the worse for you."

"Will you give me a sovereign?"

"No;—I will give you nothing. I have desired you not to come to me here, and I will not pay for you coming."

"Then I will not go;" and the woman sat down upon a chair at the foot of the table. "I will not go till you have given me something to buy food. You may put me out of the room if you can, but I will lie at the door of the stairs. And if you get me out of the house, I will sit upon the door-step."

"If you play that game, my poor girl, the police will take you."

"Let them. It has come to that with me, that I care for nothing. Out of this I will not go till you give me money—unless I am put out."

And for this she had dressed herself with so much care, mending her gloves, and darning her little fragments of finery! He stood looking at her, with his hands thrust deep into his pockets,—looking at her and thinking what he had better do to rid himself of her presence. If he even quite resolved to take that little final journey of which we have spoken, with the pistol in his hand, why should he not go and leave her there? Or, for the matter of that, why should he not make her his heir to all remainder of his wealth? What he still had left was sufficient to place her in a seventh heaven of the earth. He cared but little for her, and was at this moment angry with her; but there was no one for whom he cared more, and no friend with whom he was less angry. But then his mind was not quite made up as to that final journey. Therefore he desired to rid himself and his room of the nuisance of her presence.

"Jane," he said, looking at her again with that assumed tranquillity of which I have spoken, "you talk of starving and of being ruined,—"

"I am starving. I have not a shilling in the world."

"Perhaps it may be a comfort to you in your troubles to know that I am, at any rate, as badly off as you are? I won't say that I am starving, because I could get food to eat at this moment if I wanted it; but I am utterly ruined. My property,—what should have been mine,—has been left away from me. I have lost the trumpery seat in Parliament for which I have paid so much. All my relations have turned their backs upon me—"

"Are you not going to be married?" she said, rising quickly from her chair and coming close to him.

"Married! No;—but I am going to blow my brains out. Look at that pistol, my girl. Of course you won't think that I am in earnest,—but I am."

She looked up into his face piteously. "Oh! George," she said, "you won't do that?"

"Oh! George," she said, "you won't do that?"

"But I shall do that. There is nothing else left for me to do. You talk to me about starving. I tell you that I should have no objection to be starved, and so be put an end to in that way. It's not so bad as some other ways when it comes gradually. You and I, Jane, have not played our cards very well. We have staked all that we had, and we've been beaten. It's no good whimpering after what's lost. We'd better go somewhere else and begin a new game."

"Go where?" said she.

"Ah!—that's just what I can't tell you."

"George," she said, "I'll go anywhere with you. If what you say is true,—if you're not going to be married, and will let me come to you, I will work for you like a slave. I will indeed. I know I'm poorly looking now—"

"My girl, where I'm going, I shall not want any slave; and as for your looks—when you go there too,—they'll be of no matter, as far as I am able to judge."

"But, George, where are you going?"

"Wherever people do go when their brains are knocked out of them; or, rather, when they have knocked out their own brains, — if that makes any difference."

"George," — she came up to him now, and took hold of him by the front of his coat, and for the moment he allowed her to do so, — "George, you frighten me. Do not do that. Say that you will not do that!"

"But I am just saying that I shall."

"Are you not afraid of God's anger? You and I have been very wicked."

"I have, my poor girl. I don't know much about your wickedness. I've been like Topsy; — indeed I am a kind of second Topsy myself. But what's the good of whimpering when it's over?"

"It isn't over; it isn't over, — at any rate for you."

"I wish I knew how I could begin again. But all this is nonsense, Jane, and you must go."

"You must tell me, first, that you are not going to — kill yourself."

"I don't suppose I shall do it to-night, — or, perhaps, not to-morrow. Very probably I may allow myself a week, so that your staying here can do no good. I merely wanted to make you understand that you are not the only person who has come to grief."

"And you are not going to be married?"

"No; I'm not going to be married, certainly."

"And I must go now?"

"Yes; I think you'd better go now." Then she rose and went, and he let her leave the room without giving her a shilling! His bantering tone, in speaking of his own position, had been successful. It had caused her to take herself off quietly. She knew enough of his usual manner to be aware that his threats of self destruction were probably unreal; but, nevertheless, what he had said had created some feeling in her heart which had induced her to yield to him, and go away in peace.

CHAPTER LXXII
SHOWING HOW GEORGE VAVASOR PAID A VISIT

It was nearly seven o'clock in the evening,—a hot, July evening,—when the woman went from Vavasor's room, and left him there alone. It was necessary that he should immediately do something. In the first place he must dine, unless he meant to carry out his threat, and shoot himself at once. But he had no such intention as that, although he stood for some minutes with the pistol in his hand. He was thinking then of shooting some one else. But he resolved that, if he did so at all, he would not do it on that evening, and he locked up the pistol again in the standing desk. After that, he took up some papers, referring to steam packets, which were lying on his table. They contained the programmes of different companies, and showed how one vessel went on one day to New York, and another on another day would take out a load of emigrants for New Zealand and Australia. "That's a good line," said he, as he read a certain prospectus. "They generally go to the bottom, and save a man from any further trouble on his own account." Then he dressed himself, putting on his boots and coat, and went out to his club for his dinner.

London was still fairly full,—that is to say, the West End was not deserted, although Parliament had been broken up two months earlier than usual, in preparation for the new elections. Many men who had gone down into the country were now back again in town, and the dining-room at the club was crowded. Men came up to him condoling with him, telling him that he was well rid of a great nuisance, that the present Members for the Chelsea Districts would not sit long, or that there would be another general election in a year or two. To all these little speeches he made cheerful replies, and was declared by his acquaintance to bear his disappointment well. Calder Jones came to him and talked hunting talk, and Vavasor expressed his intention of being at Roebury in November. "You had better join our club," said Calder Jones. In answer to which Vavasor said that he thought he would join the club. He remained in the smoking-room till nearly eleven; then he took himself home, and remained up half the night destroying papers. Every written document on which he could lay his hands he destroyed. All the pigeon-holes of his desk were emptied out, and their contents thrown into the flames. At first he looked at the papers before he burned them; but the trouble of doing so soon tired him, and he condemned them all, as he came to them, without examination. Then he selected a considerable amount of his clothes, and packed up two portmanteaus, folding his coats with care, and inspecting his boots narrowly, so that he might see which, out of the large number before him, it might be best worth his while to take with him. When that was done, he took from his desk a bag of sovereigns, and, pouring them out upon the table, he counted them out into parcels of twenty-five each, and made them up carefully into rouleaus with paper. These, when complete, he divided among the two portmanteaus and a dressing-bag which he also packed and a travelling desk, which he filled with papers, pens, and the like. But he put into it no written document. He carefully looked through his linen, and anything that had been marked with more than his initials he rejected. Then he took out a bundle of printed cards, and furnished a card-case with them. On these cards was inscribed the name of Gregory Vance. When all was finished, he stood for awhile with his back to the fireplace contemplating his work. "After all," he said to himself, "I know that I shall never start; and, if I do, nobody can hinder me, and my own name would be as good as any other. As for a man with such a face as mine not being known, that is out of the question." But still he liked the arrangements which he had made, and when he had looked at them for awhile he went to bed.

He was up early the next morning, and had some coffee brought to him by the servant of the house, and as he drank it he had an interview with his landlady. "He was going," he said;—"going that very day." It might be possible that he would change his mind; but as he would desire to start without delay, if he did go, he would pay her then what he owed her, and what would be due for her lodgings under a week's notice. The woman stared, and curtseyed, and took her money. Vavasor, though he had lately been much pressed for money, had never been so foolish as to owe debts where he lived. "There will be some things left about, Mrs. Bunsby," he said, "and I will get you to keep them till I call or send." Mrs. Bunsby said that she would, and then looked her last at him. After that interview she never saw him again.

When he was left alone he put on a rough morning coat, and taking up the pistol, placed it carefully in his pocket, and sallied forth. It was manifest enough that he had some decided scheme in his head, for he turned quickly towards the West when he reached the Strand, went across Trafalgar Square to Pall Mall East, and then turned up Suffolk Street. Just as he reached the club-house at the corner he paused and looked back, facing first one way and then the other. "The chances are that I shall never see anything of it again," he said to himself. Then he laughed in his own silent way, shook his head slightly, and turning again quickly on his heel, walked up the street till he reached the house of Mr. Jones, the pugilistic tailor. The reader, no doubt, has forgotten all he ever knew of Mr. Jones, the pugilistic tailor. It can soon be told again. At Mr. Jones's house John Grey lodged when he was in London, and he was in London at this moment.

Vavasor rang the bell, and as soon as the servant came he went quickly into the house, and passed her in the passage. "Mr. Grey is at home," he said. "I will go up to him." The girl said that Mr. Grey was at home, but suggested that she had better announce the gentleman. But Vavasor was already halfway up the stairs, and before the girl had reached the first landing place, he had entered Mr. Grey's room and closed the door behind him.

Grey was sitting near the open window, in a dressing-gown, and was reading. The breakfast things were on the table, but he had not as yet breakfasted. As soon as he saw George Vavasor, he rose from his chair quickly, and put down his book. "Mr. Vavasor," he said, "I hardly expected to see you in my lodgings again!"

"I dare say not," said Vavasor; "but, nevertheless, here I am." He kept his right hand in the pocket which held the pistol, and held his left hand under his waistcoat.

"May I ask why you have come?" said Grey.

"I intend to tell you, at any rate, whether you ask me or not. I have come to declare in your own hearing,—as I am in the habit of doing occasionally behind your back,—that you are a blackguard,—to spit in your face, and defy you." As he said this he suited his action to his words, but without any serious result. "I have come here to see if you are man enough to resent any insult that I can offer you; but I doubt whether you are."

"Nothing that you can say to me, Mr. Vavasor, will have any effect upon me;—except that you can, of course, annoy me."

"And I mean to annoy you, too, before I have done with you. Will you fight me?"

"Fight a duel with you,—with pistols? Certainly not."

"Then you are a coward, as I supposed."

"I should be a fool if I were to do such a thing as that."

"Look here, Mr. Grey. You managed to worm yourself into an intimacy with my cousin, Miss Vavasor, and to become engaged to her. When she found out what you were, how paltry, and mean, and vile, she changed her mind, and bade you leave her."

"Are you here at her request?"

"I am here as her representative."

"Self-appointed, I think."

"Then, sir, you think wrong. I am at this moment her affianced husband; and I find that, in spite of all that she has said to you,—which was enough, I should have thought, to keep any man of spirit out of her presence,—you still persecute her by going to her house, and forcing yourself upon her presence. Now, I give you two alternatives. You shall either give me your written promise never to go near her again, or you shall fight me."

"I shall do neither one nor the other,—as you know very well yourself."

"Stop till I have done, sir. If you have courage enough to fight me, I will meet you in any country. I will fight you here in London, or, if you are afraid of that, I will go over to France, or to America, if that will suit you better."

"Nothing of the kind will suit me at all. I don't want to have anything to do with you."

"Then you are a coward."

"Perhaps I am;—but your saying so will not make me one."

"You are a coward, and a liar, and a blackguard. I have given you the option of behaving like a gentleman, and you have refused it. Now, look here. I have come here with arms, and I do not intend to leave this room without using them, unless you will promise to give me the meeting that I have proposed." And he took the pistol out of his pocket.

"Do you mean that you are going to murder me?" Grey asked. There were two windows in the room, and he had been sitting near to that which was furthest removed from the fireplace, and consequently furthest removed from the bell, and his visitor was now standing immediately between him and the door. He had to think what steps he might best take, and to act upon his decision instantly. He was by no means a timid man, and was one, moreover, very little prone to believe in extravagant action. He did not think, even now, that this disappointed, ruined man had come there with any intention of killing him. But he knew that a pistol in the hands of an angry man is dangerous, and that it behoved him to do his best to rid himself of the nuisance which now encumbered him. "Do you mean that you are going to murder me?" he had said.

"I mean that you shall not leave this room alive unless you promise to meet me, and fight it out." Upon hearing this, Grey turned himself towards the bell. "If you move a step, I will fire at you," said Vavasor. Grey paused a moment, and looked him full in the face. "I will," said Vavasor again.

"That would be murder," said Grey.

"Don't think that you will frighten me by ugly words," said Vavasor. "I am beyond that."

Grey had stopped for a moment to fix his eyes on the other man's face; but it was only for a moment, and then he went on to the bell. He had seen that the pistol was pointed at himself, and had once thought of rushing across the room at his adversary, calculating that a shot fired at him as he did so might miss him, and that he would then have a fair chance of disarming the madman. But his chief object was to avoid any personal conflict, to escape the indignity of a scramble for the pistol,—and especially to escape the necessity of a consequent appearance at some police-office, where he would have to justify himself, and answer the questions of a lawyer hired to cross-question him. He made, therefore, towards the bell, trusting that Vavasor would not fire at him, but having some little thought also as to the danger of the moment. It might be that everything was over for him now,—that the fatal hour had come, and that eternity was close upon him. Something of the spirit of a prayer flashed across his mind as he moved. Then he heard the click of the pistol's hammer as it fell, and was aware that his eyes were dazzled, though he was unconscious of seeing any flame. He felt something in the air, and knew that the pistol had been fired;—but he did not know whether the shot had struck him or had missed him. His hand was out for the bell-handle, and he had pulled it, before he was sure that he was unhurt.

"D——ation!" exclaimed the murderer. But he did not pull the trigger again. Though the weapon had of late been so often in his hands, he forgot, in the agitation of the moment, that his missing once was but of small matter if he chose to go on with his purpose. Were there not five other barrels for him, each making itself ready by the discharge of the other? But he had paused, forgetting, in his excitement, the use of his weapon, and before he had bethought himself that the man was still in his power, he heard the sound of the bell. "D——ation!" he exclaimed. Then he turned round, left the room, hurried down the stairs, and made his way out into the street, having again passed the girl on his way.

Grey, when he perceived that his enemy was gone, turned round to look for the bullet or its mark. He soon found the little hole in the window-shutter, and probing it with the point of his pencil, came upon the morsel of lead which might now just as readily have been within his own brain. There he left it for the time, and then made some not inaccurate calculation as to the narrowness of his own escape. He had been standing directly between Vavasor and the shutter, and he found, from the height of the hole, that the shot must have passed close beneath his ear. He remembered to have heard the click of the hammer, but he could not remember the sound of the report, and when the girl entered the room, he perceived at once from her manner that she was unaware that firearms had been used.

"Has that gentleman left the house?" Grey asked. The girl said that he had left the house. "Don't admit him again," said he;—"that is, if you can avoid it. I believe he is not in his right senses." Then he asked for Mr. Jones, his landlord, and in a few minutes the pugilistic tailor was with him.

During those few minutes he had been called upon to resolve what he would do now. Would he put the police at once upon the track of the murderer, who was, as he remembered too well, the first cousin of the woman whom he still desired to make his wife? That cross-examination which he would have to undergo at the police-office, and again probably in an assize court, in which all his relations with the Vavasor family would be made public, was very vivid to his imagination. That he was called upon by duty to do something he felt almost assured. The man who had been allowed to make such an attempt once with impunity, might probably make it again. But he resolved that he need not now say anything about the pistol to the pugilistic tailor, unless the tailor said something to him.

"Mr. Jones," he said, "that man whom I had to put out of the room once before, has been here again."

"Has there been another tussle, sir?"

"No;—nothing of that kind. But we must take some steps to prevent his getting in again, if we can help it."

Jones promised his aid, and offered to go at once to the police. To this, however, Mr. Grey demurred, saying that he should himself seek assistance from some magistrate. Jones promised to be very vigilant as to watching the door; and then John Grey sat down to his breakfast. Of course he thought much of what had occurred. It was impossible that he should not think much of so narrow an escape. He had probably been as near death as a man may well be without receiving any injury; and the more he thought of it, the more strongly he was convinced that he could not allow the thing to pass by without some notice, or some precaution as to the future.

At eleven o'clock he went to Scotland Yard, and saw some officer great in power over policemen, and told him all the circumstances,—confidentially. The powerful officer recommended an equally confidential reference to a magistrate; and towards evening a very confidential policeman in plain clothes paid a visit to Vavasor's lodgings in Cecil Street. But Vavasor lodged there no longer. Mrs. Bunsby, who was also very confidential,—and at her wits' end because she could not learn the special business of the stranger who called,—stated that Mr. George Vavasor left her house in a cab at ten o'clock that morning, having taken with him such luggage as he had packed, and having gone, "she was afraid, for good," as Mrs. Bunsby expressed it.

He had gone for good, and at the moment in which the policeman was making the inquiry in Cecil Street, was leaning over the side of an American steamer which had just got up her steam and weighed her anchor in the Mersey. He was on board at six o'clock, and it was not till the next day that the cabman was traced who had carried him to Euston Square Station. Of course, it was soon known that he had gone to America, but it was not thought worth while to take any further steps towards arresting him. Mr. Grey himself was decidedly opposed to any such attempt, declaring his opinion that his own evidence would be insufficient to obtain a conviction. The big men in Scotland Yard were loth to let the matter drop. Their mouths watered after the job, and they had very numerous and very confidential interviews with John Grey. But it was decided that nothing should be done. "Pity!" said one enterprising superintendent, in answer to the condolings of a brother superintendent. "Pity's no name for it. It's the greatest shame as ever I knew since I joined the force. A man as was a Member of Parliament only last Session,—as belongs to no end of swell clubs, a gent as well known in London as any gent about the town! And I'd have had him back in three months, as sure as my name's Walker." And that superintendent felt that his profession and his country were alike disgraced.

And now George Vavasor vanishes from our pages, and will be heard of no more. Roebury knew him no longer, nor Pall Mall, nor the Chelsea Districts. His disappearance was a nine days' wonder, but the world at large knew nothing of the circumstances of that attempt in Suffolk Street. Mr. Grey himself told the story to no one, till he told it to Mr. Palliser at Lucerne. Mr. Scruby complained bitterly of the way in which Vavasor had robbed him; but I doubt whether Scruby, in truth, lost much by the transaction. To Kate, down in Westmoreland, no tidings came of her brother, and her sojourn in London with her aunt had nearly come to an end before she knew that he was gone. Even then the rumour reached her through Captain Bellfield, and she learned what few facts she knew from Mrs. Bunsby in Cecil Street.

"He was always mysterious," said Mrs. Greenow, "and now he has vanished. I hate mysteries, and, as for myself, I think it will be much better that he should not come back again." Perhaps Kate was of the same opinion, but, if so, she kept it to herself.

CHAPTER LXXIII
IN WHICH COME TIDINGS OF GREAT MOMENT TO ALL PALLISERS

It was not till they had been for a day or two together at Lucerne that Mr. Grey told Mr. Palliser the story of George Vavasor's visit to him in Suffolk Street. Having begun the history of his connection with Alice, he found himself obliged to go with it to the end, and as he described the way in which the man had vanished from the sight of all who had known him,—that he had in truth gone, so as no longer to be a cause of dread, he could not without dissimulation, keep back the story of that last scene. "And he tried to murder you!" said Mr. Palliser. "He should be caught and,—and—" Mr. Palliser hesitated, not liking to say boldly that the first cousin of the lady who was now living with him ought to be hung.

"It is better as it is," said Grey.

"He actually walked into your rooms in the day time, and fired a pistol at you as you were sitting at your breakfast! He did that in London, and then walked off and went abroad, as though he had nothing to fear!"

"That was just it," said Grey.

Mr. Palliser began to think that something ought to be done to make life more secure in the metropolis of the world. Had he not known Mr. Grey, or been accustomed to see the other man in Parliament, he would not have thought so much about it. But it was almost too much for him when he reflected that one man whom he now called his friend, had been nearly murdered in daylight, in the heart of his own part of London, by another man whom he had reckoned among his Parliamentary supporters. "And he has got your money too!" said Palliser, putting all the circumstances of the case together. In answer to this Mr. Grey said that he hoped the loss might eventually be his own; but that he was bound to regard the money which had been taken as part of Miss Vavasor's fortune. "He is simply the greatest miscreant of whom I ever heard in my life," said Mr. Palliser. "The wonder is that Miss Vavasor should ever have brought herself to—to like him." Then Mr. Grey apologized for Alice, explaining that her love for her cousin had come from her early years; that the man himself was clever and capable of assuming pleasant ways, and that he had not been wholly bad till ruin had come upon him. "He attempted public life and made himself miserable by failing, as most men do who make that attempt," said Grey. This was a statement which Mr. Palliser could not allow to pass without notice. Whereupon the two men got away from George Vavasor and their own individual interests, and went on seriously discussing the merits and demerits of public life. "The end of it all is," said Grey at last, "that public men in England should be rich like you, and not poor like that miserable wretch, who has now lost everything that the Fates had given him."

They continued to live at Lucerne in this way for a fortnight. Mr. Grey, though he was not unfrequently alone with Alice, did not plead his suit in direct words; but continued to live with her on terms of close and easy friendship. He had told her that her cousin had left England,—that he had gone to America immediately after his disappointment in regard to the seat in Parliament, and that he would probably not return. "Poor George!" Alice had said; "he is a man very much to be pitied." "He is a man very much to be pitied," Grey had replied. After that, nothing more was said between them about George Vavasor. From Lady Glencora Alice did hear something; but Lady Glencora herself had not heard the whole story. "I believe he misbehaved himself, my dear," Lady Glencora said; "but then, you know, he always does that. I believe that he saw Mr. Grey and insulted him. Perhaps you had better not ask anything about it till by-and-by. You'll be able to get anything out of him then." In answer to this Alice made her usual protest, and Lady Glencora, as was customary, told her that she was a fool.

I am inclined to think that Mr. Grey knew what he was about. Lady Glencora once scolded him very vehemently for not bringing the affair to an end. "We shall be going on to Italy before it's settled," she said; "and I don't suppose you can go with us, unless it is settled." Mr. Grey protested that he had no intention of going to Italy in either case.

"Then it will be put off for another year or two, and you are both of you as old as Adam and Eve already."

"We ancient people are never impatient," said Grey, laughing.

"If I were you I would go to her and tell her, roundly, that she should marry me, and then I would shake her. If you were to scold her, till she did not know whether she stood on her head or her heels, she would come to reason."

"Suppose you try that, Lady Glencora!"

"I can't. It's she that always scolds me,—as you will her, when she's your wife. You and Mr. Palliser are very much alike. You're both of you so very virtuous that no woman would have a chance of picking a hole in your coats."

But Lady Glencora was wrong. Alice would, no doubt, have submitted herself patiently to her lover's rebukes, and would have confessed her own sins towards him with any amount of self-accusation that he might have required; but she would not, on that account, have been more willing to obey him in that one point, as to which he now required present obedience. He understood that she must be taught to forgive herself for the evil she had done,—to forgive herself, at any rate in part,—before she could be induced to return to her old allegiance to him. Thus they went on together at Lucerne, passing quiet, idle days,—with some pretence of reading, with a considerable amount of letter-writing, with boat excursions and pony excursions,—till the pony excursions came to a sudden end by means of a violent edict, as to which, and the cause of it, a word or two must be said just now. During these days of the boats and the ponies, the carriage which Lady Glencora hated so vehemently was shut up in limbo, and things went very pleasantly with her. Mr. Palliser received political letters from England, which made his mouth water sadly, and was often very fidgety. Parliament was not now sitting, and the Government would, of course, remain intact till next February. Might it not be possible that when the rent came in the Cabinet, he might yet be present at the darning? He was a constant man, and had once declared his intention of being absent for a year. He continued to speak to Grey of his coming travels, as though it was impossible that they should be over until after the next Easter. But he was sighing for Westminster, and regretting the blue books which were accumulating themselves at Matching;—till on a sudden, there came to him tidings which upset all his plans, which routed the ponies, which made everything impossible, which made the Alps impassable and the railways dangerous, which drove Burgo Fitzgerald out of Mr. Palliser's head, and so confused him that he could no longer calculate the blunders of the present Chancellor of the Exchequer. All the Palliser world was about to be moved from its lowest depths, to the summits of its highest mountains. Lady Glencora had whispered into her husband's ear that she thought it probable—; she wasn't sure;—she didn't know. And then she burst out into tears on his bosom as he sat by her on her bedside.

He was beside himself when he left her, which he did with the primary intention of telegraphing to London for half a dozen leading physicians. He went out by the lake side, and walked there alone for ten minutes in a state of almost unconscious exaltation. He did not quite remember where he was, or what he was doing. The one thing in the world which he had lacked; the one joy which he had wanted so much, and which is so common among men, was coming to him also. In a few minutes it was to him as though each hand already rested on the fair head of a little male Palliser, of whom one should rule in the halls at Gatherum, and the other be eloquent among the Commons of England. Hitherto,—for the last eight or nine months, since his first hopes had begun to fade,—he had been a man degraded in his own sight amidst all his honours. What good was all the world to him if he had nothing of his own to come after him? We must give him his due, too, when we speak of this. He had not had wit enough to hide his grief from his wife; his knowledge of women and of men in social life had not been sufficient to teach him how this should be done; but he had wished to do it. He had never willingly rebuked her for his disappointment, either by a glance of his eye, or a tone of his voice; and now he had already forgiven everything. Burgo Fitzgerald was a myth. Mrs. Marsham should never again come near her. Mr. Bott was, of course, a thing abolished;—he had not even had the sense to keep his seat in Parliament. Dandy and Flirt should feed on gilded corn, and there should be an artificial moon always ready in the ruins. If only those d——able saddle-ponies of Lucerne had not come across his wife's path! He went at once into the yard and ordered that the ponies should be abolished;—sent away, one and all, to the furthest confines of the canton; and then he himself inspected the cushions of the carriage. Were they dry? As it was August in those days, and August in Lucerne is a warm month, it may be presumed that they were dry.

He then remembered that he had promised to send Alice up to his wife, and he hurried back into the house. She was alone in the breakfast-room, waiting for him and for his wife. In these days, Mr. Grey would usually join them at dinner; but he seldom saw them before eleven or twelve o'clock in the day. Then he would saunter in and join Mr. Palliser, and they would all be together till the evening. When the expectant father of embryo dukes entered the room, Alice perceived at once that some matter was astir. His manner was altogether changed, and he showed by his eye that he was eager and moved beyond his wont. "Alice," he said, "would you mind going up to Glencora's room? She wishes to speak to you." He had never called her Alice before, and as soon as the word was spoken, he remembered himself and blushed.

"She isn't ill, I hope?" said Alice.

"No;—she isn't ill. At least I think she had better not get up quite yet. Don't let her excite herself, if you can help it."

"I'll go to her at once," said Alice rising.

"I'm so much obliged to you;—but, Miss Vavasor—"

"You called me Alice just now, Mr. Palliser, and I took it as a great compliment."

He blushed again. "Did I? Very well. Then I'll do it again—if you'll let me. But, if you please, do be as calm with her as you can. She is so easily excited, you know. Of course, if there's anything she fancies, we'll take care to get it for her; but she must be kept quiet." Upon this Alice left him, having had no moment of time to guess what had happened, or was about to happen; and he was again alone, contemplating the future glories of his house. Had he a thought for his poor cousin Jeffrey, whose nose was now so terribly out of joint? No, indeed. His thoughts were all of himself, and the good things that were coming to him,—of the new world of interest that was being opened for him. It would be better to him, this, than being Chancellor of the Exchequer. He would rather have it in store for him to be father of the next Duke of Omnium, than make half a dozen consecutive annual speeches in Parliament as to the ways and means, and expenditure of the British nation! Could it be possible that this foreign tour had produced for him this good fortune? If so, how luckily had things turned out! He would remember even that ball at Lady Monk's with gratitude. Perhaps a residence abroad would be best for Lady Glencora at this particular period of her life. If so, abroad she should certainly live. Before resolving, however, on anything permanently on this head, he thought that he might judiciously consult those six first-rate London physicians, whom, in the first moment of his excitement, he had been desirous of summoning to Lucerne.

In the meantime Alice had gone up to the bedroom of the lady who was now to be the subject of so much anxious thought. When she entered the room, her friend was up and in her dressing-gown, lying on a sofa which stood at the foot of the bed. "Oh, Alice, I'm so glad you've come," said Lady Glencora. "I do so want to hear your voice." Then Alice knelt beside her, and asked her if she were ill.

"He hasn't told you? But of course he wouldn't. How could he? But, Alice, how did he look? Did you observe anything about him? Was he pleased?"

"I did observe something, and I think he was pleased. But what is it? He called me Alice. And seemed to be quite unlike himself. But what is it? He told me that I was to come to you instantly."

"Oh, Alice, can't you guess?" Then suddenly Alice did guess the secret, and whispered her guess into Lady Glencora's ear. "I suppose it is so," said Lady Glencora. "I know what they'll do. They'll kill me by fussing over me. If I could go about my work like a washerwoman, I should be all right."

"I am so happy," she said, some two or three hours afterwards. "I won't deny that I am very happy. It seemed as though I were destined to bring nothing but misery to everybody, and I used to wish myself dead so often. I shan't wish myself dead now."

"We shall all have to go home, I suppose?" said Alice.

"He says so;—but he seems to think that I oughtn't to travel above a mile and a half a day. When I talked of going down the Rhine in one of the steamers, I thought he would have gone into a fit. When I asked him why, he gave me such a look. I know he'll make a goose of himself;—and he'll make geese of us, too; which is worse."

On that afternoon, as they were walking together, Mr. Palliser told the important secret to his new friend, Mr. Grey. He could not deny himself the pleasure of talking about this great event. "It is a matter, you see, of such immense importance to me," Mr. Palliser said.

"Indeed, it is," said Grey. "Every man feels that when a child is about to be born to him." But this did not at all satisfy Mr. Palliser.

"Yes," said he. "That's of course. It is an important thing to everybody;— very important, no doubt. But, when a man—. You see, Grey, I don't think a man is a bit better because he is rich, or because he has a title; nor do I think he is likely to be in any degree the happier. I am quite sure that he has no right to be in the slightest degree proud of that which he has had no hand in doing for himself."

"Men usually are very proud of such advantages," said Grey.

"I don't think that I am; I don't, indeed. I am proud of some things. Whenever I can manage to carry a point in the House, I feel very proud of it. I don't think I ever knocked under to any one, and I am proud of that." Perhaps, Mr. Palliser was thinking of a certain time when his uncle the Duke had threatened him, and he had not given way to the Duke's threats. "But I don't think I'm proud because chance has made me my uncle's heir."

"Not in the least, I should say."

"But I do feel that a son to me is of more importance than it is to most men. A strong anxiety on the subject, is, I think, more excusable in me than it might be in another. I don't know whether I quite make myself understood?"

"Oh, yes! When there's a dukedom and heaven knows how many thousands a year to be disposed of, the question of their future ownership does become important."

"This property is so much more interesting to one, if one feels that all one does to it is done for one's own son."

"And yet," said Grey, "of all the great plunderers of property throughout Europe, the Popes have been the most greedy."

"Perhaps it's different, when a man can't have a wife," said Mr. Palliser.

From all this it may be seen that Mr. Palliser and Mr. Grey had become very intimate. Had chance brought them together in London they might have met a score of times before Mr. Palliser would have thought of doing more than bowing to such an acquaintance. Mr. Grey might have spent weeks at Matching, without having achieved anything like intimacy with its noble owner. But things of that kind progress more quickly abroad than they do at home. The deck of an ocean steamer is perhaps the most prolific hotbed of the growth of sudden friendships; but an hotel by the side of a Swiss lake does almost as well.

For some time after this Lady Glencora's conduct was frequently so indiscreet as to drive her husband almost to frenzy. On the very day after the news had been communicated to him, she proposed a picnic, and made the proposition not only in the presence of Alice, but in that of Mr. Grey also! Mr. Palliser, on such an occasion, could not express all that he thought; but he looked it.

"What is the matter, now, Plantagenet?" said his wife.

"Nothing," said he;—"nothing. Never mind."

"And shall we make this party up to the chapel?"

The chapel in question was Tell's chapel—ever so far up the lake. A journey in a steam-boat would have been necessary.

"No!" said he, shouting out his refusal at her. "We will not."

"You needn't be angry about it," said she;—as though he could have failed to be stirred by such a proposition at such a time. On another occasion she returned from an evening walk, showing on her face some sign of the exercise she had taken.

"Good G——! Glencora," said he, "do you mean to kill yourself?"

He wanted her to eat six or seven times a day; and always told her that she was eating too much, remembering some ancient proverb about little and often. He watched her now as closely as Mrs. Marsham and Mr. Bott had watched her before; and she always knew that he was doing so. She made the matter worse by continually proposing to do things which she knew he would not permit, in order that she might enjoy the fun of seeing his agony and amazement. But this, though it was fun to her at the moment, produced anything but fun, as its general result.

"Upon my word, Alice, I think this will kill me," she said. "I am not to stir out of the house now, unless I go in the carriage, or he is with me."

"It won't last long."

"I don't know what you call long. As for walking with him, it's out of the question. He goes about a mile an hour. And then he makes me look so much like a fool. I had no idea that he would be such an old coddle."

"The coddling will all be given to some one else, very soon."

"No baby could possibly live through it, if you mean that. If there is a baby—"

"I suppose there will be one, by-and-by," said Alice.

"Don't be a fool! But, if there is, I shall take that matter into my own hands. He can do what he pleases with me, and I can't help myself; but I shan't let him or anybody do what they please with my baby. I know what I'm about in such matters a great deal better than he does. I've no doubt he's a very clever man in Parliament; but he doesn't seem to me to understand anything else."

Alice was making some very wise speech in answer to this, when Lady Glencora interrupted her.

"Mr. Grey wouldn't make himself so troublesome, I'm quite sure." Then Alice held her tongue.

When the first consternation arising from the news had somewhat subsided,—say in a fortnight from the day in which Mr. Palliser was made so triumphant,—and when tidings had been duly sent to the Duke, and an answer from his Grace had come, arrangements were made for the return of the party to England. The Duke's reply was very short:—

> My dear Plantagenet,—Give my kind love to Glencora.
> If it's a boy, of course I will be one of the godfathers.
> The Prince, who is very kind, will perhaps oblige me by
> being the other. I should advise you to return as soon as
> convenient.
> Your affectionate uncle,
Omnium.

That was the letter; and short as it was, it was probably the longest that Mr. Palliser had ever received from the Duke.

There was great trouble about the mode of their return.

"Oh, what nonsense," said Glencora. "Let us get into an express train, and go right through to London." Mr. Palliser looked at her with a countenance full of rebuke and sorrow. He was always so looking at her now. "If you mean, Plantagenet, that we are to be dragged all across the Continent in that horrible carriage, and be a thousand days on the road, I for one won't submit to it." "I wish I had never told him a word about it," she said afterwards to Alice. "He would never have found it out himself, till this thing was all over."

Mr. Palliser did at last consent to take the joint opinion of a Swiss doctor and an English one who was settled at Berne; and who, on the occasion, was summoned to Lucerne. They suggested the railway; and as letters arrived for Mr. Palliser,—medical letters,—in which the same opinion was broached, it was agreed, at last, that they should return by railway; but they were to make various halts on the road, stopping at each halting-place for a day. The first was, of course, Basle, and from Basle they were to go on to Baden.

"I particularly want to see Baden again," Lady Glencora said; "and perhaps I may be able to get back my napoleon."

CHAPTER LXXIV
SHOWING WHAT HAPPENED
IN THE CHURCHYARD

These arrangements as to the return of Mr. Palliser's party to London did not, of course, include Mr. Grey. They were generally discussed in Mr. Grey's absence, and communicated to him by Mr. Palliser. "I suppose we shall see you in England before long?" said Mr. Palliser. "I shall be able to tell you that before you go," said Grey. "Not but that in any event I shall return to England before the winter."

"Then come to us at Matching," said Mr. Palliser. "We shall be most happy to have you. Say that you'll come for the first fortnight in December. After that we always go to the Duke, in Barsetshire. Though, by-the-by, I don't suppose we shall go anywhere this year," Mr. Palliser added, interrupting the warmth of his invitation, and reflecting that, under the present circumstances, perhaps, it might be improper to have any guests at Matching in December. But he had become very fond of Mr. Grey, and on this occasion, as he had done on some others, pressed him warmly to make an attempt at Parliament. "It isn't nearly so difficult as you think," said he, when Grey declared that he would not know where to look for a seat. "See the men that get in. There was Mr. Vavasor. Even he got a seat."

"But he had to pay for it very dearly."

"You might easily find some quiet little borough."

"Quiet little boroughs have usually got their own quiet little Members," said Grey.

"They're fond of change; and if you like to spend a thousand pounds, the thing isn't difficult. I'll put you in the way of it." But Mr. Grey still declined. He was not a man prone to be talked out of his own way of life, and the very fact that George Vavasor had been in Parliament would of itself have gone far towards preventing any attempt on his part in that direction. Alice had also wanted him to go into public life, but he had put aside her request as though the thing were quite out of the question,—never giving a moment to its consideration. Had she asked him to settle himself and her in Central Africa, his manner and mode of refusal would have been the same. It was this immobility on his part,—this absolute want of any of the weakness of indecision, which had frightened her, and driven her away from him. He was partly aware of this; but that which he had declined to do at her solicitation, he certainly would not do at the advice of any one else. So it was that he argued the matter with himself. Had he now allowed himself to be so counselled, with what terrible acknowledgements of his own faults must he not have presented himself before Alice?

"I suppose books, then, will be your object in life?" said Mr. Palliser.

"I hope they will be my aids," Grey answered. "I almost doubt whether any object such as that you mean is necessary for life, or even expedient. It seems to me that if a man can so train himself that he may live honestly and die fearlessly, he has done about as much as is necessary."

"He has done a great deal, certainly," said Mr. Palliser, who was not ready enough to carry on the argument as he might have done had more time been given to him to consider it. He knew very well that he himself was working for others, and not for himself; and he was aware, though he had not analysed his own convictions on the matter, that good men struggle as they do in order that others, besides themselves, may live honestly, and, if possible, die fearlessly. The recluse of Nethercoats had thought much more about all this than the rising star of the House of Commons; but the philosophy of the rising star was the better philosophy of the two, though he was by far the less brilliant man. "I don't see why a man should not live honestly and be a Member of Parliament as well," continued Mr. Palliser, when he had been silent for a few minutes.

"Nor I either," said Grey. "I am sure that there are such men, and that the country is under great obligation to them. But they are subject to temptations which a prudent man like myself may perhaps do well to avoid." But though he spoke with an assured tone, he was shaken, and almost regretted that he did not accept the aid which was offered to him. It is astonishing how strong a man may be to those around him,—how impregnable may be his exterior, while within he feels himself to be as weak as water, and as unstable as chaff.

But the object which he had now in view was a renewal of his engagement with Alice, and he felt that he must obtain an answer from her before they left Lucerne. If she still persisted in refusing to give him her hand, it would not be consistent with his dignity as a man to continue his immediate pursuit of her any longer. In such case he must leave her, and see what future time might bring forth. He believed himself to be aware that he would never offer his love to another woman; and if Alice were to remain single, he might try again, after the lapse of a year or two. But if he failed now,—then, for that year or two, he would see her no more. Having so resolved, and being averse to anything like a surprise, he asked her, as he left her one evening, whether she would walk with him on the following morning. That morning would be the morning of her last day at Lucerne; and as she assented she knew well what was to come. She said nothing to Lady Glencora on the subject, but allowed the coming prospects of the Palliser family to form the sole subject of their conversation that night, as it had done on every night since the great news had become known. They were always together for an hour every evening before Alice was allowed to go to bed, and during this hour the anxieties of the future father and mother were always discussed till Alice Vavasor was almost tired of them. But she was patient with her friend, and on this special night she was patient as ever. But when she was released and was alone, she made a great endeavour to come to some fixed resolution as to what she would do on the morrow,— some resolution which should be absolutely resolute, and from which no eloquence on the part of any one should move her. But such resolutions are not easily reached, and Alice laboured through half the night almost in vain. She knew that she loved the man. She knew that he was as true to her as the sun is true to the earth. She knew that she would be, in all respects, safe in his hands. She knew that Lady Glencora would be delighted, and her father gratified. She knew that the countesses would open their arms to her,—though I doubt whether this knowledge was in itself very persuasive. She knew that by such a marriage she would gain all that women generally look to gain when they give themselves away. But, nevertheless, as far as she could decide at all, she decided against her lover. She had no right of her own to be taken back after the evil that she had done, and she did not choose to be taken back as an object of pity and forgiveness.

"Where are you going?" said her cousin, when she came in with her hat on, soon after breakfast.

"I am going to walk,—with Mr. Grey."

"By appointment?"

"Yes, by appointment. He asked me yesterday."

"Then it's all settled, and you haven't told me!"

"All that is settled I have told you very often. He asked me yesterday to walk with him this morning, and I could not well refuse him."

"Why should you have wished to refuse him?"

"I haven't said that I did wish it. But I hate scenes, and I think it would have been pleasanter for us to have parted without any occasion for special words."

"Alice, you are such a fool!"

"So you tell me very often."

"Of course he is now going to say the very thing that he has come all this way for the purpose of saying. He has been wonderfully slow about it; but then slow as he is, you are slower. If you don't make it up with him now, I really shall think you are very wicked. I am becoming like Lady Midlothian;—I can't understand it. I know you want to be his wife, and I know he wants to be your husband, and the only thing that keeps you apart is your obstinacy,—just because you have said you wouldn't have him. My belief is that if Lady Midlothian and the rest of us were to pat you on the back, and tell you how right you were, you'd ask him to take you, out of defiance. You may be sure of this, Alice; if you refuse him now, it'll be for the last time."

This, and much more of the same kind, she bore before Mr. Grey came to take her, and she answered to it all as little as she could. "You are making me very unhappy, Glencora," she said once. "I wish I could break you down with unhappiness," Lady Glencora answered, "so that he might find you less stiff, and hard, and unmanageable." Directly upon that he came in, looking as though he had no business on hand more exciting than his ordinary morning's tranquil employments. Alice at once got up to start with him. "So you and Alice are going to make your adieux," said Lady Glencora. "It must be done sooner or later," said Mr. Grey; and then they went off.

Those who know Lucerne,—and almost everybody now does know Lucerne,—will remember the big hotel which has been built close to the landing-pier of the steamers, and will remember also the church that stands upon a little hill or rising ground, to the left of you, as you come out of the inn upon the lake. The church is immediately over the lake, and round the church there is a burying-ground, and skirting the burying-ground there are cloisters, through the arches and apertures of which they who walk and sit there look down immediately upon the blue water, and across the water upon the frowning menaces of Mount Pilate. It is one of the prettiest spots in that land of beauty; and its charm is to my feeling enhanced by the sepulchral monuments over which I walk, and by which I am surrounded, as I stand there. Up here, into these cloisters, Alice and John Grey went together. I doubt whether he had formed any purpose of doing so. She certainly would have gone without question in any direction that he might have led her. The distance from the inn up to the church-gate did not take them ten minutes, and when they were there their walk was over. But the place was solitary, and they were alone; and it might be as well for Mr. Grey to speak what words he had to say there as elsewhere. They had often been together in those cloisters before, but on such occasions either Mr. Palliser or Lady Glencora had been with them. On their slow passage up the hill very little was spoken, and that little was of no moment. "We will go in here for a few minutes," he said. "It is the prettiest spot about Lucerne, and we don't know when we may see it again." So they went in, and sat down on one of the embrasures that open from the cloisters over the lake.

"Probably never again," said Alice. "And yet I have been here now two years running."

She shuddered as she remembered that in that former year George Vavasor had been with her. As she thought of it all she hated herself. Over and over again she had told herself that she had so mismanaged the latter years of her life that it was impossible for her not to hate herself. No woman had a clearer idea of feminine constancy than she had, and no woman had sinned against that idea more deeply. He gave her time to think of all this as he sat there looking down upon the water.

"And yet I would sooner live in Cambridgeshire," were the first words he spoke.

"Why so?"

"Partly because all beauty is best enjoyed when it is sought for with some trouble and difficulty, and partly because such beauty, and the romance which is attached to it, should not make up the staple of one's life. Romance, if it is to come at all, should always come by fits and starts."

"I should like to live in a pretty country."

"And would like to live a romantic life,—no doubt; but all those things lose their charm if they are made common. When a man has to go to Vienna or St. Petersburg two or three times a month, you don't suppose he enjoys travelling?"

"All the same, I should like to live in a pretty country," said Alice.

"And I want you to come and live in a very ugly country." Then he paused for a minute or two, not looking at her, but gazing still on the mountain opposite. She did not speak a word, but looked as he was looking. She knew that the request was coming, and had been thinking about it all night; but now that it had come she did not know how to bear herself. "I don't think," he went on to say, "that you would let that consideration stand in your way, if on other grounds you were willing to become my wife."

"What consideration?"

"Because Nethercoats is not so pretty as Lucerne."

"It would have nothing to do with it," said Alice.

"It should have nothing to do with it."

"Nothing; nothing at all," repeated Alice.

"Will you come, then? Will you come and be my wife, and help me to be happy amidst all that ugliness? Will you come and be my one beautiful thing, my treasure, my joy, my comfort, my counsellor?"

"You want no counsellor, Mr. Grey."

"No man ever wanted one more. Alice, this has been a bad year to me, and I do not think that it has been a happy one for you."

"Indeed, no."

"Let us forget it,—or rather, let us treat it as though it were forgotten. Twelve months ago you were mine. You were, at any rate, so much mine that I had a right to boast of my possession among my friends."

"It was a poor boast."

"They did not seem to think so. I had but one or two to whom I could speak of you, but they told me that I was going to be a happy man. As to myself, I was sure that I was to be so. No man was ever better contented with his bargain than I was with mine. Let us go back to it, and the last twelve months shall be as though they had never been."

"That cannot be, Mr. Grey. If it could, I should be worse even than I am."

"Why cannot it be?"

"Because I cannot forgive myself what I have done, and because you ought not to forgive me."

"But I do. There has never been an hour with me in which there has been an offence of yours rankling in my bosom unforgiven. I think you have been foolish, misguided,—led away by a vain ambition, and that in the difficulty to which these things brought you, you endeavoured to constrain yourself to do an act, which, when it came near to you,—when the doing of it had to be more closely considered, you found to be contrary to your nature." Now, as he spoke thus, she turned her eyes upon him, and looked at him, wondering that he should have had power to read her heart so accurately. "I never believed that you would marry your cousin. When I was told of it, I knew that trouble had blinded you for awhile. You had driven yourself to revolt against me, and upon that your heart misgave you, and you said to yourself that it did not matter then how you might throw away all your sweetness. You see that I speak of your old love for me with the frank conceit of a happy lover."

"No;—no, no!" she ejaculated.

"But the storm passes over the tree and does not tear it up by the roots or spoil it of all its symmetry. When we hear the winds blowing, and see how the poor thing is shaken, we think that its days are numbered and its destruction at hand. Alice, when the winds were shaking you, and you were torn and buffeted, I never thought so. There may be some who will forgive you slowly. Your own self-forgiveness will be slow. But I, who have known you better than any one,—yes, better than any one,—I have forgiven you everything, have forgiven you instantly. Come to me, Alice, and comfort me. Come to me, for I want you sorely." She sat quite still, looking at the lake and the mountain beyond, but she said nothing. What could she say to him? "My need of you is much greater now," he went on to say, "than when I first asked you to share the world with me. Then I could have borne to lose you, as I had never boasted to myself that you were my own,—had never pictured to myself the life that might be mine if you were always to be with me. But since that day I have had no other hope,—no other hope but this for which I plead now. Am I to plead in vain?"

"You do not know me," she said; "how vile I have been! You do not think what it is,—for a woman to have promised herself to one man while she loved another."

"But it was me you loved. Ah! Alice, I can forgive that. Do I not tell you that I did forgive it the moment that I heard it? Do you not hear me say that I never for a moment thought that you would marry him? Alice, you should scold me for my vanity, for I have believed all through that you loved me, and me only. Come to me, dear, and tell me that it is so, and the past shall be only as a dream."

"I am dreaming it always," said Alice.

"They will cease to be bitter dreams if your head be upon my shoulder. You will cease to reproach yourself when you know that you have made me happy."

"I shall never cease to reproach myself. I have done that which no woman can do and honour herself afterwards. I have been—a jilt."

"The noblest jilt that ever yet halted between two minds! There has been no touch of selfishness in your fickleness. I think I could be hard enough upon a woman who had left me for greater wealth, for a higher rank,—who had left me even that she might be gay and merry. It has not been so with you."

"Yes, it has. I thought you were too firm in your own will, and—"

"And you think so still. Is that it?"

"It does not matter what I think now. I am a fallen creature, and have no longer a right to such thoughts. It will be better for us both that you should leave me,—and forget me. There are things which, if a woman does them, should never be forgotten;—which she should never permit herself to forget."

"And am I to be punished, then, because of your fault? Is that your sense of justice?" He got up, and standing before her, looked down upon her. "Alice, if you will tell me that you do not love me, I will believe you, and will trouble you no more. I know that you will say nothing to me that is false. Through it all you have spoken no word of falsehood. If you love me, after what has passed, I have a right to demand your hand. My happiness requires it, and I have a right to expect your compliance. I do demand it. If you love me, Alice, I tell you that you dare not refuse me. If you do so, you will fail hereafter to reconcile it to your conscience before God."

Then he stopped his speech, and waited for a reply; but Alice sat silent beneath his gaze, with her eyes turned upon the tombstones beneath her feet. Of course she had no choice but to yield. He, possessed of power and force infinitely greater than hers, had left her no alternative but to be happy. But there still clung to her what I fear we must call a perverseness of obstinacy, a desire to maintain the resolution she had made,—a wish that she might be allowed to undergo the punishment she had deserved. She was as a prisoner who would fain cling to his prison after pardon has reached him, because he is conscious that the pardon is undeserved. And it may be that there was still left within her bosom some remnant of that feeling of rebellion which his masterful spirit had ever produced in her. He was so imperious in his tranquillity, he argued his question of love with such a manifest preponderance of right on his side, that she had always felt that to yield to him would be to confess the omnipotence of his power. She knew now that she must yield to him,—that his power over her was omnipotent. She was pressed by him as in some countries the prisoner is pressed by the judge,—so pressed that she acknowledged to herself silently that any further antagonism to him was impossible. Nevertheless, the word which she had to speak still remained unspoken, and he stood over her, waiting for her answer. Then slowly he sat down beside her, and gradually he put his arm round her waist. She shrank from him, back against the stonework of the embrasure, but she could not shrink away from his grasp. She put up her hand to impede his, but his hand, like his character and his words, was full of power. It would not be impeded. "Alice," he said, as he pressed her close with his arm, "the battle is over now, and I have won it."

"You win everything,—always," she said, whispering to him, as she still shrank from his embrace.

"In winning you I have won everything." Then he put his face over her and pressed his lips to hers. I wonder whether he was made happier when he knew that no other touch had profaned those lips since last he had pressed them?

CHAPTER LXXV
ROUGE ET NOIR

Alice insisted on being left up in the churchyard, urging that she wanted to "think about it all," but, in truth, fearing that she might not be able to carry herself well, if she were to walk down with her lover to the hotel. To this he made no objection, and, on reaching the inn, met Mr. Palliser in the hall. Mr. Palliser was already inspecting the arrangement of certain large trunks which had been brought down-stairs, and was preparing for their departure. He was going about the house, with a nervous solicitude to do something, and was flattering himself that he was of use. As he could not be Chancellor of the Exchequer, and as, by the nature of his disposition, some employment was necessary to him, he was looking to the cording of the boxes. "Good morning! good morning!" he said to Grey, hardly looking at him, as though time were too precious with him to allow of his turning his eyes upon his friend. "I am going up to the station to see after a carriage for to-morrow. Perhaps you'll come with me." To this proposition Mr. Grey assented. "Sometimes, you know," continued Mr. Palliser, "the springs of the carriages are so very rough." Then, in a very few words, Mr. Grey told him what had been his own morning's work. He hated secrets and secrecy, and as the Pallisers knew well what had brought him upon their track, it was, he thought, well that they should know that he had been successful. Mr. Palliser congratulated him very cordially, and then, running up-stairs for his gloves or his stick, or, more probably, that he might give his wife one other caution as to her care of herself, he told her also that Alice had yielded at last. "Of course she has," said Lady Glencora.

"I really didn't think she would," said he.

"That's because you don't understand things of that sort," said his wife. Then the caution was repeated, the mother of the future duke was kissed, and Mr. Palliser went off on his mission about the carriage, its cushions, and its springs. In the course of their walk Mr. Palliser suggested that, as things were settled so pleasantly, Mr. Grey might as well return with them to England, and to this suggestion Mr. Grey assented.

Alice remained alone for nearly an hour, looking out upon the rough sides and gloomy top of Mount Pilate. No one disturbed her in the churchyard,—no steps were heard along the tombstones,—no voice sounded through the cloisters. She was left in perfect solitude to think of the past, and form her plans of the future. Was she happy, now that the manner of her life to come was thus settled for her; that all further question as to the disposal of herself was taken out of her hands, and that her marriage with a man she loved was so firmly arranged that no further folly of her own could disarrange it? She was happy, though she was slow to confess her happiness to herself. She was happy, and she was resolute in this,—that she would now do all she could to make him happy also. And there must now, she acknowledged, be an end to her pride,—to that pride which had hitherto taught her to think that she could more wisely follow her own guidance than that of any other who might claim to guide her. She knew now that she must follow his guidance. She had found her master, as we sometimes say, and laughed to herself with a little inward laughter as she confessed that it was so. She was from henceforth altogether in his hands. If he chose to tell her that they were to be married at Michaelmas, or at Christmas, or on Lady Day, they would, of course, be married accordingly. She had taken her fling at having her own will, and she and all her friends had seen what had come of it. She had assumed the command of the ship, and had thrown it upon the rocks, and she felt that she never ought to take the captain's place again. It was well for her that he who was to be captain was one whom she respected as thoroughly as she loved him.

She would write to her father at once,—to her father and Lady Macleod,—and would confess everything. She felt that she owed it to them that they should be told by herself that they had been right and that she had been wrong. Hitherto she had not mentioned to either of them the fact that Mr. Grey was with them in Switzerland. And, then, what must she do as to Lady Midlothian? As to Lady Midlothian, she would do nothing. Lady Midlothian, of course, would triumph;—would jump upon her, as Lady Glencora had once expressed it, with very triumphant heels,—would try to patronize her, or, which would be almost worse, would make a parade of her forgiveness. But she would have nothing to do with Lady Midlothian, unless, indeed, Mr. Grey should order it. Then she laughed at herself again with that inward laughter, and, rising from her seat, proceeded to walk down the hill to the hotel.

"Vanquished at last!" said Lady Glencora, as Alice entered the room.

"Yes, vanquished; if you like to call it so," said Alice.

"It is not what I call it, but what you feel it," said the other. "Do you think that I don't know you well enough to be sure that you regard yourself now as an unfortunate prisoner,—as a captive taken in war, to be led away in triumph, without any hope of a ransom? I know that it is quite a misery to you that you should be made a happy woman of at last. I understand it all, my dear, and my heart bleeds for you."

"Of course; I knew that was the way you would treat me."

"In what way would you have me treat you? If I were to hug you with joy, and tell you how good he is, and how fortunate you are,—if I were to praise him, and bid you triumph in your success, as might be expected on such an occasion,—you would put on a long face at once, and tell me that though the thing is to be, it would be much better that the thing shouldn't be. Don't I know you, Alice?"

"I shouldn't have said that;—not now."

"I believe in my heart you would;—that, or something like it. But I do wish you joy all the same, and you may say what you please. He has got you in his power now, and I don't think even you can go back."

"No; I shall not go back again."

"I would join with Lady Midlothian in putting you into a madhouse, if you did. But I am so glad; I am, indeed. I was afraid to the last,—terribly afraid; you are so hard and so proud. I don't mean hard to me, dear. You have never been half hard enough to me. But you are hard to yourself, and, upon my word, you have been hard to him. What a deal you will have to make up to him!"

"I feel that I ought to stand before him always as a penitent,—in a white sheet."

"He will like it better, I dare say, if you will sit upon his knee. Some penitents do, you know. And how happy you will be! He'll never explain the sugar-duties to you, and there'll be no Mr. Bott at Nethercoats." They sat together the whole morning,—while Mr. Palliser was seeing to the springs and cushions,—and by degrees Alice began to enjoy her happiness. As she did so her friend enjoyed it with her, and at last they had something of the comfort and excitement which such an occasion should give. "I'll tell you what, Alice; you shall come and be married at Matching, in August, or perhaps September. That's the only way in which I can be present; and if we can bespeak some sun, we'll have the breakfast out in the ruins."

On the following morning they all started together, a first-class compartment having been taken for the Palliser family, and a second-class compartment close to them for the Palliser servants. Mr. Palliser, as he slowly handed his wife in, was a triumphant man; as was also Mr. Grey, as he handed in his lady-love, though, in a manner, much less manifest. We may say that both the gentlemen had been very fortunate while at Lucerne. Mr. Palliser had come abroad with a feeling that all the world had been cut from under his feet. A great change was needed for his wife, and he had acknowledged at once that everything must be made to yield to that necessity. He certainly had his reward,—now in his triumphant return. Terrible troubles had afflicted him as he went, which seemed now to have dissipated themselves altogether. When he thought of Burgo Fitzgerald he remembered him only as a poor, unfortunate fellow, for whom he should be glad to do something, if the doing of anything were only in his power; and he had in his pocket a letter which he had that morning received from the Duke of St. Bungay, marked private and confidential, which was in its nature very private and confidential, and in which he was told that Lord Brock and Mr. Finespun were totally at variance about French wines. Mr. Finespun wanted to do something, now in the recess,—to send some political agent over to France,—to which Lord Brock would not agree; and no one knew what would be the consequence of this disagreement. Here might be another chance,—if only Mr. Palliser could give up his winter in Italy! Mr. Palliser, as he took his place opposite his wife, was very triumphant.

And Mr. Grey was triumphant, as he placed himself gently in his seat opposite to Alice. He seemed to assume no right, as he took that position apparently because it was the one which came naturally to his lot. No one would have been made aware that Alice was his own simply by seeing his arrangements for her comfort. He made no loud assertion as to his property and his rights, as some men do. He was quiet and subdued in his joy, but not the less was he triumphant. From the day on which Alice had accepted his first offer,—nay, from an earlier day than that; from the day on which he had first resolved to make it, down to the present hour, he had never been stirred from his purpose. By every word that he had said, and by every act that he had done, he had shown himself to be unmoved by that episode in their joint lives, which Alice's other friends had regarded as so fatal. When she first rejected him, he would not take his rejection. When she told him that she intended to marry her cousin, he silently declined to believe that such marriage would ever take place. He had never given her up for a day, and now the event proved that he had been right. Alice was happy, very happy; but she was still disposed to regard her lover as Fate, and her happiness as an enforced necessity.

They stopped a night at Basle, and again she stood upon the balcony. He was close to her as she stood there,—so close that, putting out her hand for his, she was able to take it and press it closely. "You are thinking of something, Alice," he said. "What is it?"

"It was here," she said—"here, on this very balcony, that I first rebelled against you, and now you have brought me here that I should confess and submit on the same spot. I do confess. How am I to thank you for forgiving me?"

"How am I to thank you for forgiving me?"

On the following morning they went on to Baden-Baden, and there they stopped for a couple of days. Lady Glencora had positively refused to stop a day at Basle, making so many objections to the place that her husband had at last yielded. "I could go from Vienna to London without feeling it," she said, with indignation; "and to tell me that I can't do two easy days' journey running!" Mr. Palliser had been afraid to be imperious, and therefore, immediately on his arrival at one of the stations in Basle, he had posted across the town, in the heat and the dust, to look after the cushions and the springs at the other.

"I've a particular favour to ask of you," Lady Glencora said to her husband, as soon as they were alone together in their rooms at Baden. Mr. Palliser declared that he would grant her any particular favour,—only premising that he was not to be supposed to have thereby committed himself to any engagement under which his wife should have authority to take any exertion upon herself. "I wish I were a milkmaid," said Lady Glencora.

"But you are not a milkmaid, my dear. You haven't been brought up like a milkmaid."

But what was the favour? If she would only ask for jewels,—though they were the Grand Duchess's diamond eardrops, he would endeavour to get them for her. If she would have quaffed molten pearls, like Cleopatra, he would have procured the beverage,—having first fortified himself with a medical opinion as to the fitness of the drink for a lady in her condition. There was no expenditure that he would not willingly incur for her, nothing costly that he would grudge. But when she asked for a favour, he was always afraid of an imprudence. Very possibly she might want to drink beer in an open garden.

And her request was, at last, of this nature: "I want you to take me up to the gambling-rooms!" said she.

"The gambling-rooms!" said Mr. Palliser in dismay.

"Yes, Plantagenet; the gambling-rooms. If you had been with me before, I should not have made a fool of myself by putting my piece of money on the table. I want to see the place; but then I saw nothing, because I was so frightened when I found that I was winning."

Mr. Palliser was aware that all the world of Baden,—or rather the world of the strangers at Baden,—assembles itself in those salons. It may be also that he himself was curious to see how men looked when they lost their own money, or won that of others. He knew how a Minister looked when he lost or gained a tax. He was familiar with millions and tens of millions in a committee of the whole House. He knew the excitement of a near division upon the estimates. But he had never yet seen a poor man stake his last napoleon, and rake back from off the table a small hatful of gold. A little exercise after an early dinner was, he had been told, good for his wife; and he agreed therefore that, on their second evening at Baden, they would all walk up and see the play.

"Perhaps I shall get back my napoleon," said Glencora to Alice.

"And perhaps I shall be forgiven when somebody sees how difficult it is to manage you," said Alice, looking at Mr. Palliser.

"She isn't in earnest," said Mr. Palliser, almost fearing the result of the experiment.

"I don't know that," said Lady Glencora.

They started together, Mr. Palliser with his wife, and Mr. Grey with Alice on his arm, and found all the tables at work. They at first walked through the different rooms, whispering to each other their comments on the people that they saw, and listening to the quick, low, monotonous words of the croupiers as they arranged and presided over the games. Each table was closely surrounded by its own crowd, made up of players, embryo players, and simple lookers-on, so that they could not see much as they walked. But this was not enough for Lady Glencora. She was anxious to know what these men and women were doing,—to see whether the croupiers wore horns on their heads and were devils indeed,—to behold the faces of those who were wretched and of those who were triumphant,—to know how the thing was done, and to learn something of that lesson in life. "Let us stand here a moment," she said to her husband, arresting him at one corner of the table which had the greatest crowd. "We shall be able to see in a few minutes." So he stood with her there, giving way to Alice, who went in front with his wife; and in a minute or two an aperture was made, so that they could all see the marked cloth, and the money lying about, and the rakes on the table, and the croupier skilfully dealing his cards, and,—more interesting than all the rest, the faces of those who were playing. Grey looked on, over Alice's shoulder, very attentively,—as did Palliser also,—but both of them kept their eyes upon the ministers of the work. Alice and Glencora did the same at first, but as they gained courage they glanced round upon the gamblers.

It was a long table, having, of course, four corners, and at the corner appropriated by them they were partly opposite to the man who dealt the cards. The corner answering to theirs at the other end was the part of the table most removed from their sight, and that on which their eyes fell last. As Lady Glencora stood she could hardly see,—indeed, at first she could not see,—one or two who were congregated at this spot. Mr. Palliser, who was behind her, could not see them at all. But to Alice,—and to Mr. Grey, had he cared about it,—every face at the table was visible except the faces of those who were immediately close to them. Before long Alice's attention was riveted on the action and countenance of one young man who sat at that other corner. He was leaning, at first listlessly, over the table, dressed in a velveteen jacket, and with his round-topped hat brought far over his eyes, so that she could not fully see his face. But she had hardly begun to observe him before he threw back his hat, and taking some pieces of gold from under his left hand, which lay upon the table, pushed three or four of them on to one of the divisions marked on the cloth. He seemed to show no care, as others did, as to the special spot which they should occupy. Many were very particular in this respect, placing their ventures on the lines, so as to share the fortunes of two compartments, or sometimes of four; or they divided their coins, taking three or four numbers, selecting the numbers with almost grotesque attention to some imagined rule of their own. But this man let his gold go all together, and left it where his half-stretched rake deposited it by chance. Alice could not but look at his face. His eyes she could see were bloodshot, and his hair, when he pushed back his hat, was rough and dishevelled; but still there was that in his face which no woman could see and not regard. It was a face which at once prepossessed her in his favour,—as it had always prepossessed all others. On this occasion he had won his money, and Alice saw him drag it in as lazily as he had pushed it out.

"Do you see that little Frenchman?" said Lady Glencora. "He has just made half a napoleon, and has walked off with it. Isn't it interesting? I could stay here all the night." Then she turned round to whisper something to her husband, and Alice's eyes again fell on the face of the man at the other end of the table. After he had won his money, he had allowed the game to go on for a turn without any action on his part. The gold again went under his hand, and he lounged forward with his hat over his eyes. One of the croupiers had said a word, as though calling his attention to the game, but he had merely shaken his head. But when the fate of the next turn had been decided, he again roused himself, and on this occasion, as far as Alice could see, pushed his whole stock forward with the rake. There was a little mass of gold, and, from his manner of placing it, all might see that he left its position to chance. One piece had got beyond its boundary, and the croupier pushed it back with some half-expressed inquiry as to his correctness. "All right," said a voice in English. Then Lady Glencora started and clutched Alice's arm with her hand. Mr. Palliser was explaining to Mr. Grey, behind them, something about German finance as connected with gambling-tables, and did not hear the voice, or see his wife's motion. I need hardly tell the reader that the gambler was Burgo Fitzgerald.

But Lady Glencora said not a word,—not as yet. She looked forward very gently, but still with eager eyes, till she could just see the face she knew so well. His hat was now pushed back, and his countenance had lost its listlessness. He watched narrowly the face of the man as he told out the amount of the cards as they were dealt. He did not try to hide his anxiety, and when, after the telling of some six or seven cards, he heard a certain number named, and a certain colour called, he made some exclamation which even Glencora could not hear. And then another croupier put down, close to Burgo's money, certain rolls of gold done up in paper, and also certain loose napoleons.

"Why doesn't he take it?" said Lady Glencora.

"He is taking it," said Alice, not at all knowing the cause of her cousin's anxiety.

Burgo had paused a moment, and then prepared to rake the money to him; but as he did so, he changed his mind, and pushed it all back again,— now, on this occasion, being very careful to place it on its former spot. Both Alice and Glencora could see that a man at his elbow was dissuading him,— had even attempted to stop the arm which held the rake. But Burgo shook him off, speaking to him some word roughly, and then again he steadied the rolls upon their appointed place. The croupier who had paused for a moment now went on quickly with his cards, and in two minutes the fate of Burgo's wealth was decided. It was all drawn back by the croupier's unimpassioned rake, and the rolls of gold were restored to the tray from whence they had been taken.

Burgo looked up and smiled at them all round the table. By this time most of those who stood around were looking at him. He was a man who gathered eyes upon him wherever he might be, or whatever he was doing; and it had been clear that he was very intent upon his fortune, and on the last occasion the amount staked had been considerable. He knew that men and women were looking at him, and therefore he smiled faintly as he turned his eyes round the table. Then he got up, and, putting his hands in his trousers pockets, whistled as he walked away. His companion followed him, and laid a hand upon his shoulder; but Burgo shook him off, and would not turn round. He shook him off, and walked on whistling, the length of the whole salon.

"Alice," said Lady Glencora, "it is Burgo Fitzgerald." Mr. Palliser had gone so deep into that question of German finance that he had not at all noticed the gambler. "Alice, what can we do for him? It is Burgo," said Lady Glencora.

Many eyes were now watching him. Used as he was to the world and to misfortune, he was not successful in his attempt to bear his loss with a show of indifference. The motion of his head, the position of his hands, the tone of his whistling, all told the tale. Even the unimpassioned croupiers furtively cast an eye after him, and a very big Guard, in a cocked hat, and uniform, and sword, who hitherto had hardly been awake, seemed evidently to be interested by his movements. If there is to be a tragedy at these places,— and tragedies will sometimes occur,—it is always as well that the tragic scene should be as far removed as possible from the salons, in order that the public eye should not suffer.

Lady Glencora and Alice had left their places, and had shrunk back, almost behind a pillar. "Is it he, in truth?" Alice asked.

"In very truth," said Glencora. "What can I do? Can I do anything? Look at him, Alice. If he were to destroy himself, what should I do then?"

Burgo, conscious that he was the regarded of all eyes, turned round upon his heel and again walked the length of the salon. He knew well that he had not a franc left in his possession, but still he laughed and still he whistled. His companion, whoever he might be, had slunk away from him, not caring to share the notoriety which now attended him.

"What shall I do, Alice?" said Lady Glencora, with her eyes still fixed on him who had been her lover.

"Tell Mr. Palliser," whispered Alice.

Lady Glencora immediately ran up to her husband, and took him away from Mr. Grey. Rapidly she told her story,—with such rapidity that Mr. Palliser could hardly get in a word. "Do something for him;—do, do. Unless I know that something is done, I shall die. You needn't be afraid."

"I'm not afraid," said Mr. Palliser.

Lady Glencora, as she went on quickly, got hold of her husband's hand, and caressed it. "You are so good," said she. "Don't let him out of your sight. There; he is going. I will go home with Mr. Grey. I will be ever so good; I will, indeed. You know what he'll want, and for my sake you'll let him have it. But don't let him gamble. If you could only get him home to England, and then do something. You owe him something, Plantagenet; do you not?"

"If money can do anything, he shall have it."

"God bless you, dearest! I shall never see him again; but if you could save him! There;—he is going now. Go;—go." She pushed him forward, and then retreating, put her arm within Mr. Grey's, still keeping her eye upon her husband.

Burgo, when he first got to the door leading out of the salon, had paused a moment, and, turning round, had encountered the big gendarme close to him. "Well, old Buffer, what do you want?" said he, accosting the man in English. The big gendarme simply walked on through the door, and said nothing. Then Burgo also passed out, and Mr. Palliser quickly went after him. They were now in the large front salon, from whence the chief door of the building opened out upon the steps. Through this door Burgo went without pausing, and Mr. Palliser went after him. They both walked to the end of the row of buildings, and then Burgo, leaving the broad way, turned into a little path which led up through the trees to the hills. That hillside among the trees is a popular resort at Baden, during the day; but now, at nine in the evening, it was deserted. Palliser did not press on the other man, but followed him, and did not accost Burgo till he had thrown himself on the grass beneath a tree.

"You are in trouble, I fear, Mr. Fitzgerald," said Mr. Palliser, as soon as he was close at Burgo's feet.

"We will go home. Mr. Palliser has something to do," said Lady Glencora to Mr. Grey, as soon as the two men had disappeared from her sight.

"Is that a friend of Mr. Palliser?" said Mr. Grey.

"Yes;—that is, he knows him, and is interested about him. Alice, shall we go home? Oh! Mr. Grey, you must not ask any questions. He,—Mr. Palliser, will tell you everything when he sees you,—that is, if there is anything to be told." Then they all went home, and soon separated for the night. "Of course I shall sit up for him," said Lady Glencora to Alice, "but I will do it in my own room. You can tell Mr. Grey, if you like." But Alice told nothing to Mr. Grey, nor did Mr. Grey ask any questions.

CHAPTER LXXVI
THE LANDLORD'S BILL

"You are in trouble, Mr. Fitzgerald, I fear," said Mr. Palliser, standing over Burgo as he lay upon the ground. They were now altogether beyond the gas-lights, and the evening was dark. Burgo, too, was lying with his face to the ground, expecting that the footsteps which he had heard would pass by him.

"Who is that?" said he, turning round suddenly; but still he was not at once able to recognize Mr. Palliser, whose voice was hardly known to him.

"Perhaps I have been wrong in following you," said Mr. Palliser, "but I thought you were in distress, and that probably I might help you. My name is Palliser."

"Plantagenet Palliser?" said Burgo, jumping up on to his legs and looking close into the other's face. "By heavens! it is Plantagenet Palliser! Well, Mr. Palliser, what do you want of me?"

"I want to be of some use to you, if I can. I and my wife saw you leave the gaming-table just now."

"Is she here too?"

"Yes;—she is here. We are going home, but chance brought us up to the salon. She seemed to think that you are in distress, and that I could help you. I will, if you will let me."

Mr. Palliser, during the whole interview, felt that he could afford to be generous. He knew that he had no further cause for fear. He had no lingering dread of this poor creature who stood before him. All that feeling was over, though it was as yet hardly four months since he had been sent back by Mrs. Marsham to Lady Monk's house to save his wife, if saving her were yet possible.

"So she is here, is she;—and saw me there when I staked my last chance? I should have had over twenty thousand francs now, if the cards had stood to me."

"The cards never do stand to any one, Mr. Fitzgerald."

"Never;—never,—never!" said Burgo. "At any rate, they never did to me. Nothing ever does stand to me."

"If you want twenty thousand francs,—that's eight hundred pounds, I think—I can let you have it without any trouble."

"The devil you can!"

"Oh, yes. As I am travelling with my family—" I wonder whether Mr. Palliser considered himself to be better entitled to talk of his family than he had been some three or four weeks back—"As I am travelling with my family, I have been obliged to carry large bills with me, and I can accommodate you without any trouble."

There was something pleasant in this, which made Burgo Fitzgerald laugh. Mr. Palliser, the husband of Lady Glencora M'Cluskie, and the heir of the Duke of Omnium happening to have money with him! As if Mr. Palliser could not bring down showers of money in any quarter of the globe by simply holding up his hand. And then to talk of accommodating him,— Burgo Fitzgerald, as though it were simply a little matter of convenience,— as though Mr. Palliser would of course find the money at his bankers' when he next examined his book! Burgo could not but laugh.

"I was not in the least doubting your ability to raise the money," said he; "but how would you propose to get it back again?"

"That would be at your convenience," said Mr. Palliser, who hardly knew how to put himself on a proper footing with his companion, so that he might offer to do something effectual for the man's aid.

"I never have any such convenience," said Burgo. "Who were those women whose tubs always had holes at the bottom of them? My tub always has such a hole."

"You mean the daughters of Danaus," said Mr. Palliser.

"I don't know whose daughters they were, but you might just as well lend them all eight hundred pounds apiece."

"There were so many of them," said Mr. Palliser, trying a little joke. "But as you are only one I shall be most happy, as I said before, to be of service."

They were now walking slowly together up towards the hills, and near to them they heard a step. Upon this, Burgo turned round.

"Do you see that fellow?" said he. Mr. Palliser, who was somewhat short-sighted, said that he did not see him. "I do, though. I don't know his name, but they have sent him out from the hotel with me, to see what I do with myself. I owe them six or seven hundred francs, and they want to turn me out of the house and not let me take my things with me."

"That would be very uncomfortable," said Mr. Palliser.

"It would be uncomfortable, but I shall be too many for them. If they keep my traps they shall keep me. They think I'm going to blow my brains out. That's what they think. The man lets me go far enough off to do that,— so long as it's nowhere about the house."

"I hope you're not thinking of such a thing?"

"As long as I can help it, Mr. Palliser, I never think of anything." The stranger was now standing near to them,—almost so near that he might hear their words. Burgo, perceiving this, walked up to him, and, speaking in bad French, desired him to leave them. "Don't you see that I have a friend with me?"

"Oh! a friend," said the man, answering in bad English. "Perhaps de friend can advance moneys?"

"Never mind what he can do," said Burgo. "You do as you are bid, and leave me."

Then the gentleman from the hotel retreated down the hill, but Mr. Palliser, during the rest of the interview, frequently fancied that he heard the man's footfall at no great distance.

They continued to walk on up the hill very slowly, and it was some time before Mr. Palliser knew how to repeat his offer.

"So Lady Glencora is here?" Burgo said again.

"Yes, she is here. It was she who asked me to come to you," Mr. Palliser answered. Then they both walked on a few steps in silence, for neither of them knew how to address the other.

"By George!—isn't it odd," said Burgo, at last, "that you and I, of all men in the world, should be walking together here at Baden? It's not only that you're the richest man in London, and that I'm the poorest, but—; there are other things, you know, which make it so funny."

"There have been things which make me and my wife very anxious to give you aid."

"And have you considered, Mr. Palliser, that those things make you the very man in the world,—indeed, for the matter of that, the only man in the world,—from whom I can't take aid. I would have taken it all if I could have got it,—and I tried hard."

"I know you have been disappointed, Mr. Fitzgerald."

"Disappointed! By G——! yes. Did you ever know any man who had so much right to be disappointed as I have? I did love her, Mr. Palliser. Nay, by heavens! I do love her. Out here I will dare to say as much even to you. I shall never try to see her again. All that is over, of course. I've been a fool about her as I have been about everything. But I did love her."

"I believe it, Mr. Fitzgerald."

"It was not altogether her money. But think what it would have been to me, Mr. Palliser. Think what a chance I had, and what a chance I lost. I should have been at the top of everything,—as now I am at the bottom. I should not have spent that. There would have been enough of it to have saved me. And then I might have done something good instead of crawling about almost in fear of that beast who is watching us."

"It has been ordered otherwise," said Mr. Palliser, not knowing what to say.

"Yes; it has been ordered, with a vengeance! It seems to have been ordered that I'm to go to the devil; but I don't know who gave the orders, and I don't know why."

Mr. Palliser had not time to explain to his friend that the orders had been given, in a very peremptory way, by himself, as he was anxious to bring back the conversation to his own point. He wished to give some serviceable, and, if possible, permanent aid to the poor ne'er-do-well; but he did not wish to talk more than could be helped about his own wife.

"There is an old saying, which you will remember well," said he, "that the way to good manners is never too late."

"That's nonsense," said Burgo. "It's too late when the man feels the knot round his neck at the Old Bailey."

"Perhaps not, even then. Indeed, we may say, certainly not, if the man be still able to take the right way. But I don't want to preach to you."

"It wouldn't do any good, you know."

"But I do want to be of service to you. There is something of truth in what you say. You have been disappointed; and I, perhaps, of all men am the most bound to come to your assistance now that you are in need."

"How can I take it from you?" said Burgo, almost crying.

"You shall take it from her!"

"No;—that would be worse; twenty times worse. What! take her money, when she would not give me herself!"

"I do not see why you should not borrow her money,—or mine. You shall call it which you will."

"No; I won't have it."

"And what will you do then?"

"What will I do? Ah! That's the question. I don't know what I will do. I have the key of my bedroom in my pocket, and I will go to bed to-night. It's not very often that I look forward much beyond that."

"Will you let me call on you, to-morrow?"

"I don't see what good it will do? I shan't get up till late, for fear they should shut the room against me. I might as well have as much out of them as I can. I think I shall say I'm ill, and keep my bed."

"Will you take a few napoleons?"

"No; not a rap. Not from you. You are the first man from whom I ever refused to borrow money, and I should say that you'll be about the last to offer to lend it me."

"I don't know what else I can offer?" said Mr. Palliser.

"You can offer nothing. If you will say to your wife from me that I bade her adieu;—that is all you can do for me. Good night, Mr. Palliser; good night."

"Good night, Mr. Palliser."

Mr. Palliser left him and went his way, feeling that he had no further eloquence at his command. He shook Burgo's hand, and then walked quickly down the hill. As he did so he passed, or would have passed the man who had been dodging them.

"Misther, Misther!" said the man in a whisper.

"What do you want of me?" asked Mr. Palliser, in French.

Then the man spoke in French, also. "Has he got any money? Have you given him any money?"

"I have not given him any money," said Mr. Palliser, not quite knowing what he had better do or say under such circumstances.

"Then he will have a bad time with it," said the man. "And he might have carried away two thousand francs just now! Dear, dear, dear! Has he got any friends, sir?"

"Yes, he has friends. I do not know that I can assist him, or you."

"Fitzgerald;—his name is Fitzgerald?"

"Yes," said Mr. Palliser; "his name is Fitzgerald."

"Ah! There are so many Fitzgeralds in England. Mr. Fitzgerald, London;—he has no other address?"

"If he had, and I knew it, I should not give it you without his sanction."

"But what shall we do? How shall we act? Perhaps with his own hand he will himself kill. For five weeks his pension he owes; yes, for five weeks. And for wine, oh so much! There came through Baden a my lord, and then, I think he got money. But he went and played. That was of course. But; oh my G——! he might have carried away this night two thousand francs; yes, two thousand francs!"

"Are you the hotelkeeper?"

"His friend, sir; only his friend. That is, I am the head Commissionaire. I look after the gentlemen who sometimes are not all—not all—" exactly what they should be, the commissioner intended to explain; and Mr. Palliser understood him although the words were not quite spoken. The interview was ended by Mr. Palliser taking the name of the hotel, and promising to call before Mr. Fitzgerald should be up in the morning—a purposed visit, which we need not regard as requiring any very early energy on Mr. Palliser's part, when we remember Burgo's own programme for the following day.

Lady Glencora received her husband that night with infinite anxiety, and was by no means satisfied with what had been done. He described to her as accurately as he could the nature of his interview with Burgo, and he described to her also his other interview with the head commissioner.

"He will; he will," said Lady Glencora; when she heard from her husband the man's surmise that perhaps he might destroy himself. "He will; he will; and if he does, how can you expect that I shall bear it?" Mr. Palliser tried to soothe her by telling her of his promised visit to the landlord; and Lady Glencora, accepting this as something, strove to instigate her husband to some lavish expenditure on Burgo's behalf. "There can be no reason why he should not take it," said Glencora. "None the least. Had it not been promised to him? Had he not a right to it?" The subject was one which Mr. Palliser found it very hard to discuss. He could not tell his wife that Fitzgerald ought to accept his bounty; but he assured her that his money should be forthcoming, almost to any extent, if it could be made available.

On the following morning he went down to the hotel, and saw the real landlord. He found him to be a reasonable, tranquil, and very good-natured man,—who was possessed by a not irrational desire that his customers' bills should be paid; but who seemed to be much less eager on the subject than are English landlords in general. His chief anxiety seemed to arise from the great difficulty of doing anything with the gentleman who was now lying in his bed up-stairs. "Has he had any breakfast?" Mr. Palliser asked.

"Breakfast! Oh yes;" and the landlord laughed. He had been very particular in the orders he had given. He had desired his cutlets to be dressed in a particular way,—with a great deal of cayenne pepper, and they had been so dressed. He had ordered a bottle of Sauterne; but the landlord had thought, or the head-waiter acting for him had thought, that a bottle of ordinary wine of the country would do as well. The bottle of ordinary wine of the country had just that moment been sent up-stairs.

Then Mr. Palliser sat down in the landlord's little room, and had Burgo Fitzgerald's bill brought to him. "I think I might venture to pay it," said Mr. Palliser.

"That was as monsieur pleased," said the landlord, with something like a sparkle in his eye.

What was Mr. Palliser to do? He did not know whether, in accordance with the rules of the world in which he lived, he ought to pay it, or ought to leave it; and certainly the landlord could not tell him. Then he thought of his wife. He could not go back to his wife without having done something; so, as a first measure, he paid the bill. The landlord's eyes glittered, and he receipted it in the most becoming manner.

"Should he now send up the bottle of Sauterne?"—but to this Mr. Palliser demurred.

"And to whom should the receipted bill be given?" Mr. Palliser thought that the landlord had better keep it himself for a while.

"Perhaps there is some little difficulty?" suggested the landlord.

Mr. Palliser acknowledged that there was a little difficulty. He knew that he must do something more. He could not simply pay the bill and go away. That would not satisfy his wife. He knew that he must do something more; but how was he to do it? So at last he let the landlord into his confidence. He did not tell the whole of Burgo's past history. He did not tell that little episode in Burgo's life which referred to Lady Glencora. But he did make the landlord understand that he was willing to administer money to Mr. Fitzgerald, if only it could only be administered judiciously.

"You can't keep him out of the gambling salon, you know, sir; that is, not if he has a franc in his pocket." As to that the landlord was very confident.

It was at last arranged, that the landlord was to tell Burgo that his bill did not signify at present, and that the use of the hotel was to be at Burgo's command for the next three months. At the end of that time he was to have notice to quit. No money was to be advanced to him;—but the landlord, even in this respect, had a discretion.

"When I get home, I will see what can be done with his relations there," said Mr. Palliser. Then he went home and told his wife.

"But he'll have no clothes," said Lady Glencora.

Mr. Palliser said that the judicious landlord would manage that also; and in that way Lady Glencora was appeased,—appeased, till something final could be done for the young man, on Mr. Palliser's return home.

Poor Burgo! He must now be made to end his career as far as these pages are concerned. He soon found that something had been done for him at the hotel, and no doubt he must have made some guess near the truth. The discreet landlord told him nothing,—would tell him nothing; but that his bill did not signify as yet. Burgo, thinking about it, resolved to write about it in an indignant strain to Mr. Palliser; but the letter did not get itself written. When in England, Mr. Palliser saw Sir Cosmo Monk, and with many apologies, told him what he had done.

"I regret it," said Sir Cosmo, in anger. "I regret it; not for the money's sake, but I regret it." The amount expended, was however repaid to Mr. Palliser, and an arrangement was made for remitting a weekly sum of fifteen pounds to Burgo, through a member of the diplomatic corps, as long as he should remain at a certain small German town which was indicated, and in which there was no public gambling-table. Lady Glencora expressed herself satisfied for the present; but I must doubt whether poor Burgo lived long in comfort on the allowance made to him.

Here we must say farewell to Burgo Fitzgerald.

CHAPTER LXXVII
THE TRAVELLERS RETURN HOME

Mr. Palliser did not remain long in Baden after the payment of Burgo's bill. Perhaps I shall not throw any undeserved discredit on his courage if I say that he was afraid to do so. What would he have said,—what would he have been able to say, if that young man had come to him demanding an explanation? So he hurried away to Strasbourg the same day, much to his wife's satisfaction.

The journey home from thence was not marked by any incidents. Gradually Mr. Palliser became a little more lenient to his wife and slightly less oppressive in his caution. If he still inquired about the springs of the carriages, he did so in silence, and he ceased to enjoin the necessity of a day's rest after each day's journey. By the time that they reached Dover he had become so used to his wife's condition that he made but little fluttering as she walked out of the boat by that narrow gangway which is so contrived as to make an arrival there a serious inconvenience to a lady, and a nuisance even to a man. He was somewhat staggered when a big man, in the middle of the night, insisted on opening the little basket which his wife carried, and was uncomfortable when obliged to stop her on the plank while he gave up the tickets which he thought had been already surrendered; but he was becoming used to his position, and bore himself like a man.

During their journey home Mr. Palliser had by no means kept his seat opposite to Lady Glencora with constancy. He had soon found that it was easier to talk to Mr. Grey than to his wife, and, consequently, the two ladies had been much together, as had also the two gentlemen. What the ladies discussed may be imagined. One was about to become a wife and the other a mother, and that was to be their fate after each had made up her mind that no such lot was to be hers. It may, however, be presumed that for every one word that Alice spoke Lady Glencora spoke ten. The two men, throughout these days of close intimacy, were intent upon politics. Mr. Palliser, who may be regarded as the fox who had lost his tail,—the tail being, in this instance, the comfort of domestic privacy,—was eager in recommending his new friend to cut off his tail also. "Your argument would be very well," said he, "if men were to be contented to live for themselves only."

"Your argument would be very well," said the other, "if it were used to a man who felt that he could do good to others by going into public life. But it is wholly inefficacious if it recommends public life simply or chiefly because a man may gratify his own ambition by public services."

"Of course there is personal gratification, and of course there is good done," said Mr. Palliser.

"Is,—or should be," said Mr. Grey.

"Exactly; and the two things must go together. The chief gratification comes from the feeling that you are of use."

"But if you feel that you would not be of use?"

We need not follow the argument any further. We all know its nature, and what between two such men would be said on both sides. We all know that neither of them would put the matter altogether in a true light. Men never can do so in words, let the light within themselves be ever so clear. I do not think that any man yet ever had such a gift of words as to make them a perfect exponent of all the wisdom within him. But the effect was partly that which the weaker man of the two desired,—the weaker in the gifts of nature, though art had in some respects made him stronger. Mr. Grey was shaken in his quiescent philosophy, and startled Alice,—startled her as much as he delighted her,—by a word or two he said as he walked with her in the courts of the Louvre. "It's all hollow here," he said, speaking of French politics.

"Very hollow," said Alice, who had no love for the French mode of carrying on public affairs.

"Of all modes of governing this seems to me to be the surest of coming to a downfall. Men are told that they are wise enough to talk, but not wise enough to have any power of action. It is as though men were cautioned that they were walking through gunpowder, and that no fire could be allowed them, but were at the same time enjoined to carry lucifer matches in their pockets. I don't believe in the gunpowder, and I think there should be fire, and plenty of it; but if I didn't want the fire I wouldn't have the matches."

"It's so odd to hear you talk politics," said Alice, laughing.

After this he dropped the subject for a while, as though he were ashamed of it, but in a very few minutes he returned to it manfully. "Mr. Palliser wants me to go into Parliament." Upon hearing this Alice said nothing. She was afraid to speak. After all that had passed she felt that it would not become her to show much outward joy on hearing such a proposition, so spoken by him, and yet she could say nothing without some sign of exultation in

her voice. So she walked on without speaking, and was conscious that her fingers trembled on his arm. "What do you say about it?" he asked.

"What do I say? Oh, John, what right can I have to say anything?"

"No one else can have so much right,—putting aside of course myself, who must be responsible for my own actions. He asked me whether I could afford it, and he seems to think that a smaller income suffices for such work now than it did a few years since. I believe that I could afford it, if I could get a seat that was not very expensive at the first outset. He could help me there."

"On that point, of course, I can have no opinion."

"No; not on that point. I believe we may take that for granted. Living in London for four or five months in the year might be managed. But as to the mode of life!"

Then Alice was unable to hold her tongue longer, and spoke out her thoughts with more vehemence than discretion. No doubt he combated them with some amount of opposition. He seldom allowed out-spoken enthusiasm to pass by him without some amount of hostility. But he was not so perverse as to be driven from his new views by the fact that Alice approved them, and she, as she drew near home, was able to think that the only flaw in his character was in process of being cured.

When they reached London they all separated. It was Mr. Palliser's purpose to take his wife down to Matching with as little delay as possible. London was at this time nearly empty, and all the doings of the season were over. It was now the first week of August, and as Parliament had not been sitting for nearly two months, the town looked as it usually looks in September. Lady Glencora was to stay but one day in Park Lane, and it had been understood between her and Alice that they were not to see each other.

"How odd it is parting in this way, when people have been together so long," said Lady Glencora. "It always seems as though there had been a separate little life of its own which was now to be brought to a close. I suppose, Mr. Grey, you and I, when we next meet, will be far too distant to fight with each other."

"I hope that may never be the case," said Mr. Grey.

"I suppose nothing would prevent his fighting; would it Alice? But, remember, there must be no fighting when we do meet next, and that must be in September."

"With all my heart," said Mr. Grey. But Alice said nothing.

Then Mr. Palliser made his little speech. "Alice," he said, as he gave his hand to Miss Vavasor, "give my compliments to your father, and tell him that I shall take the liberty of asking him to come down to Matching for the early shooting in September, and that I shall expect him to bring you with him. You may tell him also that he will have to stay to see you off, but that he will not be allowed to take you away." Lady Glencora thought that this was very pretty as coming from her husband, and so she told him on their way home.

Alice insisted on going to Queen Anne Street in a cab by herself. Mr. Palliser had offered a carriage, and Mr. Grey, of course, offered himself as a protector; but she would have neither the one nor the other. If he had gone with her he might by chance have met her father, and she was most anxious that she should not be encumbered by her lover's presence when she first received her father's congratulations. They had slept at Dover, and had come up by a mid-day train. When she reached Queen Anne Street, the house was desolate, and she might therefore have allowed Mr. Grey to attend her. But she found a letter waiting for her which made her for the moment forget both him and her father. Lady Macleod, at Cheltenham, was very ill, and wished to see her niece, as she said, before she died. "I have got your letter," said the kind old woman, "and am now quite happy. It only wanted that to reconcile me to my departure. I thought through it all that my girl would be happy at last. Will she forgive me if I say that I have forgiven her?" The letter then went on to beg Alice to come to Cheltenham at once. "It is not that I am dying now," said Lady Macleod, "though you will find me much altered and keeping my bed. But the doctor says he fears the first cold weather. I know what that means, my dear; and if I don't see you now, before your marriage, I shall never see you again. Pray get married as soon as you can. I want to know that you are Mrs. Grey before I go. If I were to hear that it was postponed because of my illness, I think it would kill me at once."

There was another letter for her from Kate, full, of course, of congratulations, and promising to be at the wedding; "that is," said Kate, "unless it takes place at the house of some one of your very grand friends;" and telling her that aunt Greenow was to be married in a fortnight;—telling her of this, and begging her to attend that wedding. "You should stand by your family," said Kate. "And only think what my condition will be if I have no one here to support me. Do come. Journeys are nothing nowadays. Don't you know I would go seven times the distance for you? Mr. Cheesacre and Captain Bellfield are friends after all, and Mr. Cheesacre is to be best man. Is it not beautiful? As for poor me, I'm told I haven't a chance left of becoming mistress of Oileymead and all its wealth."

Alice began to think that her hands were almost too full. If she herself were to be married in September, even by the end of September, her hands were very full indeed. Yet she did not know how to refuse any of the requests made to her. As to Lady Macleod, her visit to her was a duty which must of course be performed at once. She would stay but one day in London, and then go down to Cheltenham. Having resolved upon this she at once wrote to her aunt to that effect. As to that other affair down in Westmoreland, she sighed as she thought of it, but she feared that she must go there also. Kate had suffered too much on her behalf to allow of her feeling indifferent to such a request.

Then her father came in. "I didn't in the least know when you might arrive," said he, beginning with an apology for his absence. "How could I, my dear?" Alice scorned to remind him that she herself had named the precise hour of the train by which they had arrived. "It's all right, papa," said she. "I was very glad to have an hour to write a letter or two. Poor Lady Macleod is very ill. I must go to her the day after to-morrow."

"Dear, dear, dear! I had heard that she was poorly. She is very old, you know. So, Alice, you've made it all square with Mr. Grey at last?"

"Yes, papa;—if you call that square."

"Well; I do call it square. It has all come round to the proper thing."

"I hope he thinks so."

"What do you think yourself, my dear?"

"I've no doubt it's the proper thing for me, papa."

"Of course not; of course not; and I can tell you this, Alice, he is a man in a thousand. You've heard about the money?"

"What money, papa?"

"The money that George had." As the reader is aware, Alice had heard nothing special about this money. She only knew, or supposed she knew, that she had given three thousand pounds to her cousin. But now her father explained to her the whole transaction. "We couldn't have realized your money for months, perhaps," said he; "but Grey knew that some men must have rope enough before they can hang themselves."

Alice was unable to say anything on this subject to her father, but to herself she did declare that not in that way or with that hope had John Grey produced his money. "He must be paid, papa," she said. "Paid!" he answered; "he can pay himself now. It may make some difference in the settlements, perhaps, but he and the lawyers may arrange that. I shan't think of interfering with such a man as Grey. If you could only know, my dear, what I've suffered!" Alice in a penitential tone expressed her sorrow, and then he too assured her that he had forgiven her. "Bless you, my child!" he said, "and make you happy, and good, and—and—and very comfortable." After that he went back to his club.

Alice made her journey down to Cheltenham without any adventure, and was received by Lady Macleod with open arms. "Dearest Alice, it is so good of you." "Good!" said Alice, "would I not have gone a thousand miles to you?"

Lady Macleod was very eager to know all about the coming marriage. "I can tell you now, my dear, though I couldn't do it before, that I knew he'd persist for ever. He told me so himself in confidence."

"He has persisted, aunt; that is certain."

"And I hope you'll reward him. A beautiful woman without discretion is like a pearl in a swine's snout; but a good wife is a crown of glory to her husband. Remember that, my dear, and choose your part for his sake."

"I won't be that unfortunate pearl, if I can help it, aunt."

"We can all help it, if we set about it in the right way. And Alice, you must be careful to find out all his likes and his dislikes. Dear me! I remember how hard I found it, but then I don't think I was so clever as you are."

"Sometimes I think nobody has ever been so stupid as I have."

"Not stupid, my dear; if I must say the word, it is self-willed. But, dear, all that is forgiven now. Is it not?"

"There is a forgiveness which it is rather hard to get," said Alice.

There was something said then as to the necessity of looking for pardon beyond this world, which I need not here repeat. To all her old friend's little sermons Alice was infinitely more attentive than had been her wont, so that Lady Macleod was comforted and took heart of grace, and at last brought forth from under her pillow a letter from the Countess of Midlothian, which she had received a day or two since, and which bore upon Alice's case. "I was not quite sure whether I'd show it you," said Lady Macleod, "because you wouldn't answer her when she wrote to you. But when I'm gone, as I shall be soon, she will be the nearest relative you have on your mother's side, and from her great position, you know, Alice—" But here Alice became impatient for the letter. Her aunt handed it to her, and she read as follows:—

Castle Reekie, July, 186—.

Dear Lady Macleod,—

I am sorry to hear of the symptoms you speak about. I strongly advise you to depend chiefly on beef-tea. They should be very careful to send it up quite free from grease, and it should not be too strong of the meat. There should be no vegetables in it. Not soup, you know, but beef-tea. If any thing acts upon your strength, that will. I need not tell one who has lived as you have done where to look for that other strength which alone can support you at such a time as this. I would go to you if I thought that my presence would be any comfort to you, but I know how sensitive you are, and the shock might be too much for you.

If you see Alice Vavasor on her return to England, as you probably will, pray tell her from me that I give her my warmest congratulations, and that I am heartily glad that matters are arranged. I think she treated my attempts to heal the wound in a manner that they did not deserve; but all that shall be forgiven, as shall also her original bad behaviour to poor Mr. Grey.

Alice was becoming weary of so much forgiveness, and told herself, as she was reading the letter, that that of Lady Midlothian was at any rate unnecessary. "I trust that we may yet meet and be friends," continued Lady Midlothian. "I am extremely gratified at finding that she has been thought so much of by Mr. Palliser. I'm told that Mr. Palliser and Mr. Grey have become great friends, and if this is so, Alice must be happy to feel that she has had it in her power to confer so great a benefit on her future husband as he will receive from this introduction." "I ain't a bit happy, and I have conferred no benefit on Mr. Grey," exclaimed Alice, who was unable to repress the anger occasioned by the last paragraph.

"But it is a great benefit, my dear."

"Mr. Palliser has every bit as much cause to be gratified for that as Mr. Grey, and perhaps more."

Poor Lady Macleod could not argue the matter in her present state. She merely sighed, and moved her shrivelled old hand up and down upon the counterpane. Alice finished the letter without further remarks. It merely went on to say how happy the writer would be to know something of her cousin as Mrs. Grey, as also to know something of Mr. Grey, and then gave a general invitation to both Mr. and Mrs. Grey, asking them to come to Castle Reekie whenever they might be able. The Marchioness, with whom Lady Midlothian was staying, had expressly desired her to give this message.

Alice, however, could not but observe that Lady Midlothian's invitation applied only to another person's house.

"I'm sure she means well," said Alice.

"Indeed she does," said Lady Macleod, "and then you know you'll probably have children; and think what a thing it will be for them to know the Midlothian family. You shouldn't rob them of their natural advantages."

Alice remained a week with her aunt, and went from thence direct to Westmoreland. Some order as to bridal preparations we must presume she gave on that single day which she passed in London. Much advice she had received on this head from Lady Glencora, and no inconsiderable amount of assistance was to be rendered to her at Matching during the fortnight she would remain there before her marriage. Something also, let us hope, she might do at Cheltenham. Something no doubt she did do. Something also might probably be achieved among the wilds in Westmoreland, but that something would necessarily be of a nature not requiring fashionable tradespeople. While at Cheltenham, she determined that she would not again return to London before her marriage. This resolve was caused by a very urgent letter from Mr. Grey, and by another, almost equally urgent, from Lady Glencora. If the marriage did not take place in September she would not be present at it. The gods of the world,—of Lady Glencora's world,—had met together and come to a great decision. Lady Glencora was to be removed in October to Gatherum Castle, and remain there till the following spring, so that the heir might, in truth, be born in the purple. "It is such a bore," said Lady Glencora, "and I know it will be a girl. But the Duke isn't to be there, except for the Christmas week." An invitation for the ceremony at Matching had been sent from Mr. Palliser to Mr. Vavasor, and another from Lady Glencora to Kate, "whom I long to know," said her ladyship, "and with whom I should like to pick a crow, if I dared, as I'm sure she did all the mischief."

CHAPTER LXXVIII
MR. CHEESACRE'S FATE

It must be acknowledged that Mrs. Greenow was a woman of great resources, and that she would be very prudent for others, though I fear the verdict of those who know her must go against her in regard to prudence in herself. Her marriage with Captain Bellfield was a rash act,—certainly a rash act, although she did take so much care in securing the payment of her own income into her own hands; but the manner in which she made him live discreetly for some months previous to his marriage, the tact with which she renewed the friendship which had existed between him and Mr. Cheesacre, and the skill she used in at last providing Mr. Cheesacre with a wife, oblige us all to admit that, as a general, she had great powers.

When Alice reached Vavasor Hall she found Charlie Fairstairs established there on a long visit. Charlie and Kate were to be the two bridesmaids, and, as Kate told her cousin in their first confidential intercourse on the evening of Alice's arrival, there were already great hopes in the household that the master of Oileymead might be brought to surrender. It was true that Charlie had not a shilling, and that Mr. Cheesacre had set his heart on marrying an heiress. It was true that Miss Fairstairs had always stood low in the gentleman's estimation, as being connected with people who were as much without rank and fashion as they were without money, and that the gentleman loved rank and fashion dearly. It was true that Charlie was no beauty, and that Cheesacre had an eye for feminine charms. It was true that he had despised Charlie, and had spoken his contempt openly;—that he had seen the girl on the sands at Yarmouth every summer for the last ten years, and about the streets of Norwich every winter, and had learned to regard her as a thing poor and despicable, because she was common in his eyes. It is thus that the Cheesacres judge of people. But in spite of all these difficulties Mrs. Greenow had taken up poor Charlie's case, and Kate Vavasor expressed a strong opinion that her aunt would win.

"What has she done to the man?" Alice asked.

"Coaxed him; simply that. She has made herself so much his master that he doesn't know how to say no to her. Sometimes I have thought that he might possibly run away, but I have abandoned that fear now. She has little confidences with him from day to day, which are so alluring to him that he cannot tear himself off. In the middle of one of them he will find himself engaged."

"But, the unfortunate girl! Won't it be a wretched marriage for her?"

"Not at all. She'll make him a very good wife. He's one of those men to whom any woman, after a little time, will come to be the same. He'll be rough with her once a month or so, and perhaps tell her that she brought no money with her; but that won't break any bones, and Charlie will know how to fight her own battles. She'll save his money if she brings none, and in a few years' time they will quite understand each other."

Mr. Cheesacre and Captain Bellfield were at this time living in lodgings together, at Penrith, but came over and spent every other day at Vavasor, returning always to their lodgings in the evening. It wanted but eight days to the marriage when Alice arrived, and preparations for that event were in progress. "It's to be very quiet, Alice," said her aunt; "as quiet as such a thing can be made. I owe that to the memory of the departed one. I know that he is looking down upon me, and that he approves all that I do. Indeed, he told me once that he did not want me to live desolate for his sake. If I didn't feel that he was looking down and approving it, I should be wretched indeed." She took Alice up to see her trousseau, and gave the other expectant bride some little hints which, under present circumstances, might be useful. "Yes, indeed; only three-and-sixpence a piece, and they're quite real. Feel them. You wouldn't get them in the shops under six." Alice did feel them, and wondered whether her aunt could have saved the half-crown honestly. "I had my eyes about me when I was up in town, my dear. And look here, these are quite new,—have never been on yet, and I had them when I was married before. There is nothing like being careful, my dear. I hate meanness, as everybody knows who knows me; but there is nothing like being careful. You have a lot of rich people about you just now, and will have ever so many things given you which you won't want. Do you put them all by, and be careful. They may turn out useful, you know." Saying this, Mrs. Greenow folded up, among her present bridal belongings, sundries of the wealth which had accrued to her in an earlier stage of her career.

And then Mrs. Greenow opened her mind to Alice about the Captain. "He's as good as gold, my dear; he is, indeed,—in his own way. Of course, I know that he has faults, and I should like to know who hasn't. Although poor dear Greenow certainly was more without them than anybody else I ever knew." As this remembrance came upon Mrs. Greenow she put her handkerchief to her eyes, and Alice observed that that which she held still bore the deepest hem of widowhood. They would be used, no doubt, till the last day, and then put by in lavender for future possible occasions. "Bellfield may have been a little extravagant. I dare say he has. But how can a man help being extravagant when he hasn't got any regular income? He has been ill-treated in his profession; very. It makes my blood curdle when I think of it. After fighting his country's battles through blood, and dust, and wounds;—but I'll tell you about that another time."

"I suppose a man seldom does make a fortune, aunt, by being a soldier?"

"Never, my dear; much better be a tailor. Don't you ever marry a soldier. But as I was saying, he is the best-tempered creature alive, and the staunchest friend I ever met. You should hear what Mr. Cheesacre says of him! But you don't know Mr. Cheesacre?"

"No, aunt, not yet. If you remember, he went away before I saw him when he came here before."

"Yes, I know, poor fellow! Between you and me, Kate might have had him if she liked; but perhaps Kate was right."

"I don't think he would have suited Kate at all."

"Because of the farmyard, you mean? Kate shouldn't give herself airs. Money's never dirty, you know. But perhaps it's all for the best. There's a sweet girl here to whom he is violently attached, and who I hope will become Mrs. Cheesacre. But as I was saying, the friendship between these two men is quite wonderful, and I have always observed that when a man can create that kind of affection in the bosom of another man, he invariably is,—the sort of man,—the man, in fact, who makes a good husband."

Alice knew the story of Charlie Fairstairs and her hopes; knew of the quarrels between Bellfield and Cheesacre; knew almost as much of Bellfield's past life as Mrs. Greenow did herself; and Mrs. Greenow was no doubt aware that such was the case. Nevertheless, she had a pleasure in telling her own story, and told it as though she believed every word that she spoke.

On the following day the two gentlemen came over, according to custom, and Alice observed that Miss Fairstairs hardly spoke to Mr. Cheesacre. Indeed her manner of avoiding that gentleman was so very marked, that it was impossible not to observe it. They drank tea out of doors, and when Mr. Cheesacre on one occasion sauntered across towards the end of the bench on which Charlie was sitting, Charlie got up and walked away. And in strolling about the place afterwards, and in going up through the wood, she was at great pains to attach herself to some other person, so that there should be no such attaching between her and the owner of Oileymead. At one time Mr. Cheesacre did get close up to her and spoke some word, some very indifferent word. He knew that he was being cut and he wanted to avoid the appearance of a scene. "I don't know, sir," said Charlie, again moving away with excellent dignity, and she at once attached herself to Alice who was close by. "I know you have just come home from Switzerland," said Charlie. "Beautiful Switzerland! My heart pants for Switzerland. Do tell me something about Switzerland!" Mr. Cheesacre had heard that Alice was the dear friend of a lady who would probably some day become a duchess. He therefore naturally held her in awe, and slunk away. On this occasion Mrs. Greenow clung lovingly to her future husband, and the effect was that Mr. Cheesacre found himself to be very much alone and unhappy. He had generally enjoyed these days at Vavasor Hall, having found himself, or fancied himself, to be the dominant spirit there. That Mrs. Greenow was always in truth the dominant spirit I need hardly say; but she knew how to make a companion happy, and well also how to make him wretched. On the whole of this day poor Cheesacre was very wretched.

"I don't think I shall go there any more," he said to Bellfield, as he drove the gig back to Penrith that evening.

"Not go there any more, Cheesy," said Bellfield; "why, we are to have the dinner out in the field on Friday. It's your own bespeak."

"Well, yes; I'll go on Friday, but not after that."

"You'll stop and see me turned off, old fellow?"

"What's the use? You'll get your wife, and that's enough for you. The truth is, that since that girl came down from London with her d——d airs;" —the girl from London with the airs was poor Alice, —"the place is quite changed. I'm blessed if the whole thing isn't as dark as ditch-water. I'm a plain man, I am; and I do hate your swells." Against this view of the case Captain Bellfield argued stoutly; but Cheesacre had been offended, and throughout the next day he was cross and touchy. He wouldn't play billiards, and on one occasion hinted that he hoped he should get that money soon.

"You did it admirably, my dear," said Mrs. Greenow that night to Charlie Fairstairs. The widow was now on terms almost more confidential with Miss Fairstairs than with her own niece, Kate Vavasor. She loved a little bit of intrigue; and though Kate could intrigue, as we have seen in this story, Kate would not join her aunt's intrigues. "You did it admirably. I really did not think you had so much in you."

"Oh, I don't know," said Charlie, blushing at the praise.

"And it's the only way, my dear;—the only way, I mean, for you with such a one as him. And if he does come round, you'll find him an excellent husband."

"I don't think he cares for me a bit," said Charlie whimpering.

"Pooh, nonsense! Girls never know whether men care for them or not. If he asks you to marry him, won't that be a sign that he cares for you? and if he don't, why, there'll be no harm done."

"If he thinks it's his money—" began Charlie.

"Now, don't talk nonsense, Charlie," said Mrs. Greenow, "or you'll make me sick. Of course it's his money, more or less. You don't mean to tell me you'd go and fall in love with him if he was like Bellfield, and hadn't got a rap? I can afford that sort of thing; you can't. I don't mean to say you ain't to love him. Of course, you're to love him; and I've no doubt you will, and make him a very good wife. I always think that worldliness and sentimentality are like brandy-and-water. I don't like either of them separately, but taken together they make a very nice drink. I like them warm, with —— as the gentlemen say." To this little lecture Miss Fairstairs listened with dutiful patience, and when it was over she said nothing more of her outraged affections or of her disregard for money. "And now, my dear, mind you look your best on Friday. I'll get him away immediately after dinner, and when he's done with me you can contrive to be in his way, you know."

The next day was what Kate called the blank day at the Hall. The ladies were all alone, and devoted themselves, as was always the case on the blank days, to millinery and household cares. Mrs. Greenow, as has before been stated, had taken a lease of the place, and her troubles extended beyond her mere bridal wardrobe. Large trunks of household linen had arrived, and all this linen was marked with the name of Greenow; Greenow, 5.58; Greenow, 7.52; and a good deal had to be done before this ancient wealth of housewifery could probably be converted to Bellfield purposes. "We must cut out the pieces, Jeannette, and work 'em in again ever so carefully," said the widow, after some painful consideration. "It will always show," said Jeannette, shaking her head. "But the other would show worse," said the widow; "and if you finedraw it, not one person in ten will notice it. We'd always put them on with the name to the feet, you know."

It was not quite true that Cheesacre had bespoke the dinner out in the field, although no doubt he thought he had done so. The little treat, if treat it was, had all been arranged by Mrs. Greenow, who was ever ready to create festivities. There was not much scope for a picnic here. Besides their own party, which, of course, included the Captain and Mr. Cheesacre, no guest could be caught except the clergyman;—that low-church clergyman, who was so anxious about his income, and with whom the old Squire had quarrelled. Mrs. Greenow had quickly obtained the advantage of his alliance, and he, who was soon to perform on her behalf the marriage ceremony, had promised to grace this little festival. The affair simply amounted to this, that they were to eat their dinner uncomfortably in the field instead of comfortably in the dining-room. But Mrs. Greenow knew that Charlie's charms would be much strengthened by a dinner out-of-doors. "Nothing," she said to Kate, "nothing makes a man come forward so well as putting him altogether out of his usual tack. A man who wouldn't think of such a thing in the drawing-room would be sure to make an offer if he spent an evening with a young lady down-stairs in the kitchen."

At two o'clock the gig from Penrith arrived at the Hall, and for the next hour both Cheesacre and the Captain were engaged in preparing the tables and carrying out the viands. The Captain and Charlie Fairstairs were going to lay the cloth. "Let me do it," said Cheesacre taking it out of the Captain's hands. "Oh, certainly," said the Captain, giving up his prize. "Captain Bellfield would do it much better," said Charlie, with a little toss of her head; "he's as good as a married man, and they always do these things best."

The day was fine, and although the shade was not perfect, and the midges were troublesome, the dinner went off very nicely. It was beautiful to see how well Mrs. Greenow remembered herself about the grace, seeing that the clergyman was there. She was just in time, and would have been very angry with herself, and have thought herself awkward, had she forgotten it. Mr. Cheesacre sat on her right hand, and the clergyman on her left, and she hardly spoke a word to Bellfield. Her sweetest smiles were all given to Cheesacre. She was specially anxious to keep her neighbour, the parson, in good-humour, and therefore illuminated him once in every five minutes with a passing ray, but the full splendour of her light was poured out upon

Cheesacre, as it never had before been poured. How she did flatter him, and with what a capacious gullet did he swallow her flatteries! Oileymead was the only paradise she had ever seen. "Ah, me; when I think of it sometimes, — but never mind." A moment came to him when he thought that even yet he might win the race, and send Bellfield away howling into outer darkness. A moment came to him, and the widow saw the moment well. "I know I have done for the best," said she, "and therefore I shall never regret it; at any rate, it's done now."

"Not done yet," said he plaintively.

"Yes; done, and done, and done. Besides, a man in your position in the county should always marry a wife younger than yourself, — a good deal younger." Cheesacre did not understand the argument, but he liked the allusion to his position in the county, and he perceived that it was too late for any changes in the present arrangements. But he was happy; and all that feeling of animosity to Alice had vanished from his breast. Poor Alice! she, at any rate, was innocent. With so much of her own to fill her mind, she had been but little able to take her share in the Greenow festivities; and we may safely say, that if Mr. Cheesacre's supremacy was on any occasion attacked, it was not attacked by her. His supremacy on this occasion was paramount, and during the dinner, and after the dinner, he was allowed to give his orders to Bellfield in a manner that must have gratified him much. "You must have another glass of champagne with me, my friend," said Mrs. Greenow; and Mr. Cheesacre drank the other glass of champagne. It was not the second nor the third that he had taken.

After dinner they started off for a ramble through the fields, and Mrs. Greenow and Mr. Cheesacre were together. I think that Charlie Fairstairs did not go with them at all. I think she went into the house and washed her face, and brushed her hair, and settled her muslin. I should not wonder if she took off her frock and ironed it again. Captain Bellfield, I know, went with Alice, and created some astonishment by assuring her that he fully meant to correct the error of his ways. "I know what it is," he said, "to be connected with such a family as yours, Miss Vavasor." He too had heard about the future duchess, and wished to be on his best behaviour. Kate fell to the lot of the parson.

"This is the last time we shall ever be together in this way," said the widow to her friend.

"Oh, no," said Cheesacre; "I hope not."

"The last time. On Wednesday I become Mrs. Bellfield, and I need hardly say that I have many things to think of before that; but Mr. Cheesacre, I hope we are not to be strangers hereafter?" Mr. Cheesacre said that he hoped not. Oileymead would always be open to Captain and Mrs. Bellfield.

"We all know your hospitality," said she; "it is not to-day nor to-morrow that I or my husband,—that is to be,—will have to learn that. He always declares that you are the very beau ideal of an English country gentleman."

"Merely a poor Norfolk farmer," said Cheesacre. "I never want to put myself beyond my own place. There has been some talk about the Commission of the Peace, but I don't think anything of it."

"It has been the greatest blessing in the world for him that he has ever known you," said Mrs. Greenow, still talking about her future husband.

"I've tried to be good-natured; that's all. D—— me, Mrs. Greenow, what's the use of living if one doesn't try to be good-natured? There isn't a better fellow than Bellfield living. He and I ran for the same plate, and he has won it. He's a lucky fellow, and I don't begrudge him his luck."

"That's so manly of you, Mr. Cheesacre! But, indeed, the plate you speak of was not worth your running for."

"I may have my own opinion about that, you know."

"It was not. Nobody knows that as well as I do, or could have thought over the whole matter so often. I know very well what my mission is in life. The mistress of your house, Mr. Cheesacre, should not be any man's widow."

"She wouldn't be a widow then, you know."

"A virgin heart should be yours; and a virgin heart may be yours, if you choose to accept it."

"Oh, bother!"

"If you choose to take my solicitude on your behalf in that way, of course I have done. You were good enough to say just now that you wished to see me and my husband in your hospitable halls. After all that has passed, do you think that I could be a visitor at your house unless there is a mistress there?"

"Upon my word, I think you might."

"No, Mr. Cheesacre; certainly not. For all our sakes, I should decline. But if you were married—"

"You are always wanting to marry me, Mrs. Greenow."

"I do, I do. It is the only way in which there can be any friendship between us, and not for worlds would I lose that advantage for my husband,—let alone what I may feel for myself."

"Why didn't you take me yourself, Mrs. Greenow?"

"If you can't understand, it is not for me to say anything more, Mr. Cheesacre. If you value the warm affection of a virgin heart—"

"Why, Mrs. Greenow, all yesterday she wouldn't say a word to me."

"Not say a word to you? Is that all you know about it? Are you so ignorant that you cannot see when a girl's heart is breaking beneath her stays?" This almost improper allusion had quite an effect on Mr. Cheesacre's sensitive bosom. "Did you say a word to her yesterday? And if not, why have you said so many words before?"

"Oh, Mrs. Greenow; come!"

"It is, oh, Mrs. Greenow. But it is time that we should go back to them." They had been sitting all this time on a bank, under a hedge. "We will have our tea, and you shall have your pipe and brandy-and-water, and Charlie shall bring it to you. Shall she, Mr. Cheesacre?"

"If she likes she shall, of course."

"Do you ask her, and she'll like it quick enough. But remember, Mr. Cheesacre, I'm quite serious in what I say about your having a mistress for your house. Only think what an age you'll be when your children grow up, if you don't marry soon now."

They returned to the field in which they had dined, and found Charlie under the trees, with her muslin looking very fresh. "What, all a-mort?" said Mrs. Greenow. Charlie did not quite understand this, but replied that she preferred being alone. "I have told him that you should fill his pipe for him," said Mrs. Greenow. "He doesn't care for ladies to fill his pipe for him," said Charlie. "Do you try," said the widow, "while I go indoors and order the tea."

It had been necessary to put the bait very close before Cheesacre's eyes, or there would have been no hope that he might take it. The bait had been put so very close that we must feel sure that he saw the hook. But there are fish so silly that they will take the bait although they know the hook is there. Cheesacre understood it all. Many things he could not see, but he could see that Mrs. Greenow was trying to catch him as a husband for Charlie Fairstairs; and he knew also that he had always despised Charlie, and that no worldly advantage whatever would accrue to him by a marriage with such a girl. But there she was, and he didn't quite know how to avoid it. She did look rather nice in her clear-starched muslin frock, and he felt that he should like to kiss her. He needn't marry her because he kissed her. The champagne which had created the desire also gave him the audacity. He gave one glance around him to see that he was not observed, and then he did kiss Charlie Fairstairs under the trees. "Oh, Mr. Cheesacre," said Charlie. "Oh, Mr. Cheesacre," echoed a laughing voice; and poor Cheesacre, looking round, saw that Mrs. Greenow, who ought to have been inside the house looking after the boiling water, was moving about for some unknown reason within sight of the spot which he had chosen for his dalliance.

"Mr. Cheesacre," said Charlie sobbing, "how dare you do that?—and where all the world could see you?"

"It was only Mrs. Greenow," said Cheesacre.

"And what will she think of me?"

"Lord bless you—she won't think anything about it."

"But I do;—I think a great deal about it. I don't know what to do, I don't;—I don't." Whereupon Charlie got up from her seat under the trees and began to move away slowly. Cheesacre thought about it for a moment or two. Should he follow her or should he not? He knew that he had better not follow her. He knew that she was bait with a very visible hook. He knew that he was a big fish for whom these two women were angling. But after all, perhaps it wouldn't do him much harm to be caught. So he got up and followed her. I don't suppose she meant to take the way towards the woods,—towards the little path leading to the old summer-house up in the trees. She was too much beside herself to know where she was going, no doubt. But that was the path she did take, and before long she and Cheesacre were in the summerhouse together. "Don't, Sam, don't! Somebody really will be coming. Well, then, there. Now I won't do it again." 'Twas thus she spoke when the last kiss was given on this occasion;—unless there may have been one or two later in the evening, to which it is not necessary more especially to allude here. But on the occasion of that last kiss in the summer-house Miss Fairstairs was perfectly justified by circumstances, for she was then the promised bride of Mr. Cheesacre.

But how was he to get down again among his friends? That consideration troubled Mr. Cheesacre as he rose from his happy seat after that last embrace. He had promised Charlie, and perhaps he would keep his promise, but it might be as well not to make it all too public at once. But Charlie wasn't going to be thrown over;—not if she knew it, as she said to herself. She returned therefore triumphantly among them all,—blushing indeed, and with her eyes turned away, and her hand now remained upon her lover's arm;—but still so close to him that there could be no mistake. "Goodness, gracious, Charlie! where have you and Mr. Cheesacre been?" said Mrs. Greenow. "We got up into the woods and lost ourselves," said Charlie. "Oh, indeed," said Mrs. Greenow.

It would be too long to tell now, in these last pages of our story, how Cheesacre strove to escape, and with what skill Mrs. Greenow kept him to his bargain. I hope that Charlie Fairstairs was duly grateful. Before that evening was over, under the comfortable influence of a glass of hot brandy-and-water,—the widow had, I think, herself mixed the second glass for Mr. Cheesacre, before the influence became sufficiently comfortable,—he was forced to own that he had made himself the happy possessor of Charlie Fairstairs' heart and hand. "And you are a lucky man," said the widow with enthusiasm; "and I congratulate you with all my heart. Don't let there be any delay now, because a good thing can't be done too soon." And indeed, before that night was over, Mrs. Greenow had the pair together in her own presence, and then fixed the day. "A fellow ought to be allowed to turn himself," Cheesacre said to her, pleading for himself in a whisper. But no; Mrs. Greenow would give him no such mercy. She knew to what a man turning himself might probably lead. She was a woman who was quite in earnest when she went to work, and I hope that Miss Fairstairs was grateful. Then, in that presence, was in truth the last kiss given on that eventful evening. "Come, Charlie, be good-natured to him. He's as good as your own now," said the widow. And Charlie was good-natured. "It's to be as soon as ever we come back from our trip," said Mrs. Greenow to Kate, the next day, "and I'm lending her money to get all her things at once. He shall come to the scratch, though I go all the way to Norfolk by myself and fetch him by his ears. He shall come, as sure as my name's Greenow,—or Bellfield, as it will be then, you know."

"And I shouldn't wonder if she did have to go to Norfolk," said Kate to her cousin. That event, however, cannot be absolutely concluded in these pages. I can only say that, when I think of Mrs. Greenow's force of character and warmth of friendship, I feel that Miss Fairstairs' prospects stand on good ground.

Mrs. Greenow's own marriage was completed with perfect success. She took Captain Bellfield for better or for worse, with a thorough determination to make the best of his worst, and to put him on his legs, if any such putting might be possible. He, at any rate, had been in luck. If any possible stroke of fortune could do him good, he had found that stroke. He had found a wife who could forgive all his past offences,—and also, if necessary, some future offences; who had money enough for all his wants, and kindness enough to gratify them, and who had, moreover,—which for the Captain was the most important,—strength enough to keep from him the power of ruining them both. Reader, let us wish a happy married life to Captain and Mrs. Bellfield!

The day after the ceremony Alice Vavasor and Kate Vavasor started for Matching Priory.

CHAPTER LXXIX
DIAMONDS ARE DIAMONDS

Kate and Alice, as they drew near to their journey's end, were both a little flurried, and I cannot but own that there was cause for nervousness. Kate Vavasor was to meet Mr. Grey for the first time. Mr. Grey was now staying at Matching and was to remain there until a week of his marriage. He was then to return to Cambridgeshire for a day or two, and after that was to become a guest at the rector's house at Matching the evening before the ceremony. "Why not let him come here at once?" Lady Glencora had said to her husband. "It is such nonsense, you know." But Mr. Palliser would not hear of it. Mr. Palliser, though a Radical in public life, would not for worlds transgress the social laws of his ancestors; and so the matter was settled. Kate on this very day of her arrival at Matching would thus see Mr. Grey for the first time, and she could not but feel that she had been the means of doing Mr. Grey much injury. She had moreover something,—not much indeed, but still something,—of that feeling which made the Pallisers terrible to the imagination, because of their rank and wealth. She was a little afraid of the Pallisers, but of Mr. Grey she was very much afraid. And Alice also was not at her ease. She would fain have prevented so very quick a marriage had she not felt that now,—after all the trouble that she had caused,—there was nothing left for her but to do as others wished. When a day had been named she had hardly dared to demur, and had allowed Lady Glencora to settle everything as she had wished. But it was not only the suddenness of her marriage which dismayed her. Its nature and attributes were terrible to her. Both Lady Midlothian and the Marchioness of Auld Reekie were coming. When this was told to her by letter she had no means of escape. "Lady Macleod is right in nearly all that she says," Lady Glencora had written to her. "At any rate, you needn't be such a fool as to run away from your cousins, simply because they have handles to their names. You must take the thing as it comes." Lady Glencora, moreover, had settled for her the list of bridesmaids. Alice had made a petition that she might be allowed to go through the ceremony with only one,—with none but Kate to back her. But she ought to have known that when she consented to be married at Matching,—and indeed she had had very little power of resisting that proposition,—all such questions would be decided for her. Two daughters therefore of Lady Midlothian were to act, Lady Jane and Lady Mary, and the one daughter of the Marchioness, who was also a Lady Jane, and there were to be two Miss Howards down from London,—girls who were known both to Alice and to Lady Glencora, and who were in some distant way connected with them both. A great attempt was made to induce the two Miss Pallisers to join the bevy, but they had frankly pleaded their age. "No woman should stand up as a bridesmaid," said the strong-minded Sophy, "who doesn't mean to get married if she can. Now I don't mean to get married, and I won't put myself among the young people." Lady Glencora was therefore obliged to submit to do the work with only six. But she swore that they should be very smart. She was to give all the dresses, and Mr. Palliser was to give a brooch and an armlet to each. "She is the only person in the world I want to pet, except yourself," Lady Glencora had said to her husband, and he had answered by giving her *carte blanche* as regards expense.

Alice and her bridesmaids.

All this was very terrible to Kate, who had not much feminine taste for finery. Of the dress she had heard,—of the dress which was waiting at Matching to be made up after her arrival,—though as yet she knew nothing of the trinkets. There are many girls who could submit themselves at a moment to the kindness of such a woman as Lady Glencora. Perhaps most girls would do so, for of all such women in the world, Lady Glencora was the least inclined to patronize or to be condescending in her kindnesses. But Kate Vavasor was one to whom such submission would not come easily.

"I wish I was out of this boat," she said to Alice in the train.

"So that I might be shipwrecked alone!"

"No; there can be no shipwreck to you. When the day of action comes you will be taken away, up to heaven, upon the clouds. But what are they to do with me?"

"You'll find that Glencora will not desert you. You can't conceive what taste she has."

"I'd sooner be bridesmaid to Charlie Fairstairs. I would indeed. My place in the world is not among Cabinet Ministers and old countesses."

"Nor mine."

"Yes; it seems that yours is to be there. They are your cousins, and you have made at any rate one great friend among them,—one who is to be the biggest of them all."

"And you are going to throw me over, Kate?"

"To tell the truth, Alice, I sometimes think you had better throw me over. I know it would be sad,—sad for both, but perhaps it would be better. I have done you much harm and no good; and now where I am going I shall disgrace you." She talked even of getting out at some station and returning, and would have done so had not Alice made it impossible. As it was, the evening found her and Alice together entering the park-gate at Matching, in Lady Glencora's carriage. Lady Glencora had sent a note to the station. "She could not come herself," she said, "because Mr. Palliser was a little fussy. You'll understand, dear, but don't say a word." Alice didn't say a word, having been very anxious not to lower Mr. Palliser in her cousin's respect.

None of the Lady Janes and Lady Marys were at Matching when they arrived. Indeed, there was no guest there but Mr. Grey, for which Kate felt herself to be extremely grateful. Mr. Grey came into the hall, standing behind Mr. Palliser, who stood behind his wife. Alice passed by them both, and was at once in her lover's arms. "Then I must introduce myself," said Lady Glencora to Kate, "and my husband also." This she did, and no woman in England could have excelled her in the manner of doing it. "I have heard so much about you," said she, still keeping Kate's hand, "and I know how good you've been;—and how wicked you have been," she added in a whisper. Then Mr. Grey was brought up to her, and they were introduced. It was not till some days had passed over them that she felt herself at all at her ease with Mr. Grey, and I doubt whether she ever reached that point with Mr. Palliser; but Lady Glencora she knew, and liked, and almost loved, from the first moment of their meeting.

"Have you heard the news?" said Lady Glencora to Alice, the first minute that they were alone. Alice, of course, had not heard the news. "Mr. Bott is going to marry Mrs. Marsham. There is such a row about it. Plantagenet is nearly mad. I never knew him so disgusted in my life. Of course I don't dare to tell him so, but I am so heartily rejoiced. You know how I love them both, and I could not possibly wish any better reward for either." Alice, who had personally known more of Mr. Bott than of Mrs. Marsham, said that she couldn't but be sorry for the lady. "She's old enough to be his mother," said Lady Glencora, "otherwise I really don't know any people better suited to each other. The best is, that Mr. Bott is doing it to regain his footing with Mr. Palliser! I am sure of that;—and Plantagenet will never speak to him again. But, Alice, there is other news."

"What other news?"

"It is hardly news yet, and of course I am very wicked to tell you. But I feel sure Mr. Grey knows all about it, and if I didn't tell, he would."

"He hasn't told me anything yet."

"He hasn't had time; and when he does, you mustn't pretend to know. I believe Mr. Palliser will certainly be Chancellor of the Exchequer before next month, and, if so, he'll never come in for Silverbridge again."

"But he'll be in Parliament; will he not?"

"Oh, yes; he'll be in Parliament. I don't understand all about it. There is a man going out for the county,—for Barsetshire,—some man whom the Duke used to favour, and he wants Plantagenet to come in for that. I can't understand what difference it makes."

"But he will be in the Cabinet?"

"Oh, yes. But who do you suppose is to be the new Member for Silverbridge?"

"I can't guess," said Alice. Though, of course, she did guess.

"Mind, I don't know it. He has never told me. But he told me that he had been with the Duke, and asked the Duke to let Jeffrey have the seat. The Duke became as black as thunder, and said that Jeffrey had no fortune. In short, he wouldn't hear of it. Poor Jeffrey! we must try to do something for him, but I really don't know how. Then the Duke said, that Plantagenet should put in for Silverbridge some friend who would support himself; and I fancy,—mind it's only fancy,—but I fancy that Plantagenet mentioned to his Grace—one Mr. Grey."

"Oh, Glencora!"

"They've been talking together till sometimes I think Mr. Grey is worse than Plantagenet. When Mr. Grey began to say something the other night in the drawing-room about sugar, I knew it was all up with you. He'll be a financial Secretary; you see if he isn't; or a lord of something, or an under-somebody of State; and then some day he'll go mad, either because he does or because he doesn't get into the Cabinet." Lady Glencora, as she said all this, knew well that the news she was giving would please her cousin better than any other tidings that could be told.

By degrees the guests came. The two Miss Howards were the first, and they expressed themselves as delighted with Lady Glencora's taste and with Mr. Palliser's munificence,—for at that time the brooches and armlets had been produced. Kate had said very little about these matters, but the Miss Howards were loud in their thanks. But they were good-humoured, merry girls, and the house was pleasanter after their arrival than it had been before. Then came the dreaded personage,—the guest,—Lady Midlothian! On the subject of Lady Midlothian Kate had really become curious. She had a real desire to see the face and gait of the woman, and to hear her voice. Lady Midlothian came, and with her came Lady Jane and Lady Mary. I am by no means sure that Lady Jane and Lady Mary were not nearly as old as the two Miss Pallisers; but they were not probably so fully resolved as to the condition of their future modes of living as were those two ladies, and if so, they were not wrong to shine as bridesmaids. With them Alice had made some slight acquaintance during the last spring in London, and as they were now to attend upon her as the bride they were sufficiently gracious. To Kate, too, they were civil enough, and things, in public, went on very pleasantly at Matching.

A scene there was, of course, between Alice and Lady Midlothian;—a scene in private. "You must go through it," Lady Glencora had said, with jocose mournfulness; "and why should you not let her jump upon you a little? It can't hurt you now."

"But I don't like people to jump upon me," Alice said.

"And why are you to have everything just as you like it? You are so unreasonable. Think how I've been jumped on! Think what I have borne from them! If you knew the things she used to say to me, you would not be such a coward. I was sent down to her for a week, and had no power of helping myself. And the Marchioness used to be sent for to look at me, for she never talks. She used to look at me, and groan, and hold up her hands till I hated her the worst of the two. Think what they did to me, and yet they are my dear friends now. Why should you escape altogether?"

Alice could not escape altogether, and therefore was closeted with Lady Midlothian for the best part of an hour. "Did Lady Macleod read to you what I wrote?" the Countess asked.

"Yes,—that is, she gave me the letter to read."

"And I hope you understand me, Alice?"

"Oh, yes, I suppose so."

"You suppose so, my dear! If you only suppose so I shall not be contented. I want you to appreciate my feelings towards you thoroughly. I want you to know that I am most anxious as to your future life, and that I am thoroughly satisfied with the step you are now taking." The Countess paused, but Alice said nothing. Her tongue was itching to tell the old woman that she cared nothing for this expression of satisfaction; but she was aware that she had done much that was deserving of punishment, and resolved to take this as part of her penance. She was being jumped upon, and it was unpleasant; but, after all that had happened, it was only fitting that she should undergo much unpleasantness. "Thoroughly satisfied," continued the Countess; "and now, I only wish to refer, in the slightest manner possible, to what took place between us when we were both of us under this roof last winter."

"Why refer to it at all, Lady Midlothian?"

"Because I think it may do good, and because I cannot make you understand that I have thoroughly forgiven everything, unless I tell you that I have forgiven that also. On that occasion I had come all the way from Scotland on purpose to say a few words to you."

"I am so sorry that you should have had the trouble."

"I do not regret it, Alice. I never do regret doing anything which I believe to have been my duty. There is no knowing how far what I said then may have operated for good." Alice thought that she knew very well, but she said nothing. "I must confess that what I then understood to be your obstinacy,—and I must say also, if I tell the truth, your indifference to—to—to all prudential considerations whatever, not to talk of appearances and decorum, and I might say, anything like a high line of duty or moral conduct,—shocked me very much. It did, indeed, my dear. Taking it altogether, I don't know that I was ever more shocked in my life. The thing was so inscrutable!" Here Lady Midlothian held up one hand in a manner that was truly imposing; "so inscrutable! But that is all over now. What was personally offensive to myself I could easily forgive, and I do forgive it. I shall never think of it any more." Here Lady Midlothian put up both her hands gently, as though wafting the injury away into the air. "But what I wish specially to say to you is this; your own conduct is forgiven also!" Here she paused again, and Alice winced. Who was this dreadful old Countess;— what was the Countess to her, that she should be thus tormented with the old woman's forgiveness? John Grey had forgiven her, and of external forgiveness that was enough. She had not forgiven herself,—would never forgive herself altogether; and the pardon of no old woman in England could assist her in doing so. She had sinned, but she had not sinned against Lady Midlothian. "Let her jump upon you, and have done with it," Lady Glencora had said. She had resolved that it should be so, but it was very hard to keep her resolution.

"The Marchioness and I have talked it over," continued Lady Midlothian, "and she has asked me to speak for both her and myself." There is comfort at any rate in that, thought Alice, who had never yet seen the Marchioness. "We have resolved that all those little mistakes should be as though they had never been committed. We shall both be most happy to receive you and your husband, who is, I must say, one of the most gentlemanlike looking men I ever saw. It seems that he and Mr. Palliser are on most friendly,—I may say, most confidential terms, and that must be quite a pleasure to you."

"It's a pleasure to him, which is more to the purpose," said Alice.

"Exactly so. And now, my dear, everything is forgiven and shall be forgotten. Come and give me a kiss, and let me wish you joy." Alice did as she was bidden, and accepted the kiss and the congratulations, and a little box of jewellery which Lady Midlothian produced from out of her pocket. "The diamonds are from the Marchioness, my dear, whose means, as you doubtless are aware, greatly exceed my own. The garnets are from me. I hope they may both be worn long and happily."

I hardly know which was the worst, the lecture, the kiss, or the present. The latter she would have declined, had it been possible; but it was not possible. When she had agreed to be married at Matching she had not calculated the amount of punishment which would thereby be inflicted on her. But I think that, though she bore it impatiently, she was aware that she had deserved it. Although she fretted herself greatly under the infliction of Lady Midlothian, she acknowledged to herself, even at the time, that she deserved all the lashes she received. She had made a fool of herself in her vain attempt to be greater and grander than other girls, and it was only fair that her folly should be in some sort punished before it was fully pardoned. John Grey punished it after one fashion; by declining to allude to it, or to think of it, or to take any account of it. And now Lady Midlothian had punished it after another fashion, and Alice went out of the Countess's presence with sundry inward exclamations of "mea culpa," and with many unseen beatings of the breast.

Two days before the ceremony came the Marchioness and her august daughter. Her Lady Jane was much more august than the other Lady Jane;—very much more august indeed. She had very long flaxen hair, and very light blue eyes, which she did not move frequently, and she spoke very little,—one may almost say not at all, and she never seemed to do anything. But she was very august, and was, as all the world knew, engaged to marry the Duke of Dumfriesshire, who, though twice her own age, was as yet childless, as soon as he should have completed his mourning for his first wife. Kate told her cousin that she did not at all know how she should ever stand up as one in a group with so august a person as this Lady Jane, and Alice herself felt that such an attendant would quite obliterate her. But Lady Jane and her mother were both harmless. The Marchioness never spoke to Kate and hardly spoke to Alice, and the Marchioness's Lady Jane was quite as silent as her mother.

On the morning of this day,—the day on which these very august people came,—a telegram arrived at the Priory calling for Mr. Palliser's immediate presence in London. He came to Alice full of regret, and behaved himself very nicely. Alice now regarded him quite as a friend. "Of course I understand," she said, "and I know that the business which takes you up to London pleases you." "Well; yes;—it does please me. I am glad,—I don't mind saying so to you. But it does not please me to think that I shall be away at your marriage. Pray make your father understand that it was absolutely unavoidable. But I shall see him, of course, when I come back. And I shall see you too before very long."

"Shall you?"

"Oh yes."

"And why so?"

"Because Mr. Grey must be at Silverbridge for his election.—But perhaps I ought not tell you his secrets." Then he took her into the breakfast-parlour and showed her his present. It was a service of Sèvres china,—very precious and beautiful. "I got you these things because Grey likes china."

"So do I like china," said she, with her face brighter than he had ever yet seen it.

"I thought you would like them best," said he. Alice looking up at him with her eyes full of tears told him that she did like them best; and then, as he wished her all happiness, and as he was stooping over her to kiss her, Lady Glencora came in.

"I beg pardon," said she, "I was just one minute too soon; was I not?"

"She would have them sent here and unpacked," said Mr. Palliser, "though I told her it was foolish."

"Of course I would," said Lady Glencora. "Everything shall be unpacked and shown. It's easy to get somebody to pack them again."

Much of the wedding tribute had already been deposited with the china, and among other things there were the jewels that Lady Midlothian had brought.

"Upon my word, her ladyship's diamonds are not to be sneezed at," said Lady Glencora.

"I don't care for diamonds," said Alice.

Then Lady Glencora took up the Countess's trinkets, and shook her head and turned up her nose. There was a wonderfully comic expression on her face as she did so.

"To me they are just as good as the others," said Alice.

"To me they are not, then," said Lady Glencora. "Diamonds are diamonds, and garnets are garnets; and I am not so romantic but what I know the difference."

On the evening before the marriage Alice and Lady Glencora walked for the last time through the Priory ruins. It was now September, and the evenings were still long, so that the ladies could get out upon the lawn after dinner. Whether Lady Glencora would have been allowed to walk through the ruins so late as half-past eight in the evening if her husband had been there may be doubtful, but her husband was away and she took this advantage of his absence.

"Do you remember that night we were here?" said Lady Glencora.

"When shall I forget it; or how is it possible that such a night should ever be forgotten?"

"No; I shall never forget it. Oh dear, what wonderful things have happened since that! Do you ever think of Jeffrey?"

"Yes;—of course I think of him. I did like him so much. I hope I shall see him some day."

"And he liked you too, young woman; and, what was more, young woman, I thought at one time that, perhaps, you were going to like him in earnest."

"Not in that way, certainly."

"You've done much better, of course; especially as poor Jeffrey's chance of promotion doesn't look so good now. If I have a boy, I wonder whether he'll hate me?"

"Why should he hate you?"

"I can't help it, you know, if he does. Only think what it is to Plantagenet. Have you seen the difference it makes in him already?"

"Of course it makes a difference;—the greatest difference in the world."

"And think what it will be to me, Alice. I used to lie in bed and wish myself dead, and make up my mind to drown myself,—if I could only dare.

I shan't think any more of that poor fellow now." Then she told Alice what had been done for Burgo; how his uncle had paid his bills once again, and had agreed to give him a small income. "Poor fellow!" said Lady Glencora, "it won't do more than buy him gloves, you know."

The marriage was magnificent, greatly to the dismay of Alice and to the discomfort of Mr. Vavasor, who came down on the eve of the ceremony, — arriving while his daughter and Lady Glencora were in the ruins. Mr. Grey seemed to take it all very easily, and, as Lady Glencora said, played his part exactly as though he were in the habit of being married, at any rate, once a year. "Nothing on earth will ever put him out, so you need not try, my dear," she said, as Alice stood with her a moment alone in the dressing-room up-stairs before her departure.

"I know that," said Alice, "and therefore I shall never try."

CHAPTER LXXX
THE STORY IS FINISHED WITHIN THE HALLS OF THE DUKE OF OMNIUM

Mr. Grey and wife were duly carried away from Matching Priory by post horses, and did their honeymoon, we may be quite sure, with much satisfaction. When Alice was first asked where she would go, she simply suggested that it should not be to Switzerland. They did, in truth, go by slow stages to Italy, to Venice, Florence, and on to Rome; but such had not been their intention when they first started on their journey. At that time Mr. Grey believed that he would be wanted again in England, down at Silverbridge in Barsetshire, very shortly. But before he had married a week he learned that all that was to be postponed. The cup of fruition had not yet reached Mr. Palliser's lips. "There will be no vacancy either in the county or in the borough till Parliament meets." That had been the message sent by Mr. Palliser to Mr. Grey. Lady Glencora's message to Alice had been rather more full, having occupied three pages of note paper, the last of which had been crossed, but I do not know that it was more explicit. She had abused Lord Brock, had abused Mr. Finespun, and had abused all public things and institutions, because the arrangements as now proposed would be very comfortable to Alice, but would not, as she was pleased to think, be very comfortable to herself. "You can go to Rome and see everything and enjoy yourself, which I was not allowed to do; and all this noise and bother, and crowd of electioneering, will take place down in Barsetshire just when I am in the middle of all my trouble." There were many very long letters came from Lady Glencora to Rome during the winter,—letters which Alice enjoyed thoroughly, but which she could not but regard as being very indiscreet. The Duke was at the Castle during the Christmas week, and the descriptions of the Duke and of his solicitude as to his heir were very comic. "He comes and bends over me on the sofa in the most stupendous way, as though a woman to be the mother of his heir must be a miracle in nature. He is quite awful when he says a word or two, and more awful in his silence. The devil prompted me the other day, and I said I hoped it would be a girl. There was a look came over his face which nearly frightened me. If it should be, I believe he will turn me out of the house; but how can I help it? I wish you were going to have a baby at the same time. Then, if yours was a boy and mine a girl, we'd make a change." This was very indiscreet. Lady Glencora would write indiscreet letters like this, which Alice could not show to her husband. It was a thousand pities.

But December and January wore themselves away, and the time came in which the Greys were bound to return to England. The husband had very fully discussed with his wife that matter of his parliamentary ambition, and found in her a very ready listener. Having made up his mind to do this thing, he was resolved to do it thoroughly, and was becoming almost as full of politics, almost as much devoted to sugar, as Mr. Palliser himself. He at any rate could not complain that his wife would not interest herself in his pursuits. Then, as they returned, came letters from Lady Glencora, written as her troubles grew nigh. The Duke had gone, of course; but he was to be there at the appointed time. "Oh, I do so wish he would have a fit of the gout in London,—or at Timbuctoo," said Lady Glencora. When they reached London they first heard the news from Mr. Vavasor, who on this occasion condescended to meet them at the railway. "The Duke has got an heir," he said, before the carriage-door was open;—"born this morning!" One might have supposed that it was the Duke's baby, and not the baby of Lady Glencora and Mr. Palliser. There was a note from Mr. Palliser to Mr. Grey. "Thank God!" said the note, "Lady Glencora and the boy"—Mr. Palliser had scorned to use the word child—"Lady Glencora and the boy are quite as well as can be expected. Both the new writs were moved for last night." Mr. Palliser's honours, as will be seen, came rushing upon him all at once.

Wondrous little baby,—*purpureo genitus!* What have the gods not done for thee, if thou canst only manage to live till thy good things are all thine own,—to live through all the terrible solicitude with which they will envelope thee! Better than royal rank will be thine, with influence more than royal, and power of action fettered by no royalty. Royal wealth which will be really thine own, to do with it as it beseemeth thee. Thou wilt be at the top of an aristocracy in a country where aristocrats need gird themselves with no buckram. All that the world can give will be thine; and yet when we talk of thee religiously, philosophically, or politico-economically, we are wont to declare that thy chances of happiness are no better,—no better, if they be no worse,—than are those of thine infant neighbour just born, in that farmyard cradle. Who shall say that they are better or that they are worse? Or if they be better, or if they be worse, how shall we reconcile to ourselves that seeming injustice?

And now we will pay a little visit to the small one born in the purple, and the story of that visit shall be the end of our history. It was early in April, quite early in April, and Mr. and Mrs. Grey were both at Gatherum Castle. Mrs. Grey was there at the moment of which we write, but Mr. Grey was absent at Silverbridge with Mr. Palliser. This was the day of the Silverbridge election, and Mr. Grey had gone to that ancient borough, to offer himself as a candidate to the electors, backed by the presence and aid of a very powerful member of the Cabinet. Lady Glencora and Alice were sitting up-stairs with the small, purple-born one in their presence, and the small, purple-born one was lying in Alice's lap.

"It is such a comfort that it is over," said the mother.

"You are the most ungrateful of women."

"Oh, Alice,—if you could have known! Your baby may come just as it pleases. You won't lie awake trembling how on earth you will bear your disgrace if one of the vile weaker sex should come to disturb the hopes of your lords and masters;—for I had two, which made it so much more terrible."

"I'm sure Mr. Palliser would not have said a word."

"No, he would have said nothing,—nor would the Duke. The Duke would simply have gone away instantly, and never have seen me again till the next chance comes,—if it ever does come. And Mr. Palliser would have been as gentle as a dove;—much more gentle than he is now, for men are rarely gentle in their triumph. But I should have known what they both thought and felt."

"It's all right now, dear."

"Yes, my bonny boy,—you have made it all right for me;—have you not?" And Lady Glencora took her baby into her own arms. "You have made everything right, my little man. But oh, Alice, if you had seen the Duke's long face through those three days; if you had heard the tones of the people's voices as they whispered about me; if you had encountered the oppressive cheerfulness of those two London doctors,—doctors are such bad actors,—you would have thought it impossible for any woman to live throughout. There's one comfort;—if my mannikin lives, I can't have another eldest. He looks like living;—don't he, Alice?" Then were perpetrated various mysterious ceremonies of feminine idolatry which were continued till there came a grandly dressed old lady, who called herself the nurse, and who took the idol away.

"Yes, my bonny boy,—you have made it all right for me."

In the course of that afternoon Lady Glencora took Alice all over the house. It was a castle of enormous size, quite new,—having been built by the present proprietor,—very cold, very handsome, and very dull. "What an immense place!" said Alice, as she stood looking round her in the grand hall, which was never used as an entrance except on very grand occasions. "Is it not? And it cost—oh, I can't tell you how much it cost. A hundred thousand pounds or more. Well;—that would be nothing, as the Duke no doubt had the money in his pocket to do what he liked with at the time. But the joke is, nobody ever thinks of living here. Who'd live in such a great, overgrown place such as this, if they could get a comfortable house like Matching? Do you remember Longroyston and the hot-water pipes? I always think of the poor Duchess when I come through here. Nobody ever lives here, or ever will. The Duke comes for one week in the year, and Plantagenet says he hates to do that. As for me, nothing on earth shall ever make me live here. I was completely in their power and couldn't help their bringing me here the other day;—because I had, as it were, disgraced myself."

"How disgraced yourself?"

"In being so long, you know, before that gentleman was born. But they shan't play me the same trick again. I shall dare to assert myself, now. Come,—we must go away. There are some of the British public come to see one of the British sights. That's another pleasure here. One has to run about to avoid being caught by the visitors. The housekeeper tells me they always grumble because they are not allowed to go into my little room up-stairs."

On the evening of that day Mr. Palliser and Mr. Grey returned home from Silverbridge together. The latter was then a Member of Parliament, but the former at that moment was the possessor of no such dignity. The election for the borough was now over, whereas that for the county had not yet taken place. But there was no rival candidate for the position, and Mr. Palliser was thoroughly contented with his fate. He was at this moment actually Chancellor of the Exchequer, and in about ten days' time would be on his legs in the House proposing for his country's use his scheme of finance. The two men were seated together in an open carriage, and were being whirled along by four horses. They were both no doubt happy in their ambition, but I think that of the two, Mr. Palliser showed his triumph the most. Not that he spoke even to his friend a word that was triumphant in its tone. It was not thus that he rejoiced. He was by nature too placid for that. But there was a nervousness in his contentment which told the tale to any observer who might know how to read it.

"I hope you'll like it," he said to Grey.

"I shall never like it as you do," Grey answered.

"And why not;—why not?"

"In the first place, I have not begun it so young."

"Any time before thirty-five is young enough."

"For useful work, yes,—but hardly for enjoyment in the thing. And then I don't believe it all as you do. To you the British House of Commons is everything."

"Yes;—everything," said Mr. Palliser with unwonted enthusiasm;— "everything, everything. That and the Constitution are everything."

"It is not so to me."

"Ah, but it will be. If you really take to the work, and put yourself into harness, it will be so. You'll get to feel it as I do. The man who is counted by his colleagues as number one on the Treasury Bench in the English House of Commons, is the first of living men. That's my opinion. I don't know that I ever said it before; but that's my opinion."

"And who is the second;—the purse-bearer to this great man?"

"I say nothing about the second. I don't know that there is any second. I wonder how we shall find Lady Glencora and the boy." They had then arrived at the side entrance to the Castle, and Mr. Grey ran up-stairs to his wife's room to receive her congratulations.

"And you are a Member of Parliament?" she asked.

"They tell me so, but I don't know whether I actually am one till I've taken the oaths."

"I am so happy. There's no position in the world so glorious!"

"It's a pity you are not Mr. Palliser's wife. That's just what he has been saying."

"Oh, John, I am so happy. It is so much more than I have deserved. I hope,—that is, I sometimes think—"

"Think what, dearest?"

"I hope nothing that I have ever said has driven you to it."

"I'd do more than that, dear, to make you happy," he said, as he put his arm round her and kissed her; "more than that, at least if it were in my power."

Probably my readers may agree with Alice, that in the final adjustment of her affairs she had received more than she had deserved. All her friends, except her husband, thought so. But as they have all forgiven her, including even Lady Midlothian herself, I hope that they who have followed her story to its close will not be less generous.